HEREWARD
End of Days

www.transworldbooks.co.uk

Also by James Wilde

HEREWARD
HEREWARD: THE DEVIL'S ARMY

HEREWARD
End of Days

James Wilde

BANTAM PRESS

LONDON · TORONTO · SYDNEY · AUCKLAND · JOHANNESBURG

TRANSWORLD PUBLISHERS
61–63 Uxbridge Road, London W5 5SA
A Random House Group Company
www.transworldbooks.co.uk

First published in Great Britain
in 2013 by Bantam Press
an imprint of Transworld Publishers

A CIP catalogue record for this book
is available from the British Library.

ISBNs 9780593065020 (cased)
9780593065037 (tpb)

Addresses for Random House Group Ltd companies outside the UK
can be found at: www.randomhouse.co.uk
The Random House Group Ltd Reg. No. 954009

The Random House Group Limited supports the Forest Stewardship Council® (FSC®),
the leading international forest-certification organisation. Our books carrying the
FSC label are printed on FSC®-certified paper. FSC is the only forest-certification
scheme supported by the leading environmental organisations, including Greenpeace.
Our paper procurement policy can be found at www.randomhouse.co.uk/environment

Typeset in 11.5/14pt Sabon by
Falcon Oast Graphic Art Ltd.
Printed and bound in Great Britain by
CPI Group (UK) Ltd, Croydon, CRO 4YY

2 4 6 8 10 9 7 5 3 1

MIX
Paper from
responsible sources
FSC® C016897

PROLOGUE

17 September 1071

S oon the graves would give up their dead.
   To the west, a red gash wounded the darkening sky. The cold was starting to creep across the silent wetlands. And in the cemetery beside Ely's great church shadows merged, the grassy mounds of the burials little more than smudges in the gloom.

Judgement Day was coming.

Wardric knew this was true, for the priest had announced it to the world that very morn while he sat, bored, at the back of the chill nave, watching the blood drain from his mother's and father's faces. Crouching beside the gnarled hawthorn next to the cemetery fence, the boy watched the graves with wide eyes. Soon, soon, the tumble of sod, the bony hands reaching up to the sky. And then the booming verdict of the Lord. He licked his dry lips, afraid of what he might see, but excited too.

Wardric had known eight summers, and although his kin said most of them had been hard under the grip of the cruel King William, he remembered only fishing and swimming and games and his father teaching him how to carve an angel out of deer horn. Now, though, all that was to end.

For a while he waited, his heart beating faster as the sun slipped towards the horizon. The time seemed right. The breeze smelled of endings. Ashes floated from the home-fires, and he could taste the rot drifting from Dedman's Bog. Finally he glimpsed movement.

Wardric stiffened, but his heart slowed when he realized the graves were not yawning. It was only Oswyn, old Oswyn the potter, no doubt on his way to the saint's shrine. Every day at dusk he trudged the same path. Back bowed, eyes never raised from the turf, white hair aglow, he clutched his offering, ready to mutter his prayers for the son he had lost in the spring floods.

The boy sagged back.

But only for a moment. He glimpsed another movement across the edge of his vision, a shadow taking on weight and form as it caught the dying rays of the sun. A man, swathed in a cloak, hood pulled high, striding with purpose. Curious, Wardric leaned forward.

A spear's throw away from him, the cloaked figure caught up with Oswyn. Startled, the old man spun round, but his shoulders soon slumped back under their doleful weight as he muttered a greeting and turned back to his path. The blow came from nowhere, a fist hammered into the back of the potter's head.

Wardric stifled a gasp.

Oswyn crashed across one of the graves, stunned. His attacker leaned over him, snarled his fist in the front of the man's tunic and half hauled him up. As his senses returned to him, the old man began to splutter. His fingers clawed the air. The other man shook him and murmured, 'Hold your tongue.' The words drifted across the still cemetery.

Wardric felt puzzled to hear no threat there. That command almost seemed laced with a gentle humour. Careful not to make a sound, he eased back under the cover of the hawthorn.

'What do you want of me?' the old man moaned.

'Only your life.'

Oswyn stared, baffled. 'I have done you no harm.'

'No, you have done me no harm. There is not a man or woman in Ely that you have harmed. You are well liked, old man. That is why I chose you.'

Gripped by the encounter, Wardric dug his fingers into the soft turf, squinting through the half-light to try to discern the identity of the hooded man. The attacker's back was turned, but he seemed much younger than the potter.

Oswyn reached out a pleading hand. 'I have no coin . . .' His voice wavered. Like Wardric, he could make no sense of what was happening here.

The attacker dipped a hand inside his cloak and then pulled it back. A short blade shone in the ruddy glow of the sunset. It hung in the air for only a moment before its owner plunged it into his victim's chest.

Wardric jerked back in horror, his hand flying to his mouth. How he prevented himself from crying out he did not know, but he was sure that if he made the slightest sound the hooded man would turn on him next.

The attacker pressed his free hand across the potter's mouth to stifle his cries. Wardric clutched his ears to drive out those awful muffled sounds.

'You are but the first,' the hooded man hissed.

As the potter thrashed in his death throes, his attacker removed his hand and stepped back, watching the end of the old man's days. Oswyn must have spoken, for the murderer said as if in reply, 'Your protector has abandoned you.'

'God has not abandoned us,' the potter croaked.

The hooded man laughed. 'Night is falling fast upon Ely, and upon the English. Be thankful you will not be here to witness it.'

And then he fell upon Oswyn like a wild beast, stabbing in a frenzy.

Rigid with terror, Wardric could not look away. Even when the savagery had ended and the old man's shudders had stilled, even when the murderer had swept away across the cemetery, the boy remained, staring into the dark, afraid to move. He would never speak of this thing.

The Devil had come to Ely and nothing would be the same again.

CHAPTER ONE

The wind moaned through the high branches and the skulls on the witch-charm rattled out a warning. Ravens, crows, gulls, oystercatchers and stonechats the two men spied as they looked up into the ash tree, all of them joined in death.

Madulf shuddered and pulled his cloak tighter around him. His unease only made his sullen face seem darker. 'There are things abroad that I would not see,' he murmured.

'Are you a child, afrit of the dark?' his brother Sighard said with a grin. His hair was red, his face pale and freckled, a rarity among the English rebels who had gathered under Hereward's standard in Ely. And yet even as he spoke he felt his neck prickle, and he peered into the darkening woods.

'You think the witch would have left this here for no reason?' the other man hissed. 'You are the child, simple in the head.'

'Let us not argue,' Sighard pleaded. 'These days it is all we seem to do. I worry that this struggle drives us apart.'

Madulf pushed past him back on to the track, allowing himself one last worried glance at the ghastly charm. Sighard followed. Like his brother, he had left his spear and his shield beneath his bed. Under his threadbare green cloak, he wore little more than rags. This night he would be no warrior, just a mud-spattered ceorl with straw behind his ears, and with luck no one would pay him much attention. There were eyes everywhere, even in these lonely woods. Nowhere was safe any more.

'We argue because hope fades fast,' Madulf called back, pulling up his hood as he hurried along the old straight track. 'Outside the church this morn, one of the monks cried out that it was the harvest time for man. No one spoke out against him. And now . . . now we have been abandoned by the only one who can save us.'

Another witch-charm rattled overhead. They were everywhere, a last desperate attempt to ward off what all feared.

'This night we may make things right again,' Sighard replied, hoping his brother had not seen the charm.

'Aye, crook your finger and wish,' Madulf sneered. All his worries seemed to flood out of him in one deluge and he whirled, grabbing Sighard by the shoulders. 'The End of Days has come like a midwinter gale. It howls across all England, and no man will escape its knives.'

'You do not know this to be true.'

'Can you not see?' Madulf clutched his head. 'In the far north, mortal remains clog the rivers and the streams and line the byways like markers on the road to hell. More rats than men now live in Northumbria, so say those who have fled the devastation. Hunger bloats the bellies of children and turns men and women to naught but skin upon bone. And the sickness has brought silence to whole villages, leaving black lips and black hands and feet in its passing. You know this to be true!'

'We still have hope, brother.'

'Not any more.' Madulf's shoulders sagged and he turned back to the track.

Sighard spat. It was the invaders who had brought the world to this. Those bastard Normans, with their bastard king, who had stolen the English crown. He tried to fan the flames of hatred in his heart. It had kept him warm during the bitter struggle against the enemy, but no more. These days he felt the cold touch of fear more often than not.

They paused on the edge of a black lake and looked out across the still fenlands. Wood and water, stinking bog and whispering reeds, as far as the eye could see. A treacherous landscape for any who did not know its moods, and one that changed constantly, with the tides flooding in through the salt-marshes to the north and east, and the rainfall swelling the rivers and streams to the east. Land that had been dry only a day earlier could pull a man down to his death.

Shadows were pooling under the trees. Along the western sky, a crimson band blazed as the sun slipped away. Time was short. They hurried on.

After a while, moonlight cast patches of silver among the trees. And then, through the curtain of branches, a soft golden light danced. The two brothers slowed, catching their breath. This was the place.

'Forget your fears,' Sighard whispered, resting one hand on Madulf's shoulder. 'Remember only the reason why we are here. Everyone in Ely counts on us.'

Murmuring voices drifted on the dank night air. Sighard breathed in the scent of woodsmoke. Pulling aside the hanging willow branches, he left his brother and stepped into a small clearing where some twenty folk squatted on logs around a roaring campfire. Many heads were bowed in deep reflection. Others leaned in close to whisper, as if raising their voices would bring the wrath of God upon them. He sensed a mood that was tense, almost reverent.

Through the twirl of smoke, Sighard could see a shack that had almost been swallowed by its surroundings. Yellowing grass grew waist-high on every side; the ash trees pressed so close they seemed all that stopped the bowing walls from collapsing. The roof gaped where sods of turf had fallen away. Sighard thought that it barely looked fit for pigs.

At the rear of the congregation, he dropped to his haunches and looked around the group. Worry etched deep lines into faces. They were frightened, he thought, seeking aid from whatever source they could find.

From the hut, a faint trilling rolled out. The crowd fell silent, and as the chirruping grew louder all eyes turned towards the door. Unable to look away, Sighard watched too. After a moment, he realized he was holding his breath tight in his chest.

When the door ground open, a dark shape moved in the shadows inside the shack. The trilling died away and a suffocating quiet descended on the clearing. Under his breath, Sighard muttered a prayer. These folk had heard the monks' warnings, as he had. Lives destroyed, fortunes blighted. Sickness. Starvation. Death.

In the doorway a figure loomed. For a fleeting moment, Sighard imagined all the terrors he had heard whispered. Yet it was only a woman who stepped out into the firelight. Even then he was not comforted. Like a wolf she was, lean and strong and savage, her thin lips curling back from jagged teeth, fingers crooked to tear with broken, filthy nails. Her face had been weathered by the harsh fenland seasons, her filthy dress reduced to little more than mildew-stained rags. But though her hair was streaked with grey she glowed with the vitality of a much younger woman. Sighard found himself caught in the grip of her glittering eyes. They looked all black from rim to rim, the eyes of a devil, not a woman.

As she prowled along the front row, folk reared back as one. 'Now you come,' she murmured, her voice flinty. 'In the cold of winter, you denied me food. Your children threw stones at me in the woods. You turned your faces away at the market. And your churchmen beat me with cudgels until my arms and back were blue and my blood flowed freely. Yet now you come.'

A man flushed from the heat of the fire bowed his head. He could not look at her. 'Brigid,' he ventured, 'we should not have done you wrong. All of us are in agreement.' He glanced around. Heads nodded. 'Find it in your heart to help us and we shall be in your debt.'

Brigid looked across the group. 'What would you have me do?'

'Whatever is in your power,' a wife cried. Her worries had been stifled for too long. 'The church does not help us any more. The priests either bow their heads to King William in hope of favour, or are so fearful of his vengeance they cower like mice.'

'Give us wards to keep the Normans at bay,' a man shouted.

'Make them piss blood. Make their cocks drop off with the pox,' another yelled.

'Hide our barns,' a second woman pleaded, 'so they cannot steal our food and we can live through the cold season.'

Brigid grunted. She stared into the dark beyond the circle of firelight and cocked her head as if listening to voices. When Sighard followed her gaze, he saw only gloom among the ash trees. He felt his skin crawl. Brigid prowled to the fire where a pot hung on a chain over the flames. Though the liquid bubbled in the heat, the woman dunked her fingers in and pulled out a shrivelled mushroom. 'The flesh of the gods,' she croaked. 'It gives me wings to fly to the guardian of Lugh's Spring and ask his aid, as it did for my mother, and my mother's mother, and all the mothers before them.' Brigid dipped a wooden cup into the brown stew. She let the contents cool, then began to sip. Once she had drained the liquid, she leaned her head back and closed her eyes in ecstasy. Slumping to her knees, she began to rock, humming to herself.

The moon slipped across the sky. No one spoke.

When the crack of a dry branch echoed from deep in the woods, everyone jerked and looked round. As they strained to listen, Sighard watched their fears play out on their faces. *Wuduwasa, wuduwasa*, the whispers rustled. A ceorl crossed himself, afraid he would be the next victim of the silent denizen of the wildwood who gnawed on the bones of men. They held their breaths and waited. Only when another crack echoed, this time further away, did they turn their attention back to the fireside.

Finally Brigid began to mumble. Sweat slicked her brow. 'Speak,' she breathed, her eyes still shut. 'Ask what you would.'

'Will the guardian help?' someone at the front whispered.

The wise woman nodded.

Smiles leapt to lips. Hands clasped in hope. A white-haired woman, as bent as a wind-blasted tree, leaned forward. She swallowed and her voice cracked when she spoke. 'Are these the last days?'

Brigid rocked back and forth. A tremor crossed her face. 'I see . . . fire. I see ravens feeding on a hill of bodies. A bloody sky and a bloody lake.'

In front of Sighard, a wife's shoulders began to shake with silent sobs.

'A cold wind blows from the north, and there are ashes in the wind,' Brigid continued.

A crash reverberated through the woods nearby. Men jumped to their feet, and a moan of unease rippled through the group. 'It is the *wuduwasa*,' someone gasped.

In that febrile atmosphere, Sighard could see the moment was slipping away from him. He stood up and raised his chin, trying to look commanding. It seemed to work, for all eyes turned to him.

'My name is Sighard. I come from the camp at Ely,' he announced. His mouth felt too dry. Though he dreaded the answer, he had to ask the question that all in the camp needed to know. 'Where is Hereward?'

The words seemed to hang in the air. Sighard swallowed, more afraid than at any time since he joined the rebel army.

Brigid squinted, trying to discern his face through the smoke.

'Is he alive? Or dead?' he continued, unable to hide the tremor in his voice.

There. It had been said and could not be unsaid. Though he kept his gaze upon the wise woman, he sensed the others around the fire turn to look at him. So much hope had been invested in Hereward. The leader of the uprising and the one man who could turn back the iron tide of the Normans. Who could prevent all the misery and the suffering. If the rebels had not been so desperate, he would never have said anything that would shatter that hope, which had been in such short supply for so long.

But desperate they were.

Brigid bowed her head and began to mutter to her unseen companions. Sighard held his breath, waiting for her answer.

A terrible, throat-rending scream tore through the night.

Sighard jerked in shock. Panic flooded through the congregation. Cries of 'The *wuduwasa* is coming!' rang out and within moments the terrified throng were fleeing in all directions. In the confusion, Sighard lost sight of the wise woman, and when his view across the fire was clear he saw that Brigid too was gone.

As the contagion of dread throbbed through him, he dashed away from the fireside. Bursting through the curtain of willow branches, he found Madulf crouching against a tree, hunted eyes darting.

'That scream,' his brother hissed. 'What stalks this place?'

Crashing erupted away in the trees as if some great beast raged there. The two brothers gaped at each other and then they scrambled away. In that wild flight, Sighard fancied he could glimpse bloody fangs in the dark, and feel cold breath upon his neck.

When the two men tumbled out of the trees on to a beaten surface, Sighard realized that by blind luck they had found their way to the old straight track. Pearly moonlight dappled the way ahead. Sucking in a gulp of air, he looked around, chose his direction and ran. Madulf bounded at his heels.

Behind them, breaking branches cracked.

Blinking away tears of fear, Sighard muttered a prayer. If God allowed him to slip away from the *wuduwasa*'s grasp and reach the safety of Ely's walls, he would make an offering at Etheldreda's shrine every week.

But God was not yet ready to come to his aid. Stumbling over a root, he sprawled on the track. The air rushed from his

lungs. Madulf skidded to a halt, looking all around. With
shaking hands, he grabbed Sighard and wrenched him up on to
sore knees.

'Come,' he insisted.

'Wait . . .'

'Are you mad?'

As Madulf tried to drag him along, Sighard threw him off.
His hands were wet, sticky. Raising his palm to his nose, he
recoiled from the iron stink.

'Blood,' he whispered. 'Fresh.'

'If the *wuduwasa* hunts behind us, how could that be?'

Sighard felt the uncertainty drive his terror to a new level.
Jumping to his feet, he advanced with hesitant steps, no longer
sure which way he should go.

When Madulf grabbed his shoulder, he almost cried out.
'There.' His brother's hand shook so much he could barely
point.

A dark shape lay across the path. A moan rolled towards
them. Fighting the instinct to run, Sighard crept forward and
dropped to his haunches. In a shaft of moonlight, he saw that
it was a man. A growing black pool shimmered around him.

Flashing a worried glance at his brother, Sighard turned over
the prone figure. He flinched. 'Jurmin,' he whispered.

'What?' Madulf leapt to his side. 'The scout?'

Sighard nodded. Jurmin had been dispatched to spy upon the
Normans when the worries about Hereward's disappearance
had reached fever pitch. The scout coughed and a mist of blood
settled on Sighard's arm. Jurmin blinked, forcing himself to
focus on the face hovering over him. With a burst of vigour, he
grasped Sighard's wrist and tried to lever himself up on to his
elbow. 'Run for Ely as fast as your legs will carry you,' he
croaked. 'The hour is later than we ever realized. The Normans
are everywhere.'

Still caught up in visions of the *wuduwasa*, Sighard fought to
comprehend what the scout was saying. 'The Normans?'

'You must find Hereward . . . Kraki . . . any of them . . .

warn them . . . warn them all.' He choked and spat a mouthful of blood. 'Warn them . . . the king is coming. The king!'

Sighard reeled. 'William the Bastard is making his move?'

Madulf clutched his head. 'We thought we had all the time in the world. The king would never attack before the spring floods had gone. Everyone said!'

Dry wood cracked in the trees behind them. Not the *wuduwasa* at all, Sighard realized. Something that could be far worse. He strained to hear. The clank of iron. Dim voices calling in the harsh Norman tongue.

'Go,' Jurmin insisted. 'God comes for my soul. You cannot help me.'

Sighard gave the man's arm a squeeze. He could see from the puddling blood that Jurmin was right: his days were done. Grabbing hold of Madulf's arm, Sighard urged him along the track.

As they crept away, jubilant cries rang out. The Norman hunting band had found Jurmin. Sighard glanced back and saw shapes looming over the wounded scout. Moonlight glinted off helms and mail shirts. A note of triumph rang in the harsh voices. Swords flashed up, then down. Jurmin screamed.

Consumed by terror, Sighard ran. The king was coming, and Hereward had abandoned them. A hell of iron was about to descend upon the English.

The End of Days was here.

CHAPTER TWO

In the whispering reed-beds, the English warriors were waiting to drench their spears in blood. Silent, unmoving, they crouched, breath tight in their chests, eyes fixed upon the wall of fog drifting among the willows. In that hour after dawn, the fenlands still slumbered. For too long, the only sound had been the steady patter of moisture dripping from the branches on to the blanket of sodden brown leaves. Now the muffled jangle of mail shirts rang out. The ground was throbbing with the distant pounding of hooves.

Kraki smiled. This time was to be savoured. The peace before the axe fell and the blood pumped. He could smell his own sweat, musky and comforting under the aged leather and furs. The reassuring weight of his hauberk was heavy upon his shoulders. The eyelets of his helm framed the world in iron. He always saw the world that way, a circle that was an arena, for fighting was all he had known since he was a boy. There had only been two choices in his northland home, where the sun glinted off the mountain snows and the air was as sharp as a Norman sword, and he could never have settled for the dull consistency of a farmer's life. The back-breaking ploughing, and the sowing and the praying. Life was harsh, and you had to place your hands round its neck and throttle it until the myriad riches tumbled from its purse. He remembered the first man he had ever killed, the face split in two by his axe, the glistening contents steaming in the chill air. He had felt no remorse, no queasiness at the brutal realities of death. For his lack of emotion some thought him cold-hearted, a butcher even. But in battle, he heard the song that filled the heart.

Away in the fog, a horse snorted.

Kraki glanced through the waving reeds to where Guthrinc waited. As big as an oak, the Englishman had to all but fold himself in two to hide. Guthrinc cocked his head, listened for a moment, and then nodded. It was nearly time.

Before Kraki could order his men to make ready, the sounds of a scuffle tore through the quiet. Barely able to contain his fury, Kraki bounded over to where two of his men rolled around in the reeds. He yanked the warriors apart, snarling under his breath, 'Give away our hiding place and I will cut off your cocks and feed them to you.'

Mad Hengist sprawled on his back, clearly the victim of the struggle. Bruises dappled his ratty face and blood trickled from his nose. The other man, Elstan, glowered.

'What is amiss?' Kraki growled.

'I will not call him shield-brother,' Elstan muttered. 'He murdered Oswyn the potter. He cannot be trusted.'

The Viking clanged the haft of his axe against the side of the warrior's helm. 'Have your brains leaked out of your ears?'

'His knife was found upon the body,' the warrior snapped.

Kraki snorted.

'Ask at the tavern. Ask the monks—'

The Viking rapped his axe round Elstan's head once more. 'Enough,' he spat. 'Get back to your place or you will feel the bite of this blade.'

Sullen, Elstan crawled off. Kraki eyed Hengist, who ran his fingers through his straggly blond hair, muttering to himself. Since he had seen his kin slaughtered by the Normans, Hengist had veered between madness and clarity, but he had always been loyal. 'Ready yourself,' the Viking murmured, shaking his axe for emphasis. He crawled back to the front and raised his arm. He could feel all eyes settle upon him.

After a while, grey shapes appeared in the mist. They gradually took on form and weight until three men on horse-back and five on foot emerged into the thin light. They were cloaked and hooded against the damp and the chill, but Kraki did not need to see their faces. Those on foot were guards, fodder, in case bandits attacked. Two of the riders were knights, dangerous with their double-edged swords and battle-honed skills. But it was the third man who interested Kraki the most.

He dropped his arm.

The English burst from the reeds with a throaty battle-cry. The horses reared, whinnying, as the rebels circled their prey. Their spears whisked up, their shields raised to cover their lower faces. One of the knights tumbled back on to the soft earth. The other two riders fought to control their mounts.

'Hold, if you value your lives,' Kraki barked.

He strode to the front of the war-band, swinging his axe by his side. The Normans glanced around, saw they were outnumbered.

Kraki levelled his axe at the third rider and said, 'Reveal yourself.'

The man tipped his head back in disdain and slid his cowl from his head. He showed a cold face to his captor. Unafraid, as Kraki had anticipated. He looked like a raptor, with a long, hooked nose and piercing grey eyes. His thick brown hair was shaved at the back in the Norman style.

'Abbot Turold,' Kraki noted, 'caught like a rat by a pack of mill dogs.' He looked the churchman up and down. Turold was not like any of the bent-backed, weak-armed English monks. No, he was one of the feared Norman warrior-priests, broad-shouldered and strong, as used to wielding a sword or an axe as a Bible. Kraki had heard how the English in Burgh had grown to fear this man since the king himself had sent him to take charge of the abbey. He had once raised an enemy off the ground with one hand at the throat, so tales said. And he had single-handedly slain three robbers who had attacked him while he was riding in the forest to the west of his new home. Kraki was not impressed. He could do those things himself without raising a sweat. But they were feats for a churchman, with that he had to agree.

Turold glowered. 'Dogs, you are, that you would attack a holy man.'

'Your hands are not clean,' Kraki grunted. 'Do not pretend you are close to God. Down in the mud, where you belong.'

The English rebels jabbed their spears at the abbot until he climbed off his mount. He still held his head high. Kraki nodded and Guthrinc wrenched open a chest strapped across the rear of Turold's horse. Gold plate glimmered. Guthrinc delved into the casket, tossing out jewel-encrusted chalices and silver boxes as if they were scraps for pigs. 'Here,' the big man said with a wry smile. 'Let me unburden you. You will travel much faster to Burgh without this weighing you down.'

Hengist and another man collected the treasure and stuffed the items into sacks. 'Some merchants will be regretting the day they hid their fortunes in an English church for safekeeping,' Hengist noted as he weighed his sack. 'Little did they know the king would consider it all fair game for his own coffers.'

'William the Bastard will plunder anything in England that catches his eye,' Kraki said, 'and he has more than enough lackeys to make it so.' He eyed Turold. The abbot held his gaze. The Viking grinned and said to his men, 'Get to work.'

As the English looted the treasure, Kraki prowled around the Normans. He was uneasy. Sly words were not his strength. He only truly felt comfortable when he was swinging an axe. But he had to play the game, for it was the sole reason they were there, risking their necks to rob one of the most feared Normans in the east, a man who had the king's ear.

Remembering the words he had discussed with the others at their council in Ely two nights gone, he said, 'Hereward sends

21

his greetings. He yearns for the day when he will meet you in the flesh. At the end of a sword.'

Kraki cursed silently as he saw all his men glance up at the abbot's face, though they had been warned to pretend they were engrossed in their tasks. But Turold seemed not to notice.

'If your leader was as brave as his words, he would face me this day,' the Norman abbot said with contempt. 'Instead, he hides away with the women and children at your camp.'

Turning away, Kraki kicked amongst the treasure so that the other man would not see any emotion play on his face. He had discovered what he needed to know: the invaders had not killed Hereward. Nor did they hold him prisoner. Turold would not have been able to contain his mockery if that were the case. He recalled mad Hengist's words at the council: 'Hereward *is* the English rebellion in the eyes of the Norman bastards. The king's men would have overrun Ely by now if they knew our leader was gone.' Now there was no doubt.

Kraki knelt to pretend to examine a goblet. He felt no jubilation at this news. If Hereward had not been taken by their enemies these six weeks gone, where was he? Drowned in a bog? The Mercian was no coward, that was certain. He would never have fled, no matter how great the odds. Kraki tossed the goblet to Guthrinc. 'This should buy us a few more axes-for-hire,' he said. He nodded to Turold. 'Your greed has made your work harder still. Our army grows by the day. Soon we will be coming for you. Take that message back to the snakes you call your friends.'

'I am no go-between,' the abbot roared. His sword flashed out of its sheath faster than Kraki could have dreamed. The cutting edge blurred towards his neck. His axe swung up without a thought, driven by instinct honed on a hundred battlefields. A stream of sparks. The ringing of iron. An impact jarring deep into his shoulder, forcing him back a step.

With some Norman epithet that Kraki didn't understand, Turold threw himself forward. This was madness, Kraki thought. Surely the churchman knew he would be cut down in an instant. He had thought the abbot cleverer than that.

Kraki wrinkled his nose at the stink of strange spices as the Norman slammed into him. It was like being attacked by a bear: big and strong, with a ferocious, unrelenting attack. With skilful flourishes, the sword hacked towards the few areas of exposed flesh on his body, neck, arms, calves. Kraki grunted, keeping a cool head. The priest was trying to make sure he didn't have time to think.

He swung his axe up in front of his face and hurled himself into the path of the dancing sword. The blade clanged against his weapon, more by luck than design. But he had his opening. Kraki rammed his helm into the abbot's face. He heard the Norman howl as cartilage burst. Hot blood splashed across his cheek.

With a yell, Kraki swung his axe up. He was ready to cleave Turold's head in two, the opportunity to send a message back to the king be damned. But as his weapon wavered at the apex, Turold let his sword fall to his side. Kraki glimpsed the ghost of a smile on the man's lips. He heard the sound of pounding feet in the undergrowth. One of the monks who had accompanied Turold was racing away into the woods. The fight had been a distraction. He cursed himself.

Thrusting Turold aside, he launched himself in pursuit of the darting figure. Guthrinc and Hengist crashed into the undergrowth alongside him. The monk was small and wiry, and he had a good head start. Kraki could see they would not catch him easily. And yet the churchman skidded to a halt. From a pouch at his waist, he pulled a hunting horn and raised it to his lips.

'Bring him down,' Kraki bellowed.

Guthrinc notched a shaft to his hunting bow. In one fluid movement, he took aim and loosed his arrow.

Too late; the lowing of the horn rolled through the still woods a moment before the shaft thudded into the man's back.

Away in the trees, another horn answered.

CHAPTER THREE

When the hunting horn blared again, nearer this time, Kraki, Guthrinc and Hengist jerked alert as if they had been burned. Wood cracked. Running feet thrummed on the leaf-mould.

Kraki cursed.

'We stand and fight?' Hengist peered into the mist with his unsettling pale eyes.

Turning, the Viking shook his head. 'Too many of them by the sounds of it,' he whispered. 'Back to Ely.'

'The treasure?' Guthrinc made a hurt face; he already knew the answer.

'Leave it. It will only weigh us down. We take with us something greater than gold – the knowledge that the Norman bastards have not spilled Hereward's blood.'

The horn moaned once more, closer still, and it was echoed by two more. The call and response rang across the fog-shrouded woods. Kraki frowned. This was no mere hunting band.

'Go, now,' he urged. 'Kill the knights, leave the monks. But if Turold stands in your way, gut him.'

Guthrinc darted away through ochre waves of bracken, light on his feet for such a big man. Kraki followed. Barely a spear's length had passed under his feet when he heard a cry. He whirled and saw Hengist crash down into the fern, his features contorted.

Kraki dashed back to the fallen man, fearing his spear-brother had been winged by a crossbow bolt. But as he knelt, he saw the wiry warrior only clutched at his ankle.

'Leave me,' Hengist whispered with a grimace. 'I will lie among the ferns and hope the Normans will not see me.'

Kraki grunted. 'I have heard better plans from the mouths of children.' He peered into the white cloud. The sound of running feet echoed all around now. 'Over my shoulder you will go. And no whining or I will dump you in a bog.' Hengist started to protest, but Kraki only cuffed him round the ear to silence him.

He hooked one hand in the warrior's brown tunic, the other under his thigh, and heaved him up. Hengist weighed little more than a young deer, and for that Kraki was thankful. He lumbered away from the sound of the nearing army.

Ahead, a cry echoed in the Norman tongue. Kraki recognized Turold's voice. Guthrinc must have led the English away already. That was good. Kraki veered away from where they had caught the band of churchmen. If he could reach the flanks of the approaching Normans, he could hide in the fog as he circled behind them.

Yet even that thin plan faded too fast. Grey shapes emerged from the white cloud, two of them, he saw, searching all around. Their lips curled back in glee when they saw their prey. Shrugging Hengist off his shoulder Kraki whirled up his axe. A head flew through the air before the English warrior sprawled in the bracken. As the other soldier cupped his hand to his mouth and yelled to his comrades, Kraki hacked into his neck.

Wrenching his weapon free, he scooped Hengist up and struggled on, but he could hear the calls of their enemies drawing closer.

'You are drunk or mad or both,' Hengist gasped. 'Aelfgar the One-Legged moves faster than us. Leave me now.'

'If the gods want us both, they will take us. What we do matters not. Now keep your pox-ridden mouth closed.'

Kraki heard heavy footsteps pounding behind them. Hoping their pursuer might lose them in the fog, he ran on through the white world, the bracken swaying against his knees. But when the sound of running feet drew closer, he cursed. His choice was stark: fight or die with a sword in his back.

'Hide,' he whispered to the man across his shoulders. 'Let our enemy think there is only one of us.' Once again he shrugged Hengist off his shoulders as if he were tossing down a sack of grain. When he saw his spear-brother crawl away into the willows, he nodded, relieved. He felt a calm descend on him, and turned to face his fate, good or ill. His axe felt good in his hand. His heart was full and his blood burned in his veins.

He stared into the fog, waiting.

After a moment, what he at first took to be a bear crashed out of the white folds. No Norman, this. Furs and blood-caked mail and worn leather. A helm dented by the blows of many axes. Eyes all-black, and wild hair and beard that had been dyed red by berries. Kraki recognized Harald Redteeth, the axe-for-hire who had sworn to take Hereward's life for some slight, Kraki wasn't sure what. But it must have been great indeed, for the Viking had hunted the Mercian for years to achieve his blood-oath.

Kraki lowered his shoulders and brought his blue and white shield up. His nostrils flared. He could smell the reek of the other man's sweat.

'Hereward's man,' Redteeth said, giving a broken-toothed grin. 'Where is your master?'

'I call no man master.'

The Viking shrugged. 'You would die in his place?'

'If there is death here, it will not be mine.'

Harald nodded, accepting the call to battle. Raising his rough, unpainted shield, he shook his axe. The two warriors began to circle. A track appeared through the glistening bracken.

Kraki narrowed his eyes. The rest of the world faded away. He studied Harald Redteeth's face, the scars from spear, sword and axe, the swath of pink where the skin had been burned away: a map of battles. Here was a worthy foe.

A roar shattered the moment as Redteeth swung his axe high. The two warriors clashed like rutting stags. Thrusting his shield in front of him, Kraki smashed his enemy's blade aside. The seasoned wood groaned. He hacked down with his own weapon, but the blade only bit deep into his enemy's shield. He wrenched it free and took a step back.

They circled each other again.

When next the calm broke, Kraki lunged to hook his foe. Darting in close, he swung his axe behind Redteeth's back. With a lightness of foot that belied his bulk, he leapt back, dragging his weapon with him to rip open his opponent's side. But the Viking rolled to one side as the blade came back, and there was only a trail of sparks where it raked across his mail. Redteeth threw back his head and laughed.

Kraki glowered – he saw no humour. Fighting was serious business.

Delirious with battle-fury, Redteeth's unblinking eyes were as black as coals. It was the toadstool-madness, Kraki knew, giving him a strength above all men, and a relentless ferocity. He seemed not to tire. Round and round they went, blades flashing high and low, until Kraki thought there would be no end to it.

Behind the Northman, Hengist raised his head above the swaying fronds. Kraki had no time to be shocked. The mad English warrior yanked up a broken branch that had been hidden beneath the bracken and jammed it between Redteeth's legs. The mercenary went down hard. Kraki wrenched up his axe. But when he locked eyes with the Viking, he realized he could not kill him. The fight had not been won fairly; it would be an ignoble death. With a flick of his wrist, he hammered the haft down into the fallen man's face.

Nearby, hunting horns blared and men called to each other

in the guttural Norman tongue. 'We are not free yet,' Kraki growled.

Once he was sure Redteeth was unconscious, he grabbed a handful of Hengist's tunic and hauled him effortlessly on to his shoulders. He remembered Guthrinc's words to Hereward when their leader had spared the Viking's life: *This night will come back and bite you in the arse.* Kraki feared this day would do the same. But he would not – could not – have done anything else. Without honour, a man had nothing.

On weary legs, he pushed his way through the bracken. Sounds of running feet echoed on all sides. Sweat trickled down his back. Their enemies were too close, and drawing closer by the moment.

Hengist seemed to be craning his neck, and after a moment he whispered, 'I know this place. Over there.' He waved his arm to the right.

Kraki hesitated, then lurched in the direction the other man had indicated. The fog rolled around them. Underfoot, the ground became softer, then sodden. Within a few steps, he reached the edge of black water.

He cursed. Trapped. And there was no going back. The call and response of the bastard Normans had started to coalesce behind him. Before he could berate Hengist for his stupidity, the other warrior waved his arm once again, this time directing Kraki along the muddy shore to his right.

Pushing through the curtain of willow branches, he found a pile of newly cut wood. An axe protruded from an oak that had been cut down and dragged to the water's edge. An adze and a mallet lay in a froth of curled, creamy chippings. Kraki inhaled the sweet smell of the wood. Further on, the embers of a fire glowed red. Beside it, in a wisp of grey smoke, hides dried, ready to be cured and then drawn over a willow frame to make the small round-boats the locals used for fishing in the inland sea. Kraki cocked his head. All was still. The boatmaker was no doubt in hiding, quaking at the sound of the Norman horns. The Northman edged past two half-made round-boats until he found one of the larger, flat-bottomed vessels constructed from a hollowed-out tree trunk. It had been dragged half out of the water on to the mud.

He grinned. 'Sometimes you are not as mad as you seem.'

'I have saved your life and I have saved your life,' Hengist murmured.

A yell shattered the tranquillity. Redteeth had been discovered. Kraki dumped the other man into the boat and hurried to the prow. The thick mud sucked at his feet. Heaving the vessel from its mooring, he splashed out into the shallows and clambered aboard with little grace. The fog closed around them.

Lying in the bottom, Kraki stared up at the white world. The stifled sounds of the Normans searching the boatmaker's yard floated across the gently lapping water. Relief flooded him. The bastards would never find them now.

As his rapid breathing subsided, he raised his head and glanced at Hengist. *Sometimes you are not as mad as you seem.* His own words tugged at his thoughts. 'Show me your knife,' he murmured.

The other man didn't meet his searching gaze. 'I have lost it,' he replied in a barely audible voice.

Kraki studied his spear-brother, reflecting on what Elstan had said about the murder that had cast a pall over all Ely. Oswyn the potter had been a friend to many, a gentle man. No one could imagine what kind of devil had killed him. After a moment, Kraki laid his head back, pushing the troubling notion to one side.

He drifted with the boat.

Unshackled, his thoughts took wing, back to his woman, Acha. He felt a pang of affection that surprised him. When he had first met her in Eoferwic, he had loathed her sharp tongue and contemptuous manner. Then he had wanted to tame her. But at some point on the long journey south to Ely, true feelings had stirred inside him. He hated that; it made him feel weak, like the rosy-cheeked young men who had their noses tweaked by the village girls. And he despised himself for fearing that death might drag them apart whenever he went into battle. That made him vulnerable, as if he fought without a shield.

He shook the thought from his head, for in truth it frightened him, and he had never been afrit before. Sometimes he even dreamed of fleeing Ely with her, and this cursed, never-ending fight, to see out their days together in some quiet settlement where axes and spears were never raised.

He closed his eyes. She had made a farmer of him. Cut off his head now and be done with it.

'I hear something.' Hengist was lying on his stomach and peering over the rim of the boat.

'No eel-catcher would be out in this fog,' Kraki grunted. 'Put your head down. Soon we will be far enough from shore for the king's men not to hear the splashing of our oar. And then we will be back in Ely in no time.'

He watched Hengist furrow his brow. 'Listen,' the Englishman exclaimed, cupping a hand to his ear.

Kraki heard nothing. He shook his head.

'No,' the other man protested. 'There is something out there.'

The Northman raised his head above the rim of the boat. This time he did hear something, far away in the bank of the fog. A low moan, so fleeting he could barely be sure he had heard anything. Hengist turned to him, eyes widening. Kraki could see the other man feared this was no earthly encounter. When the muffled rumbling came again, he felt his neck prickle. It did sound like the call of some great beast.

'What do we do?' Hengist whispered, his voice strained.

The Northman pulled himself up, resting his hands on the rim of the rocking boat. The sound was coming from somewhere ahead of them, but the distorting effects of the fog made it impossible to tell the exact direction. They could not go back towards the shore, that was certain.

Hengist edged backwards, raising one trembling arm to

point. A dark shape loomed away in the white bank. It towered above them, perhaps as high as the pitch of the church roof at Ely. If this were a monster, it could swallow them whole in an instant.

The boat drifted on, both men gripped by the looming shadow.

The beast's call rolled out across the water again. When the bulk finally emerged from the fog, he grew cold. This was worse than any supernatural terror.

Kraki raised his head to look up the length of a huge siege engine, a trebuchet, standing tall on a scaffold with four mighty oak legs, each one too wide for him to encircle with his arms. The long beam ending in the catapult sling hung low. He imagined the machine in action, firing projectiles that could rip through a fortress's thick stone walls as if they were made of wattle. He shivered again. The siege engine floated on several of the flat-bottomed boats bound together with rope. He marvelled at the cunning of the Normans; there was no other way to get such a vast machine across the fenlands. Several men were hard at work rowing. Another lounged among the trebuchet's legs. He raised a horn to his lips and blew, producing the deep, low blast that they had taken to be the voice of the lake monster.

As the siege engine disappeared into the mist once more, their boat bobbed across its wake.

'They did not see us,' Hengist gasped with relief. 'God has blessed us.'

Another horn blasted from a different direction. Kraki turned and looked back. Now he could hear men shouting and the creak of ropes, and more horns calling that all was well. Another vast black shape began to drift out of the fog, following the first siege engine. And another, and another, until he could see the towering shadows everywhere. With mounting trepidation, he watched the slow procession until the fog swallowed them up once more.

Doom was coming to Ely. The king's patience had grown

thin and he had sent his full might into the fenlands. And there could not have been a worse time. Their leader was missing. Their forces were in low spirits awaiting news of Hereward's fate. And like wild dogs they fought among themselves over the right course of action. Kraki gripped his axe between his legs and bowed his head, wondering what terrors the coming days would bring.

CHAPTER FOUR

Golden leaves glowed in the shafts of sunlight punching through the fading fog. The morning was growing warmer as the two men made their way through the woods on the backs of dun ponies. The scent of autumn hung in the air, the sharp tang of berries and the sweet aroma of fallen fruit turning to rot, the cloying reek of damp vegetation.

'You are well?' Alric asked. His voice sounded jarring amid the birdsong and the steady crunch of leaves under the horses' hooves. They had not spoken for long miles. He was a monk, his face thin, his frame slight, and he always looked to be three days from a good meal.

His companion, Thurstan, abbot of Ely, was older, taller and greyer, but just as lean. He jerked his head as if startled. 'Church business weighs upon me,' he muttered.

Alric was not convinced, but he did not press the matter. He wiped the sheen of sweat off his forehead and looked around with unease. He saw enemies in every thicket and ditch. Perhaps the abbot felt the same.

'We will soon be in Angerhale,' Alric said, 'and home in Ely before midnight. Our brothers will fare well without you till then.'

Thurstan inhaled a deep draught of the chill air. They had been riding through the night and their muscles ached. 'No news of Hereward?' he asked.

Alric shook his head. 'I am sure he is well.'

'But if he has abandoned us . . .'

'We have leaders of great wisdom among the rebel band,' the younger man interjected. 'Kraki. Guthrinc . . .'

'But they are not Hereward.'

Alric paused. 'No. They are not. But there is not a man there who would not lay down his life to protect the monks of Ely. The English will never forget the faith you have placed in them. We stand strong, together.'

Thurstan nodded, but he lost himself in his dark thoughts too quickly.

They guided their ponies along the track through the woods and emerged into rolling green lands lit by the morning sun. Trails of pearly mist still drifted to the hollows. Nearby was Bottisham, and on the horizon in the west was the grey fug of the home-fires of Grentabrige. They would not want to venture too near to that stronghold of the king. Once out of the trees, the riding was easier. They trundled along a road of rutted mud, weaving past a mill where hens scratched among the white dust beside a pile of sacks.

Thurstan's mood seemed to lift as they took the track past neat fields towards their destination, a hamlet of only four shacks around a dirty pond and a few outlying farms.

'May I ask, Father, now we are here, what is the nature of your ministrations in Angerhale?' Alric clambered down from his mount and tied the pony to the post.

'Aye, you may ask now.' Thurstan slipped from his pony and unfurled his long frame, stretching the cricks from his muscles. 'I am not here to minister, but to do God's business.'

'Here?' Alric looked around at the meagre shacks. He noticed a man skulking in the lee of a barn, his eyes on them.

Thurstan glanced around once to make sure they were not

being watched and then hurried over. 'Jaruman. You are well?' he enquired.

Jaruman barely came up to Alric's chest. His face was flayed pink by the wind and his hair was the colour of a fleece. He bowed his head in awe when Thurstan towered over him and muttered some words that Alric could not hear.

'You do God's work well, Jaruman,' the abbot said with a tight smile. 'You will be well rewarded in the next life. And in this one.' He pressed a coin into the ceorl's palm. When Jaruman's eyes lit up, Alric thought he might fall to his knees in gratitude. 'Make sure we are not disturbed,' Thurstan added, and without waiting for an answer he marched into the barn. Alric ran over the whorls of hard mud to catch up.

As they stepped into the dusty air of the interior, he looked around, his brow knitting again. He saw hay for a horse, a plough caked with old mud, and one of the tiny straw men that the superstitious farmers used to placate the god of the fields, and he could smell the apples in the barrels. Nothing that might have encouraged the abbot to take such a dangerous journey.

'Close the door,' Thurstan said.

Once Alric had heaved the creaking door shut, narrow beams of sunlight spiked through the gloom here and there from the unpatched holes in the barn's roof. The abbot strode to the far end and kicked aside the dry straw that covered the floor in that area. Most of the ground was packed earth, but Alric glimpsed a wooden trap. With a length of hemp rope, Thurstan pulled up the hatch. He lowered himself into the hole that had been revealed.

Following, Alric found himself in a dank chamber cut out of the earth. When his eyes grew accustomed to the half-light, he gasped. Treasure was heaped against the far wall. Gold plate, silver chalices, books and reliquaries encrusted with jewels. He snatched up a familiar gold bowl and turned it over in his hands. 'This is from the church in Ely.' His voice was dulled in the enclosed space.

Thurstan took a gold plate and a goblet from the sack he had carried from his pony and laid them carefully on the pile. 'All of it, now.'

'But when . . .'

'One or two pieces at a time, brought out of Ely hidden in sacks or tucked inside Jaruman's tunic when he came to us in the guise of a merchant.'

'Why, it must have taken weeks,' Alric marvelled. 'And yet not a word was said.'

'Our brothers think it hidden for safe keeping under the church. Only a handful know the truth.'

Alric looked over the riches. 'Father, I fail to understand. Surely this gold and silver is safer in Ely than here. This ceorl . . .'

'Jaruman fears God's judgement more than he desires any earthly reward. I have known him since he was a boy, and he would die rather than betray this trust placed in him.'

Alric replaced the bowl. His thoughts raced. 'You fear Ely will fall. You have hidden the church's gold here to prevent it tumbling into the king's hands.'

Thurstan nodded, caring little for the note of judgement he heard in the other man's voice. 'My duty is to God, and the church we have built, above all else. I must prepare for what may never come to pass, or risk failing the Lord. You know full well what the king thinks of the English church. He takes our gold for his own coffers. He steals our land. He replaces good English abbots with his own loyal Norman priests. William the Bastard would like nothing more than to sack Ely, and to smite us low for the aid we have given to the last of the English. But should he ever set foot within Ely's walls, he will find little joy.'

'Why have you brought me here?'

Thurstan hesitated before putting on a smile and taking the younger man's arm. 'I sit among Hereward's men when plans are made and I hear all. But there will come a time, in days darker than now, when news may be thin on the ground. I know, whatever your friendship with Hereward, your allegiance is to God above all. You are in my trust here. I would be in yours, if there is benefit to the church.'

'You would have me betray the trust of men I call friends?'

'I would have you be true to God, and your vows.' Thurstan peered at him, stern and unflinching.

Alric took a deep breath. How could he fault the abbot? With Hereward missing, surely it was only good sense to prepare for the worst. 'I will do what I can.'

The abbot smiled. 'Good. Then we are in agreement.'

They climbed out of the loamy atmosphere and stepped out of the barn. Jaruman waited, his hands clasped in front of him.

'You must not take the same road home,' he said in a voice so low it was almost lost beneath the clucking of the hens. 'My brother has come with news – he waits by my hearth now. This morning the Normans rode out of Grentabrige in force. They are everywhere, like flies on a dead dog. All who travel towards Ely are being stopped and turned back, or worse.'

Alric eyed Thurstan. They did not need to speak to share their concerns. It was not yet winter, but the wolves were drawing closer. What had prompted this new approach?

'There is another way,' Jaruman said. He gave directions to a secret track that only the ceorls of Angerhale knew. It would take them east, out of their way by several miles, but then they could take another hidden track that would lead them north to Ely. Alric prayed it would help them avoid the Normans.

They climbed back on to their ponies and set off across the fields. Alric's stomach was growling by the time they reached the woods. From his sack he pulled a knob of bread to gnaw on as he rode. His mood grew darker with each passing hour.

The sun had passed its highest point by the time they neared a village. He frowned. No sound of mallets or axes. No children at play. No voices of women gossiping with their neighbours. Puzzled, Alric took in the empty fields and the half-cut tree near the firewood pile. He chewed a nail in thought. The atmosphere felt strained, haunted. The abbot felt it too, for he raised himself up on his mount, his shoulders tense.

'Should we pass this village by?' Alric asked.

Barely had the words left his lips before figures began to stagger from the cluster of homes. All of them were women, he saw. They stood beside their doors, staring at the two clerics on their ponies as if they could not believe their eyes. A few children ventured out into the light, but hovered near their mothers as if they were afraid to stand on their own. No men, anywhere. Then, as one, the women picked up their skirts and scrambled towards them through the long grass. Unsettled by the sight, Alric and Thurstan brought their horses to a halt.

As the women neared, Alric saw their faces were drawn and their cheeks flushed. And as they gathered around the two men, he recognized eyes red from hard tears. Despair, that was what he sensed in all of them.

'Help us,' one of the woman pleaded, 'oh, help us,' and that seemed to release a deluge. All the women cried out as one, pent-up emotions releasing a torrent of words, all fighting to be heard. Alric could not understand a single thing they were saying. The women reached out to him in desperation and clawed at the abbot's tunic with trembling fingers, until Thurstan held up his hands.

'Daughters, hold your tongues!' he commanded. 'Let one speak, one only!'

The women fell silent. Then one stepped forward. Alric thought she seemed about his age. She wore no headdress. Her brown hair was pulled back and tied with a ribbon and she was not unattractive, he saw; her eyes were large and dark and filled with emotion. Yet she showed a face that was filled with more defiance than all the other women's put together.

'Speak, daughter, if you would,' Thurstan said. 'What is your name?'

'Rowena,' she replied. Her voice did not waver.

'What is amiss here?'

'We are lost,' one of the other women cried. Rowena gave her a rough shove before turning back to the abbot.

'The Normans came at dawn. They took our men from their beds and marched them away across the fields.'

'To their deaths?' Thurstan asked, too harshly, Alric thought.

'I . . . I think not,' Rowena replied. 'I have seen the Normans take out their anger on the English before, and they cut off their heads in front of their wives and children, or slit their throats and hang them from a gibbet beside their homes.' Her voice trembled now, but with anger, not misery, Alric noted. 'No, our husbands were taken for some other reason,' she continued, wiping away one hot tear with the back of her hand, 'but though we pleaded we were not told why, or when or if they would be back.'

Thurstan looked to Alric. There was mystery here.

'Our village is not the first to suffer,' Rowena said. 'Two others have been so afflicted, to my knowledge. More, perhaps.' She clenched her teeth. 'We have agreed to go into the fields to carry on the work, and do our own duties too, but there are not enough of us. If our husbands do not return by the time the snows come, we will starve.'

Alric looked around the desperate, tear-stained faces and felt a wave of pity. Stories of the miseries the Normans had inflicted were too many.

'Would that we could help find your husbands,' Thurstan replied. 'When we return to Ely, I will see what aid I can summon for your village. You have my word on that.'

It was thin hope, Alric knew, and he could see the women felt the same. But Rowena's eyes narrowed. 'You are from Ely?'

Thurstan hesitated, wondering if he had said too much.

'You know Hereward?' she pressed.

Excitement rippled through the throng.

'They say he kills bears with his bare hands . . .' one woman exclaimed.

'. . . and giants too. And that he chased the Devil out of Ely and stabbed his arse with a spear . . .'

'. . . and has a sword of fire that brings death to every Norman it touches . . .'

'Quiet,' Rowena ordered, her eyes blazing. 'You know him?'

'We do,' Alric replied.

'He is the last hope of the English,' she said. 'He can find our husbands.'

Thurstan's eyes flickered towards Alric, and then he put on the kind of smile he would show to a child. 'Hereward is consumed by work of great import—'

'This is of great import to us,' Rowena snapped.

'Do you think he has time to listen to your pleas?' Thurstan said, still smiling. 'Or those of every woman in England? His days are taken with great matters. Battles . . . plans . . . this is beneath him.'

Rowena flinched.

'I know Hereward well,' Alric interrupted, 'and no man or woman is beneath him. If he could help, he would. But—'

'You will not ask him.' Rowena glared.

'If only—'

'Then I will ask him.' She raised her chin, daring Alric to defy her. Thurstan laughed. The woman did not back down. 'I will travel with you to Ely and make my plea to Hereward himself.'

'You will not,' the abbot said, his humour draining away.

'I will go to Ely, whether you say so or not. I will travel through the woods, at night if I must. Would you see me killed by robbers? Or have my honour taken by Normans?' She jabbed a finger at the abbot. 'If I suffer, it will be upon your souls, know that.'

Thurstan opened his mouth, but could find no words to say. Alric raised his hand to his mouth to stifle the urge to laugh. Here the abbot had met his match.

'Good,' Rowena said with a nod. 'Then it is decided. And I will not return until Hereward has agreed to save us.'

CHAPTER FIVE

The wetlands shimmered in the fading light. Alric shielded his eyes against the glare as he looked out across the last stretch of their journey. In a smoky haze, Ely sat atop the isle rising out of the deceptively placid waters. The church tower stood dark and proud upon the summit. The woods were a blaze of gold and russet and orange, a chill breeze whispering through the branches. Winter was not far away.

He pulled his cloak tighter as he led his pony along the narrow causeway across the stinking bog. Perched on the horse, Rowena peered towards the settlement, a hopeful smile on her lips. Behind them, Thurstan sat in silence upon his own mount. He had simmered with irritation ever since he had been forced to allow the woman to accompany them on the journey home. Soon, though, they would have hot stew and bread and beer and their own beds.

'I have heard tell of Hereward's wife, Turfrida,' Rowena mused. 'Some said she was a witch.' She shrugged. 'That matters not to me. But all said she had the strength of an oak. A worthy wife for a great man like Hereward. Much can be told about a man by the woman he chooses. It is true that she is dead?'

Alric nodded. 'Slain by Hereward's own brother, Redwald.' He felt disgust burn in his chest at the foul murder. Even the fires of hell were a poor punishment for that wretched dog. Redwald had deceived them all, worming his way into the heart of the rebel camp, and then betraying everyone when he decided to throw his lot in with the Normans. Turfrida was a woman with only good in her heart, but Redwald had cut off her head and no doubt taken it to show off to his new allies. How they must have laughed at his friend Hereward's misfortune. He ground his teeth.

'I will say a prayer for him when we reach Ely,' she said.

Alric felt a pang of guilt. Sooner or later they would have to tell her that Hereward was missing. In her village, she would have thought it another excuse to deter her. He hoped she would forgive him.

Once across the causeway, they made their way up the winding path to Ely's gates. Only then did Alric feel safe. God had granted them a fortress of lethal bogs and dense woods and foul black water that the Normans could never cross in force. If they had made their stand anywhere else in England, the rebellion would already be crushed and his head would be sitting on a pole alongside Hereward's and Kraki's and all the rest. For that, he would give thanks every day and every night.

Once the gates had trundled shut behind them and the guards had set the great oak beam to bar them, Alric frowned at a babble of angry voices drifting across the hillside. A crowd had gathered along the street leading past the dwellings and workshops to the minster on the summit. Among the scowls, the monk glimpsed familiar faces, Ely folk, and others from the Camp of Refuge along the hillside, where all those who had sought sanctuary with Hereward had made their home. Kraki and a few of Hereward's men were all but encircled.

'Where is Hereward?' Rowena asked. 'I would speak to him now.'

Troubled by the confrontation, Alric guided the woman to

one side and said in a low voice, 'Go to the church and wait. I will meet you there soon.'

'I will wait. I have nothing but time.' She looked across Ely's thatched roofs, marvelling at the activity in the bustling settlement, so far removed from her own quiet village. She set off, taking a path between the houses to avoid the crowd.

Alric and Thurstan walked to the edge of the gathering. Folk were oblivious of them, their anger focused on Kraki and the warriors.

'Nothing but grief have we had since you came to Ely,' someone called.

'You hide the one with blood on his hands,' another shouted. 'Give him up.'

'Still your tongues,' Kraki bellowed, shaking his axe.

The crowd quietened. Eyes dipped down in fear of the warrior's fierce demeanour, but Alric could still see anger and resentment simmering in those faces. What could have happened while he had been away from Ely?

'We hide no one,' the Viking continued, pacing around the circle of bowed heads, 'because we do not know who committed these crimes. Nor do you.'

'The knife . . .' someone began.

'The knife was stolen,' Kraki barked. 'But we will find who spilled innocent blood, and they will be punished. That is my oath. Now, return to your homes.'

The men and women lingered for a moment, not satisfied by what they had heard. Then one by one they began to drift away, sullen eyes darting back to the band of warriors.

When the crowd had dissipated, Alric marched over to Kraki. 'What has put the fire in them?'

'Another murder,' Kraki grunted. 'A woman from the Camp of Refuge, strangled and thrown into the waters.'

The monk bowed his head. 'And they blame Hereward's army?'

'Aye. When we came here, we turned their lives on their heads.' The Viking hawked phlegm and spat. 'But mostly they blame Hengist. His knife was found by the body of Oswyn the potter. Stolen, he says.' He shrugged.

'You do not trust him? He has always been loyal—'

'I do not trust anyone any more,' Kraki snarled with such ferocity that Alric took a step back. 'Since Hereward has gone, we bicker and fight. Now this . . . Soon the folk here will drive us out of Ely. What then for the last hope of the English?'

Alric felt his heart fall. Hope was thin on the ground.

'And while we tear ourselves apart here in Ely, the king does not rest. Come with me. There is a man you must meet, a new arrival in the camp.' The Northman turned on his heel and strode up the hill, lowering his broad shoulders to thrust his way through the throng.

He led Alric and the abbot among the houses, past the piles of refuse reeking of rot, and the wells, to a hovel which looked as though it had been built in less than a day. The walls were packed with still-drying blocks of mud among the wood. Sods of turf had been laid across the low roof. They had to stoop to enter.

Smoke from the hearth hung in the air. Through the haze, the monk glimpsed a man sitting against the far wall. He barely murmured a word as they approached.

'Cuthwin, I have brought two churchmen to see you,' Kraki said in a hushed voice. 'They would hear the tales you have brought back from the great north road.'

Once Alric's eyes had adjusted to the gloom, he flinched. The sitting man was dressed in little more than filthy rags and he smelled of loam and sharp fear-sweat. His limbs hung limply, so thin the monk could have encircled his forearm in finger and thumb. But his face was the worst. Alric saw it had been ravaged by fire, one side blackened from forehead to jaw, the other bubbling with cracked blisters from the cheekbone down. One eye was milky with sightlessness, and he seemed half blind in the other. It was truly God's miracle that he still lived.

Cuthwin moistened his lips and tried to lift his head, but so weak was he it rocked back against the wall.

'Leave him be,' Alric whispered to Kraki. 'He needs rest, a chance to . . . to recover.'

'No. You must hear his words,' the Northman insisted. 'Tell them, Cuthwin, of the north, as you told me when you were carried through the gates of Ely. Tell them what William the Bastard has left behind in his wake.'

'Hell.' The word rustled out into the still of the hut. In a rasping voice, Cuthwin continued, 'The north is nothing but a wasteland, filled with the dead and the rats that feed upon them.'

'Do not punish him so,' Alric murmured. 'We know the king throttled the life out of the north.'

'Listen to him,' Kraki said, his eyes blazing. He dropped to his haunches and rested one hand on the wounded man's shoulder. 'Tell them what the Bastard did.'

For a moment, there was only the sound of the wind soughing through the roof, and then Cuthwin began in a faltering voice that took on strength as the terrible memories rushed back to him. 'The king came with his great army and destroyed everything in his path. All were put to the sword. Babes in arms and white-haired grandfathers too feeble to lift a bowl to their lips. Cut down in front of their wives and mothers. The bodies . . . some were burned, others thrown in ditches. The women and girls were raped. They were English, not Norman, you see. Then the Bastard's men burned the barns, and the houses, and destroyed all the food we had stored to see us through the winter. Then the fields were salted so that nothing would grow in the spring. Even that was not enough. The army went from village to village. They sent out war-bands to hound any men who fled, tracking them through the woods and across the hill-sides as if they were hunting meat for the king's larder. A few escaped southwards, like me, more by luck than judgement.'

'You were saved by God,' Thurstan insisted.

When Alric looked over the man's ruined face, he could not believe that was an act of mercy.

'Those who did not come south, but hid out in the hills,

fared worse,' Cuthwin croaked. 'In the bitter cold of the winter, they ate the horses, then they ate the dogs. And then, God help them, they fed on themselves.'

Thurstan recoiled, crossing himself. 'This cannot be. No man would stoop to such a foul act. Whoever told you these things was lying.'

Alric watched the wounded man's hand tremble. He had not been told these tales.

Kraki seemed to understand too. 'Go on,' he said with an unfamiliar note of gentleness in his voice.

'The sickness came soon after, taking the women who had been left to suffer. There is God's charity,' he said with bitterness. 'Now there is nothing left beyond Eoferwic.'

'Nothing?' Alric repeated, hoping he had misheard.

Cuthwin shook his head. 'Only a wasteland remains. More died in one season than in any battles I have heard tell of. This was not war, it was slaughter. This was cruelty beyond any we have ever known.' He grabbed Kraki's arm with a burst of passion. 'What man could do such a thing? A man who calls himself king! He is the Devil; he can be no other.' He pulled Kraki in closer and hissed, 'The English must never forget. Hereward must avenge us.'

He slumped back, so still once more that Alric thought he had died until he saw the barely perceptible rise and fall of his chest.

Kraki led them out into the chill afternoon. Their breath had begun to steam. 'Why do you show us this?' Alric enquired.

'So you know what awaits us in the days to come.' Kraki held the monk's gaze for a long moment, his eyes like deep water, and then he marched off towards the church on the top of the hill.

When they caught up with him, he was already seated at the table in the refectory, swilling beer. At the head of the table, Guthrinc gnawed on a goose leg. He wiped the grease from his mouth with the back of his hand and nodded as the two churchmen entered. Hengist limped around the room. His madness came and went these days – the wound left by the slaughter of his kin would never heal completely – but at that moment he was kneading his hands and muttering to himself, his filthy blond hair hanging across his face. Sighard was there too.

'Sit your arse down, monk. We have much to discuss,' Kraki growled. He called to one of the girls to bring stew to warm the bellies of the travellers, and beer. Once he was seated, Alric searched the faces of those around the table. Worry gnawed at them, as it had eaten its way into Alric's bones on the journey south.

'Close the door,' Kraki barked, yelling to the guard outside. 'Let no one come in while we talk.'

The door groaned shut.

'No news of Hereward?' Thurstan asked as he took his seat.

'Hereward is not here.' Kraki slammed down his cup. 'He has left us to fight this cursed war on our own. And fight it we shall.'

Hengist stopped his pacing and leaned on the table with both hands. 'I had a dream last night, that I walked under a hot sun and there was sand as far as the eye could see. And though I cried out for water, there was none. What does this mean? Is it a portent?' He looked to Thurstan.

'God speaks to us in dreams,' the abbot replied. 'This we are told. But I would ponder upon your vision for a while before I give you the answer you need.'

'Dreams!' Kraki said, clenching his fist. 'Let us speak of the here and now, before Ely is swamped in a tide of blood.'

Alric leaned forward and held out his hands. 'I do not understand this talk of portents and blood. When I set off for Bottisham, we searched for Hereward, yes, but we also made plans to take this war beyond the fens, to the king's door, if necessary.'

'All that has changed.' Kraki wagged a finger at Sighard and ordered him to speak. In a clear voice, the red-headed man told of the Norman force sweeping in from the west and the message of the murdered scout. When he was done, Kraki boomed his own account of the king's army venturing further into the fens than it ever had before, and in greater numbers. But when he spoke of the siege machines floating across what they had perceived to be the impassable waters of the east, Alric felt his heart sink.

'The king has sent out men from Grentabrige to close the roads from the south,' the monk added. 'He tries to throttle us . . . cut off our trade and keep out the men who come to join our army.'

'And he has tried to throttle us before,' Guthrinc mused. 'Why should this time be any different?'

Kraki poured himself another beer and hugged it between his palms as he stared into the brown depths. 'The king is cunning,' he reiterated. 'Some plan will be burning in the dark of his head.'

'The danger,' Thurstan suggested, 'is that you find out what that plan is too late to stop it.' His words might have sounded harsh, but Alric knew every man there was thinking the same thing.

Guthrinc cracked his knuckles. 'Now Earl Morcar has brought his men to Ely to stand with us, we have an army that could make the king quake. Our fangs are as sharp as the Bastard's, and we have a fortress better than any he can claim. I say we keep strong, and hold fast to the plans we have made. Soon we will be ready to strike out beyond the fens.' He looked from one man to the next. 'When we rout the king's men at our first battle, the English will race to our standard. William will be outnumbered, surrounded and driven back across the whale road to Normandy. Or he will stand and fight and his head will sit atop the gate at the palace at Wincestre. His choice.'

'I know I do not have a wise head like all others here,' Sighard interrupted, 'but we know the king cannot bring his army within a day's march of Ely. We are safe. Safe to plan. Safe to strike when we are ready.'

'The king is cunning,' Kraki insisted. 'We do not know his mind. But we must fathom it, and soon.'

The mood in the refectory had grown almost unbearable. All seemed happy to draw the discussion to a close so they could be alone with their thoughts. The council reached agreement to send out more scouts, though three had already been killed by the Normans that week. Risks would have to be taken if they were to learn the king's plans.

Before they could rise from their benches, the door crashed open and a red-faced monk raced in. 'Murder,' he gasped. 'Another murder.'

Kraki bellowed a curse. 'Take us there.'

The monk led the men beyond the gates and down the slopes to where the waters lapped against the isle. In the trees, not far from the narrow wooden jetty where the small fishing boats were moored, the shaking cleric stopped and pointed.

Kraki grabbed him by the shoulders and growled, 'You will speak of this to no one, do you hear me?'

Abbot Thurstan nodded his support for the implied threat in those words. Relieved to be released from his burden, the monk hurried back up the hill.

In the fading light, the men gathered around the pale remains. It was a man, though at first barely recognizable from his wounds. An axe had been taken to him, Alric noted with disgust.

'No God-fearing soul could have committed such a crime. This is the work of the Devil,' the abbot gasped, horrified by the extent of the injuries.

'Aye, or a madman,' Kraki snapped, whirling around and bearing down upon Hengist. 'What have you done?' he roared.

Hengist threw himself back, waving his arms impotently in front of him. 'It was not me,' he protested.

'You lie.' Lost to his rage, the Viking grabbed the smaller man's tunic and swung up his axe.

Guthrinc and Sighard snatched Kraki's arms and wrestled him back. 'You destroy all we have built here,' the Viking spat.

'I did not do this thing, I swear,' Hengist proclaimed. He was shaking.

'There is naught to be gained by tearing ourselves apart,' Guthrinc said, his quiet voice bringing calm.

Kraki let his weapon fall. 'If not Hengist, then who?' he growled. He looked around the circle of grim faces, but no one had any answers.

Alric knelt beside the corpse. 'I . . . I think I know him. A fisherman. I read the scripture to his son.'

Thurstan crossed himself. 'Another innocent. We must pray for him—'

'No,' Kraki said. 'Tie rocks to him and throw him into Dedman's Bog.'

Aghast, Alric jumped to his feet. 'We cannot do that.'

'His kin must be told, so they can mourn for him,' Sighard protested.

The Viking snatched a handful of Sighard's tunic and all but dragged him forward. 'If you weaken here, we will lose everything. Do you hear me?' He hurled the younger man to one side and strode around the others. 'One more innocent death will turn all Ely against us. They will drive us out. And once we are away from this fortress, the king will hunt us down like rabbits.'

Guthrinc nodded. 'What choice do we have?'

'This,' Alric began, 'is worthy of William the Bastard. Are we not better?'

'What do you suggest, monk?' Kraki snarled. 'Turn the other cheek and die, and have all that we fought for die with us? This war has dragged us all down into the mud. Now you have to ask yourself, do you want to win? And if you do, how far along the road to hell are you ready to walk to snatch victory?'

Alric stared down at the mutilated body, fighting with himself. How easy everything had seemed when they first rose up against the Norman invaders. But when he looked around at the others, he realized there was a bigger price to pay than he had foreseen. Thurstan frowned. Sighard looked away, disgusted. Hengist cowered. Guthrinc bowed his head, torn. The shield wall was breaking. How long before they could no longer stand together as spear-brothers?

'Do it,' he said, 'and may God forgive us.'

While Sighard, Guthrinc and Hengist hauled away the remains, Kraki pulled Alric to one side in the lee of Ely's walls. 'You are as slippery as an eel, monk,' he hissed, leaning in so close that Alric could see the bloody lines in the whites of his eyes. 'The others here may take you as a holy man, but I know the truth.'

The monk pulled his arm free. 'And what truth is that?'

'That you would lie like any thieving dog given the right moment.'

'I do not lie.'

'No? Not even to protect your friend? I do not believe your claims of ignorance. You have barely left Hereward's side in all the years since you first met him on the winter road to Eoferwic. You guide him. You hear him confess his sins. You share secrets that no other man will ever know. And now you say you know nothing of him?' Kraki adopted a mocking tone. 'One night he was in his hall, and the next morn he was gone, and none the wiser.'

'That is what happened.' Alric kept his tone gentle, knowing full well how easily the warrior was inflamed.

'Whatever lay between the two of you may have been your business once, but now it affects all of us in Ely,' the Northman growled. 'Without Hereward the fire in the hearts of the fighting men here is dying. If you know where he is, speak now, or let this always rest upon your soul.'

'If I could help, I would.' Pretending the conversation was done, Alric turned and walked through the gates. Bats flitted from the church tower in the dying light. The darkening sky was clear, the stars beginning to appear, and a chill was settling upon the isle of eels. He could feel Kraki's eyes upon his back. The workshops were all closed for the day, the hammers and looms stilled. Chatter drifted from open doors. Alric sensed peace there, and he was happy for them. But he could not feel it himself.

He wandered back to the walls as the golden strip along the western horizon started to become rosy. On the walkway along the palisade, the master of the flame lit the torches above the gates. They sizzled and spat. The smell of pitch hung in the air. Night fell fast at that time of year. Wanting to see the last of the day, Alric climbed the shaky ladder and looked out over the walls. His heart was heavy. He let his gaze drift across the woodlands where the shadows now deepened, and over the shimmering waters of the fens. The season was turning, the light was dying. And he found himself returning to the questions that had haunted him for too long: where was Hereward now? And was he still alive?

CHAPTER SIX

The sun slipped below the horizon. Darkness folded around the ship and the sea and sky became as one. Aft, the fire-pot blazed as it swung on its creaking iron hook, casting a thin ruddy light over the oarsmen hunched at their benches. Each sailor was poised for the order to guide the vessel into harbour. The sail cracked in the gathering night-wind, the boards flexed and groaned underfoot, and the waves boomed against the hull in a hymn of discord.

Deda felt that same discord as he stood at the prow, watching the torches around the quay at Hastinges flicker in the gloom. He was a knight of the great William, duke of Normandy and king of England, and he accepted this service with pride. No greater honour was there, his father had told him on the day when he had knelt in the cold church and accepted the touch of the sword on both shoulders. The spray had slicked his black hair into ringlets, and his eyes too seemed as black as coals. Taller than most, he could command with a single stare of his dark gaze.

He had seen twenty-seven summers, and was the veteran of many a campaign. His sword had carved a path to victory at Varaville, in Maine, and Brittany, and at Senlac Ridge. And yet, for all his service, he felt a weight of unease, though he was not certain why.

'Do not be so eager to reach that shore, Deda. Soon enough the women will be spitting at your back and the tavern keepers will be pissing in your beer.'

The knight turned at the familiar booming voice. The king had risen from his bench and was striding towards him along the surf-slick deck, seemingly oblivious of the rolling ship. William looked as broad as the old oak on the green at Wincestre. Some there were who thought he had grown fat, but Deda had seen him bare-chested as he donned his hauberk before battle, and nearly all of that bulk was muscle. Fifty summers had not dulled him.

Deda did not feel frightened by William as the king terrified so many of his fellow knights. True, the royal temper glowed like an iron in a forge, and more than one man had met his end for a word spoken out of turn. But Deda did not fear death and that made him free of the king's unspoken threat. If he died, he died. The next world would be better than this one.

'There is no peace for the likes of us,' the king growled. 'We have enemies everywhere we look. The Danish bastards sit in their halls and say they have no desire to attack. But you and I know they would sail the moment we turned our gaze else-where. Malcolm, king of the Scots, wants our blood and will not back down. And now I am forced to spend long weeks to keep my own home safe from Maine, listening to the bleating of Philip of France.'

'The talks went well. Normandy is safe.'

'This country torments me, also,' William muttered, glower-ing towards the nearing lights. 'The war was won five autumns gone. And yet still they fight on.'

'Not too many now, my lord,' Deda ventured, trying to keep his voice flat. 'A few in the east. Your campaign in the north crushed the heart of the English. No man lives there now, I hear. It is a kingdom of women. And rats.'

Deda tasted the tang of the salt on the spray. William's

cruelty in the north had plumbed depths he had not thought imaginable. And that was not the end of it, he had heard. The king kept his plans close, but whispers had reached Deda's ears of a coming storm of iron in the east, where the rebel leader Hereward had become a threat to the king's rule.

In a lull in the rumble of the waves, he sensed the monarch's gaze upon him. He turned and saw William watching him with narrowed eyes. The king seemed to have heard some tone that he did not like. 'You do not approve of my war in the north, Deda? Too brutal? Too cruel? I am told some think this way, although rivers of blood have drowned all but those last few angry voices.'

Deda smiled. 'My lord, you are wise. There is no other who knows better how to hold a crown and tame the newly conquered folk.'

The king smiled too, but like a wolf. He turned his attention back to the lights. Folding his arms behind his back, he said, 'You are not like my other knights, Deda. You do not flinch when I near.'

'I am a loyal subject, my lord.'

'You are a clever one, Deda. Too clever, some would say. I have spoken to many about you, but few seem to know your heart. They say you have no love for gold. The others scrabble like hungry dogs for my attention, but not you. Would you not wish to be raised up high? To earn new land ... power?'

'I am a simple man.'

Deda could sense the king shifting beside him, a hint of irritation. William liked to get the measure of every man in his court, the better to make them dance to his tune. But he had prowled around Deda time and again without ever getting his scent.

The king hawked up a mouthful of phlegm and spat it into the waves. 'And women? No lusts there? I hear you have no woman to warm your bed.'

'My wife is dead, my lord.'

The glow from the fire-pot lit William's furrowed brow. 'That was three winters gone, was it not?'

'She was taken by the sickness.' Deda winced as his thoughts flew back to his wife's bedside as he mopped the sweat from her brow and listened to her fading moans, when even the leech had fled at the sight of her blackened fingers. Deep into the watches of the night he had sat beside her, until the light in her eyes finally winked out. It was not the first time he had cried since he was a boy, but it was the only time that stayed with him.

'What drives you, then?' the king demanded.

'Honour, my lord. At the end of our days that is all a man has.'

William snorted, low and mocking. 'Ah, honour. Do you think you are better than other men, Deda? Do you think you are better than me?'

'Honour is the rule by which I live. I stand or fall by it. I do not use it to look down upon others. That would not be . . . honourable.'

After a moment of silence, William said, 'I will keep my eye on you, Deda. Perhaps I will learn something. You should do the same of me.'

'I will, my lord.'

'Hold out your hand. I would reward you for being an honourable man.'

'My lord?'

'Hold out your hand.'

Deda opened his palm. The king had kept his right arm behind his back for all the time they had been talking. He whipped it out and dropped a cold fish into Deda's open hand. It flapped around in the last of its death throes.

Laughing as he made his way back to his bench, William glanced over his shoulder to see the knight's reaction. All around, the oarsmen laughed with him, as they always did.

Deda gripped the fish until it stilled and then he bowed. The king's laughter drained away and a shadow crossed his face.

This was not the reaction he wanted, Deda could see. William slipped back into the shadows and lowered his bulk on to his bench, but as the knight turned back to the sea he could feel eyes heavy upon his back.

CHAPTER SEVEN

The shadow of the raised sword stabbed into the chest of the man kneeling on the mud of the castle's inner ward. Guards yanked his arms back as the Norman soldiers and nobles gathered round. Blinking away tears of fear, the prisoner fought to stop his mouth trembling and raised his chin in defiance.

'Loose your tongue,' the Butcher growled, still holding his blade high. Ivo Taillebois was the sheriff, but he still carried himself like the brute who had clawed his way out of the Normandy mud. His English was thick-tongued, his features like clay, his brow low. He knew how to kill, though, and how to run the king's enemies like rats.

'Norman bastard,' the man on the ground snarled. 'You will not make me break faith with my own.'

Redwald studied the confrontation. There was no doubt the spy would refuse to betray the rebels. Hereward had a skill for choosing the most loyal men to scout for him. But the Butcher would whittle him down. A finger or two here, a hand there, a nose, ears, eyes, then limbs. He would leave the tongue till last, so the screams would stir terror in the hearts of any English who heard them. Redwald had seen this enough times now, since he had deserted the rebels and his brother to advise the invaders here in Lincylene.

He smiled, his apple cheeks flushing. He had made the right choice. His road to power was clear once again.

'Where is Hereward?' Taillebois barked. 'Our eyes and ears in your camp tell us he has not been seen for many days now.'

The spy hung his head, his dark features sullen.

'He has fled, afraid of the king's might.' William de Warenne waved a dismissive hand towards the prisoner. Redwald eyed the nobleman. Like the Butcher, William was a fighting man who had earned his land in the east with the English blood he had spilled at Senlac Ridge. But he had a good length of bone, and learning, and the purple cloak tossed over one shoulder was of a finer and more expensive cloth than Taillebois's rough, mud-spattered garment.

'No,' Redwald interjected, his voice gentle and unthreatening. 'Hereward would never flee.'

William weighed the words, but he would not disagree. No one knew Hereward better than his brother, and for that Redwald was, if not trusted, at least respected. 'Dead, then,' the nobleman said. 'Either way, we are close to the end of this thing.'

The spy jerked his head around and searched the crowd of Normans until his gaze fell upon Redwald. His eyes widened. Redwald couldn't remember ever seeing the man, but clearly the prisoner knew him from the camp at Ely.

'Help me,' the spy called. 'Tell them to let me live, in your brother's name.'

William de Warenne chuckled. Behind his hand, he whispered, 'He thinks you are some messenger. He cannot have heard that you cut off the head of your own brother's wife to buy your way into our trust.' Redwald ignored the undisguised contempt he heard in the other man's voice. 'Still,' the nobleman continued in a thoughtful tone, 'if you think we should spare his miserable life, speak now and it shall be done.'

William was setting a trap with words, Redwald knew. Now

that he had secured his position among the Normans, he was not about to show any hint of weakness. 'Do what you will with him,' he replied with a shrug.

The prisoner's face crumpled. 'You are English,' he cried.

The Normans only laughed.

The Butcher rested the edge of his sword above the prisoner's ear. The spy began to whimper. When his scream rang out a moment later as Taillebois began to saw, Redwald walked away; he had no stomach for it. The sickening sounds followed him as he pushed through the crowd in the ward. After a moment, he stopped hearing them.

A firm hand gripped his arm. He turned to see Asketil, Hereward's father, his own father if not by blood, the man who had taken him in as a boy when his birth parents had died. Redwald was surprised to see the old man looking so vital. For a long time, Asketil had seemed to be fading by the day, as grey and twisted and lifeless as the lightning-blasted oak near their home. But now he stood tall and his eyes were clear and his grip was almost too strong to break.

'You bend the Normans to your will with ease. That is good,' the old man said in a low voice.

'They think themselves the masters now. They see no threat around them and so their guard is down.'

'You have not told them all you know?'

Redwald shook his head. 'A little here, a little there. A few grains of salt upon meat to make it taste the better.'

The old man nodded, pleased by what he was hearing. 'Good. Too much, and they will have no need of you.'

Redwald smiled. He would never let that happen. 'I will climb up on their shoulders and reach great heights once again. And I will raise Asketil Tokesune up with me. You will have all the gold and power you once enjoyed, Father.'

The old man grinned. His teeth were yellow and broken. But then a shadow crossed his face. 'If only you were my true son and not Hereward.'

'Hereward has failed you. He has failed us both. But we

should give him no further thought. His days are all but done—'

'Good,' Asketil spat.

'And we have our own plans to make.' Redwald grinned. 'Doom is coming for the English in Ely. They sip their beer and boast about how they will bring the king to his knees. And all the time William the Bastard circles closer, like the wolves in winter.'

'How can he bring an army to Ely across the waters and the bogs?'

Redwald glanced back at the crowd, screwing up his face in disgust at their cheers. 'Perhaps he has summoned the Devil to carry him across the fens. It matters little. The war will soon be over, the last of the English destroyed. And Ely will be a wasteland like the north, drowned in ashes, with no man standing.' He leaned in to his father and whispered, 'Some of the Bastard's most trusted men arrive in Lincylene today to prepare the way for the king . . . and I will be there to meet them.'

Asketil frowned, not understanding.

'The king will need a good Englishman to tell him the ways of those who raise arms against him, one who knows the secret paths. The Butcher . . . William de Warenne . . . we have no need of them if we can gain the king's ear.'

The old man looked shocked. 'You would dare?'

'The prize is too great not to try.' He nodded and began to walk away, saying, 'If all goes as planned, we will rise up faster than we ever dared hope, and have riches and power beyond imagining. Wish me well, Father.'

He felt a lightness to his step as he hurried across the ward. In those grey days after King Harold had fallen at Senlac Ridge, he thought his hopes had been for ever dashed. But in the years since, he had learned a hard lesson. Glory came not to those who fought, but to those who waited. A skilled tongue could loosen heads better than any axe. And if he remained true to what he believed, and patient, no obstacle would be too great. In the final accounting, nothing mattered; not brothers, not lovers, no, nor fathers. He had himself, and that was all he needed, and by his own guiles he would find peace.

Among a swirl of crisp, ochre leaves, Edoma waited in the shade beside the castle gate. Her blonde hair and angelic features conjured a vision of innocence, but he knew better. She still sported a blue bruise on her left cheek from the roughness of their lovemaking three nights ago. Whatever he wanted, she gave him, without a complaint, or tears, even when that compliance drove him on to greater excesses. Perhaps he had met his match.

'Any news?' she asked, her eyes shining.

'I swear your blood is higher than mine,' he said, amused.

'I want only good things for you. You deserve your heart's desire.' If they had been alone, she would have slipped her arm through his, he knew. Instead, she looked up at him with big eyes filled with promise.

He glanced around to make sure he would not be overheard, and whispered, 'The king's men come today.'

Edoma all but clapped her hands in glee.

'Hush,' he cautioned. 'Do not bring eyes towards us. I must speak to them before Ivo or any of the others realize.'

'Plant your seeds, yes,' she said with a quick nod of agreement. 'And they will grow fast. The others are too slow-witted for you, my love. Do not worry about them.'

He had tried to stay calm, but he allowed himself a quick grin. 'Come. We must ready ourselves. Time is short.' He took a few paces and paused, adding, 'Perhaps we should marry. Would the king trust a married man more?' Without glancing at Edoma for her thoughts, he strode off once more. There was much he had to consider.

Beyond the castle gates, the muddy road wound down the steep hill on which Lincylene sat. The streets throbbed with life. Amid the din of the workshops and folk shouting to be heard above hammers and looms, there was no point in speaking. He forced his way through the throng with Edoma at his heels until he reached the market. It was no less quiet there.

Merchants bellowed to gain the attention of any who neared their stalls. Some turned their offer of wares to song, competing in hoarse voices with the sellers nearby. A knife for two pennies, a fox skin for eight, a fledged sparrowhawk for twenty-four. A gang of boys fought with wooden swords, crying out as they clattered knuckles.

Redwald dipped into the leather purse at his waist and pressed a coin into Edoma's hand. 'Buy what you will,' he shouted. 'A ribbon for your hair, a new comb, some silk. Come to me later, after the king's men have passed through. And then, perhaps, you may buy silver or gold to wear on your breast.'

Edoma's eyes gleamed. She gave a seductive smile as she folded her fingers around the coin and slipped away. Feeling his heart swell with excitement, Redwald kicked his way through a brood of chickens pecking in the dirt around a stall, and made his way to where the swine rooted in their swill. He clambered on to a low stone wall and found a spot where he could look out over all Lincylene, to the gleaming ribbon of river with the merchants' ships moored at the quay, and across the green land beyond. His nose wrinkled at the fruity smell of dung, but it would keep him from being disturbed. He let his gaze fall upon the great south road, far below, and waited.

But not for too long. With his heart racing, he watched ten horsemen wend their way along the road and pass through the gate. When they had made their way up the hill to the market, he was there to greet them, with Frankish wine and salt pork and bread. He paid a boy to take the horses to water, while the Normans stretched their tired limbs and wiped the dirt of the road from their faces. He knew William de Warenne and Taillebois would be waiting in the castle ward, puzzled at the slow arrival of their guests for the feast that had been planned. He would deal with the repercussions of his actions later. As he moved among the black-cloaked men, constantly filling their cups from the skin he carried, he found the king's adviser, a long-faced man called Bardolph. Redwald sowed his seeds well, and in only a little time he had left the Norman commander in no doubt that he was a much valued counsellor to the sheriff and that he held vital information about the English rebels which would be of great use to the king.

Once the men set off for the castle, Redwald all but ran into the heart of the market to tell Edoma that Bardolph had insisted . . . *insisted* . . . that he be taken to the monarch to tell all he knew. But though he searched among the stalls, he could not find her anywhere. Prettying herself with her new ribbon, he thought with annoyance. He asked around the merchants until he found a man who pointed him towards the smith's workshop on the edge of the market. Edoma had sent a message that she had gone in to warm herself, for the wind had grown cold.

Unable to contain his excitement Redwald thrust his way through the market crowd. He could have found the half-timbered workshop by his nose. The acrid stink of the forge seemed to seep out of the very wood. He marvelled how the smith worked in the fug with the large door closed. Wrenching it open a little, he slipped through the gap.

Inside, the gloom was made darker still by the orange glare from the coals. He covered his mouth and nose and flapped his hand to whisk away the choking smoke. The heat in the smithy was near-unbearable and sweat prickled along his brow. Edoma was mad if she thought this was a pleasant place to warm herself. The forge hissed, but there was no thunder of hammers or sizzle of hot iron plunged into water. The smith was nowhere to be seen.

Then the smoke shifted and he glimpsed Edoma waiting on the far side of the workshop. Coughing, he stumbled towards her.

Pain flared in his head as something heavy crashed against the base of his skull. He pitched forward, seeing stars. Through the throb of his blood, he heard Edoma cry out. Her voice was muffled, as if it came from the depths of a well. Redwald clawed at the hard-packed mud floor and rolled on to his back.

Through the smoke, a figure loomed. Tears of pain blurred his eyes, but Redwald still felt his chest tighten in terror. He blinked. The glow from the forge painted his attacker's face. Shadows pooled in the eyes and the hollows of the cheeks. The Devil had come to drag him to hell for his sins.

'Now there will be a reckoning.' The familiar voice was a low growl of rage.

Aye, the Devil. For here was Hereward, his brother, filled with an insatiable hunger for slaughter in revenge for the murder of his wife.

Chapter Eight

Hereward raised his sword. 'Your days are done,' he snarled, peering down the blade to where Redwald quivered. His fair hair had been dyed by berries and dirt, and the plain brown tunic of a merchant hid the tattooed spirals of the warrior that covered his arms. But now he could forget his disguise.

The forge blazed like the sun, but he did not feel the heat. The stinging smoke swirled around him, unseen. Nor could he taste the brimstone on his tongue. The only fire that mattered in that place was the one in his heart, and that had burned bitter cold for too long.

He watched Redwald choke back his fear, but the traitor's dry mouth could not even form a plea for his miserable life. Eyes wide, his brother scrabbled away from the sword. For his revenge, Hereward could have used an axe, or a spear. But this was no faceless, meaningless battle death. It was judgement and for that it demanded ceremony and a killing tool that carried a greater import than war weapons. It demanded his wolf of wounds. He turned Brainbiter so that the sword seemed to glow in the light of the forge. The hilt was edged with gold to befit his former high standing. It had majesty, and power, and it felt so comfortable in his grip that it seemed almost a part of him. With this, he would take his brother's life.

Redwald held out his hands. 'The smith will come . . .'

'The smith is in the tavern, spending the coin I gave him on mead and mutton.'

Hereward glanced towards Edoma who cowered at the back of the workshop. She was too scared to help. And what could she do? By the time she raised the alarm, he would have his brother's head. His trap had been well set.

He looked down on the man he despised more than any other and the rush of emotion almost made him stagger. Choking on the smoke, Redwald seized the opportunity to scramble to his feet. His gaze darted to the door. Hereward grinned. His brother could not reach it before he was cut down. The younger man swallowed, his eyes moistening. Sweat trickled down his brow.

'How you must have hated me.' Hereward's voice was almost lost beneath the crackle and hiss of the forge.

Redwald looked startled. 'Hated you? I only ever had love for you, Hereward. No one else has shown me such kindness.'

The warrior snorted with derision, until he saw that his brother truly believed what he was saying. 'You killed my wife . . . cut off her head . . . to buy your way into the trust of the Norman bastards.' All he could see was the open grave beside the abbey when Turfrida's shroud-wrapped body was lowered into it. He felt a pang of loss worse than any flesh wound.

'She was a woman,' his brother stuttered, uncomprehending.

'My wife!'

Rage flared once more, and he swung his blade back. Yet even then, slaying Redwald was harder than he thought. All he could see was the boy who had sat beside him at the lake in Barholme, fishing. The lad who had hidden him in the hayrick when his father had threatened to use his fists on him again. His lifelong guide, and friend. The wound of this betrayal was almost as agonizing as his grief at Turfrida's murder. 'We were brothers,' he said. His sword wavered.

'We still are.' Redwald drew his shoulders back and put on a sad smile. 'I am weak, Hereward. You know that. You were always my strength. When the boys in the village beat me, you were the one who bloodied them in turn.' He took a step forward, wringing his hands. 'In my weakness, I chose poorly time and again. And my heart burns for what I did to Turfrida. Not a day passes when I do not pray for forgiveness. But I was afraid of the Normans and what they would do if they came to Ely.' He blinked away tears. His voice lowered until it was almost a whisper. 'I am not strong, Hereward. Not like you.'

The warrior tightened his grip on the sword. He shook his head. 'You speak as if the death of my wife was your only crime.'

'God will judge me.'

'I will send you to him.'

Redwald held out his hands. 'Remember when we were boys—'

'Aye, I do. And that makes the sting so much sharper. Kneel.'

'No!' Redwald's face flushed, making him look even more like a child. He bunched one fist. 'You would judge me? You, who have had all you ever needed. A father and a mother, land, gold, power. I was the dog who fed on the scraps from your table.' His eyes blazed.

'Kneel. I will be merciful. Your death will be swift.'

'Do you think I have paid so many high prices to die here, in this filthy hovel, like some ceorl?' Redwald's voice cracked with passion.

'If you do not kneel, I will butcher you like a pig where you stand.' Hereward felt a calm descend on him. He had reached acceptance. This day would haunt him for the rest of his life, but the deed needed doing. He had no choice.

Like a rat, Redwald darted behind the forge. The hot coals lit his face and for the first time he no longer appeared angelic.

'You cannot run,' Hereward said. He stepped to one side of the forge. His brother edged in the opposite direction.

As Hereward readied himself to rush him, Redwald lunged.

Hereward found himself wrong-footed by the movement, for it was away from the door. Edoma squealed as Redwald grabbed her wrist and yanked her through the smoke towards the forge. Snagging his hand in her hair, he rammed her head down. She screamed and struggled, but he held her fast, barely a hand's width from the hot coals. Locks sparked and sizzled as they fell on either side of her face. Hereward could smell the burning.

'Coward,' he growled. 'Leave her.'

Edoma wailed in terror, but Redwald never once looked at her. 'If you would be rid of me, do it now,' the traitor said, his eyes fixed on his brother. 'And if her face is burned away to the skull beneath, so be it.'

Soon her flesh would blister and blacken even if his brother did not force her down into the coals, Hereward saw. He put on a smile. 'You think I care about your woman?' Yet he knew his hesitation had already answered his question.

'My woman . . . all women.' Redwald grinned. 'I know you as well as I know myself.'

Edoma's cries became strangled and then died away. Hereward watched her eyelids flutter as the heat drove her wits from her.

As frustration ate away at him, his brother threw back his head and yelled, 'Murder! In here! Murder!'

Hereward stiffened, torn by his lust for vengeance and the realization that this day was now certainly lost. For a moment, he held Redwald's gaze, feeling the rage build inside him, and then he darted to the door. Outside, querying cries were beginning to respond to the shouts. He glanced back. His brother watched him through the smoke, smiling.

'Count your days,' Hereward called back. 'I will not rest until our debt has been cleared.'

'This was your one chance and you failed,' Redwald replied. 'The king is coming, as he did in the north. It is your days that are ending.'

CHAPTER NINE

Hereward bolted from the smithy. Suspicious folk milled around the anvil and the brown mounds of iron, their faces darkening. If he gave them a moment, they would be on him like wolves.

'Inside,' he cried, pointing into the smoky workshop. 'Save her.'

As the crowd surged into the smithy, Hereward fought his way through the flow. With the clamour at his back, he bowed his head and tried to look inconspicuous as he strode down the road towards the stone wall separating the high-town from the low-town. But the Norman guards at the gate had been alerted by the outcry and were straining to see what was happening. One caught Hereward's eye. The soldier's hand fell to the hilt of his sword at whatever he saw in that unguarded moment.

Spinning aside, Hereward plunged into the bustling market. A merchant stepped in front of him, thrusting a leather bridle under his nose. Hereward shoved him aside. At the smithy, a tumult erupted as the mob flooded out, baying for his blood.

He slipped behind a table piled high with beaver furs, and hovered next to two men haggling over the price of a pig, pretending he was part of the bidding. 'Twenty pennies,' the seller demanded. 'I can take no less.' The other man grunted and shook his head.

From under his brows, Hereward glanced around. He could see no way out. Soldiers had joined the guards at the lower gate, and from their gesticulations he guessed they were ordering a messenger to fetch more men from the garrison. The rabble from the smithy had started to spill into the market. He could hear Redwald whipping up the crowd to search for the English rebel leader. Gold was promised, if the Mercian warrior was found and dragged to the castle to face justice. He cursed himself for getting caught like a callow youth who had just charged into his first fight.

As he edged towards the stone wall encircling the high-town, the whirl of the market pressed in on all sides. Yelling voices, bickering and bartering. Song from the scop standing on the Speaking Stone in the centre. Lowing, fly-blown cows and a flock of noisy sheep. He stepped around two dogs snapping and snarling over a bone, his nostrils wrinkling at the competing smells of dung, hot stew, spilled beer, sweat and animal musk. Distractions assailed him as he searched for a path.

Eager for the reward, the mob pushed further into the market, spinning folk around and peering into the depths of hoods. A churn upended. Butter spilled across the mud. Pottery crashed from a teetering table. The merchant leapt out, swinging his fists.

Among the rabble, Hereward counted nine Norman guards drawing closer. More gleaming conical helmets were moving down the road from the castle. He stepped behind a fletcher showing off a quiver of newly made arrows, and edged back until he felt the cold stone of the wall.

A roar of recognition cut through the market's din. A wild-bearded, thickset Northman was pointing at him, someone he had all but knocked flat when he came rushing out of the smithy. The time of hiding had passed.

Seeing one slim chance, Hereward drew his sword and

hacked through the hemp rope tethering an ox to a post. With the point of his blade, he jabbed the beast in the haunches. The ox bellowed and kicked out, blundering across the market. Men and women scrambled out of its path. Trestles upended. Merchants threw themselves on to the mud to reclaim their precious wares.

Taking advantage of the confusion, Hereward hurled himself through the crowd. He kicked over a trestle laden with pitchers of wine and a barrel of good ale. As hands grabbed for him, he leapt on to another table, clattering from one rickety plank to the next until he dived among the pigs. He prodded each of them with his sword. Squealing and snorting, they lumbered into the throng.

Through the mayhem, he thought he glimpsed a path to the gate. He shouldered his way into the mass of folk, only to find two guards barring his way. Hereward flashed his blade into the throat of the first man. Blood gushed. As the guard fell, gurgling, more Normans ran towards the terrified cries ringing on every side.

Hereward raced this way and that. Swords whisked by a finger's width from his flesh. But soon every way was blocked. Grins leapt to the faces of the Normans as they forced him back into a corner against the stone walls. He looked across the growing numbers of gleaming helms and felt bitter that Turfrida would remain unavenged.

From the edge of the market, Redwald was watching like a hawk. No jubilation, no triumph, no anger marked his face. It was blank, as if his soul had fled his body and only the clay remained. But then his eyes flickered, and he nodded, recognizing the threat was contained, and he turned and pushed his way into the crowd.

Hereward looked back to his enemies. 'You cannot take me to your masters to be humbled. I will die here,' he said, his voice so low it was almost lost beneath the creak of leather and the clink of swords on shield rims. 'But I will not die alone. Who goes first?'

His words hung in the air. He gritted his teeth as he waited for the wave of iron to break.

Beyond the market, a scream shattered the stillness. The Norman soldiers jolted. A second cry rang out, and then another. Within moments, alarmed yells were leaping from throat to throat across what seemed to be all Lincylene. Above the rooftops, a thick cloud of smoke billowed and a roaring like a great wind echoed. A flare of orange and gold burst into view. A cart filled with hay for the castle's horses streamed flames as it careered across the ruts down the steep street.

Folk threw themselves out of its path. Plunging into the market, the blazing cart upended. Flames leapt to the dirty straw scattered where the cattle and horses had been kept, and then to trestles, and bolts of silk, and furs.

Hereward watched the conflagration, his eyes aglow.

Choking smoke swirled across the market. He could hear the cries of alarm as the folk ran to fetch water to stop the blaze spreading to the half-timbered, thatched houses. Against the danger of the tinder-dry dwellings turning Lincylene into a bonfire, he was no threat at all.

While the Normans' backs were turned, he darted round the edge of the force and tried to lose himself in the bank of smoke. Fate had given him only a sliver of hope. Soon his enemies' attention would return to him, he knew, and every bastard in the place would be hunting him down.

He pressed the wool of his cloak against his mouth and nose. The flames glowed through the wall of grey and sparks drifted through the air. The sound of running feet echoed all around. Men with eyes filled with terror lurched past, hauling buckets. He slipped away, following the slope towards the gate to the low-town.

As he neared freedom, a hand grabbed his arm. He whirled, his sword flashing up. A hooded man held him tight. Just before he struck, he peered into the depths of the cowl and saw in the light of the flickering flames a familiar face.

It was Alric.

CHAPTER TEN

The two men raced down the steep slope through the low-town. Outside their homes and workshops, folk lined the street to look up at the pall of smoke hanging over the market. Already Hereward could hear the Norman commanders barking orders as they turned their attention back to the fugitive.

'I told you to leave me well alone,' he gasped as he ran.

'Is that the thanks I get for saving your miserable life?' Alric pulled his cowl low to hide his face.

The blast of a horn reverberated from the high-town, followed in quick succession by two more. Ivo the Butcher and William de Warenne would send every fighting man in Lincylene on his trail if they thought there was a chance of cutting down their most hated enemy.

Slowing his step, he fumbled for Alric's arm to hold him back. Haste would only make them easier targets. Yet they had little time before the gates to the town were sealed and they were trapped like rats.

'Why did you come?' Hereward whispered through gritted teeth. 'Now you have put your own life at risk.'

'I gave you my word that I would leave you to follow your

own path, and I did,' the monk murmured. 'But now there is news you must hear, once we are safe.'

'Safe,' the warrior repeated with a hollow laugh. 'Have you looked around you?'

Turning the corner on the final stretch of the road, he saw the Hungate ahead of them. Beyond lay the Witham with its busy quay, packed with ships laden with goods and lined with the camps of sailors from all corners of the world. He hoped they could lose themselves there. But as he scanned the walls he spied at least eight Normans, all of them looking with unease towards the smoke.

'We may make a fighting man of you yet,' he continued, distracted. 'Only a hardened warrior would have sent a burning cart into a crowded market. Watch yourself, monk, or you might wake up and find you are me.'

With a dismissive snort, Alric looked around until his eye fell upon a dirty-faced boy jabbing a stick into a smaller lad as if he were spearing a deer. He grabbed the child by the back of his tunic and hauled him up so his toes barely scraped the mud. 'Run to the guards,' he urged. 'The sheriff has sent word that they are needed in the high-town. The fire is spreading. And in the market, thieves rob merchants under cover of the smoke.'

The boy seemed suspicious until Alric pressed a coin into his palm. He grinned, and spat, and ran to the walls. Hereward and Alric stepped back into the shadows in the rat-run between two workshops. Once the guards had pounded by on their way to the high-town, they slipped out and ran through the gate.

'You are as cunning as a fox, monk,' Hereward said.

'Where you have your sword, I have only my wits,' Alric replied. 'I must use them as best I can.'

The quayside smelled of freshly caught fish and strange spices. Hulls creaked as they flexed in the river currents. Ropes cracked and sails snapped. Swarthy-skinned men in flowing white robes called to each other in a strange tongue as they heaved barrels on to dry land. Wild-haired Northmen glowered at anyone who ventured near their ship. Other seamen, with sallow skin and heads bound with cloth, squatted on the quay, chewing vigorously before spitting wads of brown-green mush on to the timbers. In the summer, the sailors slept aboard their vessels, under the stars. But now the nights had grown colder they had erected brightly coloured tents along the harbour. Around campfires, they gathered, keeping warm. Some hunched over merel boards. Others drank or sang or argued, eyes glinting like the knives they kept tucked in their tunics.

'We must take the road south, and quickly,' Hereward insisted as Alric urged him among the tents. 'I have coin. We can buy a ride on a cart, at least to the woods where we can hide.'

The monk shook his head. 'The Normans will have ridden us down long before we reach the trees. Hark.'

Hereward could hear the calls of the Butcher's men as they searched the low-town. In no time, they would be out of the Hungate. 'Now I have damned us both,' he spat. He looked around the tents, but could see no hiding place that would survive more than a moment's inspection.

'Show faith and God will reward you.' Keeping his head down, Alric grabbed his friend's arm and steered him among the camps to the very edge of the quay.

At their backs, the sound of hooves thundered.

'Your plan had better be more than *Put your faith in God*, monk,' Hereward said under his breath. 'I see angels coming to carry us away.'

'There is one angel here, and one devil,' Alric snapped, 'and if you want to avoid the fires of hell, keep your tongue still.'

Behind them, Hereward could hear the Normans questioning the sailors along the quay. He kept his gaze fixed on the timbers under his feet. Every instinct told him to fight, or run, but the monk kept his pace steady, unrushed, and the Mercian forced himself to do the same.

The churchman came to a halt beside a plank leading up to a skiff. On board, a man with dark features and a thick mass of curly black hair cleaned the scales off a fish with his knife. Alric whistled under his breath. The sailor looked up and nodded. Satisfied the Normans could not see them, the monk urged Hereward up the creaking plank.

'Hardred the Black,' the churchman said by way of introduction.

Satisfied Hereward could be trusted aboard his vessel, the sailor grunted a greeting and proceeded to haul aside a pile of filthy fleeces on the bottom of the skiff.

'A friend?' Hereward enquired, squatting.

'Gold buys friends easily.' Dropping to his haunches, the monk peered along the dock. In their black cloaks, the Normans were like a storm cloud sweeping among the colourful tents. The sailors eyed them with suspicion, barely responding to their sharp questions.

'Now would be good,' Hereward insisted. Over the rim of the boat, he watched the Normans begin to board and search some of the larger ships. 'Now, monk. Now.'

'Hush,' Alric snapped. 'Do you think I wish to be marched in front of the Butcher on the tip of a sword?'

Hardred whistled, nodding to the space he had cleared. Once the two fugitives had crawled over the damp boards and lain down, the sailor heaped the fleeces across them. In the gloom under the heavy weight, Hereward breathed in the stink of mould and musk and the dank odours of the river. The creaking of the boards filled his head. When he heard Hardred walk away, singing, he whispered, 'You trust him?'

Alric's voice floated back to him, muffled. 'No. But what choice do we have?'

'That would have been good to know earlier.'

The monk hissed at him to be silent.

Hereward's chest tightened. He could hear the harsh voices of the Normans in the camp beside the skiff. Just when he expected to feel the weight of men boarding the vessel, the boat rocked and began to move.

An angry voice rang out. 'And farewell to you,' Hardred

called back in a cheery voice, adding under his breath, 'you Norman bastard.'

As the boat drifted, Hereward's thoughts took wing, across the years and the miles, over the whale road to Flanders, and the battle-fair on the field beside the wood outside Bruges' walls. Till that moment he had been an earth-walker, wandering through his days without direction, filled with the rage born of the thing that lived inside him. But that day Turfrida had seen something good in his heart, though what he did not know. He had all but believed in the life of peace she had promised him. But then William the Bastard had come to England with his storm of iron, tearing down all that had been built by fathers and fathers' fathers and every one who had come before. And he had returned to fight, and his wife had come with him without a single complaint, though she had traded her family and her days of comfort for worry and danger. And he remembered the last time he had seen her, in that misty dawn when he had sent her to the abbey at Crowland to hide. But even that had not saved her. Perhaps she had been doomed the moment she met him.

And then he thought of Redwald, and he knew he could never forget, never forgive.

The weight upon him began to ease as Hardred dragged the fleeces to one side. When the midday sun warmed his face, he sat up, blinking, and sucked in a breath of clean air. They were heading south-west. Lincylene had fallen from view, and the river bank was now lined with trees. Ahead was the endless sky of the flat fenlands.

Alric sat up beside him. Hereward saw he had a bemused expression.

'Your plan worked, monk.'

'Aye. It did,' Alric replied in a faintly surprised tone.

'You have your uses, then.' Hereward gave a wry smile.

'Keeping you among the living seems to be the main one.'

Hereward looked out to the trees. 'One day we will drink mead together and laugh about these days. For now, I have work to do.' He glanced back at Hardred who sat astern, one hand on the rudder. 'Take me ashore anywhere. I will live in the woods while I make new plans.'

'To kill your brother,' the monk said. His face hardened.

'My mind has not changed.'

Alric shook his head. 'You must return with me.'

Hereward sighed. 'We have spoken of this time and again—'

The monk grabbed his arm. 'The king is coming.'

'Then let him. The English have an army now. Morcar's men make it a force to be reckoned with.'

Alric gripped tighter. 'The king has plans, secret plans that we cannot divine. Siege machines . . .'

Hereward snorted. 'In the fens? He will not get them within a day's ride of Ely.'

'And yet still he brings them. William the Bastard is no fool.' The churchman leaned in, his voice heavy with passion. 'You must come back to Ely and lead the English again.'

'I cannot.' Hereward dropped his gaze and stared into the grey waters.

'They will be destroyed without you at their head.'

'I said no,' the Mercian replied, too sharply. He softened his voice and added, 'I told you, monk, there are better men than I—'

'No, there are not.' Alric leaned forward again, holding out one hand. 'And if a leader with such God-given prowess has turned his back upon his army, how, then, will his men feel? Lost. Alone. Broken.'

'You go too far.'

A dragonfly skimmed across the water's edge, glimmering in the sunlight. Astern, Hardred began to sing once more, an old song, in a tongue Hereward didn't know, which sounded like a lament to lost love.

'You do not want to hear these words because you do not wish to think of the plight of the ones you have left behind,' the churchman pressed. 'But if you would not have the doom of the English upon your soul, you cannot turn away.'

Hereward climbed to his feet and strode to the prow. He looked out across the water to the desolate lands beyond. 'Have I not given my all for the English?' he asked.

The words hung in the air for a moment, and then Alric replied, 'You have.'

'I left the English army strong and ready.'

'You put your heart into the fight. No one could ever doubt that. But this is not about an army's readiness, or spears and axes, or battle-plans and supplies. It is about you, Hereward. Though you cannot believe it, you are worth more than a hundred men. A thousand. However many answer the call at Ely, there will not be enough if you are not there to lead them.' He paused. 'Your warriors tear themselves apart. They no longer trust each other, or trust the path they are walking. And good men and women have been murdered . . .'

'By whom?'

Alric shrugged. 'But it has stirred the flames of the Ely folk. Soon they will rise up and drive the English army out.'

The Mercian frowned. 'Murders,' he muttered to himself.

'A clear head coupled with a strong heart, that is the only thing that will save the day. A leader who can soothe these passions.' Alric forced a smile. 'You. Only you.'

Hereward bowed his head. He felt as if he were drowning in the cold waters around him. 'Turfrida must be avenged. That is all that matters now.'

'And so she will—'

'Three times now she has come to me in my dreams,' the Mercian interjected, staring into the river but seeing only his wife's face. 'She cannot rest, and neither can I, until Redwald has paid for his crime.' He sensed Alric rise and stand behind him. He did not look round.

'I feel your burden.' The churchman's voice was low and filled with feeling. 'But this desire for vengeance will only draw up the devil that lives inside you. And it will destroy you. I would not see you come to harm, Hereward.'

'When we stood at the gates of Ely that dawn, you said you would not stand in my way.'

'Aye. Out of friendship, and pity for the pain that ate away at you. I was wrong. And I cannot remain silent any more.'

When the monk rested a comforting hand on his shoulder, the warrior threw it off. He whirled, feeling the anger rise inside him, the anger that would in turn summon the devil that Alric knew only too well. 'Leave me be,' he snarled. 'This is my duty. You will not stand in my way.'

'I will.'

Hereward felt the blood thunder in his head, and his hand fell involuntarily to the hilt of his sword. 'Do not push me.'

The monk bared his chest. 'Kill me, then. I would rather die than see you walk the road to hell, if there was aught I could do to prevent it.'

The Mercian took a step back, staggered by the vehemence he saw in the other man's face. He felt his anger begin to subside.

But Alric did not back down. 'Would you have the deaths of the English upon your soul? Your friends? I know you have searched for peace in your life, but peace does not come through vengeance.'

Hereward turned away, frustrated.

'Return to Ely,' the cleric said, softening, 'and lead the English into this final battle.'

CHAPTER ELEVEN

The bloated body floated face down in the grey waves. Brown hair drifted like seaweed and the tunic billowed as the swell tugged the corpse through the lonely expanse of water. The two men watched the ghastly remains bob past the prow of their small boat. Neither of them spoke. Overhead, the shrieking gulls soared, waiting to plunder the tasty morsel.

'A fisherman, claimed by the sea,' Alric said finally.

From the blackened hands, Hereward could see the body had spent a while in those tidal waters to the north-east of Ely. Taking an oar, he stood up. The craft wobbled and the monk gripped the side in fear. Leaning out, the warrior prodded the carcass. The head swayed from side to side, barely attached to the torso.

'An axe strike, or a sword,' he muttered, frowning.

'The tides have brought this poor soul out from the land where he fell,' the monk affirmed.

Hereward was not so sure. He lowered himself down, leaning on the oar, deep in thought.

Since they had left Hardred and his skiff, their circuitous journey had taken longer than they had anticipated. They had thought it better to cross the dangerous fenland currents than take the old straight tracks to the west where the king's men had no doubt set their traps. The Mercian began to worry they had made the wrong decision.

As the body drifted away, they rowed towards the south-west. After a while, the sun slipped down the sky to a point where its rays blazed off the waters and it seemed they were wafting through a world of silver. In the glare, Hereward smelled a hint of tar on the breeze. Moments later, a grey shape began to appear out of the haze. As it took on form and weight, he saw that it was a ship, one large enough to cross the whale road, its crimson sail flapping above a deck filled with men.

'Here?' Alric said, puzzled. 'A wave-skimmer that size is far off course.'

As Hereward studied the vessel, more shapes emerged from the glare on every side. A multitude. Small fishing craft, merchants' boats and ocean-going ships. The monk gaped.

'Keep your wits and put that tongue of yours to good use,' Hereward commanded. He spun round and snatched up the mooring rope. Looping it around his right arm several times, he slipped over the edge of the boat into the cold water.

As he floated unseen in the shadow with only his face above the surface, Alric appeared above him. 'What . . .?' he stuttered.

'Wits, monk. And tongue,' Hereward hissed.

Understanding lit the other man's features, and with haste he took his seat and began to row with lazy strokes. After a few moments, the warrior heard a voice hail them. He pulled himself as close to the side of the boat as he could and tried not to splash as he trod water. The sound of oars dipping into the waves drew nearer. One of the smaller vessels, he decided. That was good. Less chance that he would be seen.

'What is your business, monk?' a voice barked.

'What is your business?' Alric replied in a haughty tone.

'The king's business. Turn back now. None may approach Ely, by order of King William.'

'You are fishermen,' the cleric said with a laugh.

'Aye, were. Till we found a good catch of coin.' Laughter rippled around the other boat. Hereward guessed there were four or five men aboard.

'The king has bought the services of every boat in the east,' another voice said. 'Let the fish swim free. Silver in the hand is better than any basket of eels.'

Hereward felt his mood darken. Ivo the Butcher had raised a sea blockade of Ely before, but it had been a half-hearted venture. William the Bastard would not be so lax. If the crown had control of the waters, then the noose had started to choke the life from Ely.

'Are you not afraid of God's will?' Alric was asking the fishermen.

After a moment's hesitation, one asked, 'What do you say?'

'In the church at Ely lies the arm of St Oswald. God's power has been visited upon that relic. Have you not heard?'

'Aye,' the other man replied with a note of unease. 'I have heard of this thing.'

'I travel now to see this holy sight, for I hear tales of great wonders in Ely. It is said that God stands with the English.'

Hereward raised one ear better to hear the response. For a long moment only the creaking of the oars upon the side rolled out. He imagined the fishermen blanching and bowing their heads as they thought about opposing God's will. The monk was clever indeed.

'Aye, we are frit of God,' one of the men muttered, 'in the next world. But we fear the king in this one. All know of the doom he has visited upon the north.'

'He has already taken the heads of many who have not done his bidding,' the second man said in a low voice, as if he feared the monarch himself would overhear. 'And he has commanded us to do the same to all who disobey his order.'

'Turn back,' the first man said. 'Even a monk will not be spared.'

'Very well,' Alric replied, 'but know that you will be judged for these actions.' He began to row the boat round, but slowly enough for Hereward to keep himself hidden.

Once they were out of sight, the monk hauled on the mooring rope and helped his friend back into the vessel. The Mercian huddled in the prow, drying off in the afternoon sun.

'What now?' Alric asked. 'We would risk our necks in these currents under cover of the night.'

'The Bastard would be ready for us, even in the dark. Enough ships will be sailing these waters now. Not an eel could swim through.' Squinting, Hereward glanced back at the vessels disappearing into the glare. 'My brother will have told the Normans about all our secret paths through the wetlands.'

'Aye, and where we forage for food, and which merchants have helped us.'

Hereward clenched one fist. 'Any English blood that has been spilled because of his weakness must be paid for in full.'

'But our army is trapped within the camp, and we are shut out here.' The monk let his head sag.

'No, there is another path, one kept secret lest the English ever have to flee Ely to escape the king's wrath. It is wild in parts, through the most treacherous bogs where one wrong step means death. When the tides come in, the waters sweep across it and a man can be washed away and drowned. No one would walk it of free will. But we have no choice.' He picked up his oar and gave his friend a lupine grin. 'Where there is life there is hope, monk. You taught me that.'

They sailed back to the north and the west, dragging the boat up into the mud of the first dry land they found. Through thick sedge, dense walls of willow snarled by bramble, and sucking bogs that appeared deceptively solid, they struggled on. Begging for scraps of food on the way, the two men forged west through the chill night until they were too tired to walk any further. Then they huddled in their cloaks in the roots of a giant oak and tried to sleep until first light.

Bands of Norman soldiers roamed with increasing regularity the closer they got to Ely. The two companions would hide among the fern, or in the branches of ash trees, then run, and then hide again. When they found the secret path, they had to wait in the fading light for the tide to go out. The way was as wild and dangerous as Hereward remembered and the night was heavy upon them by the time they reached the isle of eels, hungry and exhausted. But Hereward felt his worries ebb when he saw the church tower silhouetted against the starry sky.

As the gates trundled open, they stared into a row of warriors bristling with spears. Warnings were barked. But then torches flared, and the dark swept away. Hereward saw a corresponding light spring to life in the faces of the night watch. Disbelief turned to amazement and then jubilation. Full-throated cheers rose up. Shields and weapons were thrown aside, and the men ran forward to surround the two travellers, clapping shoulders and babbling questions.

'You doubted me?' Alric said, with a wry smile. 'Here is all the proof you need.'

Hereward looked around in stunned silence, humbled by the greeting. As the circle of men herded him inside the gates, he heard the cry 'Hereward is here!' leap from mouth to mouth, rising up into the dark of Ely's streets.

'Where have you been these past days?' someone yelled as the gates rumbled shut behind him.

'Tweaking the king's nose,' he called back. Laughter rose up.

'And is it true the Bastard has come to the east?' At this, the voices quietened and an uneasy silence hung in the air.

'Aye,' Hereward said, looking around at the worried faces. 'Now we have him where we want him.'

The silence broke as another cheer rang out.

On the street to the minster, Kraki waited, his heavy gaze weighing, judging. 'You came back, then,' the Northman growled.

'Aye. I would not leave you to face the Bastard alone.'

Kraki grunted. He looked over the crowd and bellowed, 'Would you wake the dead with this noise? Back to your homes, all of you. Hereward scouted and now he is home. That is no reason for a feast. Back to your hearths, and leave us to make our plans.'

The crowd broke up. But Hereward heard the jubilation continue as he strode up the hill, and it was not until he reached the minster enclosure that silence finally fell. Thurstan waited in a knot of monks, alongside Guthrinc, Hengist and a few more of his most trusted men, eyes still heavy with sleep. Guthrinc lumbered forward and wrapped his enormous arms round Hereward, almost crushing the breath from him.

'We thought you dead,' the big man said with a grin.

'Many have wished that. Now put me down before you end my days yourself.'

Guthrinc laughed as he released his arms.

'We have news to tell and plans to make,' Hereward called to his men. 'Let us—'

'It is true, then. You are here.'

Hereward turned at the woman's voice. He half expected to see Turfrida there, waiting to greet him with a kiss as she always had when he returned from fighting.

'Her name is Rowena,' Alric whispered. ''Twas her village where the Normans took all the menfolk.' In the torchlight, the woman's dark eyes were bright with hope and her cheeks were flushed.

'I have come to Ely to plead for your help,' she said, the words loud and clear.

'And I will hear you, after I have—'

'No, you will hear me now.' Her voice cracked with desperation. Seeing she did not mean to give offence, Hereward held up a hand to stop Kraki guiding her away. 'Aid me,' she continued, defiant. 'Help me find my husband, and all the other men the Normans took from their beds.'

'I will aid you,' the Mercian replied. 'But we have a crown to claim, and that must come first.'

'Not for me, or any of the goodwives in my village.' As he turned to leave, she continued, 'I call on you in the name of your wife Turfrida.'

He glanced back, his eyes blazing. 'Watch what you say.'

'Would your wife have held her tongue if you were lost?' she said, undeterred. 'I have heard tales of Turfrida. A woman with a fighting heart as great as any man's. She aided the sick, and gave food to the hungry. And she never turned away from anyone in need. Do I speak true?'

'You do,' he replied in a low voice.

'All the wives here have heard those tales, and they have taken strength from her. The memory of her gives us courage in these dark days.' Kraki approached her again, but she threw him off. 'Do not forget the women, for they are fearsome when roused,' she said with passion.

'I will do what I can,' Hereward replied after a moment. 'We will talk. After I have met with my war-band.' He put iron in his voice so she knew he would brook no further dissent. Acha, Kraki's woman, stood nearby, her skin as pale as snow and her black hair gleaming in the torchlight. Her brow was furrowed as she sized up Rowena. Hereward called to her. 'Take her,' he commanded. 'Keep her well. Hear her tales. I will come when I am done here.'

As Acha led Rowena away, Hereward turned back to the grave-faced men gathered in the flickering torchlight. 'Let us talk now of these dark times and the worries you have,' he said. 'And then I will tell you how we can kill a king.'

Before he had taken a step towards the refectory, he heard running feet at the enclosure gate and turned to see a boy waiting there. The lad looked both frightened and eager, dancing from foot to foot and kneading his hands in front of him.

'What does he want?' Hereward asked, suspicious. Children troubled him, weak, whining things.

'It is Wardric,' Alric murmured, puzzled. 'Away with you, boy,' he called. 'Hereward has important business.'

'I must speak to you.' The lad held out one pleading hand. He seemed on the verge of tears, the Mercian thought.

'Tell me,' Alric said.

'My words are for Hereward's ears alone.' Swallowing,

Wardric glanced over his shoulder fearfully. 'Only Hereward can save us from the devil . . . the devil that walks in Ely.'

The Mercian frowned. He held the monk back when Alric would have ushered the boy away. 'Bring him to me,' he said, curious. 'I would hear about this devil.'

CHAPTER TWELVE

The ghost watched from the shadows. As he staggered out of the tavern, Harald Redteeth looked across the deserted street and into that dead, grey face, those black, unblinking eyes. Ivar, his friend, long gone from the world, but always there, always reminding him of his vow. The Viking swayed, his breath steaming in the cold morning air. He held that gaze as long as he could. There would be no peace for either of them until Ivar was avenged and the gates of Valhalla swung open to admit him at last.

The wan sun glowed over the glistening rooftops of Grentabrige. Soon the town would be waking. Finally breaking the stare, Redteeth lurched a few paces, opened his breeches and pissed into the ruts. The stream seemed to go on for ever. A night of ale would do that to a man. Even through the drunken haze, his head still throbbed from the blow Hereward's right-hand man had dealt him after the attack on Abbot Turold and his monks. He snorted in disgust. The English dogs had taken him as if he were a child. But he could afford to wait to sate his desire for vengeance. They had burned him and stabbed him and cut him. His face and body was a mass of blackened dead skin and pink scars. Yet still he came back. And he would do so time and again, until he got what he wanted – Hereward's death. The English could not kill him; the *alfar* had told him that when he had journeyed to the shore of the great black sea.

He stumbled along the street, hot under his chain mail and his furs and his helm. Sweat trickled down his back. The bitter mushrooms he had chewed in the hour before sunrise always made him sticky. Only a few had passed his lips, not enough to take him to the black sea, and certainly not enough to keep him there. He treated the mushrooms with respect. They gave him the heart of a bull in battle, and the wisdom of the world beyond.

From the thatched rooftops, he could feel the eyes of the *alfar* watching him. In the wind rustling under the doors of the workshops, he could hear them calling to him: *angr, angr.* Trouble, trouble. A warning. He wandered down to the banks of the grey Grenta. His stomach pitched and yawed, another sign of the power of the mushrooms settling upon him. At the waterside, his thoughts flew on a raven's wings, and once again he was standing before Ivo Taillebois and William de Warenne by the roaring fire in the castle in Lincylene. The Butcher was peering at him from under his heavy brow, slow in his thoughts but as hard as stone. The nobleman was pacing around the hearth. Only now did Redteeth realize how unsettled they both had looked, as if he was watching a storm approaching at sea. They were commanding him to travel south to Grentabrige, that very day, and waste no time. But they would not tell him what he was to do when he got there, or why he was needed.

'You are Harald Redteeth?'

The Viking jerked from his vision. Turning from the river, he looked into the face of a knight standing at the top of the bank. He was tall, with dark features, the kind of looks that could turn a maid's heart, the Northman decided. 'What do you want, Norman?' he said with a gap-toothed grin that held no humour.

'My name is Deda. I have been ordered to meet a mad

Viking.' He looked around at the empty streets, a wry smile on his lips. 'I see no other who fits that description.'

Redteeth looked the knight up and down. The Normans were bastards, all of them. They either swaggered like kings or slaughtered like butchers. This knight looked like one of the peacocks, he thought. They expected all to fall before them, yet most had no spine or were slippery as eels. 'They say all Norman men use sheep like women,' he ventured.

Deda smiled, refusing to rise to his taunting. 'You have no place in your heart for Normans?'

'I never met one I liked.'

'And yet you take our coin.'

'If we only took coin from folk we liked, our bellies and our mead-cups would always be empty.' Redteeth climbed the bank, sizing the other man up with each step.

'Ah, yes. Axes-for-hire know the price of everything, but the true worth of nothing at all, so they say. When everything is measured in coin, how else would it be?' Deda's smile remained lazy, but his dark eyes had a sharp intelligence. The Viking thought that perhaps this man was not a peacock at all. Yet nor did he look like one of the Men of Iron who seemed made for nothing but killing in the king's name.

'Knights with land, and great halls, and slaves, always say there is more than coin, I have found. Tell me, then. What is missing from my poor life?'

Deda held out a hand. 'I never judge a man. That is God's business. And we have only just met. Only a fool would speak so boldly at this time.' As Harald prowled closer, the knight eased back his cloak and rested his hand on the hilt of his sword. 'And I am no fool,' he added.

'I have fought beside your kind time and again,' the Viking said. He cracked his knuckles as he regarded the knight. 'I have seen into your heart, and it is a cold place. You build castles out of stone, and great churches that are chill and empty. And you kneel and you pray and you listen to the echoes come back and you shiver. You count your coin in your counting houses, and make marks upon your ledgers. You put women in their place. Not shoulder to shoulder as is their right, but lower. They should bow their heads to their husbands now, eh? 'Tis no surprise you find comfort in sheep.'

'So, we have yet to find some common ground between us.' The knight stood his ground as Redteeth prowled around him, eyeing him as a wolf might eye a lamb. 'Yet we must have trust if we are to be brothers in battle.'

The Viking ground to a halt. 'Brothers?'

'Ivo Taillebois has told the king that of all the warriors under his command, you know the enemy leader Hereward best. You know his mind, and his heart, and from that, one would think, his plans. I have been charged to ride with you in the fens. King William is about to make his move, and we have work to prepare the way.'

Redteeth nodded to himself. He liked the sound of that. Closer to Hereward, closer to taking his head and meeting the vow he had made all those years ago over Ivar's burned body.

'And yet there is this matter of trust,' the knight continued. 'Can we ride together if the only thing that binds us is the coin the king pays you?'

Harald furrowed his brow. This did not sound like any Norman he had encountered before. He shrugged, then gave a lupine grin. 'Beat me in battle, and I will bow my head to you, coin or not. You have my word on that.'

Deda cocked his head, amused. 'A fight?'

Redteeth raised the axe that hung at his side on a leather thong. 'This is Grim. It was given to me by my father, and to him by his father. When it drinks blood, it honours all who have held it before. Only through days gone by can we see the way to days yet to come. And it is this,' he shook the axe, 'that binds us to all the things that made us who we are. You Normans do not understand such things.' He snorted. 'I would not taint the blade with your blood.' He tossed the axe aside. 'Use your sword. I will defeat you still.'

Deda drew his weapon, turning it over in his hand as if it

were the first time he had seen it. 'A sword against an unarmed man? That would not be honourable.' He set the sword aside, and then drew off his mail shirt, and put his helm atop it.

The Viking was puzzled. He had heard the Norman bastards speak of honour before, but he had never met one who would risk his neck for it.

Defenceless, the knight stretched, rubbed his hands together and smiled. 'Let us fight, then. With the strength of the arms that God gave us.'

'I will not go easy on you.'

'I would expect no less.'

With a roar like a bear, Harald Redteeth threw himself forward. But his arms closed only on thin air. Deda was light on his feet, strong and agile, with the skill of a master swordsman. He stepped aside and jabbed his elbow into the Viking's back as he sped by. The Northman crashed on to the mud.

Grinning, Redteeth heaved himself up. He had a fight on his hands. That was good.

Back and forth the two men fought along the muddy, leaf-clogged river bank. Harald felt his thoughts drift away on the mushrooms' raven-wings. He saw only his enemy. His arms and legs moved as if they belonged to someone else; and they did, to Thor himself, who had given his lightning and his thunder the moment Harald had swallowed the bitter flesh. He gritted his teeth and snapped and snarled. His knuckles crashed into the other man's face. Deda spun back to his knees, then raised one eyebrow as he wiped a trickle of blood from his nose with the back of his hand.

Harald saw no fear there. Indeed, the knight seemed to see their battle as an amusement.

For long moments they tore at each other. Now Harald could see why his opponent had removed his hauberk. His own mail shirt made him lumber like a bear. But as the knight stumbled back over a stone, he saw his opening. Racing forward, he crashed into Deda and wrapped his arms around him.

Redteeth grinned as he peered into his enemy's face, their

noses barely a finger's width apart. He crushed tighter, squeezing the breath from the other man's lungs. Soon ribs would shatter, and then spine. And yet Deda's face remained calm, and an ironic smile still played on the edge of his lips. That only drove the Viking to even greater exertions.

But the knight was a head taller than him. He pressed his toes on the mud and thrust forward with all his weight. A moment later, the two men were flying down the slippery bank and into the icy Grenta. So powerful was Deda's kick that Harald realized they had spun beyond the shallows and into the deeper water. The bitter cold shocked through the numbness of his thoughts. His arms flew from the knight. Down he went, pulled to the bottom by the weight of his mail shirt. As the water closed over his head, he thought how clever the bastard Norman had been.

Just when he felt the darkness begin to close in, hands fumbled for his chest and hauled him up. He burst into the pale light, throwing back his head as he sucked in a deep draught of air. Deda had his fingers hooked in the mail shirt. He pulled the Viking through the shallows and dragged him up into the thick brown mud along the water's edge. Harald lay on his belly for a moment, catching his breath. When he rolled over, he looked at the other man through narrow eyes. The dripping Norman still sported a wry smile.

'I saved your life,' Deda said. 'I would think that would be worth something. Coin or not.'

'Aye,' Redteeth grunted. 'It has some worth.' Water sluiced out of the back of his hauberk as he pulled himself to his feet.

The knight offered his hand. 'They said you were a wild beast. I think there is more to you than that. And we shall find out the truth of the matter on the road.'

CHAPTER THIRTEEN

The lone candle flame guttered in the dark belly of the church. Shadows danced across the drawn face of the man kneeling in prayer before the altar. In the vast gulf of night, that single point of light was his sole worldly comfort. As cold sweat trickled down his back, Alric's supplication echoed more loudly. He squeezed his hands together until they ached. God would watch over him. God would keep him safe.

How long had he been alone in that deserted church? Two hours? Three? His knees ached and the cold of the stone reached deep into his bones. But he could not leave. Death was coming for him.

When the flame flickered upright once more, the monk felt his gaze drawn towards it. For a long moment, the candlelight held him fast. Then, with the prayer dying in his mouth, he moistened his dry lips and listened.

Only silence filled that empty space.

Barely a moment later, he sensed someone behind him. Crying out in shock, he threw himself aside. A glinting blade flashed through the space where his neck had been.

Alric sprawled across the cold flagstones, straining to see through the gloom. A shadow loomed over him, a cloaked and hooded man wielding a short-bladed knife. 'The king's man,' the monk hissed. The candlelight lit a long face with deep-set eyes, one he did not recognize. Not an Ely man, but one of the thousands of human flotsam who had drifted into the Camp of Refuge to seek shelter under Hereward's banner. A nobody, a nothing, the perfect disguise.

'The monk who knew how to uncover me,' the attacker spat. 'In the tavern, in every workshop, that was all I heard. No more.' Alric's heels and elbows skidded on the smooth stone as he tried to push himself away. Hereward's lie had had the desired effect, drawing the Norman bastards' rat out of its hole, though little comfort it was to him at that moment.

The knife swept up; the hooded man lunged.

With a flick of his foot, Alric kicked the candle as he rolled aside. The church was plunged into an all-consuming darkness. Scrambling away on his hands and knees, the monk heard the attacker's curse echo along the nave. A moment later he sensed frantic movement as the hooded man lashed out wildly with his blade. Time and again the monk felt the knife whistle by. Terror gripped him. Now he had seen the face of the king's spy he would not be allowed to escape with his life.

As he scrabbled through the dark, he heard a door crash open. A light flared, then another, torches dancing along the nave, the slap of running feet. His heart leapt.

Shadows flickered across the walls as Hereward and his men surged around the church. The hooded man raced to escape the trap he now realized had been set for him, but there was no way out. The plan had been too well made.

Alric pushed his way up the wall and drew in a deep breath. He was shaking. Yet he felt a surge of elation that he still lived. For a moment, he had doubted that he would ever see the day again.

The English warriors surrounded the attacker. Ranging back and forth, the trapped man brandished his knife at anyone who took a step towards him. Alric weighed the hardness he had seen in the spy's face. Here was a man who was not afraid to die. He would not give up his secrets, the monk was sure, and he would try to take some English blood before he was brought down.

Alric's attention flitted towards Hereward. The Mercian's face was unreadable as he strode across the nave. Eyes fixed upon the prisoner, he pushed his way through the ranks of warriors. At the front, he took Madulf's spear and without breaking a step drove the weapon through the hooded man.

The monk flinched. Cold, brutal and effective. Here was the leader the English needed in these dark times, a man who could match the king blow for blow. And yet he could not celebrate, for he knew the price his friend would pay.

As the Norman spy twitched on the end of the weapon, his blood pooling around him, Hereward pushed past his men and strode up to Alric with the nonchalance of a sailor who had just speared a codfish.

'You risked your life for the people here. They will never forget that,' he said, resting one hand on the monk's shoulder.

'I did only what had to be done.'

Hereward allowed himself a brief smile which said more than words, and returned to his warriors.

'Where there is one, there could be many,' Kraki said, eyeing the wounded man. 'William the Bastard will not rest. He will send more of these rats, until he succeeds in stirring the folk to rise up against us.'

Hereward nodded. 'That he will.'

'Are we then doomed to see more innocents slaughtered?' Sighard asked. 'To keep fighting this same battle over again until we are worn down?'

The Mercian stepped over his fallen enemy and glanced down at him. 'He has some life in him yet.' He looked around the gathered warriors who were hanging on his words. 'Take a wooden stake and drive it up through his arse and out of his neck. Then set him by the gates for all to see.'

'Alive?' Sighard said, uneasy.

'He will live for a day, perhaps two.' Hereward's voice was

devoid of emotion. He watched the spy's eyes widen in horror at the ordeal to come. 'His screams will do our work for us. All Ely will know what happens to any who dare attack us here, in our home. And they will warn any new arrival, and any Norman snake who slithers up will think twice before it acts.'

The hooded man held out an arm and began to plead for mercy. Turning on his heel as if he had not heard, Hereward walked towards the door. 'Our backs are safe,' he called. 'Now let us turn our spears towards the bastard king.'

Alric watched his friend depart, and then he bowed his head and whispered a prayer.

Chapter Fourteen

Across the marshy floodplain of the Ouse, a finger of solid land was growing. Around it, men toiled with shovels and hammers. They shattered flint and dragged sacks of sand. Others cut alder branches and carried armfuls of reeds as they extended the raised bank across the wet land. The rhythmic crack of hard labour rang out in the quiet of the autumn morn.

'See, was I not right?' mad Hengist hissed. 'The Normans are building a causeway.' He danced in a circle, no longer troubled by his injured ankle.

'You did well. We have no better scout.' Hereward lay on his stomach on the high ground and eased aside the brown bracken so he had a clear view of the work.

'Is this the king's great plan? That causeway is barely wide enough to take two men abreast,' Kraki snorted as he crawled beside his leader. Guthrinc, Sighard and Madulf squatted at their backs and more of their men leaned on their spears and waited for orders further down the slope.

'It may not be as bad as we feared,' Guthrinc commented, 'but that causeway will still bring his army closer to Ely than they have ever been before.'

'No horsemen will be able to use that narrow way, and the riders are their greatest strength,' Kraki growled.

Sighard laughed. 'We will pick them off, two by two, as they wander off the end. And that will leave us in a better place to launch our own attack against the king himself.'

Hereward allowed the chatter to fade into the background. He squinted, studying the activity so that he did not miss a single thing of importance. The men were Norman foot-soldiers, though they had set aside their armour and weapons as they sweated in the warm sun. The bundles of alder and rushes and reed were laid out in a line on the boggy ground so that the layers of sand and flint being shovelled on to them would not sink. At the water's edge, more wood was being lowered into the water to pile up a raised area across the river bed. Ramparts of peat were being constructed along the course of the causeway.

Kraki nodded towards the fortifications. 'Peat. If that is the best the king has, then his crown is already falling from his brow.'

Madulf had been moving along the high ground, studying the causeway from different angles. 'The defences are far from complete. With Morcar and his men beside us, we could carve through them in no time.'

'Aye,' Guthrinc agreed. 'Send a message to the king. Let him know we are coming for him.' He glanced at his leader. 'What say you? We send word back now to Earl Morcar? We could attack before nightfall.'

Hereward eyed the defences, the heaps of armour and weapons, and the few guards half dozing from boredom. 'No,' he said. He could sense the disappointment of his men. 'They outnumber us, but only by a few.' He took a handful of the black earth and began to smear it around his eyes and along the lines of his cheekbones. Slowly, the skull beneath his skin emerged under his tracing fingers, a fearsome sight. His men watched, eyes bright, and then one by one they began to do the same.

'Our enemy's defences are not done,' Hereward continued. 'They are weary and unprepared for battle. We have surprise upon our side. Let us seize our moment. We attack now.'

CHAPTER FIFTEEN

'Y̶ou have taken my balls, knight. You and that king of yours.' Harald Redteeth stalked along the causeway swinging his axe as if he wanted to lop the head off every guard he passed. 'This is work for children, not warriors.'

Deda hid his grin behind his hand. He liked the Northman. 'You are a wonder to all, Viking,' he called. 'Most yearn for peace, or gold, or women and mead. For you, only guts and blood and brains will do.'

'And they will not come soon enough,' the other man grumbled. 'Any thick-skull can guard a pile of shit in the middle of the fens.'

'But this pile of shit is the king's great plan,' the knight remarked, feigning seriousness.

Redteeth grunted. 'Aye, and there, in one, is the king's dream for England.'

Humming to himself, he wandered off, pausing only to glower at each guard he passed. Thin sport, but he took what he could find. Deda smiled. But when he looked around the causeway, he understood the Viking's concerns. Once they had been summoned to receive their orders in Grentabrige, he had expected a greater calling and worthy battles against the

English, ones in which a knight could distinguish himself. But the king had insisted they both be dispatched to this god-forsaken place. He presumed William had some deeper plan in mind, but he could not see it.

He watched the sweating men shovelling piles of flint as clouds of midges danced in the sunlight around them. The steady chink of spade on stone was lulling some of the guards into a doze. Nearby a soldier's eyelids drooped and his head began to nod.

As Deda began to turn away, he glimpsed rapid movement in the corner of his eye. The guard staggered and choked. For a moment, the knight stared with incredulity until he saw that the head of an arrow had rammed out of the man's throat. The soldier plunged forward, dead, a trail of glistening crimson following him down.

Deda jerked from his frozen moment. A throat-rending battle-cry rang out across the causeway.

Out of the shadowy wood on the high ground, apparitions burst forth, hollow-eyed and hollow-cheeked, as if the grave had recently given them up. Bristling with spears, their shields held high, they whooped and howled as they swept through the long grass towards the rooted, slack-jawed Normans.

'Arm yourselves,' Deda bellowed to the unmoving guards. 'Defend the causeway.'

In twos and threes, the king's men stumbled towards the pile of hauberks, helms and axes, but many stood as if in a dream.

'A fight, then. This is more like it.' Redteeth was grinning like a wolf, his axe shaking in his fist.

'No. You know the paths here better than any man. Take a message to the king. This may be the beginning of the English uprising. If we all die here, there will be no one to warn our army.' Deda could see the Viking wrestling with his bloodlust. 'Go,' he urged. 'Bring back fresh men.'

Redteeth hawked up phlegm and spat, but gave a grudging nod. Spinning on his heel, he raced into the ash trees and was gone.

Deda drew his sword and darted along the causeway. Those men who had managed to drag on their mail shirts and their helms threw themselves towards the ramparts. But there was no shape to the defence. One warrior found himself facing three English spears. Though he had the higher ground and a long Norman shield, it was not enough. He was cut down in a moment.

His own shield was resting against a pile of sandbags, but Deda knew he had no time to reclaim it. He leapt on to the ramparts where four English rebels were closing on a wounded soldier. As the man knelt, clutching at his side where his tunic darkened, the knight stepped in front of him and braced himself. He thrust his blade into the chest of an English fighter, then hacked through the haft of a spear.

Sensing they faced a seasoned warrior, his opponents fumbled together a wall with their three shields. It was a feeble thing. Their commander would have been furious. When they tried to advance up the crumbling peat ramparts, Deda hammered his foot into the centre shield. As the rebel stumbled backwards, he leapt into the space that had been vacated, stabbed left and cut right. The two English fighters screamed as their sides opened up.

He bounded back to the top of the ramparts. When he looked around, he saw the day was already lost. The smaller English force had already torn the heart out of his men. Bodies littered the causeway. Some of the rebels had thrown aside their spears and were shovelling aside the sand and flint with whoops of glee. In moments, they were destroying what had taken hours to build.

Hereward's men prowled towards him, white eyes staring from black sockets. They conjured a vision of death as easily as they dealt it. Deda whirled around. Barely a quarter of the men who had laboured that morning still lived, all of them trapped on that spur stretching out across the bog to the water's edge. Huddled like pigs in the butcher's pen.

Racing towards them, Deda called, 'Stand your ground. Form a shield wall. You can yet hold them off.'

But he might as well have remained silent for all the good it did. He felt his heart sink as he watched good men driven mad by fear of death. Some leapt from the causeway as if they had suddenly gained the ability to walk upon the surface of the bog. They were sucked down or managed to stagger a few paces before the mud held them fast, easy targets for the English bowmen. Others jostled for a footing on the causeway and pitched their own fellows over the side.

'Stand your ground,' Deda yelled once more.

He pushed his way into the soldiers, grabbing shoulders to try to heave them into line. But he could see their terror was too great. They threw him off so that he almost stumbled into the bog himself. Some of them raced towards the English, yelling the Norman battle-cry, *Dex aie*. A futile gesture. Each one ran straight into a row of spears.

Soon he found himself at the end of the causeway, with his back to the swollen river. The currents were strong enough to drag him to his death. Only a madman would risk them. He grinned with grim irony. Surely God was now punishing him for the way he had tricked Harald Redteeth in Grentabrige?

Tossing aside his sword and his helm, he dived into the torrent. The river was a wild beast. It dragged him down to the bed, pummelled him against the side, then spat him up for one gulp of air before thrusting him to the depths once more. His thoughts fled, dashed from his head. He felt only the fire in his chest. He saw only grey and black.

And then, just when he felt sure his time was done, something cracked against him. He flung out a hand and his fingers closed round wood. Forcing his head up, he saw he was holding on to the haft of a spear. In an instant, he was yanked out of the flow. Hands hauled him on to the river bank.

With a rush of joy that he still lived, Deda sucked a draught of air into his burning lungs. Above him, black branches hovered against a patch of silver sky. And then a head heaved into view, skull-faced as though it were taunting him with how close he had been to leaving the world behind.

'My name is Hereward,' the English rebel said. 'And your life is now mine.'

CHAPTER SIXTEEN

The ghosts were abroad in the forest that night. Rowena had seen them, standing among the willows, their eyes pools of shadow in faces of stone. Her father had told her by the hearth one midwinter night how the dead sometimes stayed close to the living, lamenting the life they had lost. 'Never look them in the face,' he had said. 'Never let them lay their hands upon you, for they will not let go.'

She pulled her cloak tighter around her and hurried along the moonlit track. Her feet whispered over the fallen leaves. Behind her, Acha kept pace. Her pale face was emotionless, but her wide eyes darted around. Could she see the ghosts too, Rowena wondered, or was it the Norman hunting bands which frightened her so? Three times they had been forced to hide in ditches until the bastards had passed by. They had lain in the mud, covered in leaves and branches, and shivered in terror for their very lives, knowing full well their fate if they were caught.

An owl shrieked and they both jumped. Their laughter was nervous, but brief, for they knew any sound would carry far in the stillness of the fenland night.

Not long after, Rowena smelled the smoke of a home-fire on the breeze. Easing aside a curtain of willow branches, she peered into a small clearing. All was as Sighard had told her. The hut looked as if it could barely withstand a hard winter.

'The wise woman's home,' Rowena whispered. Her neck prickled at the eyes of the dead upon her. She should not be here.

She felt Acha grow tense beside her, too. Putting on a brave face, Rowena turned to the other woman and said, 'You have my thanks for walking with me on the night-road. You did not have to do this. We are not kin. I am hardly known to you. But now we are here, you can return to Ely where you will be safe.'

'And walk the night-road alone?' Acha's dark eyes gave nothing away.

'Then stay here.'

'We stand or fall together.'

Rowena looked back at the hut. It seemed deserted. 'The words of Hereward?'

'He is . . .' Acha paused, searching for words that seemed hard to find, 'a good leader. A good man.' She seemed about to say more, but caught her tongue.

Rowena sniffed. 'So I have heard. But he has been no use to me. I will not sit by the hearth and stay silent like some Norman wife. If Hereward will not help, I will do it myself.'

Pushing her way into the clearing, she raised her head in a show of confidence. 'Brigid,' she called. 'We are two lost souls who would seek your guidance back to the path.'

After a moment, the door creaked open. Brigid was framed in the orange glow of the hearth-fire at her back. She had become almost a part of the wild in which she hid, Rowena could see. Sinewy, filthy, the wise woman half hunched as if ready to pounce. She looked her visitors up and down for a moment and then crooked a finger to beckon them in.

Rowena felt Acha all but pressing against her back as they stooped to enter the hovel. Inside, her nostrils flared at odd smells, unfamiliar spices, strange mixtures. A bed of dirty straw lay on the hard earth in one corner. Animal bones, charms, feathers, bundles of dried herbs and plants were scattered everywhere.

'We have brought you bread, and salt,' she said, offering the cloth-wrapped bundle.

Brigid took the gift and motioned to the two women to sit by the hearth. The wise woman squatted on the other side and they watched each other through the swirling strand of grey smoke. 'I have many questions,' Rowena began. 'This world has been turned on its head. Little makes sense any more.'

The wise woman nodded. 'This is a time of hidden things. What is seen is not all there is.' She picked up a long, thin bone and began to beat a steady rhythm on the edge of a chipped bowl filled with dried leaves. Closing her eyes, she added, 'All is changing, like the seasons. What once waited in the shadows will step out into the light. And then you should beware.'

'You speak of the king . . . coming to the east?' Acha ventured, her voice almost lost beneath the crackle of the fire.

'All here will see the skull that hides behind the face. Death is drawing closer.'

Rowena shivered. Had the wise woman seen into her own mind and read the thoughts that had passed there only moments earlier?

'All here . . . in this house?' Acha asked in a tremulous voice. 'Or all in the east?'

Brigid did not answer.

Rowena leaned forward. She could not forget the thing that had driven her to visit that dangerous place in the middle of the night, the only thing that truly mattered to her. 'The Normans took my husband. They dragged him from his bed, aye, and all the men in our village. If they were to be killed, the king's bastards would have done it there and then. I must know where they were taken, and why.' And I will bring them back, she thought, if no man is brave enough to aid me.

Brigid took a cup of brackish water and poured it into the bowl. She stirred vigorously with the bone until the leaves disintegrated, and then she peered into the contours of the sludge in the bottom.

'Do the men live?' Acha whispered.

'They live. For now.'

Rowena tensed. Her thoughts flowed back across three summers to the hall by the lake, and her handfasting. She remembered Elwin folding his fingers around her own, and looking into his smiling face and thinking her heart would burst from happiness. No other man had moved her like that. He was as strong as an ox, but he could play the harp and sing like an angel. It was the laughter she missed the most. He made a hard life sweet. Ah, how they laughed. 'For now, you say. How many hours or days do I have to find him?'

Brigid studied the paste.

Outside, a stone clinked against wood. All three women jerked their heads up. In the still night, the sound had come like thunder.

'The Normans are here,' Acha said under her breath. Her hand slipped inside her dress and she pulled out a short knife.

Rowena felt shocked to see she carried such a blade, as all the men did. The notion was lost in an instant when she saw Brigid rise. She reached out to the wise woman. 'Wait,' she said with urgency. 'Tell me where my husband is.'

But Brigid swept to the door, the other two women forgotten. Rowena felt desperation surge through her and she scrambled after the wise woman, demanding an answer.

The crack of a branch reverberated from the edge of the clearing. Now Rowena allowed herself to fall silent. There would be no saving Elwin if she died there.

Brigid turned, her eyes glowing in the reflected firelight. 'Flee,' she urged in a hoarse voice. 'Into the trees. Do not stop. Do not look back.'

She wrenched open the door and stepped out. Rowena felt Acha's fingers grip her upper arm, and then the other woman propelled her into the night. Her feet whisked across the ground. In the whirl, she sensed Acha, transformed, no longer the silent watcher with the face like stone. A wild thing, snapping and snarling and lashing out with her knife, she tore across the clearing. Nothing could stand in her way. Pulled along at her side, Rowena glimpsed figures . . . men . . . little more than smudges against the greater dark. They fell away, afraid to confront this ravening wolf ripping through their midst. And then the branches tore at her face and hair and the shadows closed around her and they were scrambling over roots and snarled brambles.

'Wait,' she gasped, tearing her arm free. 'We must help Brigid.'

Acha whirled, her face contorted, still wild with passion. 'Go back and you die,' she spat.

'I . . . I cannot leave. As God is my witness, if there is aught I can do, I must.'

The other woman must have seen something in Rowena's face, or heard something in her voice, for the beast faded from her features, and her brow knit. 'You are mad,' she whispered.

'Come. They will think us long gone.' She tugged at Acha's sleeve and eventually the other woman relented.

They crept back through the willows to the edge of the clearing. The glow from the open doorway lit a tableau of silhouettes. Brigid had been forced to her knees, a spear resting against the back of her neck. Nine men surrounded her. But as Rowena's eyes grew used to the gloom, she felt shocked. She saw no helms, no long shields or hauberks. The attackers' hair had not been shaved at the back in the Norman way. She saw English men, and five of the interlopers wore the tunics of monks. She felt Acha tense beside her, and knew the other woman had seen the same puzzling thing. One of the men swiped the back of his hand hard across the wise woman's face.

Rowena could bear no more. She pushed into the clearing and commanded, 'Leave her.' She heard Acha step out at her back and marvelled that the other woman had refused to let her face these interlopers alone.

One of the God-fearing men jabbed his spear at Rowena. 'Hold your tongue.'

'I will not.' She felt her cheeks flush with defiance.

'If you are witches like this one, you will pay a high price.'

'We are women of Ely, and you will hear us out.'

The man let his spear fall. One of the others, a priest by the look of him, stepped forward. 'We are here on the orders of Abbot Thurstan.'

Rowena frowned. 'Abbot Thurstan would not demand such a thing. A woman, beaten—'

'She is a witch,' the priest interjected. 'She sups with the Devil.'

Rowena started to protest, but the priest held up a hand and two more spears turned towards her.

'Enough,' the priest continued. 'These are the End of Days. The signs and portents are everywhere. Conquest upon the white horse, War upon the red. Famine upon the black horse, and Death. The pale horse of Death. They are abroad. You know this to be true.' His voice wavered. 'And before them, fear is driven into men's hearts.' He swept a hand towards Brigid. 'We cannot risk God abandoning us for allowing an abomination such as this so close to Ely.'

'So even Abbot Thurstan is afraid,' Rowena said.

The priest grew gimlet-eyed. 'We can take no risks.'

'And she will be killed?'

'She will be tested. And, if that is God's will—'

'Then know this woman has the protection of Hereward.' Rowena ignored the cautioning hand of Acha on her back. She watched hesitation cross the firelit faces of the men, then confusion. Rowena restrained a smile. They feared the End-Times, death and the Devil, but it seemed they were just as afraid of Hereward.

'I have heard no such thing,' the priest said. He sounded unsure.

'It is true,' Acha said in a clear voice. She stepped beside Rowena and pointed at each man in turn. 'Cause harm here and you will all pay the price. You know what that will be.'

The priest blanched. The man holding the wise woman prisoner half raised his spear and looked around for guidance. Seizing her moment, Brigid scrabbled away and leapt to her feet. But she did not dart into the dark. She threw herself at the priest and raked one hand across his face. As the wise woman pulled away, Rowena realized she had scraped some of the black paste from the bowl into the churchman's eyes. He fell to the ground, screaming.

All the other men there recoiled, crossing themselves. Brigid loped across the clearing like a wolf, spitting epithets. At the tree-line, she exchanged a fleeting look with Rowena, though whether of gratitude or warning Rowena was not sure. And then she plunged into the woods.

The priest howled for a long moment, and then his voice drained away and he began to babble. He raised both hands to the sky and cried out, 'He is coming.'

'She has made him see visions,' Acha whispered.

'He is coming. He is coming.' The gathered men began to smile, thinking the priest was speaking of the Christ. But then his voice broke, and he coughed and choked and sobbed, and finally he cried, 'The Devil is coming, on the wings of ravens. And there is thunder . . . my ears ring. This thunder! And there is fire . . .' His words drained away into an incoherent mumbling.

Blood drained from the face of every man there. One of the other churchmen turned and yelled, 'Burn this place to the ground.'

As the frightened men plunged through the door to kick the hot coals in the hearth on to the straw, Acha pulled Rowena away. They hurried into the dark, fearing retribution. Behind them, the flames roared up. Sparks swirled over the stark trees. Rowena felt cold reach deep inside her. She had not found her husband, and with each day the world was turning further from the light.

CHAPTER SEVENTEEN

The shadow of the axe carved across the bared neck of the man hunched on his knees. There, on the edge of the black mere, the world seemed to hold its breath. No breeze, no sound at all disturbed the weighted moment. In a circle, the English watched the tableau. They smelled of sweat and peat and smoke. Some licked their dry lips. Others swallowed. No one blinked. Every man wondered how the Norman knight could bear the waiting. They imagined his thoughts, the knowledge that it would take three, perhaps four strokes to separate his head from his shoulders. The agonies that would have to be endured before the end. The despair that must surely engulf him as he realized there was no hope. No escape.

Death waited at his shoulder.

Kraki's hand trembled. He itched to bring the axe down. His eyes flickered towards Hereward. But the Mercian frowned as he studied Deda's profile. Not even a glimmer of fear lay there. The knight looked at peace, as if he prayed at the altar of one of the Normans' vast, cold churches.

Hereward nodded to Kraki.

'Speak now if you would,' the Northman growled.

'I have made my peace with God,' Deda replied in a clear voice.

115

'No pleas for mercy?' Kraki shifted his feet to brace himself. 'Once more: tell us what you know of the king's plans and we will spare your miserable life.'

'I will not betray my king.'

'Aye, all cut from the same cloth, you Normans,' Kraki snarled. 'Bastards, the lot of you.'

'Wait.' Hengist danced forward, his eyes shining. He rubbed his twitchy hands together and knelt so he could peer into the knight's eyes. 'There is a better path.'

'Speak, Hengist,' Hereward commanded.

'Do it the Norman way.' Hengist lay flat so that he looked like an eager child. 'Cut off a foot. Then a hand. An ear, an eye, his nose. Whittle him down, bit by bit. His lips will be loose long before he loses them.'

'What do you say, Norman?' Hereward squatted so he could make eye contact with the knight. 'Speak now and have a clean death. Or suffer the agonies of hell before you talk. And still die.'

Deda held the Mercian's gaze. A hint of a smile crossed his lips. 'A choice like that, I would need time to think on it.'

Hereward studied the strong face, the clear eyes. He saw no cruelty there. He felt troubled, for this made little sense to him. He had been watching Deda from the moment they had fished him out of the rushing waters of the Ouse. The knight had sat calmly by while the English had set about destroying the causeway, burning the peat defences and scattering the sand and the flint to the four corners of the earth. By nightfall, the king's plan, a feeble one at best, lay in tatters. And still Deda showed no fear of what was to come for him.

'Raise him up,' Hereward commanded.

Hengist looked puzzled, but with Kraki's help he lifted the knight to his feet. The Norman warrior stood erect, still holding his captor's gaze.

'I see now there is little to gain by holding the threat of death against this foe,' the Mercian said.

'Kill him then and be done with it,' Hengist pressed, rubbing his palms together.

Hereward looked around his men. 'Are we afraid of one poor Norman? Are we afraid of *any* Normans?' He grinned. His men nodded, their mutterings of defiance rising to loud assent. 'We are English. We show kindness to all guests. That is our way. And is Deda the knight not a guest? Then let us treat him as one. Let us take him to Ely and give him a feast greater than any he would have had under the bastard king.'

The men looked at each other, unsure. But when they glimpsed Kraki's sly grin, they cheered. 'Aye. Let us show him the English way.'

Deda cocked one eyebrow. 'Mercy, then? And a full belly too.' His tone was wry.

'If we were Normans we would have strung you up alive, cut off your cock and pulled out your guts so you could watch the ravens feeding on them,' Hereward replied. 'Even taking your head would have been a mercy. You are our guest now. No more worry, or fear. You will see us as we are. But not just yet.' He nodded and Madulf and Sighard tied a strip of cloth across the Norman's eyes. Once their captive could not see, Kraki nodded to Hereward. All had gone as planned.

Grinning, Hengist and Guthrinc prodded their spears into the knight to guide him towards the secret path back to Ely. He strode ahead of them, at his own pace.

Before Hereward could follow his war-band, he heard a familiar voice hailing his name. Alric was pushing his way through the sea of bracken with Herrig the Rat at his side. Herrig was the best scout they had. The folk across the fens called the rebels the wild men of the woods, and Herrig was the wildest of all. Like his namesake, he was lean and lithe and ferocious. His long hair was lank and greasy and his front teeth had been knocked out in a fight, creating the illusion that he had fangs at the edge of his mouth. Hereward had seen him scale a soaring ash tree in a flash and then leap to the next tree from a bouncing branch. He could crawl through ditches half filled with brackish water for miles on end, and live in the woods on berries and rabbits longer than any man in Ely.

Round his neck, on a leather thong, he carried the finger bones of men he had killed, and there were now so many he rattled when he walked.

'Herrig has important news that could not wait. And a strange sight to show you,' Alric said, flushed from the haste of his journey from Ely.

The scout gave a gap-toothed grin and waved three bloody severed digits. 'The blood of good men would run cold at the screams. But now there is only silence.' He ended his words with a snicker that sounded like a pig rooting in the mud.

'Aye, there are no good men in these parts,' Hereward said. 'Speak, Rat.'

Herrig's eyes flickered from side to side. He could not help searching the trees for enemies, even when he was with friends. 'There is much to tell.' He raised a finger, choosing. 'The king is to set up camp at Belsar's Hill—'

'Close enough to strike at Ely,' Alric interjected.

'He may as well be in Wincestre,' Hereward said. 'We have destroyed the causeway which would have carried his men to our gates. He cannot cross the waters and bogs.'

'Worse news for the Bastard,' the scout said with a crooked grin. 'He tries to raise a levy, away to the west, but few men are joining him.'

'If he searches for new men,' the monk ventured, 'his army must be poor indeed.'

'It would seem,' Hereward said.

'In the villages, they are waiting for your call,' Herrig added. 'They will rise up with the English.'

'Then we should strike soon, while the king is at his weakest.' Alric looked eager. Glad to be done with all this strife, the Mercian thought. And who could blame him?

'What else do you have?' he asked.

Herrig waved a filthy, broken-nailed finger. 'Would you hear of your brother?'

Hereward stiffened. 'What do you know?'

'He travels south from Lincylene, with your father, and the

Butcher and William de Warenne and some other Norman nobles. They go to see the king.'

'How near?'

'A day away from Belsar's Hill.'

Hereward peered through the trees towards the west. He felt the flames of his anger lick up inside him. He imagined his hands round Redwald's throat, choking the life from him. He envisioned blood, to wash away the memory of Turfrida's suffering, blood spilled in front of his father. How easy it would be to give in to the devil inside him. He sensed Alric's eyes upon him and could almost read the other man's thoughts. *Do not turn your back upon the English for your own needs. You will never forgive yourself if you follow this path of vengeance.* With a struggle, he damped down his fury and said, 'There will be time enough for my brother.'

Alric flashed a smile of relief. 'One other thing,' the scout added. 'Another riddle. Come.'

Hereward and Alric followed Herrig into the trees. They skirted a lake the colour of iron and forged across a narrow cause-way through a stinking marsh. All the time, they kept their ears cocked, listening for the sound of birds taking flight. The day grew warmer. Crows called from the treetops. They smelled rotting leaves and stagnant water, but nothing of men. Finally, Herrig pushed through a line of trees snarled by bramble and came to a halt. Hereward frowned as he looked ahead.

Acres of the wooded land now lay bare. Stumps of trees dotted the land, creamy ridges revealing the axe cuts that had brought them down. Furrows led off to the west where the trunks had been dragged away.

'What is the meaning of this?' Alric asked. 'This has all been newly cut. There are no farms in these parts, no homes.'

'A riddle,' Herrig repeated.

Hereward walked to the centre of the cleared land and knelt down. He traced his fingers across hoofprints and footprints made deep by men weighted down with armour. 'The Normans did this,' he murmured.

119

The sight weighed heavily on him as they made their way back to Ely. Too many riddles circled, like ravens over a battlefield. He felt certain some meaning was attached to these things, but he could not find it, and that troubled him. A thought haunted him: if he did not find the connections soon, all would be lost.

At Ely, the sounds of carousing echoed over the walls. The men had returned home with news of the blow struck against the king. They drank in the afternoon sun, and sang, and stole kisses from the women. They deserved their joy, Hereward thought. He would not steal that from them. But he could not be a part of it. He strode up to the minster, hoping to be alone with his thoughts in the tranquillity of the church. But at the gate to the enclosure, Abbot Thurstan waited for him. From the cleric's grim face, he could see the conversation would not be good.

'You have given your protection to the witch Brigid?' Thurstan demanded.

Weary, Hereward waved a hand to brush aside this inconsequential matter. 'I have done no such thing.'

The abbot beckoned to a monk, who brought the new woman, Rowena, from the side of one of the halls. The warrior sighed. Trouble seemed to follow her like a shadow.

'This woman,' Thurstan began, his voice trembling, 'this woman has worked against God's will. She has deceived us. She has taken your name and used it to save the life of that heathen.'

Hereward narrowed his eyes at the woman. She bit her lip, then held her head up in defiance. 'Is this true?' he asked.

'Your wife was a wise woman. You have no argument with them,' she said.

'That is not the issue here,' he snapped. 'I will not have my name used without my consent. My name, and what it means in these parts, is all I have.'

Thurstan glowered. 'She must be punished.'

The Mercian hesitated. 'No more,' he said to her.

Her cheeks flushed. 'I will not be told what to do. I am not a Norman woman. And I care naught for your fight. Who wears the crown in Wincestre ...' She sneered, then spat. 'Kings are kings. My husband is *my* world. Without him, there is nothing for me. That is all that matters to me.' She walked away a few paces and then turned back. 'Pick up your spears and axes and play your games of blood and power, if it pleases you. If you will not help me find Elwin, I will do it alone. Aye, even if it means attacking the king myself.'

Hereward watched her march away and thought how much she reminded him of his wife. He ignored Thurstan's insistence that Rowena should be imprisoned in one of the church halls, for her own good, the abbot said, and for the good of them all. Instead, he walked down to the tavern and found Kraki and Guthrinc roaring with laughter as they swilled back ale.

'In days to come, we will remember this moment,' he said, looking from one man to the other as he took a cup of mead for himself. 'Today we begin to reclaim this land for the English. Drink your drinks and then come to the minster. We have plans to make. Before the cold weather comes, we will bring together our army and we will march out from Ely, into the west. The crown will be ours. And the bastard king's head will become a feast for the ravens.'

CHAPTER EIGHTEEN

Sweating and red-faced from the cookhouse, the boys carried in the glistening roasted ox on its long iron skewer. All around Abbot Thurstan's grand hall, folk cheered as the sweet aroma of the meat swept over them. The harpists plucked at their instruments, their voices soaring up to the rafters in celebration as the boys placed the carcass on the stand near the hearth. The long tables groaned under the weight of goose legs and salt pork, bread and cheese and smoked eel, strong ale and Frankish wine. Long weeks had passed since any in Ely had seen such a feast, though they were all under strict orders not to reveal such a thing.

Hereward held up his cup and roared, 'To the glory of the English.'

The full-throated response rang back.

'Good cheer is everywhere in Ely,' the Mercian said, leaning in to the knight, Deda, who sat beside him. The din of the feast filled the hall.

The two men watched as thick slabs of steaming beef were sliced off and handed out along the tables. Hereward crashed his cup against the other man's and announced, 'Fill your belly, Norman. We look after our guests well here.'

Deda furrowed his brow. 'You would kill me with kindness?'

'You are not hungry?'

'I am . . . curious. You treat all your enemies this way?'

'Is it not the Norman way?' Hereward gave a knowing grin.

'We have no enemies,' the knight replied with a wry smile. 'Only folk who have yet to discover they are friends.'

The Mercian eyed the other man, still unsure what to make of him. He thought he had the measure of all Normans, but this one seemed no different from the English knights who had smuggled him food from the king's table at Edward's court.

As a slice of gleaming beef appeared before Deda, his hand hovered for a moment before he took it with a muttered thanks. 'I keep waiting for this all to be snatched away and the laughter to begin.'

'There is no gain in tormenting you.'

'No? Not revenge for the slaughter inflicted on the north? For the land taken from the English and passed into loyal Norman hands? For the churches stripped bare . . .'

Hereward nodded, feigning reflection. 'Speak on. You may change my mind.'

Deda laughed. 'You are an odd man, Hereward of the English. I heard you were little more than a wild beast, bathing in the blood of any who crossed your path, friend or enemy alike.'

'We are all many things.' Hereward gnawed on his piece of beef. His stomach growled as the juices trickled down his throat. How long had it been since he had eaten well, he wondered.

The knight nodded. 'This is true. And there are few truths around at the moment. The English think us monsters. We think you all drunken fools, thieves and murderers.'

'We have those too.'

A juggler and a tumbler ran into the hall and began to throw themselves around, to much laughter. The women clapped. The men, already drunk, threw chunks of bread.

Deda sipped his wine and looked around the hall. 'We are

123

told you are starving here in Ely. The king has closed your trade routes and there is not enough food upon this small isle to feed the multitude that has flocked to your standard.'

Hereward held both hands out to the vast array of meats and fish.

The knight made a thoughtful noise in his throat. 'And, we are told, the men of Ely are so hungry they have no fight left in them. Soon they will throw the gates wide and creep out with outstretched hands to beg for whatever morsels we toss them. And the war will be ended without a drop of blood being spilled.'

'And this is the tale you tell your children at night to send them into sweet dreams?' Hereward laughed. 'Let your own eyes decide the truth.'

'Yet you must know it is only a matter of time before Ely falls. The king will never give up his crown. He would see all England burn first.'

Hereward put down his cup and beckoned to the other man. 'Come, let me show you the lie at the heart of the king's words.' Deda rose and followed him out of the hall into the chill wind. The cacophony of the feast faded as the door swung shut. Grey skies lowered overhead. Leaves whirled around the minster enclosure. They walked through the gate into Ely and round the hillside towards the Camp of Refuge. Deda slowed his step as the sound of many voices was caught on the breeze. And then, as they crossed on to the lee side of the isle, they looked over a vast army of men. Thousands. The smoke of scores of bonfires blackened the sky. The men warmed themselves against the flames, or formed shield walls under the scrutiny of seasoned warriors, or practised with their bows or javelins. Some were well armed with hauberks and helms, spears and axes. Some wore only woollen cloaks over their tunics and carried cudgels.

Hereward watched a shadow cross the knight's face as he looked out over the English army. 'You march on the king this day?'

The Mercian shook his head. 'We are ready if William the Bastard dares attack Ely. But we will choose our moment and rout your army when you least expect it.' He reached out an arm, raising his voice above the beat of spears upon shields. 'This is the least of it. We are receiving word by the day from all parts of the land. When we rise up, all England will rise with us, and you will be driven into the sea before us.'

A man strode up from the ranks, a fine blue cloak swirling around him. His horse-face was formed into a permanent scowl and his blond hair was thinning. 'Earl Morcar,' Hereward told his guest. 'Many of the fiercest warriors here are his men. His huscarls are feared more than those of any other earl.'

'I know of his grudge against the king. His blood had claim to the crown, once.'

Morcar eyed Deda with suspicion as he neared. He beckoned the Mercian to one side and whispered, 'What news of your brother?'

'He rides south to join the king.'

'Good. When we attack, he is mine, do you hear? He will pay for killing my own brother.' The earl blinked away a hot tear. His brother Edwin had always been the stronger of the two, Hereward knew. Morcar was weak and poor in judgement, but his men were invaluable.

'Redwald has left no small number of men wanting his blood.' He looked out at the army. 'A good show of strength. Any man would quake to see it. We are ready?'

Morcar nodded. 'We are ready.'

As Hereward led the knight back towards the minster, he said, 'Our army is not all that you should fear. God is on our side.'

Deda jerked his head round, his eyes narrowing at this suspected blasphemy.

'Aye, I wagered William the Bastard had not made it common knowledge. We have the arm of St Oswald.'

The knight bowed his head. 'I have heard many tales of this

wonder. It heals the sick, and makes the lame walk and the blind see, so they say.'

'Aye, and God protects all who carry it. God is with us, Norman. We cannot lose.'

After a moment, Deda said in a voice filled with reverence, 'I would see it, if I may, and offer a small prayer over it.'

'You are a God-fearing man. That is good. We will not deny you.'

Deda seemed grateful for this opportunity, but he kept his head bowed in reflection as they walked. News of the relic weighed heavily on him, the Mercian saw.

When they stepped back into the abbot's hall, the tumult had grown louder still. Shouts and jeers smothered the harpists' music. Kraki and Guthrinc stood on opposite tables, facing each other, heads thrown back as they drank. Ale streamed down their chests. Warriors shook their fists as they championed one or the other while Abbot Thurstan and a small knot of monks looked on wearily. A figure stood in the shadows behind the churchmen. It was Alric. He caught Hereward's eye and gave a surreptitious nod.

As Kraki crashed back off the table into the arms of four Northmen, Deda grinned, his mood lifted by the horseplay. Hereward led him back to his seat and beckoned to one of the hall women to bring more beef and wine for their guest.

'Do you not yearn for your home instead of this rain-lashed land?' the Mercian shouted over the clamour.

'Normandy is rainswept enough,' Deda said, chewing on a goose leg. But his eyes shone with a faraway look. 'Ah, but this time of year it fair glows with gold and ruby and amber across the woods. And the feasts when the harvests are brought in! You English think us a cold-hearted folk, but if you saw the maidens dance around the corn-dolls, and the children in their horse masks, and if you heard the songs of the sea and the summer gone, you would not fail to be moved.'

'Your wife waits for you there?'

'My wife is dead. Taken by the sickness.' The knight gave a

polite nod, signalling that he would talk of this no more. Hereward glimpsed a shadow of sadness tainting his faint smile. He felt some warmth for the other man, and hated himself for it. Looking away, he forced himself to remember the ravaged face of the burned man who had escaped the rape of the north.

When the food was eaten, and the warriors were slumped across the tables in pools of ale, Hereward rested one hand on Deda's shoulder, leaned in and said, 'It is time.' The Mercian knew the knight would think the worst, but he did not dispel that thought. He could still be cruel to his enemies, if he wished.

Outside, the light was thin and the world was grey. Hereward held his face to the north. 'The cold is coming.'

'For me,' Deda said, misunderstanding, though he still showed no fear.

'For all of us. Before the Christmas bells ring, the ravens will feed hard. The wars that have gone before will seem like nothing next to what is to come.' He guided Deda into the church to pray over the reliquary and then they set off down the slope past the homes and workshops of Ely. Fires glowed through the open doors. Women hunched over pots. Children chased each other, laughing, into the growing gloom. He felt his heart grow heavy. This might be the last Ely knew of peace.

When they passed the smithy, a woman strode out in front of them. Hereward saw that it was Rowena, wrapped in a brown cloak with the hood pulled up. Her face showed no emotion. She stepped up to Deda and spat in his face.

'He is our guest,' Hereward snapped and would have pushed her away, but the knight held up a hand to stop him. He wiped the saliva from his cheek and gave a bow.

'I have had worse greetings, but not many,' he said drolly. 'Still, I am honoured to know you.' For a moment, he grew serious. 'And if I have wronged you in any way, I am truly sorry.'

Rowena glared at him, then spun round and walked away.

'The king's men took her husband, and all the men in her village,' Hereward explained as they continued down the slope. 'Her heart has hardened against all Normans.'

'We are unloved?' the knight said in a sardonic tone. 'I can scarce believe it.' But the Mercian saw him frown and glance back at the woman as she disappeared among the houses.

As they wandered towards the gates, Hereward said, 'You have witnessed our might. You know that God stands with us. The season of the Normans is passing, you must see that.'

'Many before you have said the same thing.'

'If the king were wise, he would give up the crown and return to your home. See the maidens and the children, and hear the songs, not wade through blood and find peace only behind stone walls.'

A smile ghosted Deda's lips. 'You would have me take this message to him?'

Hereward smiled in turn. The knight was clever. 'It is the last chance, perhaps, for the English and the Normans,' he replied, his voice growing grave. 'They say these are the End of Days, and well they may be, for all of us. If war comes, no one will back down. The land will burn, and the rivers will run red, and the prize may not be worth the winning.'

Deda sighed and looked out across the darkening wetlands. 'I hear your words. I will speak them to the king.'

Hereward hesitated, then rested one hand on the other man's shoulder. 'And if he does not hear . . . You do not have to stand and fight beside him. You have a home across the whale road.'

The knight shook his head. 'You know that cannot be. You are a man of honour, as I am. I have sworn my sword to the king. Whatever comes to pass, I will be there at the king's side.'

Hereward understood. 'This is the measure of a man,' he said. 'We can do no other.' He waved at the guards and the gates trundled open. 'Go well, Deda. A scout waits to bind your eyes and guide you across the causeway.'

Deda searched the Mercian's face for a moment, and seemed

satisfied by what he saw there. 'Go well, Hereward. We will meet soon enough, for the last time.'

He turned and marched through the gates and away into the night. Hereward climbed the creaking ladder on to the walkway and peered over the walls into the shadowed land. Though he could no longer see Deda, he felt the knight in his thoughts.

'You used him well.' Alric had appeared at his side. 'He has seen our army. The men have returned to their homes, though they grumble at being forced to put on such a show for just one man. And now he thinks we are not short of food, though we wasted meat that was to keep us from starvation through the cold season. And God . . .' The monk's voice grew low and hesitant. 'He knows God is with us. Do you think the king will listen?'

'Perhaps.' He knew he could not have borne the weight on his soul if he had not at least tried. The waste of lives that would surely come, on one side or the other, or both, cast a shadow over him. 'And now we make ready, and hope that Herrig will soon come with news that the king has left Belsar's Hill and returned to Wincestre.' Even as he spoke the words, he felt the thin hope drain away. Deda had been right; the king who raped the north, and slaughtered folk who were now his own, would never give up his power willingly. The end was coming.

The two men watched in silence, letting the night settle on them.

CHAPTER NINETEEN

The body sagged on the pole beside the road. The empty eye-holes stared. The ravens had taken the nose and the lips and the fleshy part of the cheeks, and the stink of rot filled the chill night air. The grin was a grim warning to any who came this way.

Rowena shuddered and crossed herself. She wished the clouds had not cleared to let the moonlight illuminate such a grisly sight. The stark shadow of the hanging man fell across the silvery track in front of them as if barring their way. Ahead she could see more silhouettes of the dead on either side of the path leading to the camp at Belsar's Hill. So many. No one could pass by without hearing the grave message of these silent sentinels – or the message of the grave.

'We should not have come,' Acha whispered beside her as if she had read her thoughts.

'You did not have to come,' Rowena replied. She winced as she recognized her unkindness. Softening her tone, she added, 'I had no choice, you know that. The days rush away from me. Hereward is ready to strike, and when war begins, what hope then of finding my husband?'

'But to go into the heart of the enemy's camp – that is madness,' the other woman hissed.

Aye, madness. Rowena felt sick from fear. Her hands shook and her chest was so tight she could barely breathe. Every part of her told her to flee back to Ely, but she could not abandon Elwin. She forced a laugh to try to lighten the dour mood. 'Do you do Hereward's bidding, to be my shadow and try to turn me back whenever I risk my neck? You should know by now that there is no harder work.'

Acha snorted. 'Hereward does not tell me what to do.'

Rowena had long sensed that there was some past between the two of them, but she did not pry. 'I will not turn back. Either leave now or walk with me.'

'Through the gates of hell,' the other woman spat. 'If I die, it will be a stain on your soul.'

'I accept my burden.' Clasping her hand over her mouth and nose, Rowena set off along the road. The dead judged them as they passed. The two women kept their heads down, but Rowena could not resist glancing up into each face. As she passed the last one, she felt a flood of relief that she had not seen Elwin.

They had not gone far when they saw twin eyes of fire burning in the night. Rowena felt a chill run through her. Acha slowed her step, but only for a moment. She pushed her chin up and walked on. 'We are not mice. We are . . .'

'Rats?' Rowena ventured. 'Cats? Dogs?'

Both women laughed. They walked on and saw that the eyes were twin torches over the gate to the enemy camp. Belsar's Hill loomed up from the flat landscape, the ridges of its ramparts silhouetted against the starry sky.

Rowena pushed aside her thoughts of what lay on the other side of those gates and said, 'In Ely, some say that you are of the Cymri.'

After a moment, Acha replied, 'Tostig Godwinson took me from my folk and made me his slave.'

'And they say you have royal blood flowing through your veins.'

For a long time, the other woman said nothing. Then: 'When

this war is done, Kraki has promised that he will take me home.'

'He is a good man. You must hold him in your heart.'

Acha did not reply.

As they neared the gate, they smelled woodsmoke and the scents of the evening stews, and they could hear dim shouts and laughter. Two guards stood on the walkway looking down at them, their faces lost to shadow.

'Who goes?' one called in heavily accented English.

Rowena swirled the hem of her dress and gave a coquettish giggle. 'Comfort for fighting men, that is who goes.' She sensed Acha flinch at her side. Her companion would have no man take her for a whore. The two guards conversed between themselves in the harsh Norman tongue. Rowena sensed the discussion was not going well and called, 'Haste! The night grows old. Your brothers will never forgive you if you deny them their pleasure.'

After a moment, the gates ground open and the two women hurried inside before the guards changed their minds.

Beyond the walls, many campfires lit the dense jumble of tents and newly built wooden dwellings. Paths wound among the houses, narrow and thick with deep mud from the autumn rains. Waste choked the tracks. Smoke billowed like fog across the camp. Rowena slowed her pace as she moved through it. She felt an oppressive sense of threat. Men roamed in packs, mostly drunk. They barked abuse at each other amid gales of raucous laughter. Many were Norman soldiers, but she also saw axes-for-hire, former huscarls and Northmen with scarred, leathery faces, their hands always a whisper from their weapons. A few were levied Englishmen. They looked out of place, carrying themselves like the farmers they were, and mostly they stayed away from the groups of seasoned warriors. And yet there were fewer than she would have expected.

'Hereward was right,' Acha whispered, seeing the same signs. 'If this army is the best the king can do, this war will be over in no time.'

Rowena felt conspicuous. This was not a place for women.

The only ones she saw were whores, pock-marked, toothless, rake-thin, faces like winter fields. Through the open flaps of a tent they glimpsed two soldiers roughly taking one of the women between them. Naked, she had no shame, not caring that any might see what other women only did with their husbands in their beds. Rowena hurried on, only to find the way barred by another whore lying in the mud like a beast of the field, legs splayed for the grunting Northman atop of her.

'You would have us be whores,' Acha whispered with thick contempt as they turned along another narrow track. 'I would rather cut my own throat than fall to these depths.'

Choking from the smoke and the stink of waste, Rowena blinked away stray tears. What had she hoped to accomplish by visiting this foul place? She had kept a little girl's vision of walking through the gate to find Elwin waiting for her, and she would take his hand and lead him home. She was not prepared for this hard world.

Acha must have seen some of her thoughts in her face for she said in a gentle voice, 'We will find him. You have the strength to see this through.'

Rowena nodded, wiping her eyes dry. She pushed aside her doubts and replied, 'Let us keep looking. And if the men approach us, we must tell them we have been bought by one of the nobles. That will keep us safe, for a while.'

Through the choked camp they searched. Near the centre, they came up against another enclosure wall. Beyond it, they could see the outline of one of the Normans' wooden castles. As they looked up at the tower, they heard a shout ring out from the walls. A clamour rushed over the tents and huts. The laughter and the drunken shouts died away, and they realized men were emerging from their homes to wait and watch.

'What is this?' Rowena asked. Acha gripped her wrist to silence her. In the distance, the sound of hoofbeats grew louder.

A hush fell over the entire camp. The main gates rattled open and the thunder of hooves drew nearer. Heads dropped one by one until all the men were bowing.

Rowena held her breath without knowing why.

The amber glow of the campfires lit a column of men riding towards the castle. Knights in helms and hauberks and noblemen in fine cloaks of purple and gold and blue. At the head of the procession was an oak of a man, broad-shouldered and powerful, his mail shirt a mountain of iron atop his stallion. His expression was fierce and he levelled his gaze across the men he passed as if he held their lives in his hand.

'The king,' Acha gasped. 'It can be no other.'

As William the Bastard neared the castle gates, he turned his head and caught sight of the two women. He looked into Rowena's eyes and held her gaze for a long moment until she realized what she was doing and bowed her head.

The castle gates ground open. The procession clattered through. And then the gates shut, and after a few moments of awed stillness the clamour of the camp rose up once more.

'Then all that we heard was true,' Acha said in a low, unsettled voice. 'The king has come, and he will smite the east as he did the north. War can only be days away.'

'I care little,' Rowena said, turning back to the camp. 'Let us find Elwin, and then we can be away.'

She strode out, following the line of the castle wall in the direction of the other, unexplored side of the camp. She had been right to worry that time was short. Her husband had to be found before Hereward and the Bastard started tearing bloody chunks off each other like starving dogs.

A quiet lay over the other side of the camp. No drunken soldiers lurched along the narrow tracks, but the stink of shit and piss was, if anything, even worse. The tents here were larger, the few huts more roughly built, little more than walls of peat blocks with planks laid across for a roof. Rowena peeped inside one of the tents. Row upon row of men lay upon beds of straw. They were filthy, their clothes near rags. They seemed to be sleeping fitfully, arms thrown over their faces as they tossed and turned. A few sat up, staring blankly into space. Exhaustion had carved deep lines in their faces. 'These are English,' she whispered to Acha.

'But not levied,' Acha replied, 'not fighting men. They look as though they have been working in the fields. The king's army is smaller still.'

Rowena turned away from the tent, her brow knotted. She felt a weight of dread upon her shoulders although she did not know why. Acha felt it too, she could see.

'We must leave here soon,' the other woman murmured, looking around, 'or we may never leave at all.'

As they searched the narrow paths, they caught sight of a few men straggling back to their beds from the direction of the camp gates. A fire lit the face of one and Rowena all but cried out.

She ran over and caught his arm. 'Swefred,' she hissed. 'It is I, Rowena.' He peered at her with dazed eyes, recognition slowly lighting in their depths. 'He is from my village,' she said, turning back to Acha. Her voice trembled with excitement. 'He was taken with my husband.'

'Rowena? What are you doing in this foul place?' Suddenly animated, the man's eyes darted around as if he was afraid the wrath of the Normans would fall upon him merely for speaking to this woman.

'I search for Elwin. For all of you. To take you home.'

'There is no hope of that.' He bowed his head so she could not see his face.

'There is always hope.'

He swallowed and steadied himself. 'Leave now. This is not a place for you.'

'Where is Elwin?' she pressed.

'I cannot say.'

Rowena stifled her frustration. She could see the man was near-delirious with exhaustion. 'Why have the Normans brought you here?'

'To be their slaves.'

Acha looked around. 'The castle is built. The walls of the camp stand. Why do you still labour?'

Swefred began to stumble away, but Rowena grabbed him and shook him more roughly than she intended. She too felt they would be caught and dragged away at any moment. 'Tell us what you know,' she hissed.

'Very well,' he snapped. 'But no good will come from it. Here.'

He marched among the tents until he reached the camp's wall. Glancing around to make sure no guards were near, he clambered up the rickety ladder to the walkway. Rowena and Acha climbed after him. 'See,' he whispered, pointing over the palisade.

Rowena's breath caught in her throat. For a moment, she thought she looked out across the fields of hell. Fires blazed everywhere. Sparks swirled up in banks of black smoke. In a natural bowl, shielded by trees, a vast city of tents stretched deep into the night. Standards fluttered from poles. Along the edge, workshops squatted, and the sound of smiths' hammers rang out as if they were beating the drums of war. Rowena's nose wrinkled at the stink of brimstone from the forges. Looming over the camp, wooden towers soared up almost to the stars. They rested on platforms that could be rolled on logs. In the gloom beyond, Rowena could just discern the silhouettes of great siege machines.

Caught in the ruddy glow of the bonfires, men sat around drinking, their shields and helms resting beside them. Everywhere she looked, warriors, ready for bloodshed. The camp on the hill contained only the guard who would protect the monarch if the rebels attacked, she realized. Here was the king's true army, a mighty force that would crush the unwary English in no time.

'We must warn Hereward,' Acha said, her voice weak. 'If he rides now, unprepared, all is lost.'

'The Bastard is building a causeway to the east, a great road across the waters and the bogs that will lead his men up to the very walls of Ely,' Swefred said. 'We have laboured on it night and day. Foundations of good wood and reed, sand, peat, and flint. Strong enough to take the siege machines and as many men as the king will send. Those towers will guard its edges.' He hesitated, then added, 'All is lost.'

As the two women gaped, he scrambled down the ladder and began to trudge back towards his bed. Rowena raced after him. 'If you laboured on the causeway, Elwin must have worked beside you,' she said, grabbing his arm. 'Where is he? Tell me – I must see him now.'

'I will tell you nothing,' he snarled, trying to throw her off.

She held tight, her eyes blazing. 'Tell me,' she shouted.

Swefred flinched as her voice carried out across the camp. 'Hold your tongue. You will bring the guards down upon us.' He looked into her eyes and saw he had no choice. 'Very well,' he muttered. He turned and began to walk towards a long, low hut beside the wall. 'Elwin – he always had a fire in his heart. The Normans treated us worse than dogs. They threw us scraps of food to fight over, and kicked us, and hit us with the flats of their swords to make us work harder. Days of that, and Elwin would take no more. He tried to get the English to fight back. He stood, and raged at the bastards, and yelled at the men to join him.' His voice drained away and his head bowed. 'But none stood with him. The guards dragged him away and beat him . . . beat him harder than I have seen a man beaten.'

'Oh,' Rowena said in a small voice, choking back her pain. Her voice fell to a whisper, but it was infused with hope. 'Wherever they hold him, we must free him now. Will you aid me?'

Swefred came to a halt. After a moment, he raised his arm and pointed towards the hut. 'There is your husband.'

Rowena followed the line of the roof and came to a pole at one end. On the top of it, Elwin looked down at her, his empty eye-sockets staring.

Swefred swallowed. 'They took his head.'

Chapter Twenty

The campfire roared. Shadows danced across the tent as William the Bastard stood in the entrance, looking out across the mud of the castle ward. From the dark by the gate, Deda watched the monarch lit by the red glare. He looked like a bear waiting for prey, and just as savage when roused, the knight thought. After his long, lonely trek across the wetlands, Deda's hair was lank with grease and mud streaked his face. His tunic was still sodden from the rain and his legs felt as if they were made of lead. But he lived yet. Not too long ago that had seemed a thin hope.

Over the tent, the king's standard fluttered, two rampant golden lions against a red field. The new tower was not yet ready for living in, Deda guessed. As William turned to go back inside the tent, the knight took a deep breath, lifted his head and set off across the ward. He could hear the king's deep voice rumbling out, even above the din from the camp. Several other men seemed to be with him, giving their counsel.

'These English,' the monarch was shouting, 'what is wrong with them? Half the time they are drunk, the other half asleep. Yet they fight like wolves, even now, seasons after I took the crown. Must this be the story for all of my rule? War and bloodshed? What victory did I not win that day on Senlac Ridge, that I cannot enjoy my prize?'

Deda grinned as he heard the familiar sounds of lackeys fawning and dissembling to drain the king's anger before they suggested unpalatable truths. Soon he would be putting forward one of his own, and he expected the edge of the monarch's tongue in return. But Hereward had been right; these words had to be spoken if they were to avoid death on a grand scale. And England had seen more than enough of that in recent times.

He stepped into the tent's entrance. Before he could utter a word, every man inside reeled back in horror, the king included. Hands clutched at mouths and prayers were muttered. After a moment's bafflement, Deda realized they were seeing some terrible apparition. Bedraggled and streaked with mud as if he had climbed from the grave, haloed by the fire at his back like a vision from hell. After the slaughter at the causeway, they must all have thought him dead.

'My lord,' he said with a bow. 'I am in better health than I may appear.'

The king narrowed his eyes. 'Deda? You have the reek of the shroud about you.'

'The English spared my life at the causeway, but they seized me and took me back to Ely.'

'And you escaped?'

'I have word from Hereward.'

Excited murmurs ran through the tent. Deda looked around and saw Odo of Bayeux, Ivo Taillebois, William de Warenne and two other men he did not recognize, one aged but still potent, leaning upon a staff, and a younger man with apple cheeks and an innocent face.

'The English dog is afraid, eh?' the king roared. 'He wishes to bow his head before me and plead for his miserable life.' The monarch beckoned Deda into the tent. 'Give him wine,' he barked at Taillebois as if the latter were a slave. The Butcher flashed one unguarded venomous look before he turned to the pitcher.

Deda took the cup he was offered and said, 'The English are ready for war. Their army is larger than we thought. I have seen it with my own eyes. They have no shortage of food to see them through the cold season. And God is with them.' He eyed the king. 'They have the arm of St Oswald.'

The monarch showed no surprise. Nor did the Butcher or William de Warenne.

'If our men do not know it, they soon will. What then?'

William the Bastard took a cup of wine and swilled it back in one draught. After a moment's reflection, he said, 'They will accept peace?'

Deda was surprised by the response, and recognized the same reaction on the faces of the other men there. The king looked around, showing barely concealed contempt at what he saw.

'This is not weakness,' he snapped. 'I fought hard for this crown. It will mean naught if I have to kill every man in England to keep it.' He prowled to the trestle at the back of the tent and snatched up a chunk of salt pork. 'We have enemies everywhere. We cannot afford to waste time putting down the English. With our eyes here in the east, we are not looking to the Danes . . . or Malcolm in the north . . . If our men are dying here, who then will fight to protect what we have?' He chewed on the meat and spat out a chunk of gristle. 'A long fight across the years will drain our coffers. Think on that. We will be beggared. What say you, Deda?'

'The English are folk of honour,' the knight said, choosing his words carefully. 'The north . . . what they now call the Harrowing . . . weighs heavily on them. Many who accepted your rule have been sent spinning towards Hereward.'

'But they needed to be taught a lesson, eh, Deda? You agree with me.' The monarch glanced with cold eyes.

'They were taught a hard lesson, my lord. And the north will not rise again.'

William the Bastard threw the meat aside. 'If we offer them peace . . . if we forgive them their sins against us and spare their lives . . . we can talk until the fight is drained from them.' He noticed Taillebois's sour expression and scowled. 'There is more than one path to victory, Butcher. Winning does not need a drenching of blood to make it grow. If you had the wits to match that sword arm, you would know that.'

The young man shifted, keen to speak.

The king beckoned. 'You . . . the brother of Hereward. You know the mind of this dog. Will he talk peace?'

'My lord,' the younger man said, 'Hereward cannot be trusted. He will smile and nod and speak of peace, and once your guard is down, he will attack. A dog, you say. A wolf more like. Can a wolf be tamed? Can it be trusted? It is what it is, a savage beast filled only with hunger.'

The old man bowed his head in deference and added, 'Whatever you say, my lord, the English will see talk of peace as a sign of weakness. As one, they will rise and follow Hereward's standard. That few have yet done so is down to one thing – their fear of your wrath.'

The monarch beckoned to Taillebois for more wine. 'Speak, Deda. Give me the benefit of your wisdom.'

'Show mercy, my lord. The English have been worn down by their suffering. They yearn for peace and a return to the lives they knew. They will thank you for giving it to them. Blood will only lead to blood. If we fight on, this war may never end.'

William the Bastard laughed. 'The world has been turned on its head. The English call for war, against their own, no less. The Norman wants only peace.'

Deda watched the sideways glances the king cast in his direction, the shadow that formed at the edge of his mouth. The monarch loathed him. He did not know why. But in that moment he could see he had lost the argument. 'Let me think on this,' William the Bastard said, sipping his wine. Without gratifying the knight with a look, he flicked his hand to dismiss him. Deda bowed and stepped out. But he would not go far. However loyal he was to the king, he felt it wise to listen and learn what he could.

'This relic troubles me,' the monarch was saying. 'Even seasoned fighting men will not take up arms against God. How do we give them the strength to stand against such a thing?'

After a long moment's silence, Deda heard the Butcher reply. 'There is a witch who lives in the woods near here. The English monks drove her out and burned her hovel, so my men told me. I saw even hardened warriors pale when they spoke of her.'

William the Bastard roared with laughter. 'A witch! Aye, what better way! We will fight God with the Devil and see who wins.' An uncomfortable silence settled on his audience at the blasphemy, but the king went on, 'Have her brought here. We will feed her well and she will work her magic against the English, or at least make a show of it. That will put some fire into our men's hearts.'

The Butcher muttered his assent.

'Two years we have danced around this English dog,' the Bastard continued, his voice hardening. 'Two years, and all the Norman might here in the east has failed me.' Deda imagined Taillebois and William de Warenne squirming under the king's accusatory gaze, and smiled. 'Now it is left to me to put things right. We have tested the English strength with that feeble causeway we built to draw the curs out. I expected them to slaughter every man there. But now we know that foot-soldiers alone are no use. It taught us much.'

Deda nodded. So the king had sent him there to die. He had half thought that might be the case when the English had taken the causeway so easily. His heart grew heavier at the other lives thrown away, good men all of them, so that William could learn more about his enemy.

'Our sacrifice there will have lulled the English into thinking they are on an easy road to victory,' the monarch was saying. 'If they attack us, their chests will be swelled and their heads turned, and they will not be ready for our fury. You need to be cunning, like a fox,' he all but shouted, 'but you have been running in circles like frightened rabbits.'

The Butcher and William de Warenne must be regretting the

moment they entered the king's tent, Deda thought, not least because their humiliation was taking place before the eyes of two English.

'Now leave my sight,' the Bastard snapped.

Deda edged further round the tent as he heard the two men leaving. When he stepped out into the light of the campfire, Taillebois's face boiled with a cold fury. William de Warenne was shaking, knowing how close they had both come to feeling the monarch's full wrath. The Bastard had no friends there, the knight noted, but he needed none. He ruled by fear, and that had served him well.

As the two Normans trudged across the ward and into the night, muttering under their breath, Deda crept back until he found a place where he could see into the tent. If the king cared so little for his life, Deda felt he ought to pay even closer attention to the monarch from now on. He squatted in the deep shadows, watching the king prowl. William the Bastard poured himself more wine, then studied the two Englishmen over the lip of his cup. 'There is no love lost between you and your kin, this dog Hereward,' he said.

'He is no longer any son of mine,' the old man replied. 'He has turned against all those who have stood by him. He cares for naught but himself.'

'And yet the English flock to his banner.'

The younger man stepped forward and held out his hands. 'He has the Devil's skill at lying. We know him better than any. And we know he can be beaten.'

'Do you know how he can be beaten?'

Deda glimpsed a gleam in the young man's eyes. He had seen his opening. 'No man knows better. No Norman, of that we can be sure.'

The monarch raised one eyebrow, waiting for his guest to explain himself.

'The English are a folk like no other. You know this to be true.' He smiled – too quickly, Deda thought – when he saw the king agreed. 'I know their minds, in a way that Ivo Taillebois or William de Warenne never could. I know the weaknesses in their hearts, all the doubts and the fears, and I know how to prise them open into gaping wounds.' Growing in confidence, he continued, 'I know the plans Hereward and his men made to attack you. I know the merchants who give them food, under the noses of your men. I know their secret paths. I know everything you would ever need to crush them.'

William the Bastard drained his wine and tossed the cup aside. 'And what do you want in return? Land? Gold?'

'Only to serve you, my lord.' The young man bowed his head, humble, unthreatening. He was good at this game, Deda thought.

'In Wincestre, a loyal Englishman gave me good advice about your folk. Balthar the Fox was his name,' the king murmured reflectively. 'He is dead now, and I need a new man who can tell me of the English and their strange ways. And who can speak for me. Your folk will better listen to one of their own.' He thought for another moment, and then added, 'Let us see if you are as good as you say. If you are, you will be well rewarded. If you are not . . .' William smiled without humour. No words were needed.

Yet the younger man seemed untroubled by the implicit threat. He bowed deeply and said, 'I will not fail, my lord.'

Deda could see the audience was coming to the end. He slipped away into the dark, sickened by what he had seen. Hereward was his enemy, but he deserved better than this council of rats. To die in battle on the end of a sharp sword was one thing. But the English leader was likely to be brought down by a knife in the back, wielded by his own.

Chapter Twenty-One

High above the camp at Belsar's Hill, Harald Redteeth flew. His wings were gleaming black and the cold wind rushed beneath them. He looked down, his eyes carving through the suffocating night, and saw the fires that burned all across that part of the fens. He saw the Men of Iron walking among them, like hot coals in the glare. He saw the vast army that would crush all before it, coiled like Fafnir around his mound of gold, spewing flames and smoke. He saw the siege machines and the towers. He saw the new axes forged in the workshops, and the javelins and the crossbows. The king was going to war. He almost felt sorry for the English.

In his head, where the blood throbbed, he could hear the voice of his father, who now walked in the Halls of the Fallen, and of his father's father, and others before him whose names he did not know, but whose words came to him like a prayer from the beginning of the world. *Defend the old ways to the death*, they said. *Without them you are nothing.* And he answered them in his raven-shriek. He was a Northman, fashioned from fire and ice and blood. The weight of days gone by made him stronger. Honour made him stronger. He was not like those hollowed-out Norman bastards.

Down he flew, low over the city of tents. Warriors stuffed their charms and keepsakes in their sacks. Some paced. Others looked to the stars and the moon for portents. The swords were sharp, the horses well fed and watered. Soon, now. And up into the camp on the hill he whirled. He squatted on a post, watching the Butcher and William de Warenne brooding and plotting, their faces like slabs of granite. And on, and on, over Hereward's kin, a spring in their steps and smiles on their faces and a light shining in their hearts. All had wagered. All now awaited the outcome.

And he no less than any other. For nine merciless winters that had turned his blood to ice, and nine unforgiving summers that had boiled his brain, he had set his life aside. Across the frozen north, and Flanders where the rain came like stones, and the steaming fenlands, he had walked with only one purpose: to slay Hereward in battle. Only that English blood would melt the shackles that bound Ivar, his friend, to this world; and his own shackles too. Then they would be free. Both of them. Perhaps all three of them. Nine long years. But it was nearly done. He could smell the ending on the wind. Death, and then freedom.

His gleaming black wings melted away, and he was back in the large crimson tent in the reek of sour ale and spilled wine. His fingers gripped the mead-cup so tightly his knuckles ached. He could hear men singing about a girl drowned at sea, and the tavern keeper calling his boy for more ale.

As his gaze focused once more on his surroundings, he pushed his head up and saw a face looking down at him. It was that strange knight. 'Alive, then,' he muttered, taking a swig of his drink.

'You did not think me a ghost?' The Norman warrior smiled.

'I have seen ghosts. You are not one.' He looked the other man up and down. 'But you are a bedraggled rat. Sit. Drink, fill your belly and warm your heart. You will soon be back among the living.' He called for some Frankish wine and stew.

'Drinking with Normans,' Deda said, pulling up a stool. 'You have fallen lower than any man ought.'

'I have drunk with thieves and murderers. A Norman makes little difference.' Redteeth cocked his head to listen to the whispers of the *alfar*, then laughed long and hard.

Deda sipped his wine. 'Your spirits are high.'

'I have walked a long road, but now it is near the end.' He finished his mead and roared for more. The drunken soldiers across the tent glared at him. He lifted up his axe, Grim, to show the other man. 'Soon we will march on Ely, and the fight will be short, and sweet, and with this I will take Hereward's head.'

'I would think the king would want that honour. After he has tried to make Hereward beg for his life. And failed,' he added after a brief thought.

'If the king stands in my way, I will take his head first.'

Deda frowned, then laughed, unsure if the Viking was joking. 'And then your head will sit beside the other two.'

'So be it. Nothing means more to me than taking Hereward's life. I have made an oath.'

'Ah,' the knight said, understanding.

'When we first met, he was a wild beast. But he has grown, as have we all. He has honour. And courage. The English can be proud of him.' Redteeth nodded. 'But I will still take his head.'

'Then let us drink to a good death.'

Redteeth gave a gap-toothed grin. 'And when we are done drinking, let us find two whores and enjoy the comfort of their thighs.'

'No. Not this night. Perhaps not for many nights.' Though the Norman's voice remained pleasant, Redteeth glimpsed something in his eye, a look both faraway and pained. The Viking's gaze drifted down to the blue ribbon that the knight always wore tied around his left wrist. He saw some of the other man's life then, and though it was only an impression, he understood.

'You are the mad Viking,' another voice said.

Harald looked round. A Norman soldier swayed beside him.

147

He was two heads taller and just as broad, with hands that looked as if they could crush a man's skull.

'What of it?'

'Men say you worship the Devil, and speak to his imps.'

'Aye, I do at that,' Redteeth growled. Deda sighed. The Viking drained his cup and then looked up. 'Still here?'

The warrior leaned in. The Viking could smell the ale on his breath. 'We are godly men here,' he snarled.

'Then get back to your prayers.'

With one swipe of his huge hand, the Norman soldier knocked Harald's cup from his fingers. It flew across the tent. Redteeth lashed out so fast the other man never had a chance to react. His nose crumpled under the blow, his jaw shattering. He flew back, trailing blood.

The roar that filled the tent sounded like a cave full of bears awakening. Six warriors stormed to the aid of their friend. Harald leapt to his feet, gripping his axe. But as the Norman soldiers drew their swords, Deda stepped beside him, his own blade levelled. The Viking eyed him, puzzled.

One of the soldiers waved his sword towards Deda. 'You would stand with this heathen?' he growled.

'He is the wronged one here,' the knight replied in an even tone. 'Take our fallen brother and leave.'

Gritting his teeth, the warrior swung his sword towards the Viking and jabbed. Deda clattered the weapon aside with a flick of his wrist, then whipped the tip of his blade up to the other man's neck. He raised the soldier's head an inch and said again, with emphasis, 'One more time. Walk away.'

'You are no brother of ours.' The warrior took a step back and spat on the mud between them. 'Watch your back from this day on.' Two of the Normans grabbed the arms of their unconscious brother and dragged him out of the tent. The other four followed, casting black looks over their shoulders.

'Come back and I will cut your balls off and eat them,' Redteeth called after the men.

'I would know how you have lived to this ripe old age,' Deda said, sheathing his sword.

'A thick head and a sharp axe.'

'The first one, I agree. The second we shall see, when we face the English at Ely.'

Harald grunted. He had thought he had started to get the measure of the knight, but now he was not so sure.

The tent flap whipped open and a young messenger ran in, red-faced. He looked around, saw the two men and darted over.

'What is it?' Harald growled.

The boy leapt back as if the Viking was about to savage him.

Deda clapped a hand on the lad's shoulder and said with warmth, 'My friend is a wolf with no fangs. Speak. What message have you?'

'Ivo Taillebois has sent word,' the boy said, his eyes still flickering towards Harald. 'He has work for you. A witch, there is, roaming in the fenlands. He would have you . . . and . . . and your friend bring her here. Or kill her if she will not come.' The lad crossed himself and ran out.

Redteeth glowered. 'A witch. Mark my words, we will be toads before morn.'

CHAPTER TWENTY-TWO

The reeds were rustling but there was no wind. Under a silver sky, the rooks swooped up from the stark trees, shrieking in warning. A man stepped out from the vast reed-beds and looked across the mirrored meres of the wetlands. The whole world had turned silver. He carried a spear and a circular shield with a white cross on a red background, still smelling of fresh paint. His face was grey with ashes so that it resembled a skull. *Death*, it whispered to his enemies. *Death is coming.*

Another man stepped out beside him, and then another, and another. Ten. Twenty. A multitude. In those last days before the clutch of winter, the fenlands were waking.

Hereward felt calm. He was ready. His devil had not stirred, his anger remained unawakened. Alric had counselled him long and hard before they had set off from Ely. Here was purpose that would bring succour to the ache he felt in his heart. Here was God's plan. He would bring freedom to the oppressed English, and any pain was worth that prize. Any amount of blood.

'We are ready.' Kraki came to a halt at his side, a mountain of fur and leather, his iron mail fresh cleaned in a bag of sand

150

so that he too gleamed. He scowled, flexing the jagged battle-scar that ran from his forehead to the edge of his wild beard. 'After all the hunger and the want, the doubt, and the sweat, and the fear, finally we are ready.'

Hereward glanced back at his army as they moved out of the rushes and into the wildwood. The Normans would see a Devil's Army, skulls floating out of the half-light under the trees, mud-streaked bodies rising from the ditches and the cold lakes and the bogs like the dead emerging from their graves. He saw them through his enemy's eyes, these ghastly revenants sweeping down in silence on every side, bloodlust etched into their features. What terror they would strike into the hearts of the Norman bastards.

He watched as they surged through the sea of brown bracken, reaching deep into the woods. His chest swelled with pride. He glimpsed eyes bright with hope, and confidence forged by long days of battle-play under Kraki's cold tutorage. No leader could have hoped for better men at his back. 'We will fall on the Normans like wolves,' he said.

'Good. My axe is thirsty for blood.' Kraki shook his weapon as he marched.

Guthrinc ran up, his great feet thrumming on the soft floor of the wood. He grinned. 'Earl Morcar's messenger has brought word. His men are in place.'

Hereward caught the hunting horn that swung on a leather thong round his neck. 'Here is the sound of doom for our enemies. One blast will signal their days are over.'

The Mercian recalled how their plans had been turned over time and again through the long night. Nothing had been left to chance, and every man knew the part he had to play. When the horn sounded, the full force of the English would sweep in, half from the north, the others from the south, and the Normans would be caught as if by a smith's tongs, ready to be crushed by the hammer on the anvil.

As they marched, he peered over the black smudge of trees

into the grey distance. Belsar's Hill was still half a day away. Night would be falling when the English spectres crept out of the gloom. The enemy would be drunk, or sleeping. They would not be ready. How many Normans would be waiting, he wondered. He had sent Herrig the Rat ahead to see if, this time, he could get close to the enemy camp without getting his head lopped from his shoulders. But the only word that had come back from the villages on the edge of the fens was that the king's levy was still failing. Kraki believed that most of the king's men had been used to close the circle around Ely, to the south and west.

'No word from William the Bastard,' Guthrinc said as if he could read his leader's thoughts. 'Can we trust that knight, Deda, to have passed on your message?'

'He would. He is a man of honour. If the king has not responded, it is because he hopes we are scared rabbits who will not attack the wolf. Or he believes God will help him smite down any enemy that comes before him.'

Soon they would know for certain. And soon, God willing, they would have reclaimed the crown.

Through the woods the English army ghosted, by the edge of glassy lakes and stinking bogs. When their scouts caught sight of the king's guards roaming along the old straight tracks, the Devil's Army cut their foes down before the alarm could be raised. The bodies were thrown in the marshes. The Normans would not know what was upon them until the English were at their very gates.

When Hereward could smell the stink of Belsar's Hill on the breeze – smoke, shit and cooking meat, and other, bitter smells that he could not quite identify – he raised one hand to slow his men. Word rustled out along the lines. They crouched behind their shields, waiting. Not even the birds would have known they were there.

Kraki narrowed his eyes, then pointed. 'That is a lot of smoke.'

Hereward scanned the pall that hung above the treetops. He

began to feel uneasy. Kraki and Guthrinc both eyed him, but could read no clue to his thoughts.

A whistle rang out.

The Mercian stiffened. A friend approached, probably one of the scouts.

Herrig skidded down a muddy track. His face was drawn and worry had etched deep lines into his forehead. He was not alone.

'The ravens take my eyes,' Kraki exclaimed when he saw Acha. 'Have your wits leaked out of your ears?'

The black-haired woman flashed a murderous glare at him that would have turned another man's blood to ice. Turning her back on the Viking, she marched up to Hereward who saw Rowena was trailing in her wake. The woman looked like a spectre. She stumbled along the path as if dazed, her face bloodless, her unblinking eyes staring. When Kraki began to growl, Acha knitted her brow and nodded to Herrig. The scout led Rowena to one side. He smiled and whispered comforts, but she seemed not to hear. Acha flapped a dismissive hand at Kraki and turned to Hereward. 'Before you give me the edge of your tongue, yes, we are wilful children,' she snapped. 'We left Ely and went to Belsar's Hill.'

'Are you mad?' But the Mercian knew she was only giving him half a tale, and he felt proud of her for that. Acha would never have ventured into the enemy's camp of her own volition. She had accompanied Rowena. As her eyes flashed in annoyance, he held up his hand in apology and added, 'Your friend went in search of her husband.'

Acha nodded. 'And much good it did her.' She glanced back at the other woman who stood with her head bowed, her lank hair falling across her face.

Hereward could see the story writ large there. 'He is dead.'

She nodded. 'The Normans took his head.'

Remembering the moment he had heard of Turfrida's murder, Hereward knew every emotion that devastated Rowena, the grief sharper than any sword wound, the shock, the rage, and all for naught, for nothing could bring the lost ones back.

'There is more,' Acha said, lowering her voice so the men could not hear. She told him of all they had seen in the enemy camp, and the scale of the force that had been hidden in the vale on the far side of the hill. As he realized how close he had come to leading the English to destruction, Hereward felt a cold settle deep into his bones. He beckoned to Herrig. 'Is this true?' he hissed.

The Rat bowed his head. 'I crept as close to the camp as I could, in days gone by,' he stuttered. 'Only this day could I find a way past the guards, and then only at great risk . . .'

The Mercian held up his hand. It was not Herrig's fault. The failure to recognize the full extent of the king's cunning rested with him alone. He would never make that mistake again. 'Fly to Morcar as fast as your feet will carry you,' he ordered. 'Warn him before he risks an attack, or is discovered. Tell him to return to Ely. We must make new plans.'

As Herrig raced away, Hereward turned to Kraki and Guthrinc and whispered the bitter news. He commanded them to take the army back home, but he could see from their faces that they both realized their greatest hope for victory had been snatched away from them. He looked up to the sky and prayed this was not an omen for what lay ahead.

When he was alone, he crept through the woods until he could see Belsar's Hill rising from the flat landscape. Guards ranged everywhere. Herrig had been speaking truly. Their army would not have got close enough to fire an arrow at the enemy. Crawling through ditches up to his neck in filthy water, rats swimming past him, he circled the hill until he found a spot where he could spy on the king's secret camp. His chest tightened as he realized that what lay before him put the spear to any lingering hope he still held. An iron army of seasoned Norman warriors and axes-for-hire that dwarfed even the formidable English force. Siege machines. Wooden towers. And another army of English men carrying spoil and timber to the real, and greater, causeway.

Their expectations of an easy victory had been dashed. Now they were in the fight of their lives.

CHAPTER TWENTY-THREE

Ely was preparing for war. Under clouds heavy with rain, folk laboured with shovels along the slopes beyond the walls, piling high bulwarks of peat reinforced with fresh-cut timber. The new ramparts were taller, wider. Into the hillside, platforms were being cut from where archers could take aim and javelins and missiles could be launched. Woodworkers barked orders to sweating men as they hauled oaken beams to buttress the very walls that had stood so long. And along the walkways boys heaved barrels of pitch up from the ship-wrights' stores, to be set alight and poured over the side if the Normans dared venture too close.

When Hereward emerged from the council of war in the minster refectory, he stood outside the enclosure and looked out over the frantic activity across the settlement. He had feared that heads would droop and fire in hearts would fade once the army had been turned back from its attack. But he and his trusted men had worked hard to keep spirits high. The tale told was of a simple change of tactics. That they were luring the Normans into a trap that would see most of the bastards lost in the bogs and lakes, the better to save English lives. He cocked his head, listening to the full-throated singing from the labourers, and he was pleased.

The truth lay heavily upon him.

As he watched the work, children ran out from the homes and raced in circles around him. The boys carried wooden swords, every one named Brainbiter. The girls had spears fashioned from strips of wood. He smiled when he saw them play as fiercely as the lads. The wives brought cups of ale, and after a while he had to refuse their offers or he would have been drunk. The younger women came with tokens, lowering their eyes and smiling as they asked if they could tie their ribbons round his wrist. He grinned and winked and flirted to try to make them feel good, but he knew none of them would ever touch his heart.

When he was finally left alone, he wandered to the food stores beyond the refectory. As he examined their supplies, he saw the position was worse than he feared. The Norman blockade was taking its toll. They would not have enough to survive the winter, and once starvation began to carve its way into English hearts the rebellion would quickly crumble. Only one path to victory now remained: they had to defeat the Normans before the snows came.

He stepped outside the barn, licked his finger and raised it to the wind. How long did they have? Three weeks, perhaps a handful of days more? In the last few years, the snow had fallen heavily and early, another sign of the End of Days, so folk said. That may well be. All he knew was that their time was growing shorter.

Angry voices drifted on the wind. A man and a woman. They sounded familiar, and as Hereward walked among the minster halls he caught sight of Kraki and Acha arguing in the lee of the church. She had an arm full of firewood. Kraki was jabbing a stubby finger into her face. Hereward sighed. Surely the Viking should have learned by now that she would not respond kindly to that kind of treatment. Uncomfortable, he turned to go, only to hear a clatter and a roar. Acha had thrown the firewood at the warrior and stormed off.

Kraki turned and saw Hereward. A shadow of shame crossed his face, and then his anger surged once more as he marched over. 'Never have I known a woman so wilful,' he snarled. 'She refuses to do what I ask – and it is for her own good.'

'Would you have a Norman woman who bows her head to you and runs at your bidding like a whipped cur?'

'Aye, sometimes.'

'I think not.'

Kraki shrugged and stared at the floor. In that unguarded moment, Hereward glimpsed a look of pain that the other man had never shown from any battle-wound. He feared he was losing his woman.

Hereward rested a hand on the other man's shoulder. 'Acha has fire enough for ten men. That is why you took her.'

'She has not been the same since this other woman came to Ely, this Rowena. She fills Acha's head with too many thoughts. Of her home, and what she has lost.'

And Rowena has shown a fighting spirit that Acha realizes she has let fade, the Mercian thought. 'Let her have her thoughts. There is no threat in them,' he said. 'And then she will remember the man she found in Eoferwic.'

Kraki nodded, but the words seemed to do little good. Hereward sensed that much he did not know lay between the Viking and Acha.

After he had sent Kraki to oversee the work on the ramparts, he slipped into the church. The grey day made it like night inside. Fat candles flickered along the walls and the air was heavy with the scents of tallow and incense. He wandered up to the altar and into the abbot's rooms. Surprisingly, Thurstan was nowhere to be seen; in recent days the cleric had barely been off his knees. Monks hurried by him, barely giving him a glance. They muttered nothing but excuses in response to his questions.

Frustrated, he wandered to the shrine of St Etheldreda. He had found much comfort there in recent times. He remembered

Thurstan telling him of the saint's trials here in Ely, and how she had refused to submit to an unjust king. God had blessed her, and He blessed all those who bowed their heads to her, so it was said. Hereward cast his eyes over the many offerings, the bread and salt, the scraps of linen, the rabbits' feet and grain.

The door of the church slammed and he looked up. Head bowed in deep thought, Thurstan was making his way across the nave. Hereward saw that his shoes were filthy with mud and his chasuble dripped on the flagstones. He plucked at the wooden cross which hung round his neck, deep lines of worry drawn across his forehead. But when Hereward hailed him, he put on a bright expression and answered in a light tone.

'No prayers today, Father?' the warrior asked.

'I have been walking the shores of this isle, spreading God's word to all who would listen.'

'That is good. They need to know that God is on our side. It will keep the fire in their hearts when the days seem darkest.'

'And dark days are coming, are they not?' Thurstan fixed an eye on him.

'We always knew that this fight would be hard, Father. But we are far from done. We have only delayed our strike against the Norman bastards. Once we are sure that folk here in Ely are safe, we will march out again with a new plan, a better one.'

'And what is that plan?' the abbot asked, barely concealing his doubt.

'That will have to wait, Father, until I am returned.'

Thurstan frowned. 'From where?'

'From the very heart of our enemy's camp. I go to see with my own eyes the king's weaknesses.'

The abbot gaped. Hereward could see the churchman thought him mad, but he had the wherewithal to keep his tongue still. Instead he smiled. 'I will pray for you. I will call upon the Lord for all the aid that He might give.' His final words remained unspoken: *for you will never return alive without His help*.

Chapter Twenty-Four

A cha jerked awake in the dark. A scratching echoed from the door, as if some rat scrabbled to get in. She shook herself alert. Since she had been stolen from her home those long years ago, she rarely slept deeply. Pulling herself up, she flopped one hand on to the straw of the bed beside her. The space was cold and empty. No doubt Kraki was drunk and snoring in the tavern.

'Who goes?' she called.

A dim voice floated back: 'It is I, Rowena.'

Acha sighed, but after all the woman had endured she could not turn her away. Though a few embers glowed in the hearth, she shivered in the deep chill of the hut. Wiping the sleep from her eyes, she padded across the cold mud floor.

'What is wrong?' she asked as she swung open the door. The sky was clear and sprinkled with stars, and her breath steamed.

'A word,' Rowena said. She had pulled her green cloak tightly around her. 'A farewell.' She slipped inside, but Acha felt surprised to see that she smiled and there was a spring in her step.

'You return to your village?' she asked.

The other woman squatted by the hearth and blew on the

embers, dropping straw and kindling on them until the flames crackled and licked up. In the dancing light, Acha could see that the ravages of grief had indeed fallen from her features. That was far sooner than she had expected. For a time, she had worried that it might never happen.

Rowena smiled. 'I am to be a whore.'

Acha flinched, sure this must be some bitter joke. When she saw in the other woman's eyes that it was not, she dropped to the hearth beside her and insisted, 'Do not say such things. Your husband is not here to work the fields, I know, but there is food enough here in Ely for all.'

'There is not, as you know well,' Rowena replied, still smiling. 'Every loaf is precious. No, this is not about food, or surviving the winter.'

'What, then? Why would any woman choose to whore herself?'

For a moment, sadness filled Rowena's face, but she pushed it aside and revealed the fire that had warmed Acha from the moment they had first met. 'I am here to say farewell because you have shown me much kindness during my days in Ely. I planned to slip away in the night so none could stop me – I know Hereward watches me like a hawk – but I would not have you worrying about my safety.' She paused, moistening her lips. 'My husband is dead. I have prayed long and hard for him, but I cannot change that. Nor can I console myself with the knowledge that he only rests before he is called to heaven on Judgement Day, which will come soon enough. No, he is food for the ravens—'

Acha grasped the other woman's arm, urging her not to punish herself so.

'My life ended the day I knew my husband had died. I cannot go back. I cannot move forward.' She rested her hand on the backs of Acha's fingers. Her skin was unbearably cold. 'I cannot bring Elwin home to me,' she murmured. 'But I can seek vengeance for his unjust death.'

'When the Normans die on the ends of English spears, there will be vengeance enough for all.'

Rowena shook her head. 'Not for me. This night I travel to Belsar's Hill, and I will join the women who serve. And I will offer my thighs to any Norman who will have me.'

Acha felt sickened by her friend's matter-of-fact tone. She wondered if grief had driven the woman mad, but she had never seemed so sane.

'And I will fuck them well. I will fuck my way into their hearts and their trust.' Rowena's eyes blazed. 'And each day that passes, I will move closer to the king. And when I am ready, I will kill him.'

CHAPTER TWENTY-FIVE

Under the ruddy glare of the torches, the witch walked through the gates. She spat three times and circled her fingers around her right eye. Her dancing shadow seemed to claw at the Norman soldiers who had gathered to see her arrival at Belsar's Hill. Almost as one, they crossed themselves. She looked like a wildcat, hands hooked and teeth bared, and she snarled at anyone she caught staring at her. So filthy was she with mud and lichen stains that she could only have been living in the ditches and woods, Redwald thought as he watched her wander through the drifting smoke of the camp-fires. Behind her strode her captors – or guards, he wasn't quite sure. Deda the knight seemed amused by her reception. Harald Redteeth looked as fierce as ever. Redwald didn't like either man.

Trying to ignore the choking stench of shit and rotting food, he pushed his way back through the tents. When he was in the employ of Harold Godwinson, he had never been forced to endure such privations. But his discomfort was a small price to pay. He smiled to himself. He had already begun to inveigle his way into the king's confidence. Day by day he was dragging his way up to the position he deserved.

Edoma waited for him by the gate to the castle ward. He thought how beautiful she looked. Her blonde hair gleamed in the torchlight and her skin was as pale as snow. She was a prize worth having, he supposed. He looked her over and nodded, pleased that she had recovered from the burn he had inflicted on her in Lincylene. She had forgiven him. What else could she do? Now the only blemishes she sported were the bruises from his fists during their lovemaking.

'I saw the witch,' she said, swallowing. 'What if she brings the Devil to the camp?'

'Look around. There are devils everywhere.' He laughed. When he saw she was truly concerned, he took her hand and kissed it. A little charm never hurt. 'I know you are scared,' he whispered, 'but that is the king's plan. Fear is his sword, and he has used it well to gain the power he has.'

'The king is wise.' She smiled. 'But not as wise as you.'

'Hush,' he urged, glancing around. 'Do not let any hear you say such things.'

Her eyes gleamed with pride. Edoma was cleverer than most women, he thought. She recognized that he would rise quickly in William's court, given half a chance, and she had shackled herself to him.

She looked around to make sure no one was watching, leaned in and kissed him on the cheek. 'Come to me tonight,' she breathed in his ear, 'and I will show you pleasures beyond your imagining.' She skipped away, flashing one seductive look over her shoulder before the night swallowed her.

Redwald had forgotten her by the time he reached the king's tent. William was in good spirits. He could hear the monarch's roaring laughter echoing across the ward. As he stepped into the tent, he was surprised to see his father, Asketil, astride a stool, sipping from a cup. He seemed more upright, his face less lined, his hair more lustrous, as if the old man were drawing strength to him by the day.

'Ah, Redwald,' the king boomed. 'Join us. Sup some wine. Your father is spinning some tales from the court of old king

Edward. He is better than any scop. Now it seems I have two good men who will advise me on the ways of the English.'

Asketil grinned and raised his cup to his son. A silent communication passed between them. The old man was playing his part. Soon they would have the king in their thrall.

A girl came over with a pitcher of wine. She had sleek black hair that reminded Redwald of Acha, and fine bones. She gave a shy smile as she filled his cup. But when she moved to Asketil, the old man was too drunk to hold his cup still, and she slopped wine into his lap.

A shadow crossed Asketil's face. Redwald knew what was coming before the old man raised his arm. Lashing out with the back of his hand, he struck the girl so hard across the face that she all but flew across the room. She screamed. The pitcher upended, flooding good Frankish wine across the mud. For a moment, Redwald was back in the thegn's hall in Barholme, not long after he had watched his mother and father die. Asketil was much younger then, his hair like spun gold and his body as strong as a bull. The young man had watched him rain blows down on his true son, Hereward, beating him until the blood flowed and his wits had been knocked out of his skull. How many times had Redwald witnessed that brutality? And yet Asketil had never raised a hand against him.

Even the king looked shocked by this violence. But then he nodded and grinned, and offered his own hand to help the woman to her feet. Dazed, she put her fingers to a swollen lip and felt blood trickling down her chin. As tears started to form, William urged her out, with more gentleness than Redwald had ever seen him display. He turned back to his two guests and shrugged. 'There is more wine where that came from.'

They all laughed.

Once their cups had been filled once more, the king's grin faded and his mood grew grave. Redwald knew it was time for serious business. 'The witch will be given her own tent, and as much food and drink as she wants,' he said. 'She will have pride of place to work her magics here.'

Redwald smiled to himself, recognizing the brilliance and cunning of the king's plans. How alike they were.

'I have work for you too,' William continued, pointing at the younger man. 'A great settlement has grown up along the causeway we are building. Merchants and craftsmen, whores and beggars, and any who think they can gain a few scraps from our table. Move among them. Spread fear of the witch, and with any luck they will take their knowledge of her presence out among the English. And then, in time, it will find its way back to Ely.' Another grin appeared, but this one was sly. 'On the morrow, she begins her spells. The Devil is on our side. Let every man be afraid.'

CHAPTER TWENTY-SIX

A growing shadow was carving its way across the muddy fenland. The ground shook in its wake, as if the very heavens were tumbling. In the jumble of huts and workshops beside the new causeway, awed folk stopped what they were doing and craned their necks up to watch the tower move. Ropes creaked. Drums beat a steady rhythm. And inch by inch, the sun itself was consumed. On that chill autumn day, the king prepared for a war the like of which men had never seen before.

The air was sharp with the bitter sweat of the Englishmen who strained their sinews to drag the soaring timber structure on its platform across a row of slowly rolling tree-trunks. Once the tower reached the end of the row, four men would haul the last of the trunks to the front so the process could begin again. A Norman commander bellowed his orders and the red-faced, shaking men pulled as one. As he looked up the height of the tower, Hereward imagined archers at the summit picking off any attackers long before they reached the causeway. William the Bastard left nothing to chance.

Here Hereward was nothing but a lowly potter, clay-stained and insignificant in his brown cloak with its deep hood that shrouded his features in shadow, a threadbare tunic and breeches. He carried only a short-bladed knife. No one, he hoped, would give him a second look.

Keeping his head down, he pushed his way through the crowd. He felt staggered by the size of the community that had grown up in such a short time. Folk thronged past merchants perched on bales and barrels proclaiming their wares in booming voices. Makeshift workshops had been thrown up, some almost overnight by the look of them: clay walls, heaps of sod, straw and timber, some of the building materials clearly stolen from the supplies destined for the causeway. Under the rickety roofs, looms rattled and hammers fell. Leatherworkers scraped hides with their curved blades and metalworkers hunched over pieces of gold and silver, engraving intricate designs. Smoke from the fires mingled with the meaty scents of hot pies and bubbling stews from the food sellers. Cattle lowed and pigs grunted. Hens scratched among the feet of the jostling multitude.

Amid the confusion of sensations, Hereward smiled to himself. The press of bodies and the constant din made his work easier. The Norman guards patrolling nearby were more concerned with the causeway than the mass of folk attempting to scrape a living from the vast army that had descended on the wetlands.

Once he had a good view he came to a halt, pretending to delve into the depths of his leather sack. He let his gaze run along the length of the causeway as it stretched into the misty distance. The Normans were widening and strengthening the existing track from Belsar's Hill to the West River, not far from Alrehede, so that it would be broad enough and stable enough to take the Norman cavalry. Here the fen was probably only eight or nine furlongs wide, he estimated, with less water and marsh than in most other parts of the wetlands. The best and narrowest place for a crossing. And beyond it, Ely was in easy reach.

Walking along the line of the causeway, he flashed glances at the men at work. Their faces were drawn from too much labour and too little food and sleep. The Normans drove them like animals. They dragged tree-trunks and great pieces of timber, lashing them together with cowhide to form the base of the road. And as the work moved across the marsh, English captives laid sheepskins filled with sand on the track to keep the top layer clear of the surrounding bogland. From the mountains of stone and wood heaped along the way, the men formed a chain to pass buckets of material to form the solid surface. Other filth-streaked, bare-chested labourers dug out deep, rolling ramparts of peat along the route. And on the waters beyond the scene of hard labour Hereward could discern many moored boats. More wood and stone was being unloaded.

His thoughts whirled. There could be no doubt now that the feeble causeway they had destroyed had been one of William the Bastard's deceptions. This one would not be so easy to wreck. If he set his men to work with shovels for a week, they would barely have torn it down. And yet he had seen one weakness that he might be able to turn to his advantage, if fortune smiled upon him.

Ahead, three Norman soldiers were swaggering towards him through the stream of bodies. His neck prickled; he could take no risks that might uncover him. One of the warriors stopped to examine a linen merchant's wares. When he rubbed the end of the cloth between his thumb and forefinger, his nose turned up as if he could smell something foul. Tossing the linen aside, he muttered to the others. The soldiers barked with laughter. The merchant's cheeks reddened. As they moved on, Hereward lowered his head and retreated into the shadows of his hood. He turned left, only to find his path blocked by two men arguing over a goose. The soldiers drew nearer. One looked directly at him, and then glanced away at a comely girl helping her mother carry a churn.

'Pots,' Hereward mumbled, his eyes darting. 'Good pots.'

When the soldiers were only steps away, an outcry erupted nearby. A boar had broken free from its pen. Folk scurried in all directions from the squealing beast. Seizing his moment, the

Mercian plunged off the track and into the filthy, ramshackle settlement.

For a while, he hid among the mass of huts and tents. More of the defences still needed to be examined before he could creep away. Yet as he prowled closer to where the settlement pressed hard against the slopes of Belsar's Hill, he glimpsed two figures through a gap between the huts. He felt his senses start to jangle, though he was not sure why. Keeping low, he slipped from wall to wall in their wake.

As he peered round the final hut, he stiffened at the sight of two men he had never thought he would see together: Deda the knight and Harald Redteeth. They were so close that his nose wrinkled at the lamb-fat the Viking used to grease his furs. He threw himself back into the shadows, hoping they had not seen him.

The two men walked on a few paces, and then Redteeth came to a sudden halt. He cocked his head as if listening to some unseen companion. Hereward felt his neck prickle. He had seen the Northman do this before and it never failed to unnerve. The knight turned, frowning, asking what was wrong. Redteeth ignored him. He spun round and looked directly at Hereward.

And as the Mercian darted away, an angry cry rang out at his back and feet thundered in pursuit.

171

CHAPTER TWENTY-SEVEN

The throng jostled by. Hungry, most of them. Fearful that the End of Days was drawing in and hopeful that the Normans would offer them some shelter from the storm of want, sickness and death. The Normans who had brought all those things to England's door. Rowena forced a smile, trying not to let those sour thoughts show on her face.

'This is the third time you have accompanied me into danger. Do you wish to lose your life?' Rowena asked as she examined the fine silver jewellery on the metalworker's trestle.

Scowling, Acha looked past her to the Norman soldiers patrolling the causeway. 'If I die, it will be you who will have killed me.'

Rowena eyed the other woman as she turned a silver bracelet over in her hands. It gleamed in the light, showing off the black runes carved around its band. She wished Acha had not accompanied her. Soon her life would be over, and with any luck, the king's with it. There was no other course. But now she had to think about Acha's safety, and that was a distraction she did not need.

She thought back to that cold hut where she had tried to say her farewell. Barely had the words left her lips before Acha was dropping a few meagre possessions into a sack and insisting she come with her. She could not understand it. But she had been glad of the company through the night-dark fenlands. The wolves would soon be venturing out of the woods in search of food. And there were worse things abroad in the east.

She put the bracelet down and nodded to the sallow-faced metalworker. Pushing her way through the crowd, she raised her head to study Belsar's Hill looming up ahead. A pall of black smoke from the campfires hung over it.

'And you are to whore yourself as well?' she asked Acha.

'I will not.'

'Then where will you sleep and what will you eat?'

'I can still pour wine and serve meat.' The other woman's voice was flinty.

'The invaders are not kind to English women. They think we are all whores compared to their cold, obedient Norman wives.'

'And you think all English are kind to Cymri slaves?' Acha snapped. 'I have survived. I will do so again.'

Rowena hoped the other woman was right. But as she looked around at the grim faces of the soldiers, and the drunken axes-for-hire knocking folk out of their path, she feared the worst. There was little kindness in this place. None of the comforts she knew from her home. And away from the scrutiny of their nobles, the Normans made their own laws. Death came easy.

Suddenly afraid that she had made the wrong decision, she turned away from the crowded track and walked among the huts. Her chest felt tight and she thought that she might cry. Barely had she gone ten paces when she heard angry shouts ring out. A man was weaving among the dwellings, his cloak flying behind him. In his haste, his hood flew back and she was shocked to see that it was Hereward. He glimpsed her too, and his own features lit with surprise.

At first she thought he had come hunting for her. But then Acha exclaimed and pointed. A Northman was pursuing the

Mercian, his face a mass of burns and scars. Roaring like a wounded beast, he gripped his axe as he pounded along the muddy track.

'We must help,' Acha gasped.

Without thinking, Rowena darted in front of the fierce Viking warrior. He bellowed, 'Out of my way,' and attempted to thrust her aside, but she tangled herself in his arms. They all but fell to the ground.

'I am hungry,' she cried. 'Oh, aid me, I beg you. And I will give you a night of joy that you will never forget.'

'Out of my way, whore,' he yelled. He hooked an arm round her and flung her to one side with such force that she crashed against the wall of a hut. She felt dazed, and winded, but when she looked up she saw the Viking roaming back and forth searching for his prey. Hereward was nowhere to be seen. And nor was Acha.

Throwing his head back, the Northman shook his fist at the heavens and roared curses until his throat was raw. When he stormed past, he glared at Rowena with murder in his eyes, but she sensed he would not harm her. He hailed someone in his angry, rumbling voice. Rowena turned and saw it was the knight, Deda. He stared back at her.

Her heart pounded. She walked away as quickly as appeared seemly. She could not be sure whether the Norman had recognized her. The last time they met, when she had spat in his face, she had been hooded. But she knew if word got out that a woman of Ely was in the camp she would be branded a spy, and she would pay the price.

The knight did not follow, for which she was thankful. For a while, she searched among the huts until she saw Acha beckoning from the rear of one of the makeshift workshops. When she hurried over, she found Hereward crouching beside a barrel of stagnant water.

Rowena waited for the edge of his tongue, but he only said, 'I am in your debt.'

'Is Kraki with you?' Acha whispered.

The Mercian shook his head. 'I am alone. There is less danger that way.'

As he looked from one woman to the other, Rowena blurted, 'I am here to kill the king.' She expected shock, or anger, or ridicule, but the warrior only nodded his head. He seemed to understand her. She found that strange. She barely understood herself.

He stood up, still keeping his head down. 'It is not my place to tell you your business,' he said in a gentle tone, 'but take care. And do not throw your life away needlessly.'

She stuck out her chin. 'You risk your own neck.'

'So that others may live without the yoke of the Normans around theirs.' He hesitated, choosing words that did not seem to come easily to him. 'I know what is in your heart,' he began. 'There are days when I would throw my life away in an instant to find vengeance for the murder of my wife. But I have been shown there is no gain in that, and, if I could, I would show you the same.'

She looked into his face. Turbulent emotions moved just beneath the surface. In days gone by, she had been angry with him, and scared of him, but now she felt sorry for him. Whatever he was fighting seemed great indeed.

'Would Elwin wish you to die to avenge him?' he asked.

She winced. Tears flecked her eyes at the memory of her husband.

'Even if you would live . . .' he held out a hand to her, 'there is a danger in allowing yourself to be consumed by such a desire. The prize you seek may be more painful than the hurt you now feel. And success may not be the salve you hope.'

She nodded. 'You are kind.'

'I know my words will not turn you from your path here and now.' He smiled. 'I have lived through this. But I would hope you will think on what I have said, and in days to come see the truths of it. I would not see you harmed,' he added, then turned to Acha. 'Nor you. Kraki needs you.'

The other woman looked down, chastened. 'I cannot return to Ely until I am sure Rowena is safe,' she said quietly.

Hereward frowned, puzzled by what he was hearing. 'That is a noble cause. But again, take care. You are in a nest of vipers here.' He glanced around to be sure they were not being watched. Then he pulled up his hood, nodded his thanks once again, and slipped away.

Dusk came too fast.

Once Acha had found work with a noble newly arrived from Normandy, Rowena said farewell. Her friend's new master was an ascetic man, not given to grand displays, and Rowena walked away in confidence that Acha would be safe with him. Yet she felt unprepared for the pang of loneliness she felt as she trudged up the track to Belsar's Hill, or her apprehension at the enormity of what lay ahead. At times, she paused by the side of the road, afraid she might lose her stomach. Hereward's words haunted her, but she forced herself to carry on.

As night fell, the whores waited under the torches by the gate. They were a poor band. Some missed eyes, or hands. Others bore the scars of the pox on their faces. Their dresses were filthy and threadbare. Most were drunk. As Rowena drew near, two women rolled in the dirt, biting and scratching and tearing at their hair. Their curses were worse than any she had heard the Norman soldiers utter.

On the edge of the group, she stood with her head lowered. She hoped she would not draw attention to herself, but she could feel eyes upon her, and when she glanced up the stares were murderous. As she heard the guards drawing the bar on the gates, she turned away and muttered a prayer. What she was about to do was a sin and she would pay with her soul; the churchmen had said that time and again. Endure a man's affections only to quicken with child, they said. Most of the wives she had spoken to laughed at such things. They rolled with their husbands by choice. They did not lie there and cry, as the Norman women did, or so it was said. But still she feared God's wrath for her whoring. Yet doomed though she felt herself to be, still she believed it a price worth paying.

As the gates trundled open, she turned back and put on a smile that promised much. She noticed the other women doing the same. The two whores who had been fighting jumped up and brushed themselves down. Dragging fingers through their tangled hair, they darted into the camp.

Rowena shuffled in behind them, feeling her panic rise with each step. As the other women dashed along the narrow tracks, trilling and calling, she walked slowly, sizing up the men who watched her with lascivious eyes. She ignored the brutish and the low-born. Though her cheeks flushed at their cruel insults when she spurned their advances, she walked on, searching for the commanders or the noblemen who might bring her closer to the king's gyre.

In the end, she smiled at a high-ranking soldier who had a tent close to the castle enclosure. He was gentle and he had an easy nature, but as he lay atop her thrusting and grunting she closed her eyes and ran with visions of stabbing her knife into his neck until she was drenched with his blood. Afterwards, they talked for a while, and she learned how the king would sometimes wander through the lower camp, booming encouragement to his men. She felt better for that, for it was something she thought she might be able to use. But after she had taken his coin, she stumbled out to the dark near the walls, where she sat and heaved silent, juddering sobs long into the night.

When she had dried her eyes, she stood up and wandered back through the camp. The coin she had earned would buy her a berth in one of the tents the other whores used, and some warm food for her belly the next day.

Choking smoke swirled across the camp. The fires glowed in the dark wherever she looked. But now that most of the men were sleeping or drunk or both, an uneasy stillness had fallen across the hilltop. At least the din that rang out during the day had distracted her. Now she had only her thoughts for company, and they were the last thing she needed.

As she wandered towards the torches over the gates, a tremendous exhaustion settled on her. She glanced up at the vast vault of heaven and felt an aching loneliness. The hopelessness of it all was near too much to bear.

'You are far from home.'

Her heart pattered as she whirled around, looking for the source of the voice. 'Who goes?'

A figure was silhouetted against one of the fires. 'There is no need to be afraid. It is only I.'

She clenched her fingers around the knife in her cloak. When he turned slightly and the orange flames lit his face, she saw it was Deda. 'I do not know you,' she said.

'I think you do.' He took a step forward.

'Stay back,' she snapped. The knife felt hard in her hand. 'I have never seen you before.'

He laughed, though gently. 'I never forget any woman who spits in my face. That seems only courteous.'

'I fled Ely,' she said, changing course. 'There was nothing for me there.'

'You are looking for your husband. Did you find him?'

'Yes,' she lied. 'He works on the causeway.'

He nodded, but she could see in his eyes that he didn't believe her. Glancing around the camp, he said, 'And you are here to . . . spit at me again?'

Rowena couldn't think what to say. He stepped forward another pace and she saw his nose wrinkle. He could smell the musk of fornication upon her. He frowned, puzzling over some thought or other.

'Please, I must go,' she said, attempting to push by him.

He did not move. 'You have nothing to fear from me.' She was surprised to hear a note of compassion in his voice. 'Many women in these parts have had their menfolk taken from them. It is a harsh treatment. You . . . all you English . . . deserve better.' He stepped aside and bowed, sweeping out one arm to guide her way. 'Go in peace.'

Rowena hurried by. She did not look back until she reached

the gates, and by then Deda was nowhere to be seen. And yet his words echoed in her head, and they troubled her in a way she did not understand.

She did not want his pity. It was his kind that had slain all the joy in her life. And if she had to, she would kill him as well.

CHAPTER TWENTY-EIGHT

'The king has signed a pact with the Devil,' the white-haired tanner hissed. He looked around the sullen faces gathered by the campfire in the dawn chill of the causeway settlement. The men jeered, their breath steaming. He had a reputation for tall stories, this one. Scowling, the leatherworker shook his fist. 'The Bastard's men stopped by my workshop at first light and paid good coin for new scabbards,' he insisted. 'A witch has come forth to aid the king, they said. Her spells will win the war for the Normans.'

'You are frit of an old wise woman?' Hereward held his hands to the flames, warming the chill from his bones after a sleepless night in the reed-beds. He had expected Harald Redteeth to turn the settlement upside down searching for him. But the Viking must have believed any sane man would have fled this nest of vipers, and so he should have, but there was still too much to learn.

'I am frit of the Devil.' The tanner circled his finger and thumb to ward off evil.

'The English have the arm of St Oswald,' the Mercian murmured as he felt the life come back to his numb fingers. 'God is on their side. What is a witch next to that?'

'Aye, all well and good,' the tanner replied. 'In days gone any Norman would have been afrit of that.' He lowered his voice to a conspiratorial whisper. 'But they are scared of this witch more. I could see it in their faces. Each warrior wore a new wooden cross round his neck, and they touched it whenever they spoke of her. And if the Normans are frit of her . . . the Normans . . .' He let his words tail off, knowing that every man there could complete the sentence.

'I will believe this when I see it with my own eyes,' Hereward said. He pulled his cloak tighter around him. The wind was raw that morning.

Beyond the crackle of the campfire, footsteps were pounding down the track from the camp atop Belsar's Hill. Clutching their ale-cups, the men rose, squinting through the twirling smoke. A group of the king's men swept by.

'Trouble,' someone muttered.

Hereward watched the warriors race to the waterside. Bleary-eyed sailors, their faces leathered by the wind, stirred from their morning bowls as a line of long shields locked into a wall along the quay. Under the sullen gaze of the fisher-men, a gang of the soldiers began to search all the vessels moored along the wharf.

'What are they looking for?' another man grunted.

High up on the hill, a steady beat like a war-drum thumped. The Mercian stiffened. He recognized that sound. The Normans were clashing their swords upon their shields, ready for battle and blood.

He had been too confident, he knew that now. The king's men surely were coming for him.

Darting on to the track beyond the workshops, he peered up to the camp. Sure enough, a war-band was heading his way. Only ten of them, but it was enough. The soldiers plunged into the edge of the settlement, tearing open tents and dragging men, women and children from the warmth of their huts. Any who complained were hauled to the side of the rutted track and beaten until they could not stand. One man shook his fist. Four soldiers grabbed him and pinned him down, arm outstretched. A fifth took his blade and hacked through the wrist. The man's screams silenced the growing outcry.

Hereward turned away, trembling with fury. To stand by and do nothing in the face of such cruelty was almost more than he could bear.

More clashing shields echoed from the camp gates. He wrenched around and saw soldiers gathering across the north road. The noose was slowly tightening about his neck.

He loped to the edge of the huts and peered across beds of reeds and patches of long, yellowing grass stretching out to the willows in the distance. The ground was swampy. Even if he could make his way across it, a lone figure in that desolate waste would be easily visible. Like a wolf at bay, the Mercian felt his savage nature call to him. If his devil rose there, with no way to turn, it would only make things worse for him, of that there could be no doubt.

Behind him he could hear the sound of the raid drawing ever nearer.

A screech rang out across the settlement, like an owl at hunt. He jerked around. Another shriek echoed, and then another, until a constant shrill stream silenced every other voice. In that discordant sound, he began to hear a chilling music.

Folk began to creep towards the track and he slipped in among them.

A wild-haired woman was making her way out of a large blue tent towards the causeway surrounded by a band of warriors. Every now and then she would throw her head back and make that throat-rending screech. The crowd watched her, rapt. After a moment, men and women crossed themselves, or made the sign to ward off evil.

At the nearest wooden tower, the woman clawed her way up the rickety ladder. Once she reached the summit, she raised her arms to the heavens. The icy wind tore at her hair and plucked at her filthy dress. Hereward looked from her to the horizon.

Black clouds were roiling and lightning flickered over the wetlands. After a few moments, thunder boomed, and every man and woman in the crowd below cried out as if the Devil had called out their name and theirs alone. Hands clutched for crosses, or rabbit's feet, or charms in the shape of a hammer. Even the Norman soldiers stared up at the spectacle with unease.

Along the horizon the storm surged, looking for all the world as if the witch directed it with every sweep of her hand. Hereward brooded. Here was a weapon deadlier than any Norman sword, for it struck straight into a man's soul. He could not let it stand.

Pulling his hood low, he pushed his way to the back of the crowd and edged among the huts and tents. Thunder cracked in the distance. The cold wind stripped the leaves from the trees. Yet the storm would not come this way, he could see that. Soon the witch would be forced to leave her high perch, pretending that she had sped the tempest on its way. And then he had no doubt that she would seek to hide away from curious eyes so that the spectacle of her display was all that lingered in the mind.

Slipping his hand inside his cloak, he drew out his knife and kept it hidden in his palm until he came to the blue tent. Glancing around once to be sure he was not being watched, he darted inside.

His nose wrinkled at the odours of sweat and urine mixed with the pungent aroma of unfamiliar herbs. A three-legged iron brazier hissed in the centre. Most of the smoke swirled up out of a hole in the tent roof. A bed lay on one side: fresh straw and warm woollen blankets. Around it, the wise woman had scattered the accoutrements of her trade: a human skull marred by a jagged black hole where a spear had plunged through the bone, and many smaller animal skulls; posies of woodland flowers and bunches of dried herbs. Pots and bowls were scattered everywhere, some covered with a foul-smelling residue. But there was salt pork on a trestle, and fresh bread and ale and a pitcher of wine. Hereward guessed she had never lived so well.

He stepped into the crook of the tent beside the entrance. Outside, he could hear her shrieks begin to subside as the wind died. The thunder rolled away. He waited, holding the knife close to his chest.

Not long after, the tent flaps were thrown aside and the witch swept in. She ranged over to the brazier and tossed a handful of herbs into the hot coals. A sweeter smell filled the tent.

Hereward made no sound, but she must have heard something for she whirled. Her eyes flashed. 'Who are you?' she snarled.

'An earth-walker seeking the aid of a wise woman,' he said in a placid voice.

For a moment, she sized him up, then clawed her finger to beckon him to the brazier.

'Many speak of blood and war and sickness and hunger in days yet to come. Is this what you see?' Hereward asked.

'All those things.' The witch snatched a chunk of salt pork and devoured it. 'In the coming war, the English will be crushed. The king will be victorious. But then there will be food for every belly, and peace, everywhere. The *alfar* have whispered these things to me.'

Hereward flinched. Was she merely sowing seeds of despair, as William the Bastard would have wanted, or were these things to be? He thought back to the times he had sat with Turfrida in a hall of scented smoke, sweating in the heat from the stoked hearth as she rolled her eyes back and repeated the *alfar*'s whispers. Turfrida always believed those words to be true.

The witch must have seen his drifting gaze, for she furrowed her brow and asked, 'These things weigh heavy on you?'

He shrugged off her question and stepped closer still. 'Tell me more,' he murmured, his fingers tightening on the knife's handle. 'This time of gold you say yet awaits. Food in every belly and mead in every cup, and God shining His light down upon all England. Then will we see the beatings stop, and the thefts, and the gibbets?' He smiled. 'For that would be heaven indeed.'

'Aye, peace for all,' she replied, distracted. She leaned over the brazier and inhaled the fragrant smoke. Her eyelids fluttered.

One swift slash across the throat would do it. She would not be able to cry out for aid, and there may yet be time for him to slip away.

He shuddered. In his cloak, his hand trembled, and he realized he could not use his knife. His stomach clenched at the thought of killing her. Yet he had slaughtered so many men he could not guess the number, and all without a second thought.

She opened her eyes and creased her brow once more. 'What ails you?' she spat.

A tremor ran through him, and he turned his head away from her. Yes, he had killed many a man, but no women. Never a woman. He thought of his mother's blood draining through the boards of Asketil's hall after she had been beaten to death by his father's fists. He remembered his first love, Tidhild, dead at his feet. And Turfrida too, lying in her grave. Three women, three unjust deaths. No more.

The witch spat into the brazier. Her phlegm sizzled.

Hereward gritted his teeth, fighting with his very nature. But he could not bring himself to release that terrible devil that lurked inside him; or rather, it refused his summons. Mocking him, he thought. Showing him who was master.

He reeled back a step, grimacing. The time had passed. Aware that the witch was watching him like a hawk, he turned and strode across the tent. 'I must take my leave,' he mumbled.

'Stay,' she called after him. 'The *alfar* still whisper. There is much you should learn here.'

He threw aside the tent flap. Grey light flooded in.

185

She spat in the brazier once more, and hissed, 'What say you, Hereward?'

Startled, he turned back at the sound of his name.

The witch grinned.

CHAPTER TWENTY-NINE

Hereward crashed out of the tent and into a gathering crowd drawn by the witch's shrieks of alarm. As folk hovered around the entrance, as fearful as they were curious, he shouldered his way into the mass, cursing himself. He had been too weak, too slow-witted. And now he would pay the price, and all the English with him.

Diving into one of the narrow, waste-strewn tracks among the huts, he picked a winding route that he hoped would confuse anyone on his heels. A voice in his head whispered that his exertions were all for naught – there was no way out of that place, and all he had was his knife, a child's weapon. He could not even fight his way to freedom. But he pushed it aside and shrugged off his cloak, hoping that at least would make him harder to identify.

At the rear of a workshop, he paused to catch his breath. Cries rang out across the settlement, but now there was no order to the Normans searching for him. He hoped he could use that confusion to his advantage. But as he glanced towards the causeway, he saw two men standing on the peat ramparts, gaping back at him. He felt a rush of heat as he locked eyes with Redwald. His father, Asketil, stood beside his brother, his face ragged with hate.

And then his devil did stir. Blood thundered into his head, and all he wanted at that moment was to plunge his knife into his brother's chest. What cared he if the Normans caught and killed him? He would have vengeance, finally.

A woman's cry jerked him from his fury. 'He is here! He is here!' she yelled, and he realized it was Acha. Her exhortations seemed to come from far away, near the end of the causeway closest to Belsar's Hill. The sounds of pursuit moved away from him and towards those increasingly insistent cries. Hereward felt a chill when he realized that she was buying him time to escape, probably at the cost of her own life. His kin forgotten, he peered round the edge of the workshop and watched Norman warriors flood towards her, and the English too. Bafflement filled their faces as they looked around in vain, then anger when they sensed they had been deceived. Two of the warriors dragged her away. The crowd yelled and shook their fists, as if she were the enemy, not the bastards who had seized her.

Even as the Normans wrenched her along the track to the camp, showing no mercy with their fists and feet, even though she must know only death awaited her, she allowed herself to smile because her ploy had worked. Hereward stared after her, stung by that simple, selfless expression. Never had he thought her capable of such an act of sacrifice. He felt remorse that he had so underestimated her.

There was nothing he could do to save her. As the search began again, he forced himself to turn away. Redwald and Asketil were gone too, and he raced away to the very edge of the settlement before they could raise the alarm.

Ahead of him, the reed-beds rustled, a sea of creamy-brown stretching out to the willows where he could lose himself. He glanced back. No eyes were on him. Acha's ruse had worked. Murmuring a prayer for the woman, he dived into a ditch half filled with freezing, filthy water and clawed his way along.

Barely a moment had passed when he heard a shout. The

tanner from the campfire was peering down at him from the ditch's edge.

'Hold your tongue,' the Mercian urged. 'I am Hereward of the English. I fight so you might be free of these bastard Normans.'

For a long moment, the leatherworker held his gaze as this information settled on him. Then he spun round, put his hand to his mouth and began to yell for aid.

Snaking up one arm, Hereward grabbed the tanner's ankle and yanked him into the ditch. The man flailed as he fought to keep his head above water, but Hereward pressed him down. Filthy ditchwater flooded the leatherworker's mouth. Like a madman, he thrashed out, trying to claw at the Mercian's face.

'I fight for you,' Hereward protested when the spluttering tanner gulped a mouthful of air. But still the man tried to cry out, and still he struggled.

'I fight for you,' the warrior repeated. His anger surged. 'I fight for you. I fight for you.' And on and on, his words growing with passion until his voice cracked. He thrust the tanner's head underwater to try to quieten him, and then again. Finally he accepted he had no choice. Putting iron into his arms, he pinned the man down until the wild thrashing turned to twitches, and the viscous bubbles stopped breaking the surface, and all movement finally ebbed away.

His fingers slipped away from the tunic. The body sank down into the muddy depths. Sickened by what he had done, Hereward peered into the black water. Once he had gathered his thoughts, he crept away. His conscience dragged his gaze back one final time, and he regretted it. The ditch-rats were already beginning to feast.

By the time he crawled out of his hiding place and into the reeds, the light was dimming. From the settlement, the voices of the men searching for him still rang out, but there seemed a dismal tone to them now.

Yet as he crawled away into the twilight, he felt no joy at his escape, only a grim resignation and a sense that more misery was yet to come.

Acha was lost. She could be cold, and hard, and selfish, and proud, and sharp-tongued. And yet she had given up her life for him. He could not understand why she had done such a thing, nor why it troubled him so.

As the night closed in, her final, lingering smile haunted him.

CHAPTER THIRTY

The mournful howls of the hunting dogs echoed across the desolate wetlands. Deep in the dark, torches flickered as bands of Normans searched the edges of meres and dense woods. The night was chill and moonless and all of the fens was a sea of ink.

Hereward scrambled over tangled roots, all but feeling his way through the inhospitable landscape. Blood dripped from his hands where he had torn them on the flints of causeways. His tunic was sodden, his hair plastered to his head, his limbs were like lead and his chest was afire. Yet he never slowed. But as he clawed his way through a willow copse, his fingers closed around the way marker near-hidden in the sedge. Only then did he allow himself to pause and glance back at the bobbing lights.

'Come, you bastards, and drown in the bogs,' he snarled. 'You will not catch me now.'

Here was the secret path back to Ely. He had walked it enough times to navigate its lethal turns without need of eyes. But so well hidden was the start of the track, the Normans would never find it unless someone placed his foot upon it.

As he sucked in a deep draught of the cold night air, he noticed another light – smaller, perhaps no more than a lantern-candle in the trees. It was moving away from Ely, away from the start of the secret path. Was it someone searching for him, he wondered. Only Alric knew he had been risking his neck at the causeway – he had not wanted his men to fear for his safety and lose heart – and even the monk would not be fool enough to venture out alone after dark. He opened his mouth to call out and then thought better of it. He could not risk alerting the Normans to his presence.

Before he could search for the light's owner, it disappeared. Perhaps whoever it was had thought better of his impetuous journey, or had seen the Norman lights and decided to turn back. There was nothing he could do now. With a shrug, he set off along the path.

The journey was treacherous, but the waters were low and soon he set foot upon dry land. Ahead, the torches glowed over Ely's gate. He hailed the guards, who were shocked by his bedraggled appearance so late at night. By the time the gates had trundled open and he had stepped inside, Alric was running down the track from the church, beaming.

'You have the luck of the Devil,' the monk exclaimed. His grin faded when he saw the Mercian's solemn expression.

'Fetch my war-band to the minster. And bring Earl Morcar too,' Hereward commanded. 'We have much to talk about. But first I must have speech with Kraki.'

Alric frowned. Hereward knew his friend had learned to read every secret in his face, however hard he tried to hide it. 'What is amiss?'

The warrior only clapped the monk on the arm and strode off through the settlement.

He found Kraki sitting alone in the dark of his hut. Only a few embers glowed in their hearth. By their light, Hereward could see the dark rings of worry under the Viking's eyes, and the deep furrows in his forehead. He held a cup of ale loosely as he peered into the coals.

'You would drag me from my hearth now?' he rumbled, looking up at the disturbance.

Hereward squatted next to him.

'You look like a drowned rat.'

'Better that than a dead one.' For a moment, Hereward struggled to find the right words. 'I have grave news.'

Kraki raised his bushy eyebrows.

'About Acha,' the Mercian continued. 'The Normans have taken her.'

At first, he thought the Northman had not heard. The Viking stared into the embers, his face like stone. Then he roared and hurled his cup across the hut. Ale splashed up the walls.

'Where is she?' he snarled, his eyes glittering. 'I will carve through ten men, a hundred, to bring her back.'

In quiet tones, Hereward told him what had transpired at Belsar's Hill. When he was done, Kraki nodded. 'Aye, that is like her. More fire than sense.' He bowed his head, then looked Hereward full in the face. 'She yet lives?'

'She lived when I last saw her.'

They both knew what remained unsaid.

'I will go to bring her back,' Kraki said, climbing to his feet. His tone seemed to suggest that his woman had only wandered down to the waterside. 'And I will go alone. No other man should risk his life.'

'No,' Hereward replied. He laid a reassuring hand on the other man's shoulder. 'You will not go alone. You will go with an army at your side, the greatest army the English have ever known. I have found a crack in the enemy's defences. We leave Ely after the second sunrise and we will crush the Normans before us. They will pay for all the cruelties they have inflicted on the folk of England. And if God is willing, we will pluck Acha from the wolf's jaws or die trying.'

CHAPTER THIRTY-ONE

The woman cowered away from the blade of rosy dawn light that sliced across the mud floor of the gloomy hut from the open door, where Deda watched with pity. She huddled against the far wall, her knees tucked up to her chest, her face hidden by her raven-black hair. Her dress was torn, her bare feet filthy and criss-crossed with scratches. The guards had not been gentle with their gauntlets or their shoes. But they had not shamed her, not yet at least. She was too valuable to the king, and he needed at least one knife to hold to her throat.

The camp on Belsar's Hill was waking. Kindling crackled and smoke twisted up into the pink-tinged sky. Pots of yesterday's stew began to bubble over the flames, the sticky scents clouding the ever-present odour of rotting vegetation drifting in from the wetlands. The men farted as they pissed by their tents, bleary-eyed and reeking of vinegar-sweat.

Deda stepped into the hut and looked around. There was nothing in it, not even a bed of straw or a blanket to keep out the night's cold. Barrels of wine had been stored there until it had been decided it would make a better cell for their new prisoner. The ghost of the sharp scent hung in the air.

'I have brought bread,' he said. He removed the chunk of

loaf and held it out. He had not been told to bring her vittles, but it seemed only right. The guards would not feed her.

She turned her face towards him, the matted hair falling away. Her creamy skin was dappled with bruises. He had expected some frightened girl, tearful and pleading for release, but her eyes glinted like a cornered wolf's.

'Have you come to gloat? Or have your way with me?' Acha snarled.

'I have come to give you bread.'

She looked him up and down with contempt, then took the morsel of loaf without thanks. She watched him with those cold eyes as she chewed on it. He imagined she was probably enjoying a vision of slitting his throat.

'They have not knocked the fire from you, then,' he said.

'I have taken many a hand in my life, and suffered much hardship. Last night was naught.'

He tried to place her accent. She had taken on the tones of the English she had lived with, the harshness of the Northfolk, and the rolling sounds of the east, but he heard a more melodic cadence beneath it all. 'And given many a hand too, I would wager. Although they say you can measure a man . . . or a woman, I would think . . . not by the blows they give, but the ones they can take. You have a warrior's heart.'

'Would that I had a warrior's axe.'

'That would not be so good for me, I think.' He smiled, hoping it might raise her spirits, but they both knew that what was to come would be worse yet. 'I have been sent to ready you for the king.'

'Let the bastard come.' She gnawed on the bread.

'A word to the wise. Hard knocks come often enough. It is best not to call for them while they still sleep.'

Acha levelled her cold gaze at him. He could see she had nothing more to say to him. 'I am glad you are well,' he said with a bow, stepping to the door. 'It is my deepest wish that you remain so.'

On the threshold, he glanced across the castle ward and saw

the king stride out of his tent, his breath steaming in the chill air. He crossed the muddy waste like a bear, and clapped his huge hands together when he arrived at the hut.

'Deda. You have softened her up?' he said.

'She is more flint than clay, my lord. But she awaits you.'

William forced his broad shoulders through the doorway and marched across the floor. He loomed over the prisoner, his hands on his hips. She pushed herself up against the wall, her back straight, and held his gaze with defiance.

'You still have your life,' the monarch said. 'I have shown mercy. And I can show even greater kindness.'

'You have nothing that I want.'

Her tone was level, and Deda felt pleased that the woman was taking his advice. The king's rage was terrifying indeed.

For a moment, the king sized her up. Then he nodded and began to pace around the hut, one finger against his lips in thought. 'Not gold?' he suggested. 'Not food for your belly, not relief from hunger for the rest of your days? Not a place at my court? I need good women to bring me my wine.'

'I have been a slave. I would not be one again.'

'Your pride may be your downfall, as it has been many a man's. Nothing, then? Safe passage to any part of this land? You have no kin who can care for you?'

Deda watched a tremor cross the woman's face. It was barely perceptible, and he was sure the king had not seen it, but he thought it seemed that William had found his lure. And yet Acha still shook her head. She must know that her life hung in the balance. Why would she not take something of value to her?

'The English cannot win. You must know that,' the monarch continued. 'Hereward and his pack of wild dogs have only thrived at Ely because I have not turned my gaze towards them. You have seen my army. We have greater numbers, better weapons, enough food to ensure that no man will starve. They will stay strong. They will not back down. And what have the English? Thin hope and nothing more.'

'They have Hereward.'

William came to a halt. A shadow crossed his face. Deda flinched. He felt that he was watching a dam flexing under a spring torrent; with one more droplet it might break. 'One man,' the king said.

'More than that. His army will follow him into hell.'

'Aye, that they will do.' He strode towards her, his lips tight. Acha kept her head high. Deda admired her for that. 'This war could be done in a day, or it could drag on into the cold season, if those farmers that he calls an army continue to hide away like whipped curs. But it will be done, and I will win. I have other things of greater import to occupy my days. I would not waste hours here.' He towered over the woman once more and slowly lowered a finger to point at her. 'Now *you* show mercy. Tell me of the secret path that the English use to come and go as they please, so this matter can be finished quickly. If you do, I will spare the lives of the folk at Ely. You have this chance to save them. Take it.'

'I know of no secret path,' Acha said without hesitation.

The king searched her face for a moment and then said, 'Very well.' He turned on his heel and walked out. Deda closed and barred the door behind him. He knew what was to come next.

'Spare her life,' he urged as they walked away. 'She is no threat.'

The king came to a halt, eyeing his knight. 'You are starting to appear weak, Deda. This troubles me.'

'There is strength in mercy, my lord. The English are like dogs. They flinch from a hard hand, but after too many blows they grow used to their treatment, and resentful.'

'There are some who say you grow too close to these English.' The king did not break his penetrating gaze. 'And that is not a man I want close to me.' He walked away a few paces, and then turned back. 'Prove to me that you are loyal. Slay this woman yourself, then throw her remains into the bog.'

Deda grew cold as he watched the king make his way back to the tent. If he did not do as his monarch asked, it would be his remains in the bog, he knew that.

'Norman bastard.'

The knight turned to see Harald Redteeth striding towards him. Once again the Viking's eyes looked all black. It seemed he had been catching birds. Some more skulls had been threaded on the leather strips hanging from his hauberk, and he had re-dyed his beard red with woodland berries. 'A fine greeting.'

'But true. You are all bastards. No escaping that.'

Deda shrugged. He could not argue with that. What the king had done in the north hung over as many Normans as English. For the first time he had been hearing whispers of criticism and doubt about the man who had led them to so much plunder.

Redteeth glanced towards the king's tent as William parted the flaps and went inside. 'Watch your back,' he said. 'The worst enemies are not always the ones you face across a battlefield.'

'All life is a battle, my friend, from womb to grave, and the best weapons are not always the ones made of iron.' Deda smiled and swept one arm for the Viking to walk with him. 'And sometimes a swift retreat is the best route out of trouble.'

'You will return to Normandy once this war is done?'

'If I live that long.' They wandered through the castle gate and into the camp. 'And where will your axe take you?' Deda went on as they warmed themselves by the nearest fire. He smiled, but his thoughts were away in the hut, with Acha, and what he would have to do.

The flames danced in Redteeth's eyes as a log crackled and spat. 'I have had my fill of your ilk,' he replied, his gaze far-away. 'I would be with men who know honour. Who understand the ties of days gone by.'

'No offence taken,' Deda said with a wry smile.

'Constantinople,' the Viking said with a thoughtful nod. 'There is good coin for a sharp axe there, I have heard tell. Northmen and English alike have set sail to join the emperor's Varangian Guard. Once I have slain Hereward and my oath is fulfilled, I could happily end my days there, knee-deep in mead and women. A life that is true to the ways of my father and my father's father and all before him, that would be my wish.' He glanced sideways at the knight. 'Far away from England, where your kind are bringing in a long night.'

Deda grew wistful. 'A good dream,' he said. 'I may join you there.'

They stood in silence for a long moment, and then Deda took his leave and wandered across the camp to the gates. He could not face returning to the castle ward and the act that weighed so heavily on his soul. While he brooded, Rowena came over. These days she looked hollowed out by life. Her face was drawn, her step leaden, her shoulders hunched. The fire he had seen that day in the English camp was gone. He knew why, he thought. In the early hours, he had seen her leaving the tents of some of the other knights. She was not a whore, could never be one, and he could not understand why she was attempting to ruin herself. But she seemed to have a taste for those who wielded power, so perhaps that was what drove her.

'Good morn, Rowena,' he said.

She started. 'You know my name?'

'If your name is Rowena, I do.'

Her look of bafflement faded quickly and she lowered her eyes. 'I would ask for your aid,' she said.

'I have little coin to spare and no need of comfort at night,' he replied, and instantly regretted his sour tone. She did not deserve such cruelty.

Her cheeks flushed. 'That . . . that was not my meaning. I would offer my plea for mercy for the Ely woman.'

Deda regretted his harshness even more. Rowena must have struggled greatly to make such a request from a man she clearly hated. More, she had placed herself in danger. 'You would do well not to speak of this woman with any other,' he whispered, glancing around. 'She is an enemy who sought to betray us to the English, and if you acknowledge her you would be seen in the same light.'

'I know not why she came here,' Rowena lied. 'We spent our days together for the short time I was in Ely and I do know she is a good woman.'

'Why have you come to me? You have other . . . friends in this camp.'

She looked up at him, her brow furrowing. It seemed she had no answer to his question.

'I do not want to see this woman harmed, we are in agreement there,' he said in a quiet voice. 'But I do not have the ear of the king. Far from it.'

She all but grabbed his hand in desperation. 'If there is anything you can do . . . anything that might save her life . . .' she pleaded.

Deda lowered his head. The weight on his shoulders seemed to have grown heavier still. 'I will see what I can do,' he sighed. But what could he do? To broach the matter with the king once more would probably end in his own death.

Rowena looked surprised at his response. But she smiled with relief and said, 'You have my thanks.' As she took her leave, she glanced back at him once, her brow knitted. Flashing another smile, she hurried away.

Deda looked back to the tower at the summit of the hill and the hut that stood in its shadow. A chill wind blew. A few fat drops of rain spattered in the mud. And in the distance a dog howled as if it had been whipped.

Chapter Thirty-Two

Redwald cloaked himself in the shadows in the corner of the tent. The din of the feast swirled all around him and out into the still fenland night. Cups clashed together accompanied by loud oaths and raucous laughter rolled out like waves upon the shore. Every Norman noble and knight in the east was there, it seemed. Servant girls whirled with hot beef and smoked eels, and pitchers brimming with ruby wine. The succulent scents of the fine food would have drawn water from the mouth of any man. But Redwald ate nothing, nor allowed one drop of drink to pass his lips. He only watched.

The king roared with laughter, swilling wine across the table. Beside him, Abbot Turold, newly arrived from Burgh, leaned in and whispered, his eyes glittering with glee. At one of the far tables, Redwald could just glimpse Ivo Taillebois, glowering, and a sullen William de Warenne. Once they would have been supping at the king's right hand. No more. He had supplanted them.

As he studied the king, Redwald unconsciously traced a finger over his new linen tunic, expertly dyed madder red. It had been provided by William himself, for a monarch's close adviser could not be seen to dress like a common mudhopper.

He had a new leather belt too, engraved with whorls. Edoma had gasped with delight when he had shown the gifts to her.

The monarch threw back his head and laughed once more. Redwald frowned. He could see no reason for his master's uncommon high spirits. Keeping to the shadows, he edged around the tent so he could more easily overhear the king's conversation in the cacophony of voices.

'Never would I have thought the English would take so long to break,' William was saying. 'They have fought like starving rats at every turn.'

'Aye,' Turold slurred as he beckoned for more wine. 'We thought that day at Senlac Ridge was hard-fought. It was as nothing to the battle we have fought every day since then.'

William nodded. 'The sword is sharp, but it takes a keen wit to win this war.' He smiled, almost to himself, Redwald thought. 'But we are close now, God willing.'

Redwald prowled around the fringes of the tent, listening where he could. No one seemed to notice his presence. The nobles were all caught up in their drink, and filling their bellies to bursting, as if they could not get enough each day of their lives. Hereward would have been contemptuous of them, these conquerors growing fat off the labours of the broken-backed English. Redwald felt nothing. They were of use to him, or they were not. No other measurement was necessary.

As the night drew on, the king drank more than Redwald had ever seen him consume. He swilled wine, and ale, and mead, calling for oaths as if all was right with the world, and he was not on the brink of a bloody battle that would tear apart the armies of both sides. But then some nobleman rose on shaky legs and held his cup high, promising that after the English the Normans would vanquish all their enemies: the Danes who brooded in the cold lands, biding their time, with their fleets of dragon-ships; and Malcolm in the north with his army of wild men.

Everyone there roared. Some stood and threw back their cups. Others clambered on the tables and stamped their feet.

But Redwald watched the king's face. The humour flooded away and for one moment he looked like an old man. He caught himself soon enough, laughing too loud as he demanded more wine, but his eyes shifted uneasily now.

Redwald smiled to himself. Here, then, was something of value. The king, so strong and forthright in everything he did, felt the weight of his crown. Did William regret invading England, he wondered? He shrugged. The Bastard could have taken no other course. It was in his nature, and every man was driven by that beast inside him.

He took a few steps back until the cloth of the tent brushed his back. He guessed the monarch's temper would be quicker now, and sure enough he was glowering at the drunken men around him. They were oblivious of the change in his mood, still roaring with laughter and yelling across the tent at each other.

When William hurled his cup at one man's head, the din ebbed away. Heads lowered, eyes darted around. Redwald watched him scan the ranks for someone he could taunt. His gaze settled on Ivo Taillebois, the only one there who refused to avert his gaze.

'Come, Butcher,' the king called, 'show us your fangs.'

Hesitating for only a moment, Taillebois pushed himself up. No man could refuse the king and live. But Redwald watched the sheriff's glower and knew that he would rather be turning his sword upon the monarch himself. The king looked along the tables until his gaze alighted on another commander, a slender man with greying hair. Redwald didn't know his name, but he had heard whispers of the warrior's reputation as an adept swordsman.

'Swords,' the king said with a lazy wave of his hand. 'Let us see who has true skill with the blade.'

As he rounded the table, Taillebois lowered his eyes. He knew he had been set up to fail. Another humiliation. Redwald wondered how much more the Butcher could take.

The two men faced each other in the centre of the tent. The

grey-haired man bowed. Taillebois showed no such courtesy. With a roar, he hacked with his sword as if it were an axe. Caught off guard, the other man reeled back, swinging up his own blade to block by instinct alone. His eyes flickered with unease. The Butcher knew he could not compete on skill alone. Ferocity was his only path to victory, even if it meant lopping off his opponent's head.

For a while, the two men danced around each other. Redwald watched the grey-haired man try time and again to turn this into a display of swordsmanship. But Taillebois had no qualms at all about his tactics. Redwald smiled to himself with new-found admiration for the man.

As he swept by a table, the Butcher snatched up a pitcher of wine and hurled it into his foe's face. The grey-haired man staggered back, blinded. Taillebois saw his opening and hacked down.

A gasp of horror ran through the guests. As the grey-haired man half skidded on the pool of wine, the blade missed splitting open his skull by a whisker and ripped down the side of his head. His ear flew off on to the mud. Howling, he reeled on to his back, clutching at his wound.

The Butcher lunged forward and pressed his blade against his opponent's throat. For a moment, Redwald thought he was going to follow through, even then, with his enemy disabled. He seemed to catch himself at the last, and glanced over to where the monarch sipped from his cup.

The king flapped a hand to end the contest, bored now that his desire to humiliate Taillebois had been thwarted. As the Butcher swaggered back to his seat, the servants helped the wounded man to his feet. He staggered out in search of a leech, and with him went all the exuberance of the feast. Voices remained hushed, the mood as damp as a fenlands autumn. But the king didn't seem to care. Redwald stayed to watch him drinking and laughing for a while longer, and then he crept out into the night.

A little later he glanced around and saw the monarch

lurching from the tent. William stood by the entrance, swaying as he pissed.

'My lord, the feast goes well,' Redwald called, painting a beaming smile on to his face.

The king looked over and grinned. 'You are a sly one. If you truly thought the feast went well, you would be in there feasting instead of warming yourself by the fire.' He winked. 'But that is where a wise man would be. Out here you do not have to listen to the whining of dogs and the hissing of snakes.' He glared into the tent and then clapped an arm across Redwald's shoulders and urged him towards the campfire. The reek of the tavern floor floated off him.

'The minds of the English are a mystery to me,' William slurred. 'Here you have riches that are the envy of every man in Europe. Treasure . . . trade . . . the jewellery and the statues and the . . . fine cloth . . . and those laws that keep your folk on the right path. They are a monument in themselves. All those things you have made across the seasons, great things. And yet . . .' He peered into the flames, his brow creasing. 'It seems that you English are only interested in ale, and fucking, and music. This makes little sense to me.' He shook his head in incomprehension.

'We are a strange breed.'

'Strange, yes, and treacherous too.' William bowed his head, his thoughts seemingly miles away. 'Long ago now, Harold Godwinson came to me in Normandy. We went hunting together,' he said in disbelief. 'And he told me that the English crown would be mine once Edward died.'

'Harold could not be trusted,' Redwald replied. Since Senlac Ridge, he had barely thought of the man who had first raised him up.

'And then my messengers told me Harold had taken the crown himself in Edward's new abbey,' the king continued as if the other man had not spoken. His lips curled back from his discoloured teeth. The wound was still raw. He glanced at Redwald and demanded, 'Tell me about Hereward. Not as the man he is now, but as the brother who shared your father's hall.'

'Hereward is a good man,' Redwald replied. 'He is a loyal friend. He is brave. He has more honour than any other Englishman I know. I hold him in the highest regard. I could never reach his heights.'

The king frowned, baffled by this glowing account. 'And yet you aid me in bringing him to his doom?'

Redwald shrugged. 'He is all those things, and he is wrong.'

The king looked back to the fire, still struggling to comprehend. 'What do you want, above all else?' he demanded. 'Speak truly. I will know if your tongue lies.'

'Power,' Redwald answered without guile. 'And . . . to feel safe in this harsh world.'

William grinned. This he understood. 'Power,' he mused. 'When this war is done, I will grant you that, and more.'

Redwald was surprised.

It must have shown on his face, for the king continued, 'I know your heart better than any man on this hill. Trust we will never have, but I do not need to trust you if I know you. Unlike all those who lay claim to moral purpose and godly ways, I can foresee every move you will make.'

He laughed, then, and clapped Redwald on the shoulders. As he made his way towards the tent, he glanced back and said, 'Men always think they have the measure of me. But I did not become king and conqueror by being so easily understood. I have plans in place that even those dogs in there do not know.' He grinned. 'This war is all but done, and before long we will be on our way to Wincestre.'

'Plans?' Redwald said.

The king shook his head, taunting. 'The English do not realize that doom is stalking them even as we speak. And soon the end will come.'

CHAPTER THIRTY-THREE

A thin crack of light glowed under the door. A beacon, it seemed, compared to the swimming darkness of the hut. Acha huddled against the timber wall, her arms around her knees. She shivered. No blanket had she, no straw, and the mud floor felt like ice beneath her bare feet. Winter was coming in hard, but she would never see the snows, she knew that now. Her belly rumbled. Her Norman captors had not brought her food for a full day, and that told her all she needed to know. She watched the door like a hawk, knowing that when it was flung open and the dawn flooded in, it would signal the end of her.

Her thoughts flew away, across the fens, and the forests of Mercia, to Gwynedd and the great snow-capped mountains of the west, the desolate uplands and the deep river valleys, as wild in their own way as the wetlands that were now her home. She remembered sitting by the hearth of her mother's hall, listening to the rain rattling on the thatch and the sound of the men singing as they quaffed their ale. She recalled the smell of damp fern, and the smoke. It reminded her of peace. There was no want in their hall. Meat when they needed it, and clothes and coin. Slaves to service their every need.

Acha flinched. Her head filled with a vision of her giving the edge of her tongue to the young girl who was sewing by the fire. From the hot lands across the whale road she had come, bought in the markets to the south and sent to their hall. Acha had made the girl cry. And two days later Harold Godwinson had come with his war-band, and the hall had been burned, and her mother raped, and she had been carried away, to Mercia first, and then to Eoferwic, where she had been made slave to Harold's brother Tostig. Hot tears of shame burned in her eyes. A slave! They knew full well that royal blood flowed through her veins, she was sure. Her father was Gruffyd ap Llywelyn, a prince, the greatest prince that her folk had ever known. No man had done more to unite the Cymri.

She bowed her head. Aye, royal blood, and little good it had done her, in Northumbria, or even in Gwynedd. The English had always gossiped behind her back about her lineage, but she had never spoken of it to anyone, not even Kraki, and for good reason. In part, she had feared the knowledge of her high-born status would bring more suffering upon her head. But in truth, it was the shame. For she was a bastard. Her father had always cared for her and her mother, but she could never claim his heritage, or take the hand of a son of another great family. She was everything yet she was nothing, always happy yet always miserable, bound to days gone by, but with no days to come unless she made them herself.

She raised her head until it bumped against the wood. And there it was. She had royal blood, and she would never forget that. For a while she had done so, through all the sour days, when it was a struggle to reach the night. But now she had been forced to remember that she was the daughter of Gruffyd ap Llywelyn, and if she died this day, it would be with head held high.

Footsteps approached the door. She stiffened. The time had come. She had always known it would end this way, from the moment she had cried out to save Hereward's life. Her legs shaking, she pushed herself up the wall. She would meet her fate eye to eye, not cowed.

The door rattled open and once more the knight was framed in the rosy light. Deda was his name. She showed a cold face to him.

'You will come with me,' he said. His voice was not unkind, but she thought she saw doubt in his eyes, or worry, or unease. The confidence she had seen there before was gone, aye, and the compassion too. Norman bastards, they were all alike.

She lifted her chin and strode forward, trying not to tremble. When she stepped out into the chill dawn, her breath steamed. Under the pink sky, the camp was dark and still. Beyond the palisade, the wetlands lowered, the meres blushing amid acres of shadow.

'You are not to make a show of it, then?' she said. She felt grateful for that, although she would not reveal it.

Deda leaned in. She could feel his warm breath on her ear. 'Heed my words,' he whispered. 'If you would keep your head on your shoulders, do as I say. Do you understand?'

She nodded, puzzled.

'I will take you out of the camp and past the causeway to the edge of the lake. And there I will set you free. You will go back to your home, and if anyone asks, you will tell them you escaped from my grip. You were fast and clever. I was slow and stupid, like all Normans. Do you hear me?'

She flinched, thinking this was some cruel trick. The Normans were skilled at drawing out agonies. She looked into his eyes. His gaze was clear and honest. 'Why do you do this?' she asked.

He looked away across the lonely landscape for a moment as if trying to find the answer for himself. Then he only shook his head. 'Come,' he whispered. 'We must not be seen.'

Further across the ward, in the deep shadow by the castle, a squat man waited, a Northman, by the look of him, in furs and mail shirt. As she neared, she noticed the dyed red beard and the small skulls hanging from thongs at his chest, and she recognized Harald Redteeth, who had offered his axe in service to Tostig Godwinson in Eoferwic. He was a loathsome man, unpredictable and brutal, and mad some said. She looked to Deda, but he walked on seemingly unperturbed that this man, at least, had seen them.

Her chest tightened as they neared the castle gate. She waited while Deda slid the bar, her toes clenching on the dewy grass. He eased the gate open a crack.

Before they had taken one step, a voice boomed out. 'Deda.'

Her heart fell. She watched the knight's features tighten and for one moment he closed his eyes in despair before he turned to look back across the ward. The king stood beside his tent, looking down at them. He was a dog that slept with one eye open, she thought, stirring at the first whisper that something was amiss.

'Bring me her heart,' William called in a sardonic tone. Acha felt that the monarch knew what his knight had been planning.

'My lord,' Deda replied with a curt bow. He wrenched the gate open and ushered her through.

As they walked the winding track to the palisade, Acha sensed the weight that had descended on the knight. His shoulders were hunched and his gaze was fixed ahead. She knew he would not be able to continue with his deception. She was to die after all. Somehow the knowledge of her fate stung harder this second time. She blinked away hot tears.

'Do not punish yourself,' she said. 'You did what you could.'

Her words did not seem to comfort him. He remained silent to the camp gates and beyond. As they trudged down the track towards the causeway, she thought how peaceful the world looked. Perhaps it was better to lose her life than see the End of Days ushered in.

A foot crunched on the packed mud behind them. Acha reeled back as Deda pitched forward on to the track. Blood trickled from the side of his head. He did not stir.

She whirled. Harald Redteeth shook his axe in her face. She

realized he must have struck the knight with the flat of his blade.

'Deda does not have the stomach for killing you,' the Viking growled, his eyes pockets of shadow under his heavy brow. He gave a wolfish grin. 'Now you will come with me.'

CHAPTER THIRTY-FOUR

Mist drifted across the water. The muffled splash of dipping oars rolled out. All was still in that hour after dawn. A shadowy shape eased from the pearly wreaths, a fishing boat, five figures hunched aboard. Then another followed, and another. Across the grey mere, the fishermen made their way towards the quay by the causeway with the night's catch. Their thick woollen cloaks were wrapped around them, their hoods pulled low against the morning cold.

Ashore, the smoke from the morning fires was starting to rise. Voices echoed among the huts and tents of the causeway settlement as waking men hailed their neighbours. And on the hill beyond, the camp of William the Bastard brooded.

Hereward stood in the prow of the lead boat, peering out from the depths of his hood. He smiled to himself. They had their moment of surprise. Along the timber decking of the new harbour stood only a handful of guards. Most of them looked half asleep, leaning on their spears. He lowered his hand to the hilt of Brainbiter, soothed by the cool touch of the gold.

The oars slipped into the water, slow and easy. A few dead fish lay in the prow of every boat, their scent drifting on the air. Everything would seem normal. He glanced back at Kraki. The

Northman kept his head bowed. In the boat behind, the huge shape of Guthrinc loomed out of the mist, pulling on the oars with steady strokes.

Hereward grinned at the audacity of his plan. The king had commandeered all the vessels in the east to keep the English locked in Ely. Only a few had been allowed to supply fish to his camp at Belsar's Hill. And now the English had taken those very ships in turn. The Mercian thought back to the shock on the fishermen's faces as his men intercepted their boats. Spitting epithets and complaining about lost coin, the men of the sea had been rounded up and held at spear-point so they could not spread word.

On the quayside, none of the guards stirred. The mist was a cloak that hid the extent of his army, more than a hundred men drifting in, as silent as death. Not enough to defeat the king's great host, but that was not his plan.

Cries and yelled orders echoed from the direction of Belsar's Hill. The guards on the quayside jerked alert, craning their necks towards the tumult. Hereward imagined the pandemonium in the Norman camp. Bleary-eyed men torn from their morning bowls, snatching up swords and helms as their commanders strode among them, yelling. Sure enough, he heard the gates trundle open, as clear as if it were only a spear's throw away in the stillness of the morning. The column of men would be flooding out of the camp along the road to the north where Earl Morcar waited with the rest of the English army. Morcar was sly and untrustworthy, but he hated the king more than Hereward did and he had his eyes set on a greater prize, perhaps even the crown itself. That had been enough to convince him to take the brunt of the Norman attack, if only for a short while. In the hours before dawn, his men would have slaughtered one of the king's scouting parties, allowing one man to flee and take the word of the impending English attack back to Belsar's Hill. And so William the Bastard and his hated rule would be caught betwixt hammer and anvil as they had once planned; and this would be an end to it.

213

Hereward gritted his teeth. He was ready.

The boats slid through the water to the quay. Once the harbour loomed up over him, he stepped on to the ladder and clambered up the few rungs to the top. A guard stood nearby, still peering at Belsar's Hill. Kraki threw the rope and Hereward moored the boat to the post. One by one his men climbed up to the quayside. Not a word was uttered. They kept their heads down, their faces hidden in the shadows of their hoods. For all the attention the guards paid them, they might as well not have been there. Along the quay, three other boats swept in. Hereward pretended to busy himself with the knot on the mooring rope until all the men had climbed up on to the waterside.

His eyes locked on Kraki's in a moment of silent communication. Pulling himself upright, he turned and drew his blade. In one fluid motion, he thrust Brainbiter through the nearest guard. Blood gushed from the man's chest and he crumpled to the boards.

The other guards jerked round. The English fell on them like wolves, hacking them down with axes. Hereward nodded, pleased. So swift was the attack, not a sound escaped the Normans' lips. Blood ran along the lines of the timber and dripped through the cracks into the water below.

Guthrinc stepped to the edge and cupped his hands round his mouth. His keening gull-call sang into the mist. Crouching on the quay, their eyes darting all around, the English watched as dark smudges appeared in the haze. The boats swept in.

Once his army had gathered on the waterside, Hereward threw off his hood. Every man followed his lead. He looked across the grim, committed faces and then raised his arm to beckon to his men to follow him. In silence, they surged away from the quayside.

When they emerged from the mist that clung to the mere, Hereward looked along the vast causeway with its enormous rolling ramparts of peat. Six wooden towers soared up to the pale blue sky. Ballistae and catapults sat on mounds. He watched as the guards wrenched round to stare aghast at the English army. Their cries rose up, rippling back towards the enemy camp. He waved his hand towards the reed-beds and two men dashed off to follow the commands they had received earlier that morning.

Time was short.

Hereward whirled, thrusting his blade towards the sky. 'We are the English,' he yelled. 'The Norman bastards have slaughtered our brothers and stolen our land. But we will not bow down. We will not be beaten. We have fire in our hearts, and today, by spear and axe and sword, we will bring about Judgement Day.'

CHAPTER THIRTY-FIVE

'Still your tongue. I am trying to save your life,' Harald Redteeth growled as he hauled Acha along the track from the camp. 'Though why Deda thinks it is worth saving, I cannot fathom.' He ground to a halt and frowned as he listened. Dim cries rolled up from the jumble of huts along the causeway. He peered towards where the carpet of mist rolled across the wetlands, but could see nothing amiss.

Acha tried to wrench her wrist free from his grasp, but his fingers were like iron. 'You lie,' she spat. 'Deda was already leading me away.'

'Deda was walking towards his own death.' The Viking glared at her. 'I know his mind well enough to know he could never have slain you. And if he had set you free, the bastard king would have taken his head. Now he has good reason. You had a friend who struck him from behind, and then you escaped together.'

The woman narrowed her eyes, still unsure. 'Why would you risk your own neck to aid him?'

The Viking snorted. She would never understand. But he could hear the words of his father echoing across the seasons and he knew the right path to take, as he always knew. 'Keep up,' he growled, dragging her on. 'We cannot afford to be seen.'

Down the track they hurried, towards the settlement and the empty marshland beyond. More cries rang out, death-screams this time, and the clash of iron.

Cursing under his breath, Redteeth ground to a halt. Fighting. Would the English be so foolish as to risk an attack? He looked back towards the camp and heard a yell. The lookouts upon the walls had seen some threat.

'What is wrong?' Acha asked. She looked around with unease, no doubt worried that she would be recaptured when she was so close to escape.

Before the Viking could respond, he heard the sound of feet. Glancing back, he saw warriors streaming out of the camp towards him. With a snarl, he scooped the woman into his arms and ran among the huts. Stopping at the nearest workshop, he wrenched open the door. It was deserted. Prized woodworking tools were scattered across the ground. The owners had fled when they heard the sound of fighting, he guessed.

Nodding his approval, he thrust Acha inside. She sprawled across the straw. When she looked up, she bared her teeth and glared at him.

'For your own good,' he growled. 'Do not step outside or you will be seen and taken back to the camp. Do you hear?'

After a moment, she gave a sullen nod.

'I will fetch you when it is safe.' He slammed the door and dragged a water trough in front of it for good measure. Battle-cries rang out all around. Norman soldiers raced along the track beside the causeway. Redteeth cursed once more at the bad timing, and ran to join the fight.

CHAPTER THIRTY-SIX

Smoke whipped up in the wind. Bright blades of flame
flickered among the field of trembling reeds as the blaze
caught hold. Amid a swirl of sparks, two English warriors
clambered out of the dry beds and darted towards the
jumble of ramshackle huts lining the causeway. Jerking open
the door of the nearest, one hauled out a yelling woman
and a young girl. The other dashed inside. Once he had kicked
the embers in the hearth across the straw beds, the two men
raced on to the next hut. The crowd swelled. Terror lit
faces.

'If you want to keep your lives, leave now. Return to your
villages,' Hereward bellowed. 'All here will burn.'

The Mercian watched the panic begin as anguished folk
scrambled to save their meagre possessions. They would hate
him, for now. But all their lives would be better once those
flames had consumed everything the Normans had planned.
For a moment, he watched the choking clouds billow up and
the orange glows start to shine through the open doors. He
grinned, satisfied. Fire was the greatest weapon of all. Deadlier
than Brainbiter, axe or spear, more destructive than the siege
machines William the Bastard had amassed to crush the

English. And with it he would cleanse this good, black earth of its foul infestation.

Above the din from the burning settlement, Hereward could hear clamour drawing near as the Norman reinforcements hurried down the track from Belsar's Hill. They were as unprepared as he had hoped, pulling on their helms and hauberks as they came, stumbling and crashing into each other. Their commanders ran behind, yelling instructions to try to bring some order to the confusion. But the men saw they were racing towards not only an English attack but a growing inferno, and their ears were deaf to their leaders' exhortations. Yet when the Mercian squinted through the smoke, the stream of enemy warriors seemed to be unending. They outnumbered the English ten to one.

'We have a fight on our hands,' Kraki yelled as he kicked a dismembered body down the ramparts.

'We expected no less.' Leaping to his side, Hereward raced along the causeway to where the king's men were clambering up to defend their prize.

The Viking swung his axe with such force that the first man's helm spun into the air, his head all but sheared from ear to ear. Hereward glanced at the Northman. No battle-lust glowed in his eyes, only grim determination. His thoughts were with Acha.

The Mercian opened up the next soldier's throat. The Norman stumbled back into the men climbing behind him, clutching at his neck as blood gushed between his fingers. Hereward thrust down into the yawning mouth of a warrior yelling the Norman battle-cry, then rammed his foot into the chest of a third as he yanked his blade free.

At the foot of the causeway, the king's reinforcements milled, bewildered. Behind them, the conflagration swept through the huts and workshops and across the reed-beds so that it seemed a sea of flame was about to engulf them all. Along the causeway, shields slammed together in a wall of blues and reds and yellows, spears thrusting through the gaps at any Norman brave enough to attempt to attack. And on either flank, the English archers thumped shafts into the surging mass of soldiers. Men fell by the dozen, plunging under the feet of their brothers and stirring greater panic.

Sighard yelped with glee as the battle unfolded just as Hereward had told them. But beside him, Madulf only glowered. No smile would reach his lips until victory was assured, his brother knew. Hereward yelled out and the two men looked to him. He whirled his hand and they ran to their positions among the piles of timber assembled for the causeway construction.

Above the roar of the fire, a distant rumble echoed. Messengers had reached the Norman force sent out along the north road and they were returning to join the fray. On either side, Hereward saw the faces of his men harden. So few, they were, and their enemies so great in number, they seemed little more than straws about to be washed away by the spring floods.

He ran along the rear of the shield wall, punching the air as he urged his men to greater efforts. 'Courage, brothers,' he roared. 'One Englishman is worth ten of the Norman bastards. When we stand shoulder to shoulder our spears can thwart any attack, no matter how great.'

At the far end of the causeway, a group of the king's men had gained a foothold. Hereward glimpsed them hacking a path to one of the towers. As he tried to second-guess their tactics, Guthrinc ran up behind him and jabbed a finger. The Mercian followed the line of his arm to the summit of the tower, where the witch clawed her way from the top of a ladder on to the flat platform. 'Is she mad?' the tall man shouted above the din.

'Aye, mad, and crazed with hatred for the English church-men who drove her from her home.'

In front of him, one of his men fell back, his ankle hacked to the bone. Hereward thrust his way into the position, slotting his shield into the wall, and not a moment too soon. An axe crashed against the boss, jolting every bone in his body.

Gritting his teeth, he hacked down into the soldier's neck and kicked the body on top of the warriors beneath.

A cheer rang out along the English line. Disturbed by the sound, the Normans craned their necks round to see what had caused the jubilation. Hereward grinned; all was going as planned. The distant thunder grew louder still, and as the wall of smoke parted, he caught sight of Morcar and his army racing towards Belsar's Hill. The enemy was in disarray. From the edge of the camp, the music of war swelled, the clash of iron upon shields, the screams of the dying and the battle-cries of the English. All around, his men's faces flushed with fierce determination.

Behind him, another cry rang out. He glanced back to see Sighard and Madulf had set alight the causeway timbers. Some they had stoked around the foot of the nearest towers and the flames were already licking up the sides.

But that was the least of it, he saw. The two brothers had succeeded in the plan that had come to him when he had first spied the building of the causeway. The dry peat of the ramparts was on fire, the peat that ran under most of the fens in these parts.

His men had set the world itself alight. The Normans, and their hopes of victory, would be engulfed in the flames of an English-made hell.

CHAPTER THIRTY-SEVEN

By the gates, Deda jerked from his daze into a world gone mad. Black smoke swirled overhead, agleam with sparks. Cries of alarm echoed, and the din of battle hung over all. Pulling on their helms, warriors raced across the camp and out beyond the walls. The ground throbbed with the beat of hooves as five knights leaned across the necks of their horses and drove them on at a gallop from the castle ward.

Hauling himself to his feet, he tried to make sense of this madness. The last thing he recalled was a feeling of impending doom while he led Acha to the gates. Now he could see no sign of her.

Through the stream of soldiers, he caught sight of Rowena. Her head was bowed in deep reflection, or worry, and she seemed oblivious of the steeds thundering towards her.

He yelled a warning. Still she did not look up.

Within a moment she would be crushed beneath the horses' hooves. As she stepped out on to the track, Deda hurled himself in front of the chargers. The deafening rumble enveloped him. He sensed the steeds a whisker away, could almost feel their hot breath upon him, and then he crashed against Rowena, pitching her out of the path of danger.

With a cry, she jolted from her dream and gaped at the disappearing knights. As she realized how close she had come to death, she fell into Deda's arms in shock.

'My thanks,' she gasped.

Her head rested against his chest for only an instant. Then she recognized where she was and yanked herself back in embarrassment and discomfort. Running her fingers through her hair, she refused to meet his gaze.

'You must take care,' he began, silently cursing himself for his awkwardness.

'I know.' She kneaded her hands, a sign, he thought, of her self-loathing. He bowed and stepped away, not wanting to see her suffer any more.

Another horse thundered by, and when Deda looked up he saw that the rider was William de Warenne. The nobleman looked afraid for his life. At the gates, he urged his mount west, away from the camp, and the fens.

Fleeing, the knight thought, puzzled.

A moment later, the king stormed past with a face like thunder. Odo of Bayeux, the Butcher and four more of his closest advisers swirled in his wake.

Glancing back only once to see Rowena hurrying away, Deda ran after the monarch. Outside the gates, William looked out over the scenes of battle in horror. 'How has it come to this?' he roared.

'We were unprepared,' Taillebois said. 'The English are cunning bastards.'

The monarch shook his fist in the air. 'We had them by the balls! This should not be!'

Deda looked at the devastation the English had wrought already and saw that the king's men were in danger of being crushed, as William himself must surely have recognized. Should they fight, and risk being torn apart, or run?

He searched the monarch's face. Behind the fury, he thought he glimpsed the first flicker of doubt he had ever seen William display. The Bastard had underestimated the English, and he knew it.

'My lord,' the Butcher pressed. 'What do you command?'

The king snarled. 'I will have Hereward's head if it cost me all the gold in England.'

CHAPTER THIRTY-EIGHT

The fenlands were burning. Silhouetted against the wall of flames that seemed to soar up to the very heavens themselves, Hereward looked out across the destruction he had wrought. Reed-beds and willow woods, ash trees and sedge, the makeshift settlement and the causeway, even the very earth itself, all was ablaze. There was no sky, only a suffocating pall of smoke from horizon to horizon, swirling with vast constellations of golden sparks. Along the track to Belsar's Hill the Norman army cowered, a river of iron grown slow and turgid amid the conflagration. The king's men milled about in terror, not knowing which way to turn. The English archers rained arrows down upon them. The roaring of the inferno drowned out the screams.

On the hilltop, the camp shimmered in the heat haze. As Hereward squinted, trying to see William the Bastard's standard flying above the castle, he shuddered. A troubling notion gripped him that he had lived through this moment many times before. In truth, he realized, he had been dreaming it all his life. Here was his destiny: a burning world and he the devil that oversaw it.

'We have the bastards,' Kraki yelled beside him. His face was flushed and sweat streamed down his brow. He flashed a questioning glance.

'We will find her and bring her home,' Hereward replied, clapping a hand on the Viking's shoulder. He spun round and thrust his sword into the air. With a roar, he slashed his sword towards the enemy. His warriors answered him with one voice, their thunderous cry rolling out as they threw themselves down the ramparts. Spears rammed into the churning soldiers, ripping through chests and necks and faces. The shield wall held firm. Back the Normans were driven, and further back still, until those at the rear of the enemy ranks were plunged into the fire sweeping through the causeway settlement. Some ran, pillars of flame setting alight their brothers. Most were consumed in moments in the furnace heat.

The Mercian almost felt pity for the hated enemy. They fought battles the way they made their ledgers and raised their taxes, line by ordered line, a relentless procession that crushed all before it. They were not ready for this madness of the English wild men.

Hereward dashed along the burning causeway to find a better vantage point. Once the billowing smoke had cleared, he could see that Morcar's seasoned warriors were carving through the king's men near the camp.

The Normans were being routed. The causeway was crumbling. Victory was near.

But not yet assured. A shriek rang out across the din of battle. Hereward craned his neck up and saw the witch poised at the top of the nearest tower. Her skirts were raised and she was showing her arse to the English warriors. When her contempt had been seen by all, she spun round and threw her arms towards the heavens. In a voice that was near a scream, she intoned the words of her spell. The Mercian did not recognize the language, but he saw the effect it had upon his men. As they fought, they twisted their heads up towards the witch as if they expected to be struck by a lightning bolt or turned to salt. Fear was sapping the passion from them, he could see. Their attack slowed. The shield wall buckled here and there. Spears danced off mail instead of tearing flesh.

And as the English courage ebbed, flashes of determination lit the faces of the Normans as they redoubled their efforts. Swords and axes crashed against the English shields, at first holding the advance, then driving it back. Soon the greater numbers of the Normans would prevail.

Wrestling with his conscience, once more he looked up at the witch yelping her spells. It mattered not whether the Devil answered her calls as long as his men and the Normans believed it would be so. Sickened, he glanced around until he saw Guthrinc. Beckoning the tall man over, he pushed aside his guilt and pointed at the witch. 'Take your bow and end her days,' he yelled.

Guthrinc nodded. Nocking a shaft, he took aim and fired. The arrow fell short. The witch shrieked louder at his failure. The Normans must have believed her protected by the Devil himself, for they crashed against the shield wall like a winter sea. The tall man remained as calm as if he were hunting grouse. He selected another arrow and braced himself.

This one rammed into the wise woman's chest. She must have died instantly, for her shrieks snapped off and she pitched over the tower's edge into the inferno. Hereward's stomach clenched and he turned away. Never before had he caused any woman to be killed.

'The Devil has called her home,' Guthrinc muttered with a shrug. 'And all is well with the world.'

As the flames surged up the footings of the tower, Hereward watched the Norman blades slow once more. Their hope had died with the witch. Much good would come of this crime, he tried to tell himself. Forcing his thoughts aside, he roared, 'We are English. We will not be broken. Run before us, you Norman bastards. Flee for your lives.'

Whipped up by the wind, the walls of flames rushed towards Belsar's Hill along both sides of the fighting. The English kept their heads low, grimly fixated upon the enemy. Hereward felt proud. He had told them all that fire was their friend. If they put their faith in God, they would have nothing to fear. But the Normans saw only a vision of hell. Stupefied by terror, many could not even lift their weapons. Spears tore them apart. Others ran, consumed by madness, and trampled their own brothers or fell into the conflagration that they were trying to escape. And still the English arrows rained down upon them.

'This is a slaughterhouse,' Madulf said, gaping.

'No worse than what they planned for us,' Hereward shouted. His throat was hoarse from calling above the deafening roaring of the blaze. 'Let them die, as they let the north die.'

A messenger scrambled along the burning causeway, his face streaked with soot. He was barely more than a lad, who had spent most of his days carrying wood for the hearth-fires in Ely. 'I have word from Earl Morcar,' he cried, his eyes darting all around as he tried to shield his face from the heat. 'The king is running!'

Word must have reached the Normans at the same time, for Hereward could see those at the rear of the ranks taking flight in all directions. Some fled into the marshes, others raced towards the camp, where Morcar's men were waiting to pick off any they encountered.

'Kill every Norman you find,' Hereward bellowed to his warriors. 'Leave no man standing.'

Consumed with blood-lust, he hurled himself into the battle. But barely had his sword cut down two Normans when Sighard grabbed his arm.

'There is a woman screaming,' he cried, pointing towards the last of the huts and workshops standing in front of the wall of fire. 'They say it is Acha, trapped.' Hereward glanced to where Kraki was carving a path through the fleeing Normans, and then threw himself towards the fire. Sighard tried to block his path. 'You are mad. You cannot save her – no one can. The fire is moving too fast. You will be burned alive.'

'If I do not return, tell Kraki I tried,' he shouted, and then he thrust the other man aside and raced into the smoke.

Chapter Thirty-Nine

The inferno scorched Hereward's lungs as he dashed among the last of the huts and workshops not yet alight. His skin seared as if he had been suspended over a smith's forge. Around him, the world shimmered in a glassy haze, a world of towering flame and walls of sparks and choking smoke, all of it pressing so tight against him he could barely draw a breath. Sighard had been right; he would not last long in that heat of a thousand suns.

Driven by the wind, the flames leapt from hut to hut faster than a man could walk. He blinked away stinging tears and yelled Acha's name, but the roaring of the fire snatched his voice away. All around him, Norman soldiers staggered. They would rather try to pass through hell than be caught between his men and Morcar's, and put to the spear in the slaughter.

Hereward ignored them, whirling back and forth until he glimpsed a familiar face struggling through the stifling smoke. Clutching a hand across his mouth and nose, Redwald was fleeing towards the marshland. All thoughts of Acha flooded from the Mercian's head. Only the lust for vengeance remained.

With a snarl, Hereward snatched out his sword. His

brother's eyes widened in shock and he lurched back. The blade cleaved only smoke.

Redwald ran like a rabbit trying to escape a fox, but he could see no way out. The fire reached out its arms to encircle them both. Hereward felt pain blaze through his chest, but he was in the grip of his devil now. He cared not that the inferno was sapping his life as long as his brother was made to pay.

He hacked again. Redwald ducked beneath his sword and rolled across the ground. Strands of smoke rose from his hair where the sparks singed, but it was terror of Hereward that the Mercian saw in his brother's eyes.

When the warrior advanced, Redwald scrambled into a stumbling dash, but fell once more. He wrenched his head round to gape at the demon behind him.

As Hereward took a step towards his prey, a hand grasped his arm. He whirled and saw Harald Redteeth, the red glow of the conflagration reflected in his black eyes. Hereward's sword flashed up, but the Viking clashed his axe against it and shook his head. He yelled something that was lost to the roaring and pointed through the blazing huts. Hereward felt baffled by the actions of his hated enemy. The Northman tried to drag the Mercian a few paces before shouting again. This time Hereward thought he understood the word 'woman'.

Concern for Acha rushed back into his mind and he felt a pang of guilt that he had given in to his own desire for vengeance with such ease. As the Viking ran off, he followed, pausing only once to look for his brother. But Redwald was nowhere to be seen.

He caught up with Redteeth at a workshop at the centre of a firestorm. Flames consumed the huts all around and one of the blazing shacks had collapsed against the door. Shrouded by smoke, the Northman was slamming a foot repeatedly against the wall. Sparks glowed in his beard. His lungs afire, Hereward hurled himself at the hut. Flames already danced across the roof, the wood blackening and sagging.

Time and again, the two men crashed against the steaming

wood. Each time, Hereward reeled. In the heat delirium, he dreamed his father stood at his shoulder, watching his failure. But then the wood splintered, and cracked, and with a final heave it shattered inwards. The two men sprawled atop the broken boards.

As he pushed himself up, Hereward glimpsed Acha lying face down on the far side of the workshop. She was not moving.

Smoke rushed in. Above his head, the roof split and shards of burning wood began to rain down. A moment before the roof collapsed, the Mercian hurled himself across the workshop. He choked on a searing blast of air as a wall of flames roared up, trapping him. No longer able to see Redteeth, or the way out, he dropped to his knees and grasped Acha's hand. Her skin was scorching. He scooped her up into his arms. Surrounded by fire on three sides, he turned and faced the remaining wall. Smoking and charred, it bowed out.

He could hear his father now, cursing him, cursing his mother. His legs felt drained of strength and his chest ached from the effort of breathing. He knew his life was draining away. Wrapping his body around Acha, he threw himself at the wall. It folded before him as if it were made of parchment. Spikes of wood tore at his face and arms.

The last of his breath slammed from his lungs as he rolled across the ground only a hand's width from the next burning hut. Somehow he found the strength to haul himself to his feet.

Redteeth was watching him from the other side of the bank of flames. The Viking nodded, seemingly pleased with what he saw, and then he turned and loped away into the smoke.

Lost in a daze where his father and his brother circled him, Hereward staggered away from the inferno. After a while he realized he was on the edge of the marshland. He slipped into cooling water, and splashed handfuls upon Acha's face and arms. For long moments he lay there, recovering. Asketil and Redwald faded away. Only the roaring of the fire remained inside his head.

When Acha's eyelids fluttered open, he helped her to her feet. 'God watches over you,' he said.

Coughing the smoke from her lungs, she eyed him. 'No. The Devil.' She forced a smile.

He had seen the effects of fire and smoke upon men before, and thought that God had indeed watched over them both that day. With heavy steps, they trudged back towards Belsar's Hill.

As they climbed the slope, Hereward looked around and saw the scale of their victory. He could scarcely believe that all the long hours he had spent planning that day's attack had paid off so well. The causeway was destroyed. Norman bodies littered the track so thickly that it was impossible to walk without stepping on a corpse. The English army milled around as if at the midwinter fire feast.

A figure detached itself from the other men and hurried towards them. When the strands of smoke separated, he saw it was Kraki. The Northman all but swept Acha into his arms. The Mercian grinned at his dour friend's joyous relief and turned away, leaving them to their reunion. Wearily, he made his way to Guthrinc at the summit of the hill.

The tall man swept out an arm and said, 'Look on your works.'

Hereward looked back. The whole of the fens was alight. The peat was burning, deep down into the ground, and would burn for months, if not years, to come.

'Surely no man, not even a king, would challenge a warrior who could do such a thing,' Guthrinc added with a wry smile. 'Be assured, Hereward of the English, the memory of this day will live for ever. The Normans have fled. You have won.'

CHAPTER FORTY

England had become hell. Where once there would only have been a sea of shadow, the entire western wetlands glowed orange and gold. Flames surged up to the vault of heaven. Where once there would only have been silence, the night shuddered with the roaring of the inferno, and the spitting and cracking as the ancient woodland was consumed. The meres shone like the sun. A pall of smoke choked out the stars. And the wind whisked sheets of glimmering sparks through the night.

Hereward stood on the Speaking Mound at Ely, entranced by the destruction he had wrought. He felt the call of the fire deep in his gut where his devil hid. Let all the world burn, it whispered, for it will be a kinder place in the ashes.

He jerked from his dream as a woman plucked at his hand. Ely rushed in, a whirl of song and laughter and thunderous life. More flames danced, this time before his eyes. The bonfire whooshed up higher as red-faced boys hurled more wood upon it. As he peered down the slope, it seemed for a moment as if all the English had gathered there. Ely folk and the multitude who had swarmed to the Camp of Refuge covered every patch of mud and grass on the isle, among the houses and down to the very walls themselves. They swilled back ale and mead and wine looted from the Norman camp, and gnawed on slabs of hot beef and pork from the row of carcasses turning slowly on spits over the beds of hot coals. They sang and danced and cried and kissed.

Music throbbed into the night. Ten men drummed on hides pulled taut over casks. Others plucked at lyres as they sang songs from days long gone, of victory, fire and blood. A white-haired man leapt around the fire. His wolf-like howls punctuated the words of the singers as he drew a bow across a three-stringed instrument that Hereward had never heard played before, a rebec. As the player sawed, the music reeled with flourishes that made the heart swell.

Hereward grinned. The folk had earned their jubilation. They had stood by him through all the hardship, the long seasons of want and the oppressive terror that the Normans would sweep in and slaughter them all. They had placed their trust in him, and he had not let them down. He would thank God for that, with an offering at the shrine of St Etheldreda later that night.

The woman, bright-eyed and pink-cheeked, plucked at his hand once more, urging him to join the dance. He smiled and shook his head.

'Join them. Let them carry you on their shoulders. It will be good for them, and you too.' Kraki clambered up the mound to stand beside him. His eyes gleamed in the firelight. A cup of mead sloshed in his hand, but he was not yet drunk.

'There is still work to be done.'

'Your trouble, you Mercian bastard, is that you know only how to fight, not to feast.' He downed his drink, then raised the cup into the air with a roar. 'Drink. Let your worries wash away. Let your heart rise up. These times come few and far between in this grim life, and we should hold them to us as much as we can.'

Hereward smiled, knowing the other man was right. But Kraki was correct, too, that celebration did not come easily to him. He was always looking beyond the next ridge to where the ravens gathered. 'One battle has been won, and a great one,' he replied. 'The king has been sent away with his tail between his legs, and we stand on the brink of all that we have fought for – the bastard Normans driven back across the whale road and the crown once again upon a deserving head. We cannot rest until we have walked that last mile.'

Kraki sighed. 'You are a miserable bastard. You would have us all brooding over our cups, and silence in the feasting halls, I suppose.'

Hereward laughed. 'There will be time enough for feasting. When the Normans are gone, we can lay down our arms for good and enjoy the peace that will come.'

Kraki's smile faded, and he eyed Hereward from under his heavy brows. 'You think there will be peace for men like us? We were born with axes in our hands.' He nodded towards the surging crowd. 'Peace is for those folk. So they can raise their children and fill their bellies and tell tales of these dark times by the hearthside on winter nights. But for us?' He shook his head.

Hereward watched the feast. 'There is some wisdom in that thick head of yours. You hide it well.'

Kraki grunted. 'I drink to forget these things, and on the morrow I will have a sore head to end them all.' He shrugged, not caring. 'You have plans to finish off the Normans?'

'In the morn we send messengers to Malcolm in Scotland, and to the Danes. If William the Bastard is attacked on two or more fronts, as Harold Godwinson was, he will be torn asunder if he tries to resist.'

Kraki frowned. 'You do not fear we are inviting two devils to sup by our hearth?'

'If devils they be, they sit at the feet of William the Bastard. Once Malcolm and Sweyn Estrithson have seen how we have crushed the Normans, they will tread carefully.' He took a cup of ale from a girl of barely fourteen summers. She blushed and bowed her head as if he were some king, and not a warrior with blood under his nails. 'And as those messengers set sail, we will send others out across England, to Mercia, and Northumbria, Wessex and beyond, and we will bring the English to their feet. On this axis England turns, and turn it will.'

'The English will for ever praise the day you came home, and brought your sword with you,' Kraki said, clapping the other man on the back. In search of more mead, he took a few steps down the mound and then turned back. His scarred features had softened, an unfamiliar sight. 'Hereward . . .' he began in a hesitant voice. 'You have my thanks . . . for Acha . . .'

The Mercian nodded, holding his gaze for a moment, and then the Viking trudged on his way. Hereward watched him push his way through the throng to where Acha danced. A nod, a smile, a moment of tenderness without words. The Mercian felt warmed to see his battle-brother finding such unexpected comfort amid the bloody life they had shared.

Hereward drained his cup and then turned towards the minster lowering on the top of the hill. Candlelight glowed in the windows. He winced, his burns still sore despite the unguents the leech had slathered all over him.

As he began to climb the slope, he spied Morcar sitting among some of his most trusted men. The horse-faced earl's features were dark. No jubilation there, the Mercian thought. Abbot Thurstan stood beside him, his head bowed in reflection.

'You have the thanks of the English. This great victory would not have been earned without you,' Hereward called. Morcar always had to be treated like a maid on the night of her handfasting.

The earl looked up. 'Would that my brother were here to see it.'

'Think of days to come. Soon you will be back in Wincestre, at court, with the cheers of all ringing in your ears.'

Morcar's eyes gleamed, no doubt with thoughts that one day the crown would be his. 'Whatever God wills,' he said. 'And yet I see storm clouds ahead. If the king had been killed here, all would have been well. But the Bastard yet lives, and worse, he has been humbled. His vengeance will be terrible indeed.'

'Let us not sour this night with such talk,' Thurstan murmured. 'I will pray for us all.'

'Fair advice, Father,' Hereward said. 'We will deal with the king in good time.'

Leaving the earl to his brooding, the Mercian climbed the hill towards the minster enclosure. In his pouch he had plunder, a ring of silver taken from the finger of one of his Norman victims. He hoped it would be an acceptable offering at Etheldreda's shrine.

The church smelled of fresh incense. Lit by a halo of candle-light, a figure was hunched on its knees in front of the altar. Alric looked round and smiled.

'Has the feast ended so soon?' he asked in a sardonic tone.

'The mead will not be gone before I return.' Hereward grinned. 'You will be pleased, monk. I come to offer tribute at the shrine of Etheldreda.'

As Alric walked along the nave, Hereward thought he looked more at peace than he had ever seen him.

'It has been a long, hard road to this night.' The monk shook his head with disbelief. 'After our first meeting in Gedley, who would have guessed we would be standing here, together.'

'I remember it well. Blood and wolves and fire and a monk who whined like a child with a thorn in his thumb.'

'We have both learned much along the way.' Alric smiled to himself, remembering.

'From each other.' Hereward winced as he recalled the bloody trail he had carved across England when his devil rode him freely. Would he ever have learned the skills he needed to win such a great victory . . . would he even have survived . . . without the monk's influence to help him tame that part of him? 'I owe you much,' he said, for the first time.

The monk looked surprised, as if this was some great revelation. 'All you did, you did yourself. If I nudged the tiller here and there on the course of your life, then I am happy, but it was no more than that.'

'We can argue about this until dawn, monk, and God knows we like to bicker,' Hereward said with a laugh.

Alric's smile faded and he grew serious. 'Dare we dream, then, of an England free from the conqueror's yoke? Aye, and an end to this struggle?'

'We are closer than we have ever been since we took up arms. We have William the Bastard on the run. Now we need only to harry him.'

The monk raised his eyes in thought, marvelling at what crossed his mind. 'And what then for us? Days without want and war? What will we do with the hours?'

Hereward forced a smile, but Kraki's words still weighed on him. 'What will you do?'

Alric furrowed his brow. 'I have given it little thought. Perhaps return to the monastery at Jarrow . . . ? His voice tailed off. Hereward thought he saw a shade of sadness in his friend's face, as if the monk had recognized something that he had not yet found the words to define.

The sound of running feet echoed off the stone.

'What is amiss?' the churchman called, peering into the gloom beyond the candlelight.

Five monks came running along the nave, calling the name of Abbot Thurstan. Alric caught one of them by the arm.

'The bones of St Oswald are gone,' the man cried out, 'taken from the locked and hidden relic box.'

'Who did this?' Hereward growled. He sensed a looming disaster a moment before the monk gave words to it.

'God has withdrawn His support for the English,' the man gasped. 'We are abandoned.'

The Mercian thrust his way through the knot of monks and strode to the door. Alric hurried after him. At the enclosure fence, they slowed their step. The music died away, the drums stilling one by one. The singing and the cheering and the chatter ebbed. A great silence was falling upon the English.

Hereward stood at the gate and looked down the slope. Word of the theft was rippling out across every man and woman there. God had abandoned them, that was what they were hearing. At the moment of their greatest victory, they had been judged and found wanting.

'This is not God's work,' Hereward said, his voice hardening. 'No, there is a Judas among us, someone who, even at this late hour, does not want the English to be victorious. We cannot rest until we find him.'

CHAPTER FORTY-ONE

Frost glistened on the sunlit grasslands. In the enclosure, the horses stamped their hooves and snorted, their breath steaming as the boy tossed hay for their feed. The sharp apple tang of their dung drifted in the air. Rowena pressed her cheek against the rough wood of the barn door. Her chest felt tight, her breath short, and her hands trembled. Here was the moment of reckoning.

She shivered and pulled her cloak tighter around her. The cold had come early that year. It did not bode well. Peering out from her hiding place, she watched the serving girls hurrying with eggs held in the folds of their skirts. From the hut closest to her, she could hear the sound of rhythmic hacking as the butcher carved the carcass for the day's meal. Across the royal manor at Branduna, all were busy with their tasks.

Shielding her eyes against the bright morning sun, Rowena looked beyond the palisade to the dark smudge of trees that circled the great hall and its outbuildings. In times of peace, the king would be preparing to ride out there to hunt the deer that roamed in abundance among the dense woods. But now he brooded alone, worrying, no doubt, that power was slipping from his grasp. She smiled to herself. Hereward had done what she had not believed possible. These were the last days of the Normans, and even William the Bastard knew it. Soon her husband would be avenged.

Within her cloak, she closed her fingers around the hilt of the knife. It was a good blade, with a sharp edge and a handle of bone carved in the shape of a falcon. She had taken it from the chest of Galien, after they had lain together that last night in his tent. She had run him well, like a hungry dog eager for a bone. His wife cared little for him, and lay like the dead when he sought the comfort of her thighs, or so he had said. She remained at his manor, sewing away the days and nights, and he had brought Rowena with him to the king's war-court. No longer a mere whore, she was now the consort of a nobleman, and he had placed her among the king's serving women so she could supply his needs whenever he required.

She pushed aside her anger, and the queasy turn of her stomach, at the thought of lying with him. Her plan had worked as well as Hereward's. She had whispered honeyed words, and kissed demanding lips, and stroked arms and necks. She had flattered and feigned amazement at their strength and wisdom and prowess. And with every stinking, thrusting Norman bastard that had lain atop her, she had moved closer to the king himself.

Stepping out from the shelter of the barn, she hurried across the enclosure. She kept her head down, seemingly busy with her work. As she passed the brewhouse, steaming with sweet scents, she glanced over the wall to where the army was camped. Tents flapped in the chill breeze. Standards fluttered. The whipped Norman soldiers were licking their wounds and waiting for the king's next orders. Flee or fight, none of them seemed sure. Since the invasion, they had swaggered across the land with chins thrust high. An army that had never been, could never be, beaten. Now they walked with heads low and shoulders hunched. She had never seen them so dispirited.

She skirted the edge of the horse enclosure and slipped into the shade of the great hall. While the king agonized over his plans, he demanded solitude. Few of the army's commanders ventured to that place, and that had given her the opportunity for which she had been waiting for so long. The two-storey timber and wattle hall reeked of age. The Bastard had not yet begun to replace the old king Edward's hunting lodge with one of his new stone buildings. The doors were worn and badly fitting, so that draughts howled through when the wind was strong, and the thatch was thinning here and there. In the storm two nights gone, the rain had puddled on the boards.

Easing the rear door open, she stepped inside. She was in one of several small single-storey rooms attached to the main building. She smelled dust and woodsmoke. Once her eyes had adjusted to the gloom, she looked around. A broom leaned against one wall. Fresh logs had been piled high for the hearth. She crept through into the next room where a trestle was laid out with pitchers of wine and ale and fresh cups. The two serving girls who usually attended the monarch had gone off to fetch bread and cold stew for his meal. Only a short while remained before they returned. She hoped it would be enough.

Crouching beside the next door, she peered into the great hall. The vast space was filled with shadows. No candles flickered. The only light came from the fire crackling in the hearth. Long feasting tables stood to the sides, and tapestries hung along the walls, faded and threadbare now. Some seemed to show scenes of hunting and battle. At one end was a large chair of blackened oak on a dais.

The king had his back to her. Silhouetted against the fire, he looked as big as a bear. One foot rested on the stones around the hearth as he peered into the flames, brooding. He was wearing an orange tunic and brown breeches. That was good. She had only ever seen him in armour and always imagined him as the great war leader. Now he was just a man. She pricked her index finger on the tip of her knife to test its keenness.

Rowena's breath burned in her chest and she was almost afraid to take another for fear the monarch would hear. Though she had planned this strike for so long, she was afraid;

242

she could not deny that now. Not of being caught. She fully expected to be dragged out of that hall drenched in the king's blood and to be executed for such a terrible crime. After the murder of her husband, her life meant nothing. No, she was afraid of killing a man. She had never even raised a hand against anyone before.

For a moment, she closed her eyes and remembered Elwin's face. As she steeled herself, aware that time was short, the king hurled his cup across the hall in anger or frustration. He spun round, the fire lighting his glowering face so that for a moment he resembled a wild beast. Rowena almost called out in shock.

Muttering to himself, he began to prowl around the hall. One huge hand smashed into the palm of the other. His gyre grew wider with each circle of the hearth, and Rowena saw that soon he would draw close enough to her hiding place for her to strike.

She withdrew her knife.

The king's footsteps echoed nearer. Her body felt rigid, but her hand shook.

For Elwin, she thought, and crossed herself. *May God forgive me.*

She listened to the steady pace of his heavy tread. She watched his bulk block out the firelight. Soon, soon.

A hand clamped over her mouth and dragged her backwards. Her thoughts whirled away in shock, and by the time she had gathered herself enough to fight back, she been pulled through to the next room. Another hand gripped her wrist and shook it hard until she dropped the knife. Vainly, she tried to wrench herself free, but her captor was too strong. He spun her round to face him.

It was Deda.

When she saw him she was so surprised the fight went out of her. He released his hand from her mouth and pressed a finger to his lips.

'Are you mad?' he whispered, his face dark with disbelief.

She stuck out her jaw, trying not to show her dismay. All was

243

lost. But she would not give the Norman bastards any satis-faction. She would face her death with dignity. 'Call the guards,' she spat. 'I am not afraid.'

'If your tongue flaps any louder, you will summon the guards yourself.' Easing her into the corner of the room, he plucked up her knife and weighed it in his palm. 'I ask again: are you mad?' he said, shaking his head. 'You think you can kill a king?'

'All men can be killed. And he is a man, no more. One who has stolen the crown.'

Deda peered into her face, trying to make sense of what he had discovered. After a moment, his features lit. 'This was why you whored yourself. To get close to William so you could stick your blade into him.'

'For the murder of my husband.' She glared at him.

The knight softened. 'Your husband is dead. I am truly sorry,' he said with pity.

Rowena gaped. 'What kind of Norman are you?'

'One who would not see you harmed.'

Her mind reeling, Rowena stepped back and looked into the knight's face. Still she could see no cruelty there. 'Do not taunt me. Take me to the guards. I am ready for my punishment.'

'You have suffered enough.' He stepped to one side and swept out an arm to guide her through the door.

'Where—'

'We cannot talk here. We will be discovered.' He looked around the enclosure, making sure they would not be seen. When the butcher's boy had passed by, hauling a boar's carcass, Deda ushered Rowena past the horses and back to the shade of the barn.

'Why do you care if I am discovered?' she snapped.

'You are the eyes and ears of the English, here among us.' He smiled. Trying to show he is a friend, she thought. She looked away, refusing to be taken in. 'And the king has a nose for such a person,' he continued. 'Sooner or later you will be caught, and then you will be killed. And then I will be filled with sadness.'

Rowena shook her head. 'Someone must make William pay for what he has done.'

'There is no hope for your plan,' Deda said quietly.

She blinked away tears of frustration. 'I mean to do this, come what may. If you do not give me up I will come back again, and again, and again, until the Bastard is dead.'

'Then I will step in your way again and again and again.'

She stamped her foot and shook a finger in his face. 'Why are you tormenting me so? Do you take joy in my anger?'

The brewer appeared carrying a sieve filled with mash to take to the breadmakers, and Deda stepped in closer and hooked his cloak over his raised arm to hide her from prying eyes. Rowena looked up into his face, feeling the weight of his presence so close to her.

'Some say that trying to rule England will be punishment enough,' he said in a sardonic tone. But then his smile fell away, his features darkening. 'If William is to suffer, it will be God who makes that decision.' He glanced around the enclosure and seemed to reach a decision. 'I will take you back to your own folk, in Ely, so you will be safe.'

'Why would you risk your life to aid me?'

Deda only looked into her face, his features unreadable. Rowena felt the tears that had been building for so long rise up. The dam broke. In one rush, she remembered all that had been torn away from her, and the terrible sacrifices she had made, the throwing away of her future and her honour and her dignity, and all of it for naught. It had been hopeless from the very start. Shuddering, she felt her knees buckle, and she collapsed against him. And in that moment she felt even more sickened, for she was being comforted by one of the very dogs who had slaughtered the man she loved more than anything in the world.

CHAPTER FORTY-TWO

Waves of grey ash drowned the coals in the hearth. The hall was cold and dark, and Hereward's breath steamed as he clambered from his bed. Through the wattle walls, distant voices thrummed, too many for such a chill dawn. He felt uneasy, those anxious tongues caught up in the skeins of his troubled dreams. Stamping his feet for warmth, and clapping his hands, he pulled on his clothes and shoes and a thick cloak, and stepped out into the thin grey light.

The hubbub was rising from somewhere near the gates. He shook the last of the sleep from his head and tried to comprehend what he was hearing. The rest of Ely still slumbered. No smoke rose from the hearth-fires. As he trudged over curled leaves crisp with frost, he decided the voices were not urgent enough to signify an attack. Names were called. Orders were shouted.

The sound of running feet drew near, and Sighard and Madulf dashed from among the huts. Worry cast a shadow over their features.

'Hereward,' Sighard called. 'We were coming to wake you.'

'What is amiss?'

'It is Morcar,' Madulf gasped, resting his hands on his knees to catch his breath. 'He is taking his leave of Ely. And his army goes with him.'

Hereward frowned. Morcar, never trustworthy, always seeking his own gain. What was he hoping to achieve now?

He pushed past the other two men and loped down to the gates. Morcar's men milled around the walls, spilling out on to the track leading down the slope away from Ely. They were bleary-eyed and sullen at being stirred to action so early. Hereward thrust his way into the throng, throwing bodies aside as he searched for the earl.

He found the nobleman in deep conversation with one of his commanders. When the warrior neared, Morcar eyed him slyly, running one hand through his straggly blond hair.

'What is the meaning of this?' Hereward tried to keep his tone civil. The earl was thin-skinned and easily aggrieved. If Morcar took offence, there would be no reasoning with him.

'We have fought well together as brothers,' the earl replied with an unconvincing smile, 'but it is now time for us to part ways.'

'We have won a battle, not the war. There is still fighting to be done,' Hereward said, too sharply. He tried to read the plan he saw flickering behind the other man's eyes. Was this some ploy to gain a greater commitment from Hereward, perhaps the support of the English for Morcar's own bid for the crown?

'Our fighting is done,' Morcar replied, swinging one arm out to indicate his army. 'I gave my spears to you, as promised. But this agreement was not for all time.'

Hereward leaned in and said in a low voice so the others would not hear, 'You know we cannot defeat the king without your force.'

Morcar laughed. 'Where is the fire in your breast? The great Hereward! You can do aught that you set your mind to. The English will rise when you call to them. You will have an army greater than the few you see here. No, you have no need of us.'

Hereward gritted his teeth. Not a word that left the earl's lips rang true.

Kraki pushed his way alongside, scowling with fury. 'They have robbed us of our supplies,' he snarled.

'A few morsels for the road.' Morcar showed an innocent face. 'Would you see us starve?'

'Morsels? There is barely enough left to feed us,' the Viking raged. Hereward stretched out an arm to hold him back.

'The king is wounded, not dead, and that is when he is at his most dangerous. You said so yourself,' Hereward insisted. 'If you think this business done, or if you think you can bargain with him, you will find his teeth sunk in you in no time.'

Morcar only laughed. Hereward fought to hold back his rage. They were so close to victory he could almost taste it, yet in playing his games of ambition Morcar could snatch it away from them. His hand closed on the hilt of his sword.

Morcar saw the move and the false humour drained from his face. 'It will only benefit the king if we slaughter each other,' he said.

'It would be worth any price to see a snake put to death,' Kraki raged.

Hereward withdrew his hand. Morcar was right. The earl would fight out of pride, and they would tear each other apart. He had no choice. 'Let them go,' he said.

'And leave us short of food and men,' Kraki protested.

'Let them go,' Hereward thundered.

'I am taking one of your scouts to lead me along the secret path,' Morcar said. 'Those waters are treacherous and I could never navigate them alone.' Hereward felt sickened to see that triumphant grin.

'May they suck you down to Hel,' Kraki snarled.

Hereward drew the Northman away, barely able to control his own anger. When they were out of the crowd, he said, 'Morcar is right about one thing. Once our messengers spread the word and the English rise up, this morn will be forgotten.' He forced a grin, knowing he would have to work hard to keep spirits high. Kraki grunted, unconvinced.

As he walked up the slope, Hereward refused to look back.

He could hear Morcar's men beginning to sing as they started their long trek away from Ely. First the arm of St Oswald was stolen, and now this. But he would not be downhearted. Victory was still within their grasp.

CHAPTER FORTY-THREE

Blood streamed down the man's face. He blinked away the puddle in his socket and looked up into the face of the devil. Harald Redteeth grinned.

The Viking's fingers were knotted in the front of the wounded man's stained tunic and he raised him up slowly, staring deep into those terrified eyes. There was a power in watching a man die, in seeing the light slowly fade in the black of the pupil. It was an honour too. For that privilege, every warrior owed a debt to those they had slain, and in return should take a moment to usher them over the threshold into the Hall of the Fallen.

'You are not the first messenger to die,' he said, giving the man a shake so that droplets splattered from the gaping wound on the side of his head.

Behind him, horses snorted. The Norman hunting band waited further along the track that this man would have taken to Mercia. Redteeth could feel the eyes of Deda upon his back.

'Do not mourn for the life you have lost,' he continued. 'Nor should you think you have failed. There was never any hope of success.'

The man whimpered. Blood bubbled between his lips.

The Viking tapped the blade of his axe against the side of his victim's head. 'The English will never hear the call from Ely. We knew Hereward would send you messengers out. We knew when, and we knew where. We have eyes and ears in your camp. Every one of you who set forth now lies dead.'

In his last moments, the messenger seemed to find some depths of courage. His mouth hardened and his eyes grew cold. Redteeth felt proud of him for that. 'You will never defeat the English,' the man said.

In the trees waving in the breeze, Harald could hear the *alfar* laughing. He laughed too. 'The English are doomed. The king has sent out his own messengers, and they will tell all they meet that the men at Ely have been routed. No one will answer Hereward's call. What is left of your army is trapped on that isle. Time is short. The end of their days is close.'

The bravado drained from the messenger's face. His sacrifice was for naught.

'You will have a good death,' Redteeth said. Snagging his fingers in the man's hair, he yanked, and swung his axe.

With a grin, he held up the head for the Normans to see. Their faces were like granite. Deda, though, looked away into the willows. Something had been troubling him ever since they had left Branduna.

Redteeth wandered back to the knot of riders, swinging the head beside him. He hummed the tune that the *alfar* had taught him, the song of the dead as they walked the grey roads. 'We are done here,' he called to Deda, ignoring the other men. 'Let us ride hard. We can be drinking before the sun sets.'

Deda forced a smile. 'A day well spent at harvest,' he said with little humour.

Hoofbeats echoed from further along the road. Another band of Normans rode up, ten of them, and at their head was the king's new dog, Redwald. Redteeth spat. The man had the face of an innocent child and a heart as rotten and black as any man the Viking had encountered.

Redwald brought his mount to a halt. His gaze flickered over

Redteeth, as suspicious of the Viking as Harald was of him. Then he turned his attention to Deda. 'You are to come with me,' he said. 'The king's orders.'

'I do not hear the king's voice,' Redteeth said. He raised the head he was holding and peered into the dead eyes.

'I speak for him. You know that,' the younger man said, his cheeks colouring.

The Viking feigned distraction. He imagined hauling the Englishman into the trees and hacking his head from his shoulders. The notion pleased him.

His faint smile must have offended Redwald for he snapped, 'You have no voice here. I could see you killed.'

Redteeth looked up at him and grinned. He would not be able to rest until this bastard was dead, he knew that. And he could see from the other man's eyes that Redwald felt the same. The Northman turned his gaze to Deda and communicated his thoughts with a smile and a nod. The knight sighed and shook his head.

Annoyed, Redwald snapped, 'Follow me,' and urged his horse away. Redteeth clambered on to his own mount. Before they rode off, Deda leaned in and whispered, 'Every thought that passes through your head does not need to crawl out of your lips. You would do well not to anger that one needlessly.'

The Viking snorted. 'He is nothing. Less than that.'

'Still, I would take care. I know his kind. He is a viper, and you may well find that his poison will kill you days after the bite.'

They rode east along the road, deep into the fenlands. The growing shadows had begun to pool among the trees when Redwald brought them to a halt. He beckoned Deda over and exchanged a few words with him. Suspicious, Redteeth watched as the Normans tethered their horses and then slipped into the woods until they were lost in the gathering gloom.

'Follow my lead. Say nothing,' Redwald muttered to the Viking. 'You will not need your axe unless I am attacked.'

'You trust me to defend you?'

'You are responsible for me. If I die, the others will tell the king and he will hunt you down like a rat.'

'You think the king cares aught for you? You serve his purpose, for now, like the girls who bring him wine.'

Redwald ignored him, coaxing his horse into the gloom. They followed the track until it began a slow descent into a hollow. Through the ash trees ahead, Redteeth could see a campfire flickering. The whistle of a sentry rang out. Within moments, a wall of spears encircled them. Puzzled, the Viking looked around at the cold-eyed Englishmen peering at him over their shields.

'I am here for Earl Morcar,' Redwald said in a clear voice.

The Viking frowned. More of the king's manipulations? Had he truly prised Hereward's closest ally away from the fold?

Soon enough, the earl wandered from the direction of the campfire, surrounded by six of his huscarls, Northmen all, in furs and mail shirts and helms. He looked Redwald up and down with some suspicion, but Redteeth saw that the noble-man's eyes gleamed with hunger. 'You have news?' he said.

'Aye, but not here.' Redwald looked at the rows of spears and held out his hands. 'I have come unarmed, alone apart from this one guard who will protect me from the thieves who roam in these woods.'

'Where, then?' the earl asked.

Redwald pointed up the slope. 'Bring your huscarls, if you are afrit.' He smiled, pretending to be warm. Morcar's cheeks flushed, but he nodded.

The Viking rode close enough to the two men to eavesdrop as they rode back the way they had come. 'All is in place?' the earl asked with a sly smile.

'The king's power is fading fast,' Redwald replied. 'Many nobles are ready to move against him. You know these Normans . . . they plot and kill their own in search of power. That is the Norman way.'

'And this disarray will leave the way open for me to claim the crown,' the nobleman affirmed with a nod.

'The English have not forgotten the name of Earl Morcar, or the power you wielded alongside your brother Edwin. It will take a strong hand to hold the crown. Who better than you?'

'First, I must talk to those who will support me.'

Redwald nodded. 'I will give you their names when we have reached our agreement.'

'I remember you from the court,' Morcar said, glancing up at the other man. 'You had the ear of Harold Godwinson. He thought you loyal.'

'Aye, loyal I am,' Redwald replied.

To yourself, the Viking thought.

They reached the lip of the hollow and continued through the growing gloom. Redteeth watched Morcar smile to himself, his hunger growing with each step. No doubt he was lost to visions of a gold crown sitting on his head as he took the throne in Wincestre.

One of the huscarls muttered in his master's ear, and the earl asked, 'How much further?'

'I have made camp here,' Redwald said, pointing into the dark among the trees. 'There is salt pork and bread and ale.'

Licking his lips, Morcar nodded. 'My huscarls will keep watch so we are not disturbed. And once we have agreed . . .'

His words died in his throat as grey shapes rose up from the bracken on every side. The Normans rushed the group, swords drawn. Two huscarls were dead before they even realized they had been attacked. The others whipped up their axes, but they were surrounded in an instant. Swords flew up and came down, again and again. Redteeth glanced back to see if any of the army had heard the attack, but Redwald was clever. He had put enough space between them.

Morcar gaped, scarce able to believe he had been betrayed.

'Take him back to Branduna,' Redwald said to the Normans. A small smile flickered on his lips as he looked across at his captive. 'The king wishes to make you his guest in Wincestre. For many days to come.'

Horror dawned on the earl's face.

Once he had been herded away, Redwald grinned to himself. He seemed oblivious of anyone else's presence, the Viking thought. As the traitor faded into the dark of the woods in the Normans' wake, Redteeth heard his voice float back: 'And so begins the end.'

CHAPTER FORTY-FOUR

Six dead rabbits swung from the stick. Waterfowl hung from another rod, swaying as the men carried them along the narrow flint causeway. Guthrinc hummed to himself as he looked towards the dark clouds gathering in the north. Nothing seemed to trouble this giant of a man, Hereward thought, not hunger, not the hardship of a long trek through the wetlands nor the threat of more fighting to come.

'Rain is on the way,' Guthrinc mused to himself, cracking the knuckles of his large hands. 'And a lot of it, I would wager. But better that than an early snow.'

Hereward glanced back along the secret path through the wetlands. The waters lapped at the edges of the track and soon, as the tidal flow changed, they would submerge huge lengths of it. Little surprise that the Norman bastards had not been able to discover it.

Ahead of him, Madulf came to a halt and put down his basket of eels. He stretched his arms, frowning. 'This will not last long,' he said, eyeing his catch. 'There are many hungry mouths in Ely.'

'If God smiles on us, we will not be hunting for food for much longer,' Hereward replied. 'We can eke out our meagre supplies until the messengers return. And then . . .' He grinned.

Madulf looked up as a flock of rooks took wing from the stark ash trees lining the finger of solid ground to the west. As they blackened the sky, their harsh shrieks rang out. Guthrinc followed their flight, his features darkening. He turned to peer back along the path.

'What do those good eyes of yours see?' Hereward asked.

The tall man cocked his head. 'These good ears hear someone coming.'

At first the Mercian could only hear the wind rushing through the reeds, but then the beat of running feet came to him and he felt his neck prickle. He spun round and hissed to Madulf, 'Find your brother. Tell him to lead the men back to Ely as fast as he can.'

The sullen man screwed up his nose. 'Why? No one can find us here.'

'Wait,' Guthrinc rumbled. 'It is Herrig the Rat.'

Relieved, Hereward peered into the grey distance. A dark smudge loped into view. At first he could barely tell if it was man or beast. It kept low, bounding along the winding causeway, head twisting and turning. As it neared, he smiled. It was Herrig – Guthrinc's eyes never failed him. The rat-faced scout's tunic was filthy with the mud of the ditches that were his beds; his face was streaked with it and his hair matted.

'He is fast,' Madulf marvelled.

'Hungry to tell us what he has learned,' the Mercian replied. His brow knitted. Herrig *was* running fast, and something in his gait was troubling. The Rat glanced back, again, and again, almost tumbling off the edge of the track. When he was only two spear-throws away, Hereward saw that his eyes were wide with fear. He whirled. 'Run,' he barked at Madulf. 'Find your brother.'

Wind whistled past his ear. He jerked to one side instinctively.

A crossbow bolt slammed into the centre of Madulf's forehead. He reeled back from the force of the impact, his eyes rolling up until only the whites were visible. Blood trickled down his pale face, and he fell, dead.

'Run,' the Mercian yelled. 'The Normans are coming.'

Rabbit and fowl carcasses splashed into the dark water as the men sprinted along the narrow causeway. Hereward snatched up Madulf's body and flung it over his shoulder. Herrig scrambled at his heels.

'An army,' the scout gasped. 'The Normans have sent their whole army to close off the path.'

Blood thundered through Hereward's head. He pushed aside all thoughts of how their hated enemy could have found the sole route out of Ely, and his grief at Madulf's death. Survival was all that mattered. He waved Herrig ahead of him, knowing the weight of the body would slow him, but he could not leave their fallen brother behind.

Another bolt whisked by.

Hereward glanced back. A stream of Normans rushed along the flint track. He could see no end to the line. Yet their heavy armour would hinder them, he knew, and whenever the cross-bow men stopped to load and fire they would grind to a halt.

The causeway curled through dense reed-beds and across a rot-reeking bog. At times, the stones were lost beneath the mud and the sluice, so high was the water-line. He felt as if he were skimming across the surface of the marsh itself. Behind him, the pounding of feet and the rattle of mail shirts never let up for a moment. When he reached the isle of Ely, his breath was burning in his chest. He hauled his aching legs up the winding road to the gates. Rows of anxious faces waited.

Once he was inside, the gates trundled shut behind him. The oaken bar crashed into place. Around him, the crowd pressed close, but all he could hear was a susurration of fearful mutterings. No one would dare give true voice to what they knew was coming.

'Make room,' he shouted as he laid Madulf upon the ground and snatched out the bolt. Sighard thrust his way through the crowd and fell to his knees beside his brother. At first, he could only stare in shock, and then grief tore through his features.

'It is true,' he cried. 'Oh, Madulf. Madulf.'

Hereward bowed his head. They had lost so many since the war against the Normans began, but he felt this brother's grief touch him more than most. After a moment, he tore himself away. From beyond the walls the sound of thunder echoed, a steady beat as the Normans clashed their swords against their shields. They were hungry for the fight, and for revenge for their humbling.

The Mercian clambered up the ladder to the walkway along the walls. Fat drops of icy rain began to fall. Guthrinc hauled his towering form up beside him and said, 'How did they find the path? Morcar?'

Hereward shook his head. 'He never learned its twists and turns, and I would never teach him. I knew he could not be trusted.'

'Then how?'

'The same one who stole the arm of St Oswald.' As heavy cloud lowered overhead and the light grew thin, he peered down the slope. The Normans were still out of sight, but the war-beat drew closer by the moment. If the enemy could keep the English contained, they could bring up their siege machines and supplies without fear of being attacked.

He stared out, trying to comprehend how their fortunes had turned so quickly. Victory had been so close. Now they were under siege in Ely, with a fractured army, little food and no way out.

The day of judgement was upon them.

CHAPTER FORTY-FIVE

Hard rain lashed the fenlands. Under a slate-grey sky, the icy water sluiced off helms and rattled against mail shirts as the iron army thundered out of the west. Each man was hunched into the storm that had turned day into night. Their black cloaks hung sodden, their pale faces ghosts in the gloom, their pace as relentless as the onset of winter. Through a sea of mud they tramped, the ground throbbing beneath them. The clash of swords against shields rang out even louder than the howling wind that tore through the leafless trees.

War was coming. Nothing could turn it aside now, not prayer, not plea. Days would end, for many.

Riders flanked the marching men. One thousand knights, there were, the most seasoned warriors in all Europe. Fighting men from Flanders and France, axes-for-hire from Rome and the hot lands beyond. The full force of the king's might bore down upon Ely.

Redwald wiped away the rain streaming down his face. When he looked across the sea of men, he felt a shiver of awe. He had ridden beside the old king, Harold Godwinson, to victorious battle at Stamford Bridge. That army had greater numbers, but most of the men were filthy ceorls wielding sticks and rocks. It had been nothing like this.

'Do you tremble to see the power I have?' The king's voice rumbled out above the blasting wind. He was a mountain of iron upon his chestnut stallion, his broad chest and shoulders straining at his hauberk. His mail gleamed in the half-light. His boy must have spent the entire night cleaning the rust and blood off it with sand and a cloth.

'It is great indeed. The English will surely throw down their arms the moment they see this army.'

William laughed without humour. 'If you believe that, I know your brother better than you.'

Glancing out at the desolate woods and bogs, Redwald shuddered from the cold. This world felt as though it was dying. All the colour was gone. Only dark browns and muddy greens and shadows remained, and all of it drenched. He should not be there. He wanted to feel the warmth of a hearth-fire and to sip wine and make his plans.

When he had woken to the confusion of snorting horses and many feet and competing voices, he had thought that Hereward had come for him. He still felt the weight of that moment of panic. Perhaps he had been caught up in the last of a nightmare. But no one could have been more surprised when he peered out of his door at Branduna and saw the army readying itself in the field beyond the king's lodge, with more reinforcements arriving by the moment. He had convinced himself that the king had been broken by his defeat at the causeway. The days brooding alone in his hall, refusing to speak to Redwald, or Asketil, or any of his other advisers. Redwald remembered worrying that all his dreams of advancement might be dashed. He had allied himself with yet another man of straw.

But when he had dressed and stumbled out into the cold to investigate, he had seen a different monarch. That morning William had been roaring orders across the enclosure, and laughing with dark amusement, filled with a vitality that had not been evident since the retreat from Belsar's Hill. What could have transformed him? He had tried to get close to him, but the king was too engrossed in his preparations, and he had been forced to return to Edoma's fussing and chattering. When she had demanded to know the king's plans, he had laid his hand across her face. She did not cry, though he had raised blood. She took the blow, as she always did, and she would be waiting for him in bed when he returned. But her questions had stung him. He hated not knowing what was happening. It made him feel weak.

He glanced back. The trail of soldiers reached as far as he could see, perhaps all the way back to Cotingelade. As he took in the numbers, he realized these new recruits could not have been brought up overnight.

'This plan has been long in the making,' he said, nodding to himself.

The king laughed. 'You are like a little spider, or you believe yourself to be. Sitting in your web, waiting for the flies to crawl closer as you watch all that transpires. But you do not see everything, little man.'

Little man. Redwald felt the heat rise in his cheeks. The king had never spoken to him that way before.

William eyed him, a faint smile on his lips. 'Clever men always think they have more wits than those around them. It has been the downfall of more than one who aspires to scramble to great heights upon the shoulders of others.'

Redwald felt a prickle of unease. He did not recognize the odd tone in the king's voice, but he felt there was a weight there.

'Do you think me clever?' the monarch continued.

Redwald squirmed. He could see the trap in those words. 'Your skills are many and great, my lord.'

'And you are as slippery as an eel. It has served you well, so far.' Shielding his eyes from the driving rain, William searched the landscape, for what, Redwald did not know. 'Here is a lesson for you,' he continued. 'Power is not won by armies alone, nor held by swords and axes. If that were true, Ivo the

262

Butcher would be king. Shake a fist in the air and all will look at it. But it is the hand behind the back that they should be watching.'

'Then at Branduna you were—'

'Waiting. Bartering. Some men must be led by honeyed words to the place where you want them to be.'

Redwald frowned. He could not understand what the monarch was saying.

'The walls of the English fortress at Ely were built by God. Water and wood, treacherous bogs. As long as those walls stood, the dogs were safe. I tried to break them down with a ram. But a man cannot bring down God's works.' He raised his hands, making a show of whatever was amusing him so. 'Only God can do that.'

'And God has shown you the way?'

William laughed long and hard. Unable to see the joke, Redwald felt his cheeks colour.

'Ely is no longer secure,' the king said when he had calmed.

The road petered out on the edge of the fens. Ahead lay only a vast expanse of perilous bogs and dark water reaching to the very shores of the whale road. Surely William did not plan to take his army along the old straight track and the causeway to Ely. Hereward had long since protected that route. The Normans would be picked off before they could get within an arrow's shot of the English stronghold.

The king urged his horse on, beckoning for Redwald to follow. Heads were raised as the two men rode by to the front of the column. Redwald looked away when he saw Harald Redteeth eyeing him. He hated the Viking without quite knowing why. When the king slid down from his mount and strode to where Ivo Taillebois waited, Redwald followed.

'Here?' William asked.

The Butcher pointed to a dense copse of ash trees. 'One warband has already gone ahead. The secret path is narrow and dangerous, but it is as we were told.'

A murmur ran through the men and Redwald realized they

JAMES WILDE

were looking out across the waters and pointing. He turned and peered through the downpour into the gloom. Torches flickered. A huge, dark shape was floating by. He squinted and saw it was one of the siege machines on a raft of hollowed-out logs.

The king nodded, pleased. 'You will reach Ely before the ballistae,' he said to Taillebois. 'Make sure they are well protected.'

Ivo grunted his assent.

William turned to Redwald and said, 'Go with him.'

Shocked, Redwald stuttered, 'I am no fighting man.'

'Would you not give up your life for me?' the monarch taunted.

Redwald gaped.

'Did you think you would find your way to the comforts of my court at Wincestre while all the hard work was being done?' the king enquired with a cold smile. 'No. I would think you would want to look in the eye of the brother you have betrayed and make your peace with him.'

Redwald felt a deep cold settle upon him.

'If God wills that you survive the coming battle, then so be it,' the monarch continued. 'And if not, your sacrifice will not be forgotten.'

Laughter rippled around. Redwald felt his cheeks colour once more. As the king was summoned away by one of his commanders, the Englishman turned and looked straight into the face of Harald Redteeth.

The Viking leaned in and whispered, 'It seems you do not have the power you thought. Not a master now, eh?' He shook his head, then gave a gap-toothed grin. 'We shall walk through the dark and the wild as brothers.'

Redwald felt queasy. It seemed that a shadow was falling over him, and he could not escape the feeling that he would not be returning from this battle.

Behind him, the king gave a cheery hail. He turned to see a group of men arriving, all of them cloaked and hooded. For

264

a moment, Redwald was not sure what he was seeing. But when the towering leader of the group threw back his hood, realization dawned on him. It was Thurstan, abbot of Ely, and the other men were monks.

William clapped the cleric on the shoulders, dispelling any notion that the churchmen had been taken prisoner. Redwald all but gasped aloud. The monks were now betraying Hereward and the English rebels whom they had once offered safe haven in Ely. This was why the king had laughed so loud when he had asked if God had shown him the way – Thurstan must have revealed the location of the secret path that would take the Normans to the walls of the English camp, bypassing all the defences. Scarcely could he believe the scale of this treachery. He edged closer to eavesdrop.

'You are satisfied with our agreement?' the monarch was saying.

'I have prayed hard and listened to God's counsel,' the abbot replied.

'And what does He say?' Redwald recognized the fleeting smirk he saw on William's lips. If anyone here was a spider at the centre of its web, it was the king.

'I have a duty placed upon my shoulders,' Thurstan began. He raised his head, trying to show strength.

William must have seen through the disguise as easily as Redwald, for he waved a dismissive hand. 'You will keep your land,' he said. 'You have my word on that. And your treasure . . . your crosses, and reliquaries and holy books,' he corrected himself with a smile, 'wherever you have hidden them, will be given safe passage back to your church, and they will not fall into any other hands, I will see to that.'

'The English cannot win,' the abbot said as if he were trying to convince himself.

'The English cannot win now you have revealed the secret path past their defences,' Redteeth muttered at Redwald's elbow.

'And I would not see the folk of Ely harmed in the coming

fight,' Thurstan continued, his voice faltering. 'I will deliver them to you. My word carries weight. If I say I will no longer support Hereward, all will turn their backs upon him.'

'And you have a gift for me?' The king held out his hand. His gaze never left the abbot's face, until the other man was squirming. Redwald watched as the monarch humbled the churchman, sucking out what little remaining power the cleric clung to. There was a lesson for him here.

Thurstan bowed his head for a moment, then turned and beckoned. Two monks stepped forward, heaving a chest between them. 'Here, then. The arm of St Oswald.'

The king's smile grew broader still. He turned and raised his arm. When the Butcher saw, the monarch snapped his hand forward.

Taillebois bellowed an order and the column of men began to move towards the copse. The soldiers surged around Redwald, carrying him along with the flow. He wanted to resist. He was afraid. But there was nothing he could do.

The rain lashed down. The gale ripped at his face. The murky light seemed to be fading fast. The tramp of feet and the steady crash of swords upon shields enveloped him as he was swept away from safety and the days that he had dreamed for himself. But even then he could hear the king's jubilant voice booming out above the storm: 'Now God sides with the Normans!'

CHAPTER FORTY-SIX

The tents billowed in the howling gale. Lines cracked. Beyond the walls at Branduna, sheets of rain whipped across the grasslands. Pools of grey water spread under the blackening sky, and the tracks that criss-crossed the near-deserted camp were little more than streams of brown mud.

Rowena pulled her cloak tightly around her. Buffeted by the wind, she was soaked to the skin by the stinging rain within moments of slipping out into the storm. She closed the enclosure gate behind her and set off among the tents. Only the serving girls had stayed behind in the hall, huddled around the hearth, sewing and singing. Some of the men were in the brewhouse drinking. But she could see boys running errands for the nobles who had not joined the king's foray into the east. The lads looked like drowned rats, tunics clinging, hair plastered to their heads, while the masters sat warm and dry awaiting their return.

Wiping the rainwater from her eyes, she tried to peer through the torrent. Deda was nowhere to be seen. Her heart fell, a little. She was not sure why. Since Elwin had been taken, she could barely understand any of her motivations.

She was lost, of that she could be sure.

Taking care not to slip, she crept along the track. If Deda still planned to aid her, she could not afford to raise any suspicions. In the febrile atmosphere that had hung about the king's men since the defeat at the causeway, a knight spiriting away a serving girl could be seen as a traitor helping a spy. She tried to tell herself that he was a Norman. What did she care if he suffered, or even died?

'Woman. Here.'

Rowena jerked round as the voice boomed out above the din of the downpour. An old man swayed drunkenly in the entrance to a tent. She recognized the English thegn who seemed close to the king: Asketil was his name. His hair was white and thinning and red veins threaded across his nose and cheeks, but there was a power to him that she found unsettling.

She hesitated, wondering if she should simply run away. Surely he would not pursue her through the storm. But then he barked his command again and she found herself drifting towards him. He held the flap aside and she stepped into the tent.

'Pour me wine,' he said, waving towards a pitcher.

With a trembling hand, she snatched up the ewer. The quicker she could do it, the quicker she could be away. Lowering her eyes, she handed the old man a cup of wine and then turned to leave.

'Wait,' he demanded, his voice hard. 'Stay.' He swilled back his wine and held out the cup again.

'My lord, I have duties—'

'Stay.' He glowered at her, the snap in his voice suggesting he would brook no dissent.

Rowena poured another cup. As she offered it, Asketil grabbed her wrist and yanked her towards him. She gasped and tried to pull free, but his grip was stronger than that of a man half his age.

'You would question my order?' he growled, his breath sour. 'You are here to serve. You do as I say.'

'Yes, my lord.'

When his face darkened, Rowena realized her eyes must have flashed with contempt at the suggestion she should bow to his wishes. She regretted it instantly. Asketil lashed out with the back of his hand. She spun away, dazed, and fell to her knees. As she gathered her wits, she tasted blood. And when she looked up into the old man's face, she all but gasped. His features were contorted with rage. It seemed to her at that moment that a devil had taken control of him.

Rowena raised one arm to plead for mercy, but the old man thumped his hand down again, and this time it was a fist. Her head snapped to one side. Pain lanced through her. Her face numb, she blinked away stars and tried to scramble to her feet.

Fingers snarled in her dress and hauled her upright. Asketil pressed his face close to hers. 'Women must be trained, like dogs, or they will bite the hand that feeds them,' he growled.

As she stared into his bloodshot eyes, she felt something break inside her. In a flood of emotion, she reeled once again from the torment she felt when she looked upon her husband's head, and from the sickening indignities heaped upon her by the men who had lain between her thighs, and from the disdain the old man had shown her, and from his blows. She rammed her hand between his legs and squeezed as if she were breaking the neck of a rabbit.

Asketil howled.

Her eyes stung with tears at the rush of euphoria she felt at this grand release and she wrenched free of his grip, her dress tearing. But as she scrambled to flee the tent, she heard a roar behind her that made her blood run cold. The thegn fell upon her like a wild beast. He threw her across the tent like a straw caught in the wind. Blows rained down. Feet crashed into her belly. The breath rushed from her, and then her wits.

When she came round, she was lying on her back in a cloud of agony. There seemed to be blood everywhere. She blinked the haze from her eyes and saw Asketil wiping his mouth with the back of his hand. He was shaking, though not from the exertion, she thought. His eyes gleamed with a strange hunger. He poured himself a cup of wine and downed it in one.

'I look at you and I see my wife,' he said, peering down at her. His voice rang with contempt. 'She failed me time and again. She bore me a son who was too weak to be of my blood. Then she would shield him each time I tried to teach him a lesson, and thereby drove that weakness deep inside him where it could never be healed.' He spat. 'Boys learn to be men through pain. A fist. A knife. A sword.' His eyes took on a far-away look. 'There was a chance to save the boy, but she took him away from me, that cunt. And then, when I had made her pay, he hunched over her body like a wolf, spitting and snarling, fingers crooked like claws and threatening to tear out my throat. There was no hope for him.'

Rowena levered herself up, wiping the blood from her eyes.

'Bow your head to me and call me master,' he said in a wintry voice.

'I will not submit to you.' She raised her head with defiance. 'Even though it should cost me my life.'

'Then cost you it shall.' He tossed his cup aside and advanced.

'Leave her.'

Rowena glanced back and saw Deda standing in the entrance to the tent. Rain streamed from his cloak into a puddle around his feet. She had never seen his face so hard, his eyes so cold. His right hand rested upon the hilt of his sword.

Asketil only laughed. He grabbed a handful of Rowena's hair and yanked her to her feet. She cried out and fought, but he shook her until her head rang.

'I said, leave her.' Deda's voice cracked with an anger that surprised Rowena. Never had she heard him anything but gentle, even when she had spat in his face. He flung back his cloak to show his now half-drawn blade to the thegn.

Asketil's features darkened. 'You would threaten me? I have the ear of the king. And you . . . you are nothing.'

'The king would take little convincing to loose my head from its shoulders, that is true.' The knight took a step forward. 'But

I will not . . . cannot . . . stand by and watch you harm a woman.'

The old man frowned, incredulous. 'You would risk your life for her?'

'For any woman.'

'You Normans keep your women in their place.'

Deda shrugged, said nothing.

Realization dawned on Asketil's face. 'I see it now. You are like my son, an infant mewling for his mother. Weak.'

'I would not wish to harm an old man,' the knight said, ignoring the taunt. 'There is no honour in this fight. Do as I say. Let her go.'

'I am still strong,' Asketil snarled. He shook Rowena again, with force, and as she cried out he snatched a short-bladed knife from the folds of his tunic. 'Boy,' he yelled. 'Boy!'

One of the serving lads ran in and stared at the tableau, aghast.

'You know this knight?' the thegn snapped.

'It is Deda, my lord,' the lad stuttered.

'If I am found harmed, or dead, you must tell the king. Do you hear?'

'Y . . . yes, my lord.'

'Go!'

The boy ran out from this tent of mad folk.

Asketil turned his attention back to Deda. 'Now you are unmanned. Draw your sword, wave it around and know that it is useless.' He laughed at his own words until the grim humour drained from his face. 'I will show you what it means to be weak. Watch.'

Rowena screamed as the old man swung back his knife hand to slash her across the face.

From the corner of her eye, she glimpsed Deda as he lunged, drawing his sword and hacking down in one fluid motion before the thegn could complete his strike.

The old man's own scream rang out and Rowena flew from his grasp. When she glanced back, she gaped in shock. Asketil's right arm lay on the ground. The thegn sprawled beside it, twitching as blood pumped out from the stump. The gore puddled around him so fast that Rowena could see he would be dead within moments. And yet still he showed a defiant face.

'You would kill an old man,' he croaked. 'There is no honour in you.'

Deda hovered over the thegn, watching the life-blood spill out of him. Rowena thought how devastated he looked, as if he had failed, not saved her life at all. He rested the tip of his sword against Asketil's chest. The old man never blinked, never showed anything other than contempt. The knight bowed his head and then leaned on the hilt of his blade. It slid into the heart, putting the thegn out of his suffering. A low, last breath rustled out of the old man's lips. Deda hung there for a moment, his head still lowered, his eyes closed.

After his silent prayer, he stood up and withdrew his sword. He wiped the blade clean on his cloak in what Rowena thought was almost an act of sacrament. Once he had sheathed the weapon he turned to her, and with tenderness helped her to her feet. When she peered down at Asketil, she felt oddly empty. No rage burned inside her at the brutality the old man had dealt out, nor did she feel any pity for his plight. He seemed a husk, nothing more. How could she or anyone have been frightened by him?

Her legs almost gave out beneath her, but Deda slid an arm round her shoulders and helped her to walk. 'You have doomed yourself,' she croaked. 'By this action, you have challenged the authority of the king. He will see you hunted down and killed.'

'A man is nothing if he does not have his honour. Whatever the cost, I must remain true to myself.' When she looked up at him, he smiled back.

Rowena felt emotion well up in her, and for a moment she thought she might cry. She rested her head on his shoulder and allowed herself to be led out into the storm. The icy rain seemed to numb her pain and she found renewed strength inside her. By the time they had crossed the camp, she was walking unaided.

Deda looked around to make sure they were not being watched, and then guided her to where two horses were tethered.

'Are you well enough to ride?' he asked. When she nodded, he continued, 'We cannot go to Ely. It is no longer safe there. But I will take you to your village and leave some coin with your neighbours so they can keep you through the cold season.'

'And what now for you?' she asked, trying to hide her worry.

'I have sworn my sword to the king,' Deda replied. 'I must fight for him at Ely.'

Rowena stared at him in disbelief for a moment, but she thought she understood. 'I . . . I would not see you harmed,' she blurted, surprising herself.

The knight grinned. 'Ah, that is one of my greatest wishes too.' He bowed. 'You have brought some light into my life, Rowena of the English. If you knew me, you would realize that is a wondrous thing.'

She felt puzzled by his words, but he would say no more. Within moments, they were riding into the storm. Branduna fell behind her, and the miseries of the life she had created for herself. What lay ahead, she could not tell.

CHAPTER FORTY-SEVEN

At the edge of the minster enclosure, black smoke swirled up into the storm. Roaring flames lit grim faces as a small crowd of mourners stared into the searing heart of Madulf's pyre. Pounding rain drenched them all, but none cared. Every loss felt like a knife to the heart, for they were kin in all but name, with bonds forged by suffering and sacrifice, Hereward thought, looking around.

His silver hair plastered to his scalp, Thurstan stood head bowed and hands clasped in the shadow of the church. Exhausted, it seemed. He had said his godly words, but whether they had brought any comfort to Sighard the Mercian could not tell. The young man stood closest to the fire, seemingly oblivious of the heat. His eyes were hollow and he stared too long and too hard.

Alric leaned in and whispered, 'If only we could have given Madulf a good Christian burial.'

'We do what we can. In flames, he is still committed to God. This is the old way.'

The monk nodded. Since the streams of English refugees had flooded to Ely, the churchyard had filled to the brim. And so, at Kraki's suggestion, they had set aside a corner of the minster enclosure for the burnings. But this pyre had been arranged with what could have appeared unseemly haste in other, more peaceful times. This day they could not even allow Sighard time to grieve.

Hereward half turned and peered through the sheets of rain down the slopes of the isle to the walls. Somewhere in the gloom beyond, the Normans were gathering. Still he could not believe that it had come to this. From near-victory to a desperate defence in the time it had taken for the storm to sweep in. Now they were no longer the masters of their days yet to come. They could only pray.

He strode forward and rested a hand on Sighard's shoulder. Rigid beneath his touch, the young man did not turn or even acknowledge his presence. Hereward winced at the sharp memory of his own grief at Turfrida's graveside. Sighard would not recover easily from this day.

He pulled up his hood and turned away. As Alric followed Thurstan into the church, the other mourners took his lead and in ones and twos they drifted away from the pyre and out of the minster enclosure. Only Sighard remained, an unmoving figure silhouetted against the flames.

Beyond the minster gates, Hereward heaved in a deep breath. The thatched roofs of Ely fell away from him down the hillside. In the eyes of the king, every man and woman there was as much an enemy as the English warriors. Leatherworker and smith, goodwife and farmer, all would pay the price.

'Worry not. They knew.' Acha appeared at his shoulder, following his gaze down the hillside. 'Everyone who answered your call knew. We had our hopes of a life free of the Norman yoke . . .' she paused, her eyes growing faraway, 'and of a return to the days we once lived . . . but none had any doubt that the risk was great.' She nodded to herself. 'It was a risk worth taking.'

'We are not done yet.'

She smiled in agreement, refusing to acknowledge the lie in his words. 'We still have fight left in us.'

Kraki, Guthrinc and Hengist strode up. 'What now?' the Viking said.

'We ready for battle,' Hereward replied. 'Gather the army, here, on the slope facing the gates. The Normans will attack from the front. It is the easiest route up, and they will have the numbers in no time. Our shield walls will remain strong?'

Kraki nodded.

'I will gather the woodworkers and their men, and any timber they have. The walls are solid, but the Normans will try to break them or burn them and we must be ready,' Guthrinc said.

Hereward scanned the hillside. 'I have work for you, hard work,' he said, turning to Hengist. 'Bring as many men as you can with shovels. We will arrange a surprise for the bastards should they enter Ely.' He grinned. Hengist clapped his hands with glee like a child. 'The Normans will expect us to lie down like lambs,' the Mercian continued. 'But the isle will run red with their blood. Are you ready?'

The three men grinned in turn. To their credit, none asked if they would win. No warrior went into battle thinking of victory, only of the fight itself. Fired up by the thought of the coming war, they set off down the slope, laughing with each other. Hereward saw Acha slip a hand through Kraki's arm as she joined them; a small thing, but he felt it warm his heart.

As he watched them disappear among the storm-lashed huts, he realized how much the gyre of his life had turned. In the hall of his father, he had never felt more alone. The hours had been filled with pain and he had come to believe he would never find anything of value in the grim procession of days. And yet here, at the end, he felt something like peace. He marvelled at the strangeness of it.

A moment later, Alric hurried from the church and together they walked down the road through Ely. 'Thurstan would know your plans,' the monk said.

'If he is a part of my plans, I will tell him.'

'He is afraid, you know that.'

'Then he must put his faith in God, and in the men who will give their lives to defend him from the king's wrath.'

At the walls, they clambered on to the walkway. The gusting wind met them, tearing at their hair and lashing their cloaks.

'Here we are, two drowned rats,' Alric said. 'A fine sight to greet the king.'

Hereward looked out across the fenlands. 'I have only one regret – that I did not make my brother pay for his crime.'

'You must put that out of your mind.' The monk shook the rain from himself. 'You think it will make amends to end your brother's days with your sword. It will not. Turfrida will still be dead, and you will carry with you for the rest of your days the knowledge that you have slaughtered someone you once loved. You will never escape that. It will gnaw away at you, and given time it will destroy you. I would not wish that on any man.'

The Mercian heard the pain beneath the other man's words and knew he was speaking from experience. 'Good words, but they matter little now. I will not see Redwald again. At heart he is a coward and he would not risk his neck in the battle we are going to see here.'

After a moment, the monk said, 'If that is your only regret, you have had a good life.'

'Aye,' Hereward replied. 'I have had a good life.'

The Mercian stood in silence, watching the ash trees thrash and the water stream down to the black meres, remembering. Only the days since Alric had joined him on the road seemed to be bright with colour. All that had happened before had faded into a fenland mist.

All endings came too soon, but this one sooner than most.

Chapter Forty-Eight

Cold sweat trickled down Redwald's back. He glanced this way and that as he loped along the narrow track through the desolate wetlands. Threat was everywhere. An English arrow whisking out of the gloom of the storm. An unseen enemy in the tangled willow copses or the sedge or the reed-beds that seemed to stretch for miles, ready to rise up with a spear and rip him apart. He choked back his fear but his throat felt too narrow.

Even the natural world seemed to be conspiring against him. Under the lowering black clouds, it had grown so dark he could barely see to put one foot in front of the other. The torrent turned the water to his left into an angry sea and made the bog to his right even more fluid. One wrong step and he would be gone. The raindrops rattled off his helm like hailstones, blinding him. The bitter cold numbed his body until he could barely feel the flints beneath his feet.

Amid it all, he felt alone in the whole world. The path wound round obstacles through the half-light so that he could not see the men ahead or behind. He could not hear the thunder of their feet, or the rattle of their shields. Only the rushing of the storm throbbed in his ears.

Redwald swallowed. How had it come to this? Why would the king wish to punish him by sending him into the very heart of a battle that would be bloody indeed? He had only ever been loyal.

As he rounded a leaning ash tree, he scrambled to a halt, almost plunging into the churning grey water. Three Norman soldiers and the mad Viking Harald Redteeth clustered on the track. Just beyond them he glimpsed another soldier hesitantly walking towards a copse. He seemed taller than the others and his gait was rolling as if he walked upon the deck of a storm-tossed ship. Redwald gagged and covered his mouth as he breathed in the fruity stink of rot.

The Viking glanced back at him and grinned. 'Death is always closer than you think, and sometimes he is a friend.'

Redwald leaned forward to see why the men had come to a halt. The waters had risen, making a stretch of the causeway ahead impassable. But the cunning Normans would not be deterred. They had made a bridge of dead horses – no doubt killed in the English attack on the causeway – each one strapped to the next with hemp rope, the bellies bloated with the gases of decay. As one knight crossed to the higher ground beyond, the next soldier clambered on, holding his arms wide to balance himself.

When it was Redwald's turn to cross, he screwed his eyes shut and felt with his feet. The corpses shifted and belched beneath him. His gorge rose at the reek. Halfway across, his shoes slid out from under him and he crashed down, his face pressing deep into hide slippery with putrefaction and squirming with maggots. As he choked and clawed his way like a babe over the remaining bodies, Harald Redteeth's mocking laughter rang through the storm.

'How do you like life as a warrior?' the Viking taunted.

Redwald collapsed on to solid ground, his forehead almost touching the sodden earth as he sucked in clean air. Hunched over him, Redteeth yelled above the pounding of the rain, 'This is the world of a fighting man: sweat and terror and blood and shit and piss. How do you like it, eh?' The Northman laughed with contempt and stalked away. Redwald would have killed him then and there, while his back was turned, if he could have got away with it.

With his heart sinking, he joined the flow of men weaving along the next leg of the track. After a while, he heard a tremendous roaring rushing through the trees. As he stepped out of the gloom of the woods, he found himself on the muddy bank of a swollen river. Stretched out on either side of him, the soldiers who had preceded him stared into the treacherous grey waters.

He wiped the driving rain from his eyes and followed their gaze. Several small boats had been lashed together and fastened to stakes hammered into the bank. Some of the soldiers had started to fix timber across the boats to create a makeshift bridge. But the rushing currents tore at the feeble structure. Redwald heaved a sigh of relief when he saw it would not survive much longer. They would have to turn back.

As he edged away he looked upriver, through the sheets of rain, and glimpsed pinpricks of light glowing in the grey distance. They were drawing closer. Soon enough he saw they were lanterns swinging in the prows of boats sweeping along in the raging torrent. Cloaked and hooded men hunched over their oars, heads bowed into the blasting storm. Astern, another man struggled with the tiller.

'Hands to the bridge,' a voice boomed. 'We will not be turned back by a little water.'

Redwald was astonished to see the king striding up from the track. He could have been warming himself at Branduna while he waited for the route to Ely to be made secure, yet there he was, near the front of the attacking force. The soldiers parted as the monarch marched to the river's edge and scrutinized the first section of the bridge. His nose wrinkled in disgust at what he no doubt considered was a pitiful effort, and then he roared his disapproval at the commander he had placed in charge. Redwald watched the hardened soldiers cower.

'We have tamed the great seas,' the king bellowed. 'And you say this stream of piss will stop us reaching our prey?' Redwald marvelled at the monarch's determination. Now he understood how the Normans had crushed everything in their path. Not even the fury of the elements would force William off the course he had chosen.

'The waters are too dangerous,' the commander protested. 'A man must wade through them to anchor the boats.'

'Then be that man,' William bellowed. He hooked his huge hands in the commander's hauberk and heaved. So great was his strength that the soldier flew through the air, crashed on to the slick timbers of the bridge and skidded towards the rushing grey river and certain death. Flailing, he managed at the last to find a handhold and jerked to a halt half over the end, his nose a hand's width from the torrent.

The king had already forgotten him. He yelled for the boats to be brought in. Struggling against the current, the oarsmen steered in the first of the vessels. They fought to keep it in line with the already-moored boats.

Standing on the edge, the commander peered into the river. He had only moments before the boat would be torn away. He flashed one despairing glance at the king, and, with shaking hands, grabbed the end of a rope and lowered himself into the current. Instantly, the river threatened to tear him away. Clawing at the edge of the bridge, he made a feeble effort to loop the rope around the boat.

A moment later the torrent sucked him beneath the surface. Drowned. *Madness*, Redwald thought. Would the king sacrifice all of them to see the English destroyed? He glanced around at the drawn faces of the soldiers and guessed that they were thinking the same. Not Harald Redteeth, though. The mad Viking was sitting on a fallen tree as if he had not a care in the world. He put his head back and opened his mouth to catch the raindrops.

'You,' the king yelled, pointing at another man. The soldier blanched, but knew better than to show even a hint of doubt.

He clambered on to the swaying bridge and leapt into the water. Within a moment, he too was gone. Two more soldiers were claimed by the raging torrent before the monarch roared his frustration.

'I will not be denied,' he bellowed, thrusting aside the men along the bank. Snatching up the rope at the bridge, he stepped into the shallows.

Redwald gaped. What possessed the monarch that he would risk his own life? He had felt he had the measure of this man, but now it was as if he did not know him at all. But then a thought struck him with such force, he almost reeled back. In his mind's eye, he was sitting beside a tabula board in a warm hall, and Harold Godwinson, the man who would . . . should . . . have been wearing the English crown, had decided to impart his wisdom. *How far will you travel along the road to damnation to achieve your heart's desire?* he had said.

Redwald realized those words had been the great rule of his life. Perhaps he had lived by them even before Harold had given them voice. But now he could see that William held by them too. Perhaps all great men did. He smiled to himself. They were one and the same, the king and he. He should not have let himself become so downhearted. Great things still waited for him in days yet to come.

Weighed down by his vast hauberk and his helm and still carrying his sword, William waded out into the flow. One boat had drifted away and another floated in to take its place, the flickering lantern-glow lighting the lines of determination on the king's face. The water rose to his chest, and then his neck.

Some of the soldiers fell to their knees in the mud and clasped their hands together in prayer for their lord. Others stared in horror or marvelled at his courage. William seemed to care naught for the fate that awaited him. Pushing his chin up, he looped the rope around the boat. As the oarsmen battled to make it tight, he waved a hand to beckon to the next vessel.

William the Bastard waded on. The rushing water gushed around his chin, and then washed over his face. With only his helm visible, he flung the rope over the next boat. Another had already sculled into place.

And then the helm itself disappeared beneath the torrent. Silence fell across the soldiers gathered along the bank. They stared at the river, wishing their lord to live. After a moment, a cry rang out, and then another. 'The king is dead. God save the king.'

Redwald narrowed his eyes and watched.

When the helm broke the surface of the water, a cheer roared along the water's edge, drowning out the storm itself. Once the king had dragged himself a few more paces, he thrust his head up and sucked in a huge lungful of air. Still holding the rope, he turned and looked back at his men.

Redwald felt entranced. *Look upon me*, that fierce gaze said. *I am a god. Nothing can kill me. Nothing can stop me from gaining my heart's desire.* A grin spread across the king's face as the cheers continued to ring out. Redwald felt his knees go weak. Here was his destiny. Here!

As if possessed, the soldiers threw themselves at the bridge. They fastened the timbers to the boats, clawing their way along the edge as other vessels floated into place. In no time, the structure was complete. The army flowed across the bridge and on to the isle of Ely.

Caught up in the flow of determined warriors, Redwald had to fight to break free when he passed before the gaze of the monarch. He stepped forward and bowed his head, his eyes closed. 'Your servant,' he said in a trembling voice. He stayed there for a long moment, and when he looked up the king had gone. But he knew William had heard his voice. All would be well.

Grinning, he pushed his way back into the stream of fighting men.

When night fell, the rain still pounded. In the leafless woods clustering on the lower slopes where the Norman army sheltered, few could sleep from the constant drumming on their makeshift sailcloth shelters. The men huddled around smoking fires built in rudely constructed ovens of carved peat blocks, the water puddling at their feet. The orange glows dotted the hillside like summer fireflies.

Redwald could not sleep either. After his revelation at the river, he felt as if a furnace roared in his head. He had been too patient, too slow and stumbling, he could see that now. If he wanted to achieve his heart's desire, he needed to grab life by the throat, as William had done, as Harold Godwinson had done. He wandered among the knots of hooded men, their sodden cloaks pulled tight around them, their faces pools of shadow, long shields resting against their backs to give some respite from the bitter wind. The army seemed to go on for ever.

From further down the slope, he could hear the thud of mallets as soldiers worked through the night to fix the siege machines in place. Twenty good men had been lost to the swollen waters as those great wall-breakers had been floated to Ely across the treacherous fens, he had heard. Soon the pounding would begin. There could be no hope for the English now. With their cold-hearted, clear-eyed desire to keep their grip on land and power, Morcar, and the monks, had put the spear to that. The walls would fall and Ely would burn and every man, woman and child within that place would be put to the sword. It would be a Norman world then.

A figure made its way up the slope from the track. As it neared, he saw it was the knight Deda. He looked troubled, his face deeply graven. As the knight passed, he paused and held Redwald's gaze as if he were about to speak. But it seemed he could not find the words, for he only nodded and moved on. He made his way to where the mad Viking Harald Redteeth sat, chewing on the contents of the leather pouch that hung at his hip. Redwald could not understand the unlikely friendship that seemed to have grown between the two men, but they instantly fell into a deep and intense conversation.

He walked on a while and then stopped and looked up the slope. In the distance, he could just make out a flickering light, perhaps one of the torches over Ely's gates. He shivered. The last light in the deep, dark night of the English and soon it would be extinguished. Aye, it would be a Norman world, but there would be a place in it for him.

When the walls fell, he would be one of the first into Ely, whatever the risk to himself. Only a grand gesture would earn the king's favour. And in all the fighting and the heroism of that moment, only one thing would shine out like a beacon: if he could deliver William's heart's desire, the thing that had driven him to risk everything, even his life. The head of the leader of the English rebels, his own brother, Hereward.

CHAPTER FORTY-NINE

Fire was falling from the grey sky. The heads of the terror-stricken English snapped up to watch, and for a moment the hellish judgement seemed to hang above them. A terrible hush fell across Ely. And then the blazing ball plunged down. Shards of burning wood thundered against the walls. A scorching spear of timber rammed through the chest of an archer guarding the ramparts. In an instant he was alight from head to toe, his throat-rending screams tearing out across the hillside.

As flames licked up one section of the wall, Hereward scrambled from the walkway and raced across the mud, yelling, 'Bring water.' Snatching up pails filled from the wells that morning, boys stumbled after their leader. Well rehearsed, they formed a chain. But even when the blaze was quenched, there was no chance to rest. The air whistled. Hereward bellowed for the lads to take cover, but too late.

A storm of flintstones boomed from the heavens. Most of the missiles crashed against the walls, but some whipped over the top. One lad was too slow in fleeing to the shelter of the buildings. A flint cracked against the back of his head, felling him. Hereward sprinted from the cover of the palisade and scooped him up in his arms as another barrage hammered against the defences.

He laid the lad down behind a hut. The other boys gathered round, staring, wide-eyed. They all wanted to be warriors, but they had not yet made friends with death, the Mercian thought. He held the fallen boy's hand, touched his head, his lips. He eased open the eyelids, but there was no light there. One of the boys began to sob silently. A high-pitched cry rang out as a woman thrust her way through the crowd, the dead lad's mother, Hereward guessed. She fell to her knees and pressed her head against her young one's chest, weeping.

There was nothing he could say.

Feeling the weight of the lad's passing, and of all the lives that were fated to end in Ely, he stood up and turned away. His burden, and his alone.

Kraki stormed along the walkway, roaring orders at the archers and javelin-throwers they had placed along the ramparts beyond the palisade. Hereward felt pleased he had good men at his side whom he could count on. They would make it a fight. The Normans would rue the day they came to Ely.

Another crash boomed out over the settlement. The wall bowed, and Kraki had to grip the timber to keep his feet. The thunder seemed as though it would never stop.

The king's siege machines had started their relentless barrage of burning wood and hails of flint at dawn. After so many hours of punishment, Hereward wondered how much more the Ely folk could take. Each new crash against the palisade brought a cacophony of shrieks. Men who had never fought before hunched their shoulders and ran wildly and cried prayers. Even seasoned warriors winced and looked down. In Flanders, he had seen men driven mad by the constant pounding. Everyone inside the walls felt the shadow of doom upon them.

Under the eye of mad Hengist, a team of men ran to the damaged palisade with split timbers. They set to work with shovels and saws and mallets. Hereward clambered up the ladder and crouched beside Kraki.

'The bastards,' the Northman muttered. 'Enough of rocks and wood. Let me face them over my axe.'

'They will come soon enough,' the Mercian replied. 'Once they think they have softened us up.'

'At least the damned rain has let up.'

Hereward pointed to a flurry of movement further down the slope. 'Be careful what you wish for.'

Two groups of soldiers ran out from behind their defences, speeding to the right and left. Each man carried one of the deadly Norman longbows.

The Mercian leaned over the walls and yelled, 'Bowlines.' In the shelter behind the high ramparts, archers nocked their shafts and leapt up to the top of the earthworks. The javelin-throwers ran to their positions. Hereward raised his right arm.

As the Normans pounded up the slope to get close enough to loose their arrows over the walls, Hereward squinted, judging the distance. 'Now,' he bellowed.

The English arrows whisked down. One rammed into a chest, another into an eye. Norman bowmen flew backwards, crashing on to the ground, dead.

The Mercian kept his arm raised until the king's bowmen came to a halt and nocked their own shafts. He whipped it down. The javelin-throwers launched their weapons. The Normans scattered as the missiles arced towards them. One was too slow. A javelin rammed through his chest, out of his back and into the ground. Impaled, he twitched as if he had the palsy while the life drained from him.

The English archers let fly again. This time six Normans fell. But the king's men were too battle-hardened to run scared. Once they found their position, they raised their bows and loosed their shafts. Ely's defenders dived behind the ramparts, pressing their backs against the walls of earth. Hereward and Kraki dropped to their knees as the arrows thumped into the walls just below where they stood.

When they peered back over the palisade, the Norman bow-men were retreating down the slope, dragging their fallen brothers with them. The creak of straining ropes echoed as the arms of the siege machines were drawn back once more.

'William the Bastard is trying to drain all our arrows and javelins,' Kraki grunted.

'As we try to drain theirs.' Hereward grinned, but they both knew time was on the king's side. His army could sit for days if necessary, pounding the walls until they were turned to splinters, waiting for the barns to empty and bellies to rumble with hunger. But the monarch surely could not expect the folk of Ely to wander out and plead for mercy. They all knew there would be none.

When he heard his name called, he turned and saw Alric waving at him frantically from the edge of the huts. He climbed down from the walkway and ran over.

'You must see this,' the monk said in a grave tone.

'I want no bad news,' Hereward warned him.

He followed Alric across Ely to the Camp of Refuge. Since the English army had gathered on the slopes of Ely, only the sick and the wounded, and the women and children, still waited among that sprawling jumble of huts and reek of waste. For hours, the camp had been still with worry and prayer, but now Hereward could hear a passion-filled voice ringing out, a familiar voice, and the words he snatched from the wind troubled him.

In the centre of the Camp of Refuge, a large crowd had gathered around Abbot Thurstan. Hands raised to the heavens, he stood on a barrel surrounded by a wall of monks, their heads bowed in prayer.

'God will deliver you from death,' the abbot proclaimed. 'Though it seems all hope is lost, you will be saved. He will save you. Not Hereward, not any mortal men, but God Himself. You must place your faith in Him alone.'

The Mercian gritted his teeth. While he fought to keep spirits high, the cleric spoke only of coming disaster. What good would that do? But Alric waved a cautionary finger. There was more.

'Bring your men back to your hearths and tell them to lay down their arms,' Thurstan went on. 'Do not let them give their lives in vain. They will not be harmed if they bow to the king. What gain is there in the slaughter of your husbands? Save them, save yourselves.'

Hereward had heard enough. He thrust his way through the crowd. 'Make way,' he called. 'Words of cowardice will not avail you. Now hear the truth.' As Thurstan glared down at him, the Mercian realized that his enemy within Ely had been revealed. He grabbed the abbot's sleeve and tugged him from his perch, then climbed on to the barrel in his place.

He looked around at the rapt, frightened faces staring up at him. They wanted hope, nothing more, he could see that. He wished he could offer it to them. 'You know the Norman bastards,' he snarled. 'Have they ever shown mercy to any English? For five summers now, they have stolen our land and our food. They have murdered our loved ones and hanged them on gibbets as food for the ravens. Not even dogs would be left that way. We have suffered misery heaped upon misery, but we have endured. And here in Ely we have stood shoulder to shoulder and we have been stronger for it. We have defeated the king himself at Belsar's Hill. Great things remain within our grasp, as long as we stay strong.'

He could see from the relief in some faces that this was what they wanted to hear. But others still furrowed their brows and eyed him with dark suspicion. 'What will you do?' a woman called. 'How will you deliver us from the wolves?'

'I will fight, as I always have done,' Hereward called back. 'And I will give my life for you.'

A murmur of approval ran through the throng.

But Thurstan raised his arms in the air and announced, 'What good will one dead Mercian do you? I will deliver you to the king and I . . . only I . . . will protect you.'

Hereward leapt down from the barrel and caught the abbot's elbow. He steered the churchman through the crowd, whispering, 'Walk with me, Father. I would talk to you.'

'What will you do? Kill me, a man of God?' Thurstan snapped. 'Folk will turn on you in an instant. Already they cannot decide if you are devil or the leader who will carry them to the promised land.'

'Oh, I am devil, Father. Have no doubt of that.'

The monks trailed along behind as Hereward led Thurstan out of the Camp of Refuge. 'Return to the minster,' he said. 'I will have Guthrinc set men to guard you. For your own safety.'

The churchman snorted with derision. 'And would you have us slaughtered if we refuse to be your captives?'

'Aye, Father, I would,' Hereward replied without hesitation. 'I would have you cut down in the church itself and mount your heads on spikes at the door if it served to keep the folk of Ely safe.'

Thurstan blanched. He turned on his heel and marched up the slope, his monks hurrying behind him.

'What has become of him?' Alric asked. 'Thurstan is a kind man, and he has always stood by the English. We would not have survived long without his hand of friendship.'

'The abbot has stared long and hard into the dark of the night and found himself wanting,' Hereward murmured as he watched the monks walk away. 'He has not the strength to stand by the consequences of his actions. He thinks he has too much to lose . . . his power, or gold . . . He sees it slipping through his fingers.' Hereward shrugged. 'And he values that more than his honour.' He spat, adding, 'The snakes in our home have proved worse than the ones beyond the walls.'

'Many times I have looked for Thurstan,' Alric said, dazed, 'but he was nowhere to be found. The monks told me he was walking beyond the walls, seeking God's advice in solitude—'

'Meeting the king and his men, more like. Or he would not have offered safe passage so easily. He has sold us like a pig at market.' Feeling his devil stir, Hereward bunched his fists. He imagined throttling the abbot at the altar and hurling his body over the walls as a sign to the Normans that the English would brook no betrayals.

The monk rested a concerned hand on his friend's arm as if he could read his thoughts. 'Vengeance will gain us nothing,' he said.

Another thought struck Hereward and he frowned. 'The guards at the gate said naught of Thurstan's comings and goings. They would have told me, and this betrayal would have been halted long ago.'

Alric shook his head. 'What matters that now? Unless God brings a miracle, all is lost.'

'You pray to God, monk,' Hereward replied after a moment's thought, 'but the miracle might already have been delivered.'

CHAPTER FIFTY

In the gloom of the church, a few candles flickered. Shadows swooped across the walls as the two men made their way through the scent of incense to the shrine of St Etheldreda. The rain had started again, harder than ever, and the drumming upon the roof echoed along the nave. Behind it, Hereward could hear the steady pounding of the Norman siege machines beating out their rhythm of destruction. He felt that cadence match the throb of blood in his head. The end was coming, he could sense it in his bones.

In front of the shrine, the offerings left by the Ely folk were now inches deep across the flagstones. Hereward felt the weight of his burden. He had thought his purpose was to lead the English out of the dark that the Normans had set upon the land. But in the end, all he had done was lead the folk who had trusted him to disaster. He sank to his knees and bowed his head, asking the Lord for forgiveness.

Alric knelt beside him and rested a hand on his friend's shoulder. 'You have not failed,' he murmured. 'No man could have done more.'

'There is nothing to show for the sacrifice I have asked of the people who followed me.'

'You are wrong. What you have done here will flow out across England for all time. Whenever the English feel a boot upon their neck or a spear at their back, they will think of Hereward, and they will know they do not have to bow their heads. They can fight back, aye, even if they are few and the forces against them are many.' Alric smiled, his voice filled with respect. 'You have given them a gift beyond all value, Hereward. The knowledge that one man can bloody the nose of even a great and powerful king. That will never be forgotten.'

Hereward turned over Alric's words for a moment, and then said, 'Do not belittle the part you have played in this. You have helped tame a wild beast and turn it into this leader of which you speak so highly.'

His cheeks colouring, the monk shook his head. 'It is you who have aided me, and for that you will always have my loyalty. When I killed Sunnild, the woman I loved—'

'An accident—'

'The stain upon my soul was no less for that. I thought I would never wash the blood from my hands.'

'But you have made amends.'

'For the taking of a life? No. But I have tried.' He bowed his head for a moment, the weight of his emotions heavy upon him. 'Sunnild's death is a burden I will never escape. I could never take another life. It would destroy me. But in this struggle of the English . . .' he hesitated, then added in a quiet voice, 'in you, I have found a purpose.'

Hereward grinned, trying for a light response. 'You have tried to save my soul.'

Alric showed no humour. His eyes gleamed in the candle-light. 'No. I have tried to show you the path. You have saved your own soul.'

The Mercian felt humbled by the faith the other man showed in him. He broke off a chunk of the gold ring round his arm and laid it upon the shrine. As he whispered a prayer, he felt something deep shift within him. When he was done, he rose, offering a hand to help the monk to his feet. 'If we die this day, my life has been better for having you in it,' he said.

'If we die this day, my life has been better for having you in it,' the monk repeated.

Hereward smiled. 'Good. Then come, for the hours are running away from us.'

He led the way along the nave and out of the church. The rain sheeted across the minster enclosure and the day had once again become like night. At the gates, Hereward looked out beyond Ely. Fires raged along the palisade. Black smoke swirled up to the storm-clouds, and he could smell the bitter reek of burning on the wind. His men had fought hard to maintain the defences, but it had always been only a matter of time before the walls fell.

With Alric beside him, he made his way to the speaking-mound. A constellation of torches danced across the whole of Ely, sizzling in the downpour. His army waited for him in silence, faces turned towards him, lit by the glow of the flames. Pale, frightened, hopeful, desperate. Once again he felt humbled by the weight of faith that had been placed upon him. So many of them, from all parts of England, north and south and east and west, all of them fleeing the Normans to shelter under his standard. Some wanted only food and security. Others wanted vengeance against the invaders. They all counted upon him.

He could not lie to them.

'Though we lose this day,' he said in a voice that somehow carried above the roar of the storm, 'it is not because our arms have not been strong enough, or because there has not been enough fire in our hearts. Some of those we once called friends have failed us. They have shown weakness where you have shown courage, greed where you have made only sacrifices. You, all of you, deserved better than their betrayal. But we will not bow our heads. We will not be broken-hearted.'

A roar rose up from the army.

'We are wolf-brothers all, fierce and brave. And like the wolves of winter, we will fight to the death.'

The cheer grew louder still.

'Stand firm,' Hereward yelled above the clamour. 'Those who survive this battle must spread the word of our fight far and wide. Let it grow in hearts and flourish in words. And let all know, now and for ever more, the English will never be defeated.'

The deafening roar of defiance drowned out the very storm. Spears jabbed towards the heavens and fresh-painted shields swayed overhead, a sea of colour in the gloom of the day. Hereward felt his heart swell.

But as the cheer died away, he heard a corresponding roar from far off in the storm. The time of waiting had passed. The Normans were coming.

As one his army turned, and with a battle-cry that must have chilled the blood of the king's men they thundered down the slopes towards the wall and the final battle.

CHAPTER FIFTY-ONE

The gates of Ely splintered. A sound like thunder boomed time and again as the Normans rammed the felled tree against the entrance to the English stronghold. Beyond the palisade, an ocean of iron washed as far as the eye could see. Norman knights and foot-soldiers in black cloaks and helms and hauberks, and wild-haired axes-for-hire in furs and leather, all swelling up from the water's edge to the walls around the hilltop settlement. The rain lashed down and the wind howled and the dark seemed to close in around them until men and storm became as one.

The air was thick with arrows, whipped through the gloom from the Norman longbowmen. As Hereward crouched on the walkway, he watched the shafts punch through throats and chests and eye-sockets. A mist of blood was caught in the wind as bodies were torn apart. Dying men wheeled backwards into the void, slamming into the warriors below. Their screams were swallowed by the din of battle, the clatter of iron and the exhortations and the battle-cries and the constant whistle of the arrows.

Along the palisade, his own archers rose up, loosing shafts into the Normans below. The king's army pressed forward so hard, the fallen were carried along in the flow, the arrows protruding from their sagging bodies.

Wiping the streaming rainwater from his face, he peered along the walkway. Under the weight of the English ranks, the wall had started to sag. Whole sections creaked and wavered, blackened from the burning caused by the fire-missiles.

The Mercian dropped from the wall and forced his way through the ocean of waiting warriors. Faces etched with fear loomed out of the driving rain. Eyes darted. Hands trembled. They knew their fate would be decided within moments.

In front of the bowing gate, his most trusted men gripped their spears and shields. Kraki, black-eyed and glowering; Guthrinc, towering over the others, as calm as if he were setting out to fish the mere; mad Hengist, who seemed to be laughing at the confusion that swirled around him; and Sighard, head raised in defiance but his eyes still hollow.

'The whole wall will be down before we know it,' Hereward bellowed.

'Good,' Kraki spat. 'I am sick of this waiting.'

'Your axe will taste Norman blood soon enough,' Hengist said, his eyes sparkling.

Guthrinc caught Hereward's eye and nodded towards Sighard. The Mercian clapped a hand on the younger man's shoulder and grinned. 'Are you ready for this glory?'

'I am ready. I think a hundred dead Normans is fair price for my brother's life.'

'Only a hundred?' Guthrinc rumbled. 'Aim higher, lad. I am going for two hundred myself.'

The oak bar across the gates strained and then a loud crack echoed. It bent, splintering. Through the growing space between the gates, Hereward could see rain-slick helms and hungry eyes.

'Time,' he yelled, turning and thrusting his spear into the air. 'Shield wall.'

Across the slopes of Ely, the English army broke into well-rehearsed groups. Lines formed, shields slotted into place, spears bristled out.

In front of the gates, Hereward thrust his way into the centre of the line. Kraki stepped to his left, Guthrinc to his right. Others fell into place on either side and behind. They would be the first to meet the Norman bastards, that was only right. He raised his shield and peered over the rim. The world closed in around him.

The gates bowed, fell back, leaned in once more, each time the gap between them growing wider. How many Normans waited only a spear's throw away, Hereward wondered. Thousands? He cared little. Let them swarm in their multitude. All the more for the slaughter.

And then, with a resounding crack, the oak bar shattered and the gates burst open. Hereward heard the roar of hell awakening. A torrent of knights swept through the gap. Double-edged swords hacked and stabbed. Shields splintered and groaned, but the wall held. And as the knights swung their blades up once more, Hereward and the English warriors thrust their spears. Sparks glimmered in the half-light as iron tips glanced off mail shirts. But there was blood too. Hereward's spear drove up under the chin of the Norman in front of him, through the fleshy part of the neck and into the skull. The Mercian yanked back his weapon in a shower of crimson and his opponent crumpled.

And still the Normans swarmed through the gates. Whole sections of wall were collapsing on either side. The king's army flowed out on both flanks, crashing across Ely. So many there were, it seemed the deluge would never end.

Kraki stabbed his spear into the foot of the warrior in front of him. As the knight's knee buckled in agony, the Viking rammed his weapon into his opponent's eye socket. The Norman tumbled back on to a growing pile of bodies. On Hereward's other side, Guthrinc stood like an oak. However hard the king's warriors slammed against his shield, he never budged an inch. When he drove his spear forward, he lifted a man off the ground, the weapon punching through solid mail and into the heart. At his feet, the spreading pool of rainwater had turned the colour of rust. The air became thick with the reek of loosened bowels and bladders.

In front of him now, the wall of Norman soldiers was so dense Hereward could not see the other side of it. Under their slashing swords, shards of wood flew off his shield's rim and a crack had begun to grow towards the central boss.

His head throbbed. His vision began to close in. And with each death he claimed, he felt his devil rise higher, calling to him to set it free. The clamour of the battle faded away until there was only the steady, rapid beat of blood in his head. Faces swam before him. They fell like the wheat before the farmer's sickle. As his heart swelled, he thought that he could slaughter every man there; no amount of blood could sate his hunger.

But the shield wall was starting to fail. He sensed gaps around him, good English men cut down by Normans hacking for their shins and ankles. As he prepared to give the order to fall back, a familiar face flashed across his vision and a rush of cold flooded through his hot passion.

Redwald caught his eye and held it for a long moment. A hint of a taunting smile. And then his brother moved away, glancing back only once. That lure was enough. Hereward felt his devil leap into his head.

With the shocked cries of Kraki and Guthrinc ringing in his ears, he tore away from the shield wall. 'Give the order to retreat now, as we planned,' he yelled to his shield-brothers. He tossed aside his spear and snatched up the axe hanging from his waist. Hacking, he carved a path through the Normans. They fell away from his blade, as afraid of the madness they saw in his eyes as of his weapon.

And then he was through the flow of bodies and sprinting in pursuit of Redwald.

If he was to die that day, he would take his brother with him to hell.

CHAPTER FIFTY-TWO

The hunting horn rang out, low and mournful. Through the blaze of his rage, Hereward heard the insistent tone rise above the furious clash of battle and was pleased. Now his plan had been set in motion, he could give himself to vengeance. He threw himself up the hill. A Norman warrior rounded on him, growling. Without even slowing his step, Hereward hacked down. His speed caught the soldier unaware. The blade sliced through the neck and down to the collarbone, and the Mercian had wrenched his weapon free and was running up the slope before the man even knew he was dead.

Ahead of him, he could see Redwald scrambling among the huts, avoiding the worst of the fighting. A coward to the last. He didn't care that his brother had seen him. Let the traitor know that death was on his trail.

Hereward splashed through pools of rainwater as he sought out the fastest route. He knew these narrow, muddy tracks well. On every side, fighting men flashed by, barely silhouettes in the gloom. The Mercian ignored them all. He clambered over waste heaps and edged round obstacles, all the time keeping his eyes on his prey. Redwald seemed to be moving up the hill with purpose. Where he was going, Hereward could not guess, but his brother knew Ely well from the seasons that he had lived there.

As he emerged from the huts close to the minster wall, he saw that the gates to the church enclosure hung open. That had to be his brother's destination. Drawing his sword, he prowled forward.

Through the pulse of his blood, he made out someone calling his name. He ignored it. But as he reached the gate a hand grabbed his arm and he whirled without thinking, swinging his sword in an arc. Whoever was there reeled back, crying out. Somehow he halted his strike. As his vision cleared, he realized he was looking at Sighard.

'You could have taken my life,' the young man snapped. Hereward lowered his blade. 'Why do you hide here?' Sighard continued. 'Your army needs a leader.'

'Leave me,' the Mercian growled, turning back to the minster gate. His devil would not let him rest.

Sighard threw himself in Hereward's path. 'You cannot abandon us. Only you know the plan. Men are dying – do you hear me?'

As Hereward somehow shook off the grip of his rage, he felt a moment of clarity settle on him. He looked across Ely and saw only carnage. The shield walls were failing fast. Fewer men than he had hoped maintained the positions upon which he had painstakingly decided. Thurstan's call to surrender must have worked, he realized, feeling his anger spike once more.

Thrusting Sighard to one side, he ran to the speaking-mound and crouched on top, scanning the settlement. His men had heeded the first horn and were retreating up the hill step by step. But their progress was too slow.

'You have your horn?' he called back to Sighard.

'As you commanded.'

Hereward looked up at the heavens. The rain was beginning to ease. Perhaps God was on their side after all. 'Blow it now,' he said.

Sighard put the horn to his lips and a moment later the low, mournful sound rolled out across Ely.

Pushing aside his lust for vengeance, Hereward threw himself down the hill to aid his men. Barely had he reached the nearest half-timbered hall than he heard a crackling resonating above the clash of sword and shield. Smoke billowed into the air near the wall, and a moment later fingers of flame reached up. One of the barns was alight. It was only the first. Columns of smoke whipped in the wind everywhere he looked. The crackling became a roaring as the fires rushed up, whisking great clouds of sparks over the settlement. Soon every barn was burning. As planned, the lads he had positioned in each one had ignited the dry winter feed at the signal of the second horn blast. Even at the minster the stores were burning. Fire had served them well once before, and it would do so again.

Cries of alarm rang out from Norman soldiers still haunted by the inferno at Belsar's Hill. Hereward watched as panic tore apart their formations. His men were ready. They had not known when and where, but they had all been told to expect a conflagration. He nodded to himself. Now it was in the hands of God.

Ely was burning. Everything had been wagered in one last, desperate attempt to save the folk who had sheltered him. The heavy rain over the last few days would stop the fire spreading among most of the houses, he had hoped, but he could not be sure.

Among the huts he raced, with Sighard close behind. Dense, choking smoke provided all the cover he needed. A knight staggered out from beside a workshop, searching around for his fellows. He half turned, fumbling to raise his shield; too late. Hereward's blade sliced through his neck, almost severing his head. As another soldier ran out to aid his brother, Sighard rammed his spear into the man's back. A vengeful fury filled the young Englishman's face.

'For Madulf,' he shouted.

'Remember, stay away from the main roads,' the Mercian

yelled as the two men raced on. 'And blow your horn again.'
The smoke folded around them.

As the third blast echoed, Hereward ran towards the largest
fire glowing through the smoke. Kraki and Guthrinc waited
with a horde of their best fighting men, shielding themselves
from the searing heat.

The Viking eyed him with suspicion. 'I thought you had
abandoned us.'

'Never.' The Mercian pushed his way among them and
stabbed his axe ahead. 'Now,' he shouted, 'let us send some of
these bastards to hell.'

With a roar, he threw himself forward. His men charged
behind. Norman soldiers scattered ahead of the racing wall of
spears and axes. Hereward whipped his arm right and left,
urging his warriors to form a wider line. As they thundered in
an arc, they herded their enemies up the track to the minster.
Behind the roaring of the fires, he could hear the battle-cries of
his other men, ten well-drilled hordes driving the Normans in
the direction he wanted.

As the hated enemy ran ahead of the English through the
billowing smoke, the ground opened beneath them. Mud-
covered branches shattered underfoot, plunging the running
soldiers into Hengist's pits. Screams tore from the depths.
Hereward ran to the edge of one and looked down on men
writhing on spikes. He wrinkled his nose at the stink. Each
sharpened branch had been smeared with shit so that even if
the soldiers survived their impalement their wounds would
fester and sickness would eat them from within. He spat into
the hole. They deserved no less.

'You learned your lessons well in Flanders,' Guthrinc said
beside him as he too looked down.

'We do what it takes to survive this battle,' he replied.

A rolling cacophony of screams echoed from all across Ely.
The pits would claim a goodly number of the enemy, but not
enough. Up the hill they raced, avoiding the main thorough-
fares where more pits had been hidden. The rain had stopped

by the time they reached the minster enclosure. They had been fortunate. The fires were still burning.

When he reached the gate, he looked down the slope. The fires glowed through the dense bank of smoke covering everything. He hoped he had done enough. His men streamed up the hill from every direction to the agreed meeting place. Guthrinc and Kraki urged the remnants of their army into the enclosure, where four more stores burned brightly.

'Make ready,' Hereward called to Sighard. 'We must hold the bastards back for just a little longer.'

Sighard called twenty of the fiercest warriors to form a line across the hilltop. When three Norman knights burst from the smoke, the fighting men hacked them down in an instant.

Hereward tested the uneven timbers beneath his feet and nodded to Hengist, who crouched like a hungry dog next to the enclosure fence. With a laugh, the Englishman bounded a few spear-lengths away and began to tear up some of the planks to reveal the hidden ditch. He dropped into the hole and a moment later white smoke swirled out. Hereward heard the crackling as the pitch-soaked straw caught alight. Across a long line in front of the minster enclosure, more trails of smoke rose from the ground.

Further down the hill, lost in the grey cloud, the voices of the Norman commanders could be heard as they tried to direct their bewildered men. Soon the attack would begin again in force.

'Back now,' Hereward yelled, 'but keep your weapons at the ready.'

The last line of warriors retreated through the thickening smoke just as the covering timbers began to crack and fall. Flames licked up, gained life and power, and rose into a wall of fire.

Hereward led the men through the gate into the minster enclosure where his army waited, looking to him with worried eyes. Too few of them remained.

'An unwise man would think we have trapped ourselves in the church,' Guthrinc said, one eyebrow raised.

'Aye, he would,' Hereward replied, giving nothing away.

'Is this our last stand, then? A prayer to God for some miracle?' Sighard asked.

'A hard word for God's servants, more like.' The Mercian glanced back at the sheet of flames. 'The fire will not hold the king's men back for long. Let us see how Abbot Thurstan likes the cold iron of my sword.'

CHAPTER FIFTY-THREE

The church door crashed open. Hereward stalked into the candlelit nave, Kraki, Guthrinc and a knot of other warriors trailing behind. He smothered the anger burning in his chest. Their footsteps echoed off the stone walls as they marched through the chill to where Thurstan and a group of monks knelt in front of the altar. At the interruption, the abbot jerked round. The Mercian saw fear light the churchman's face before he regained control. He was right to be afraid.

'Praying for our souls, Father, or your own?' Hereward called.

Thurstan struggled to his feet, his arthritic knees cracking. 'This is a house of God,' he called, waving a finger. 'You have no right to intrude.'

'You were not so harsh in your judgement when you thought my army would save your land, your gold and your power from the king's grasping fingers.' Hereward flicked his right hand forward. As the monks rushed to form a barrier in front of the abbot, Kraki and the others stepped forward and thrust them aside.

Hereward drew his sword and levelled it as he walked. Thurstan threw himself back, almost tipping the altar over as he crashed against it. Without slowing his step, the Mercian pushed the tip of his blade against the abbot's throat. A bubble of blood rose.

'Blasphemy,' the cleric gasped. 'God will punish you—'

'I have been punished enough in my life, and I am sick of it.' Hereward fought to hold his rage in check. At that moment, he wanted nothing more than to take the churchman's head. 'I would linger over these questions . . .' he jabbed the sword a little to emphasize his meaning, 'but time is short. You have sold us to the Normans, Father. Men you called friends. Men you prayed with. You have sold the last hope of the English and now you think to instil a fear of God in me to save your worthless neck?'

Thurstan screwed up his eyes. 'Mercy . . .'

Hereward laughed without humour. 'You will buy your mercy with two gifts.'

The abbot nodded in agreement, wincing as the blade bit into him. Blood trickled down to the neck of his tunic.

'Your first gift: you will swear now, before God and here upon His table, that you will plead with the king to spare the lives of all plain folk in Ely. You will tell him that I forced them to do my bidding, through fear of death. That they are good-hearted and loyal to the crown. And that they despise me as a thief and a murderer. That should not be hard for you. You have his ear, do you not? He will listen to you.'

'I will do so,' the cleric gasped.

Hereward felt relief ease his simmering anger. If the lives of the good folk could be saved, his defeat would not taste so bitter.

'Your second gift: you will tell me the secret way out of the minster.'

Thurstan flinched with surprise.

'You think me a fool, Father?' the Mercian said with a tight smile. 'You have been coming and going from Ely as you please . . . meeting William the Bastard to make your foul deal . . . and you have not once passed by the guards at the gate. I have spoken to them. No, you have a passage out of here and I would know it.' He sensed the surprise and hope of his men as they looked round at him, but he did not take his gaze from the abbot's darting eyes.

The abbot swallowed, nodded. 'Very well. I will lead you to it.'

Hereward lowered his blade. Thurstan sucked in a juddering gasp of air and stepped forward on shaking legs. Blood-roses now bloomed on his tunic. The Mercian swept his blade towards the door and the abbot staggered ahead. Hereward glanced at the trembling monks. 'Where is Alric?' The church-men gaped or shook their heads. Hereward cursed under his breath. 'Find him,' he commanded Guthrinc. 'He was meant to be here, keeping an eye on Thurstan.'

Guthrinc nodded and hurried off.

'Stay where you are,' Kraki growled at the terrified monks, shaking his axe, 'or we will cut off your bollocks and feed them to you.'

Hereward herded Thurstan out of the door into the chill day. The abbot choked on the thick smoke, pressing one hand to his mouth. With shocked eyes, he stared at the burning stores around the minster enclosure and then at the conflagration beyond the gate. Hereward could see that the flames were already lower and he could hear the angry voices of the Normans rising up the hill. Thinking their prey trapped, the king's men were taking their time.

He jabbed the abbot in the back with his sword to urge him on. The cleric hurried across the enclosure to the bakehouse, which was set against the minster wall, and the Mercian allowed himself a moment of pleasure at how things were turn-ing out. His plan had been long in the making, and though many had known a part of it no one had the whole. He knew he could not risk word reaching the monks, and the betrayal that would clearly have ensued.

Thurstan eased open the door to the bakehouse and picked up the candle flickering just inside. Swirls of white flour covered the boards, ghostly footprints tracking here and there. The smell of fresh bread hung in the air, and the ovens were still warm from that morning's baking. The abbot hurried across the bakehouse. The dancing light of his candle lit an old door pressed against the wall by a pile of flour-sacks.

Hereward snapped a finger towards the heap. Two warriors heaved the sacks to one side and pulled the door from the wall. A blast of cold air rushed in. Hereward leaned against the edge of the hole and kicked at the timber of the enclosure wall beyond. A section fell away with ease. He peered down the slope, dark under the lowering storm clouds. A track had been worn in the grass leading past the huts to the palisade.

'Your monks have been busy,' he said, turning back to the abbot.

'There is a tunnel under the Ely wall,' Thurstan said, his voice cold. 'You will find it at the end of the track, covered with timber.'

Hereward lifted his blade to the churchman's chin. 'You have earned your mercy, Father. Now keep your tongue still until we are gone and then do as you have been commanded. If not, I will return when you least expect it and take your head.'

The abbot's face was like stone.

The Mercian turned to Kraki. 'Send the men through now, and be fast about it. Once they are beyond the wall, they are on their own. They must lose themselves in the fens. They are good men. They know how to hide from the king's eyes.' Yet even as the words left his mouth he knew many would not escape, for the king's war-bands would be roaming the wet-lands searching for any stragglers. At least he had given them a chance.

Kraki nodded, and the Mercian followed him out into the minster enclosure. He watched as the gathered warriors streamed into the bakehouse. At the gate, the fire was lower still. It would not be long before the Normans surged in.

As the Viking waved a furious hand to speed up the tramp-ing men, Hereward turned and saw Guthrinc hurrying up with a lad beside him. When the Mercian noticed the worried look on the tall man's face, his heart began to hammer and he knew what was to come.

'Tell him what you told me,' Guthrinc murmured.

'I have a message,' the boy began in a faltering voice as he struggled to recall what he had been told. 'You must follow me and you must come alone if you would see your friend alive.' The lad swallowed and added, 'He . . . he . . . the quiet man told me to say, "I have destroyed everything you have ever loved. You know I will not turn away from blood." He said you should come now . . .' His voice trailed away as he waited for his answer.

Hereward looked deep into the frightened boy's face, but his thoughts were racing back to Lincylene when he had tried to lure Redwald to his death. His brother was taunting him with the same game, and the same intended outcome.

CHAPTER FIFTY-FOUR

Hereward peered into the depths of the silent hall. The orange light from the fire crackling at his back glowed only an arm's length across the threshold. Beyond, shadows swam. He sniffed, smelling the iron reek of blood. This was where the butcher prepared meat for the monks' table. He took one step inside and let his eyes adjust to the gloom. Shapes emerged from the dark: trestles where the carcasses would be heaped, barrels filled with salt, pails to catch the draining blood for the pudding. Redwald could be hiding anywhere.

'I have come, as you asked,' he called. 'Now set the monk free.'

As his words died away, only silence followed.

Steeling himself, he gripped his sword. His instincts urged caution, but there was no time. The fires across the enclosure gate would be dying down soon and then the Normans would flood in. A part of him regretted sending Guthrinc on ahead with the others. Two of them could have caused enough of a distraction to flush his brother out into the open.

He strained to hear any rustle of linen, a faint exhalation, the scrape of a weapon being readied. When he took one more step, he felt something sticky underfoot. Eyes darting around, he crouched and dipped two fingers to the wet floor. He touched them to his tongue. Fresh blood. His heart began to pound. Inside his head, his devil whispered what terrible thing could have happened here. Snarling, he pushed the thought aside.

'Brother, come out,' he called once more. 'Speak, and I will lay down my blade.'

When no reply came, he strode deep into the hall. Puddles of blood sucked at the soles of his shoes. As his eyes adjusted further to the shadows, he glimpsed a shape on the floor at the far end. His breath caught in his throat. It was a body, he was sure, covered by a cloak.

Choking back a curse, Hereward lunged, and with his free hand he yanked the cloak back. A pale form lay beneath. Relief flooded him. It was too small to be a man. Dropping to his knees, he scraped his fingers across the body of a young pig, its throat cut.

With a roar of frustration, Hereward leapt to his feet and kicked over the trestles. The crash of falling wood shattered the silence. His brother was not there.

As he stormed out of the hall, he tried to calm himself. Redwald knew him too well. This trick had wasted time, and in doing so it had made him angry. And that was when he threw caution to the wind, and made mistakes, and lost what little control he had, all to his brother's advantage.

Glancing at the blaze beyond the gates, he thought he could now see the glint of helms above the flames. He sucked in a deep breath of smoky air as he struggled to steady himself. He could not afford the indulgence of rage. This time it was not only his life at stake.

The church door hung open. It had been closed before, he was sure.

Desperate now, he raced across the enclosure and slipped into the nave. Candles still shone along the walls, but some had been extinguished to create pools of shadow. That told him all he needed to know.

Fat candles glowed beside the altar. In their dancing light, he could just make out a figure, bound by the look of it. He was sure it was Alric. His devil urged him to race the length of the church to free his friend, but he fought against it. That was what Redwald wanted: remember the dead pig, the blood, and run without thinking.

Crouching against the wall, he looked around the heaps of reliquaries and chests and trestles until his gaze fell upon Etheldreda's shrine. Darkness shrouded it. Was that where his brother hid? Time was short. If he was to save them both, he had to gamble.

Standing tall, he strode towards the altar, making it easy for his brother to creep up and attack him from behind. Halfway along the nave, he glimpsed a shadow moving beside the shrine and whirled. A crossbow bolt whisked past his face and cracked against the stone wall. One more step, one unguarded moment, and it would have thumped into his head.

Bellowing his fury, he hurled himself towards the shrine. Redwald cried out in shock. There was no time to reload the crossbow, Hereward knew. His brother would have to fight like a warrior, and he had never been any good at that.

Redwald raced out of the shadows and towards the door, throwing trestles and chests behind him to try to slow Hereward's pursuit. The Mercian bounded over them. Now unshackled, his rage throbbed in his head. He was stronger than his brother, faster, he would not be denied his vengeance. Hurtling across the flagstones, he leapt between the other man and the door. Redwald weaved away, his eyes now wide with fear.

'You wanted me. Here I am,' Hereward yelled. 'Face me, you coward.'

Backed against the wall near the shrine, Redwald drew his blade, weaving it from side to side. Hereward laughed. He could see in his brother's skittering gaze that he had no hope of victory. The Mercian threw himself forward. His brother whipped up his sword at the last and the weapons clashed, but the force of Hereward's attack pinned Redwald against the wall. With their swords trapped between them, the warrior pressed harder until his face was barely a hand's width from the other man's. He peered into eyes flecked with tears of terror. Against him, he could feel Redwald shake.

'I will take your head for what you did to Turfrida,' he snarled.

'You . . . you cannot slay your own brother,' Redwald gasped.

Hereward felt stunned by the honest disbelief he saw in the younger man's face. He leaned on his sword.

'Wait,' Redwald choked. 'The monk . . . he is dying. If you waste your time with me, you will cost him his life.'

'You lie,' Hereward snarled. 'What will I find there? More pig's blood?'

'He is dying,' the younger man cried.

At the intensity in that voice, Hereward craned his neck round. Seizing the moment, Redwald hurled him off and scrambled towards the door. The Mercian hesitated, sword raised, torn between his lust for his brother's blood and his fear for Alric's safety. Cursing, he realized it was no choice at all. As he raced along the nave, he heard the door crash. He felt sick with fury that he had let his brother slip through his fingers once more. But his bitterness slipped from his mind when he saw the pool of blood surrounding the prone figure in front of the altar.

Dying? he thought with shock as he took in the size of that crimson puddle. *He is dead.*

Despair clutched at his heart. He hacked through the ropes binding the monk and spun him on to his back. His face was pale, his chest still. A dark stain had spread across his tunic from a wound in his side. Hereward was caught between wretched grief and a searing hatred for his brother. He snarled his hands in the monk's tunic and shook him. Blood spattered on the flagstones, but he heard the faintest exhalation too. Barely daring to believe, he pressed his ear against Alric's lips. He felt warmth.

Snatching the monk up in his arms, he raced along the nave and out into the deserted enclosure. He imagined Redwald cowering somewhere, praying for his new allies to save him, but his brother was the least of his priorities now. The flames across the gate were nearly out and beyond he glimpsed the ranks of Normans waiting to break in.

'Stay alive, monk,' he muttered. 'I will not lose you too.'

Dashing into the bakehouse, he slipped through the gap in the wall and careered down the slope. His friend's blood soaked into his tunic. Behind him, a roar rang out into the night. The Normans had rushed into the enclosure. Soon they would be swarming out across the fenlands to capture the escaping English army. Hereward felt the darkness close around him.

CHAPTER FIFTY-FIVE

Under the lowering black clouds, Ely was burning. Pinpoints of fire glowed through the pall of smoke billowing over the summit of the isle of eels. All around, the wetlands were still and quiet. The only sound was rainwater dripping steadily from the stark branches of the ash trees. On the far side of Dedman's Bog, dank and reeking of rot, Hereward craned his neck back for one final look at the place that had been his home for so long. Ely was burning, and with it the last hopes of the English were turning to ashes.

The last of his men, too, were scattered around, twenty of them, his true brothers. They crouched among the willows, pretending to catch their breaths rather than watch their dream die. Only Guthrinc and Kraki followed his gaze. Brought low by betrayal. The cruelty seemed too great after they had fought so hard and sacrificed so much.

And yet all that they had lost paled into insignificance in his thoughts compared to the form hanging limply in his arms. Alric's breathing was shallow. The dark stain was spreading across his tunic too fast.

'We must get the monk to a leech,' he said, 'or find a wise woman in the woods, with her pastes and her brews . . .' His voice trailed away when he looked into the faces of Kraki and Guthrinc. They nodded, trying to show quiet agreement, but he could see from their eyes that they thought it was hopeless. 'I will not let him die,' he insisted, the passion burning in his voice.

Sighard stepped over, his face and hair streaked with blood and dirt. 'Hereward is right. We have lost so many this day. If we can save even one life, it is a thing of value. And Alric is as much a brother as . . .' He choked on his words and looked away.

'The king's war-bands will be everywhere, hunting us down,' Kraki growled. 'They will never allow the leader of the English to escape. They will chase us to the ends of the earth, if need be, and they will only stop when they have our heads.' He paused, eyeing the monk's fluttering eyes. 'I know him. If he were awake now, he would tell you to leave him. His weight will only slow you down. We cannot risk your capture, not at any cost. The king will make a show of your death, and the English will be broken for all time once they have seen it.'

Hereward felt his frustration simmer. Kraki was right, he knew. But his heart told him that his friend's life held more value than all the things for which he had fought. He could not understand why that should be so; the notion seemed to make no sense. But he felt it none the less.

'My life means nothing now,' he said in a low, strained voice. 'I have given my all to this war, and we have gained naught. This . . .' He held out Alric's still form. 'This, here, is something I can save. I would have a victory today, just one, however small. And if we are to talk of another fight against the Bastard, then let it be tomorrow.'

After a moment's reflection, Kraki whistled through his teeth. 'Then save the monk we shall, or die trying,' he said with passion, shaking a fist at the fates. He stood up and began to walk among the other men, jerking the flat of his hand up to urge movement. 'Time is short, you lazy curs. We have a life to save and the hounds of the Norman bastards at our backs. There is no rest for us.' The men clambered to their feet, pushing aside their despondency.

Kraki beckoned to Herrig the Rat, and sent him ahead. When Hereward had cleaned the monk's wound, he lifted him in his arms once more and loped off through the woods. Keeping low, the others followed, eyes darting this way and that.

Barely had they travelled more than a few spear-lengths when they heard the sound of branches breaking underfoot. They whirled, levelling their spears. A cloaked and hooded figure swept through the trees towards them.

Kraki gaped. 'Are you mad?'

Acha threw back her hood, glancing over her shoulder. 'You must hurry. The king has already sent out men searching for you, and they are close behind.'

'You should be safe with the women in the Camp of Refuge,' Kraki said, throwing his hands in the air. 'They would have hidden you well. We made our plans—'

'And now they have changed.' She set her jaw in defiance. 'I will come with you.'

'There is too much danger here,' the Viking began.

'There is danger everywhere,' she interrupted. 'You waste time. Or would you rather stand here arguing and die?'

Hereward watched worry carve lines in Kraki's face. 'Let her come,' he urged. 'We will watch out for each other.'

Kraki let out a roar of frustration, then spun on his heel and marched ahead. Acha shrugged and followed. As he set off behind them, Hereward hoped he had not made the wrong decision.

As the light began to thin, it grew colder. A harsh wind rushed through the trees. Winter was not far off now, he knew, and they had no home and no food. But he had suffered through worse and lived. He glanced down at Alric. In his stupor, the monk mouthed words that appeared to be in the Roman tongue, some prayer, perhaps, that he learned when he first joined the monastery at Jarrow. Hereward hoped God would hear. But worry had made his chest tight and he had started to fear the worst. 'Stay strong, monk,' he muttered as he ran.

As the shadows pooled beneath the willows, the Rat came scampering back. His grin told them all they needed to know. 'The track north is free of Norman bastards,' he called. 'There is a wise woman's hut not far from here. We can reach it before full dark, if we are quick.'

CHAPTER FIFTY-SIX

Gleaming in the light of the burning barns, the axe hung in the air. A silence fell across the vast crowd gathered inside Ely's gaping walls. They could not tear their eyes away from that weapon and all that it signalled. No more feasting. No more hope of a time free of the yoke of the Normans. All had become ashes.

William the Bastard looked across the raised, despairing faces and smiled. His face was smeared with smuts and sweat and his hauberk was brown with dried blood. Under his arm, he cupped his helm, now dented by the blows of numerous axes and spears. But his eyes shone with joy, and perhaps no little relief. Five long years after he had slaughtered a king at Senlac Ridge and stolen the crown for himself, England had finally succumbed to his will.

Perched upon a heap of bodies, both Norman and English, Harald Redteeth hummed to himself. He could see the king's jubilation as if the monarch were bellowing it to the heavens. He shrugged. If William thought the struggle would ever end he was deluding himself. The Viking chewed slowly on his dry, bitter mushrooms and uttered his prayer that their magic would not take his life this day. Death had been close throughout this long battle and he had been forced to fight hard for his days yet to come. There had been no respite from the thrusting spears and swinging axes, from the bodies falling around him in showers of crimson, not a moment to seek out Hereward in the carnage. Once the English had fled, he had searched all the corpses and examined every man the Normans had captured beyond the walls, but there was no sign of the Mercian. His quest would continue.

He grinned, listening to the first whispers of the *alfar* drifting on the breeze. He watched their messengers, the ravens, pluck at eyes and lips on the fallen littered across the hillside. And he knew that now he was closer than he had been in nine long years. Somewhere in the desolate wetlands, Hereward was taking flight like a wounded deer. No allies, no fortress to protect him, as lost as the wild youth he had first encountered in the Northumbrian hills.

The king raised one arm and swept it down. The axe fell. The scream of the warrior tore across the hillside as his right hand flew from his wrist. The Normans who had been pinning him to the block stepped back and the man fell to the mud, convulsing. Pulling an iron rod from the red heart of one of the burning barns, the axeman's helper gripped the wounded man's forearm and pressed the glowing tip against the bloody stump. The warrior howled once more as his flesh sizzled.

Once the prisoner had been dragged away, the axeman plucked up the fallen hand and tossed it on to a pile of ten more. Six bloody feet were heaped beside it.

Redteeth looked along the line snaking across the slopes. Not only broken-spirited English warriors waited for their fate, but men who had been leaders of the Ely folk, wise ones who had given counsel and comfort to Hereward and had maintained the support of the common men and women. The day would be long.

Two Norman soldiers grabbed the next in line, a grey-haired man who held his head high. They forced him to his knees in front of the monarch.

'Ordric of Ely,' one of the soldiers announced. 'He would speak on Hereward's behalf to the folk and pass on his demands.'

William made a show of fingering his chin as he weighed his response. 'Take his eye,' he said.

The man blanched, but tried to keep his trembling chin raised. Yet when the axeman took out his knife and dug it into the eye socket, Ordric screamed like all the others. They always screamed, Redteeth mused. For a moment, he closed his eyes and drifted with the music he heard in that sound. When he opened them again, the axeman held the orb, slippery with blood, and tossed it towards the pile of body parts. A raven swooped down and tried to snatch the choice morsel from the air. The eye bounced and rolled and the bird set about it with its beak.

'The king is merciful.' Deda had appeared at the Viking's shoulder and was watching the next prisoner yell and fight as he was dragged to the block. Blood caked the corner of his mouth and mud streaked his forehead. A gash marred his cheek. 'There was a time when this hill would have run red. Every man, woman and child here would have been slaughtered.'

'He knows the time for killing is done,' Redteeth grunted. 'He has made the English fear him. Now he needs to make them love him if he wants a few years of peace to enjoy his spoils. He is no fool, your Norman king.'

The knight shrugged. 'Still, this is strange to my eyes. I do not recognize the man I know.'

'He is not changed. He makes his deals with the one inside him. And the one beside him.' The Viking nodded towards Abbot Thurstan, who stood behind the monarch. 'The churchman pleaded for mercy for the mass of common folk. They have suffered enough under the cruelty of Hereward's rule, he says.' Redteeth spat. 'Good Christian men. Lies spring as easily to their tongue as prayers.'

Deda scanned the fires blazing across the devastated

settlement, then looked towards the minster, shrouded in a thick pall of smoke. 'God has turned his back upon this place, that is certain.'

His voice sounded weary, Redteeth thought. 'What now for you?'

The knight shrugged. 'I foresee long miles of riding, perhaps a sea journey.'

'What about that woman who has caught your eye?'

Deda shook his head, feigning ignorance. He glanced askance at the king. 'I killed the old man, Asketil. William will demand a high price for that crime. My life, I would think.'

Redteeth snorted. 'The old man was a bastard. He had it coming.' With his foot, he rocked the head of one of the bodies underneath him so that it looked to be nodding assent. 'Once we are done here, I have a trail to follow and an English warrior to kill. I will need good men to watch my back. Join me. There will no doubt be coin and adventures along the way, a good life for a Norman bastard like yourself.' He shrugged. 'Though just as likely hardship, suffering and death.'

The other man smiled. 'You have inflamed me with your honeyed words.' After a moment, though, his face grew serious. 'And there is nothing for me here.'

The pile of hands, feet and eyes grew larger. The screams seemed to roll on for ever. But finally the king was done with his judgement. While the soldiers collected the bodies of their fallen brothers for burial, William, the abbot and a few other knights strode up the slope to the minster. Curious, Deda and Redteeth followed.

'My men will take from Ely anything of value,' the monarch said. 'That will go some way towards paying for the horses I have lost, and the time I have wasted bringing peace to the east.'

'But the church will keep its treasure, of course,' the Viking heard Thurstan reply. The cleric looked anxious.

'That is the agreement we reached,' the king said as he walked into the minster enclosure. He paused in front of the church and looked up the length of the tower to where the smoke swirled around the top. A shadow crossed his face. 'I would pray,' he said, his voice hard. He nodded to the abbot. 'You will stay outside while I am speaking to God.' He called to two soldiers and ordered them to stand guard at the church door. 'Keep the monks out,' he demanded. 'I will not be disturbed by churchmen processing with crosses and relics.'

He marched inside, followed by the Norman knights. Redteeth slipped in at the back. If there was any gold in the church, he would have it. The king's footsteps echoed across the nave. He glanced at the pile of offerings surrounded by lit candles. 'That is the tomb of the holy virgin Etheldreda,' he said, seemingly to himself. 'I have heard much of it, and the glory it contains.' He took a few steps towards the shrine and then shuffled to a halt. The Viking watched him knit his brow in apprehension, then raise a hand to the side of his head as if to shield himself. He spun away from the shrine and hurried towards the altar. Dipping into his pouch, he found a gold mark and flipped it on to God's table. With undue haste, he dropped to his knees, clasped his hands together and bowed his head, muttering his prayers in a drone that seemed to go on for ever.

Redteeth grinned. The king feared God's judgement after all.

Once he was done, William seemed to have grown angry. He marched along the nave and threw open the door with a crash, bellowing for the abbot. 'Where are your monks?' he demanded.

'They eat their stew in the refectory,' Thurstan stuttered.

William's face blackened. 'They would rather eat than bow their heads to their king,' he roared. The abbot shook. 'This insult demands a price. Only a payment of seven hundred marks will suffice.'

Thurstan gaped in shock. 'That is much of the church's treasure,' he stammered.

'Take your plate and chalices and bowls to Grentabrige and have them weighed,' the king said. 'And if you are short, my wrath will be great indeed. You will pay another three hundred marks to make peace with me. So count well.'

The abbot hurried away. His face was creased with anger at this betrayal but he could not say a word. Redteeth had no doubt that the moneyers in Grentabrige would find the church offering short, no matter how much treasure was piled high on their scales.

'Thurstan would have done better to throw in his lot with Hereward,' Deda whispered. 'The English were never as grasping as William. Wherever the abbot has hidden the church's gold, it would still remain.'

'Betrayal always earns betrayal,' the Viking replied, laughing to himself. 'That is the way of men without honour. Now, let us be away. I have warriors to buy and food to steal for the road.'

As they made their way towards the enclosure gate, a messenger ran up and headed straight to the king. They paused and watched as the man whispered. The monarch listened intently, then furrowed his brow as he looked around the minster. When his gaze alighted on Deda, he grinned. Redteeth needed to know no more. Glancing at his friend's grim expression, he could see the knight felt the same.

'There is no time to waste,' the Viking whispered as they walked away through the billowing smoke. 'Go from here now. Do not look back. I will meet you at the quay with my men.'

Deda nodded and peeled away among the huts. The Viking spat. He would have to snatch what supplies he could, but there was nothing he could do about that now. As he began to ransack the nearest house, he glanced out of the door and saw a lonely figure trudging past.

He stepped out and called a greeting. The English bastard, Redwald, looked round. His face was mottled with bruises and he had the stink of failure around him. 'Your father is dead,' Redteeth called. 'Cut down like the dog he was. And now the king no longer has need of you, you will likely be next.'

If the whipped dog felt grief, he did not show it. Nor could the Viking see any sign of shock. Redwald stared with dead eyes for a long moment, then turned and disappeared into the folds of smoke.

CHAPTER FIFTY-SEVEN

The chill wind sighed in the high branches of the ash trees. Deda clung on to the damp trunks as he skidded over sodden leaves down the steep slope. He'd kept well away from the rutted mud road in the hope that he could slip away without being seen. The more miles he could put between himself and the king before his disappearance was noted the better.

The knight felt weary from the battle, and weary from life. He had fought alongside the king at Senlac Ridge with little enthusiasm. He had no desire for land, or gold or power; he had lost the only thing that mattered to him long ago. But now that the English had been routed, he had done his duty. His oath had been met, and he could, if he wanted, leave behind the life he knew. But what then? Earn coin as a sword-for-hire alongside Harald Redteeth, in Flanders, and further afield, perhaps Constantinople? He was weary of fighting too.

As he neared the edge of the trees, he peered out at the deserted quay, little more than a short timber pier where a few boats were moored. He sniffed the odour of rotting vegetation from the marsh that bordered the mere. His hiding place was good enough for now, and the Viking would soon be there.

Behind him, dry wood snapped. His battle-honed instinct

threw him aside just in time. The flat of a blade clattered against the side of his head, a whisper away from hacking into his skull. Dazed, he reeled back, slamming into trees as he spun down the slope.

Coming to rest on his back, he jerked up, only to look along a blade pointed towards his throat. A red-haired man loomed over him, no doubt one of the monarch's axes-for-hire.

'There is no honour in attacking a man while his back is turned,' the knight said.

The mercenary shrugged. 'My only thought is for the coin I will receive when I take your head back to the king.'

'Surely I am not the man you want,' Deda said with a smile. 'I am a loyal knight.' With his sword still in its scabbard, he could only play for time.

'Enough talk,' his captor spat. He braced himself to lunge.

The knight began to mutter his final prayer.

The tip of an arrow burst from the mercenary's throat. Blood splattered across Deda's hauberk. He rolled to one side as the dead man crashed face down into the rotting leaves, the shaft protruding from the back of his neck.

Nocking another arrow, the archer slid down the slope towards him. Words of thanks died in the knight's throat. His saviour was Rowena.

A surprised smile leapt to his lips. Pulling himself to his feet, he bowed. 'You saved my life.'

'No,' she said, her voice as cold as her face. 'I came to kill you.' She raised the bow and loosed her shaft.

The arrow whisked past Deda's ear and thudded into a tree trunk. If her hands had not been shaking so much, it would surely have ended his days. As she fumbled for another shaft, he saw that tears were streaming down her cheeks. He leapt forward and snatched the bow. She did not resist.

'What is the meaning of this?' he said in a hoarse voice.

She tried to answer him, but she could only gulp in mouthfuls of air to stifle her racking sobs. He felt surprised at the strength of his urge to hold her, but he could not. Instead, he reached out his hands in a heartfelt plea. 'Tell me what I have done.'

'You are a Norman bastard,' she sobbed, 'and you killed my husband.' She whipped up her hand to strike him, but it only hovered in the air for a moment and then dropped to her side. She sagged, her chin falling to her chest. 'I despise you,' she whispered.

Behind her words, Deda sensed a different meaning. He could not hate this lost soul for trying to take his life. He felt only pity. 'You have ventured to the shores of hell to make sense of the miseries that have afflicted you,' he said in a quiet voice, 'and still you have found no answers, only more pain.'

She jerked her head up, her tear-streaked eyes blazing. 'I am not weak,' she spat, 'and I will not have you think of me that way.'

'I have never met a woman with more fire in her heart.'

She jolted at his words.

'You will not ease your misery by killing me, or any Norman. To lose someone so close to your heart is . . .' He looked up into the branches, his thoughts flying across the years. 'Unbearable. There is no easy escape from it. Only time. Only time.'

Rowena frowned at him as if seeing something new and puzzling.

'I saved your life at Branduna and now you have saved mine. Our account is clear.'

She bit her lip to stifle another sob, and he felt dismay at the despair he saw in her eyes. 'I cannot live with myself,' she croaked. He remembered the terrible things she had done at Belsar's Hill as she sought to get close to the king, and he understood.

Once again he reached out to hold her, caught in the rush of emotion, and only stopped himself at the last. 'We are not prisoners of days gone by,' he murmured. 'All that matters is days yet to come.' He could not help but glance at the ribbon tied to his wrist and was surprised to feel the sting of his own words.

Rowena searched his face, seemingly hanging on his every word. 'I . . . I do not know what to do . . . where to go . . .' she began, blinking away her tears.

'Go home, to your village. For a while, each day will be as hard as if you dug the fields in winter with your bare hands. But in time, peace will come.'

'You vow that this is true?'

He nodded. 'I have walked your road.'

She kneaded her hands, reflecting on his words. He knew he could not put right what she had given to the men at the camp, but he was sure that too would fade, if only she could look forward with hope. 'You do not stand alone,' he said with a deep bow. 'I am at your service. Your champion.'

She gaped.

'Send me to the ends of the earth to pluck a flower for you, and I will do so.' He slid his sword from its sheath and offered the hilt to her. 'This I vow.'

'Stop,' she said, taking a step back. 'Do not treat me like a child.'

'This I vow,' he repeated.

She shook her head, conflicted.

'Think on my offer,' he said, pleased to see some of the darkness had lifted from her features. 'I have offered my service to a friend, for now. But when I am done, I will seek you out to hear your answer.'

'You will come back to me?'

'God willing.'

Her brow furrowed.

He bowed one final time. 'I must take my leave now. Fare well, Rowena.'

As he stepped over the mercenary's body and made his way out of the trees to the quay, he could feel her eyes upon him. But when he looked back she was gone.

CHAPTER FIFTY-EIGHT

Silhouetted against a sky the colour of bones, Death crested the high ridge and looked down upon them. He never stopped, never slowed, not for food nor drink nor sleep. His judgement would be passed come hell or high water. Overhead, ravens swirled, their hungry shrieks carrying deep into the wildwood that sprawled for mile upon mile ahead of the band of weary men. Deep snow billowed across the land behind them, the first of that winter. Snowflakes settled into their trail of footprints.

At the tree-line, Hereward leaned on a twisted oak and glanced back at the stark figure. His breath steamed and he could no longer feel his feet. Axe in hand, the figure plunged down the white slope as more men swarmed over the ridge.

'Redteeth, you bastard,' he hissed through gritted teeth. How long had that madman and his hunting band been pursuing them across the bleak fenlands now? Three days? Four? He had gone so long without sleep he could barely think straight. 'It feels as though I have spent half my life running from you,' he muttered.

On burning legs, he threw himself into the trees. His warriors fanned out among the oaks, kicking their way through snarls of bramble. White flakes whirled through the branches around them. Deep in the forest, a wolf howled. From danger into danger with no respite.

Guthrinc and Hengist hefted the willow frame on which Alric lay, wrapped in a threadbare woollen blanket. His skin was almost the colour of the snow that crunched under their feet.

As he loped alongside, Hereward studied the frail figure. His friend had grown thin – he had begun to see the outline of the bones through the skin – and his hair was plastered to his head with sweat. Though Alric shivered, his cheeks and forehead burned to the touch. Herrig had said the monk was growing weaker by the day. Hereward could not find it within himself to believe that was true.

His thoughts flew back to the reeking hut where the wise woman had hunched over his friend smearing thick paste on his wound. The *alfar* had told her Alric's spark was weak. His survival now remained in God's hands. But for a piece of gold broken off Hereward's ring she had given them the blanket, enough of the stinking paste to last two weeks and instructions to clean the wound every day and apply a new coating. Once they had built the frame, they took it in turns to carry him across the wetlands. Day and night, they had dripped cold spring water into his mouth, and every now and then he had woken enough to chew on a knob of bread or cheese. But he never seemed to know who they were or where he was. And all the time they struggled to stay one step ahead of the Norman hunting band. Harald Redteeth had appeared with his horde of warriors on a cold dawn as the English camped beside a lake. They had been making plans to travel to any English landowner who might contribute fighting men or coin to the cause. But since that moment they had done nothing but run and hide.

Behind him, the call and response of the hunting band rang out, stirring memories of a day long gone. Redteeth's blood-lust had brought him and Alric together and forged the bonds of a friendship that had never failed to surprise him. But now it felt as though the circle was closing, and they would be torn apart for ever.

He skidded down the frosted slope of a hollow. At the bottom, the snow was calf-deep. Barbs of pain from the cold lanced up his legs. As he scrambled up the other side, he plunged into the densest part of the forest. The trees here were ancient, many of them too large even for four men to encircle with their arms. Their thick branches spread out to form a canopy that even without leaves left the interior as gloomy as twilight. Faces loomed up at him from the cracked bark, the *alfar*, Turfrida would have said, trying to speak to him. Here in the Brunneswalde they had at least a thin hope of evading their pursuers.

Ahead, Kraki waved a hand to beckon him over. 'We must rest soon or we will drop,' he hissed. Hereward saw that the Viking all but carried Acha now. She had shown enough courage for two men, refusing to complain once about the exhaustion that engulfed her.

The Viking pointed to Sighard. Near delirious with tiredness, the young warrior followed an erratic path through the brown bracken fronds poking through the carpet of snow. 'Our tracks will lead those bastards to us whatever we do,' Kraki snarled.

'Then we must lose our tracks.' Hereward looked around for inspiration.

For the next hour they limped on, twisting and turning among the soaring oaks and ash trees and hawthorn. The wind had grown harsher. The branches groaned, the tallest trees complaining as they thrashed. Snow stung their eyes. The whistles and bird-calls of the hunting band seemed to fade.

As they struggled on into the blizzard, Hengist stopped and pointed down. Prints dappled the snow, moving in all directions. They had entered the territory of a wolf pack.

'We have no choice,' Hereward said. 'Move on.'

Moments later, he heard the dim sound of a babbling stream. Leaping into the freezing water, they splashed along the centre of the brook as it wound among the trees and bracken. In Flanders, Hereward had seen warriors lose their toes by submitting to such cold, but if they were to hide their trail they had little choice.

After a while, the trees pressed close against the water's edge. Stooping, they struggled on along a dark tunnel under the overhanging branches. The white world fell behind them. Soon they were all but crawling along the stream. Spikes of hawthorn tore at their backs and raked their scalps. But just when the way seemed to be becoming impassable, the landscape altered. They found themselves in a crevice carved in the earth by floodwaters rushing from the confluence of several streams. On either side, flat banks stretched for a spear's length until the walls rose up steeply. At the top, the branches and vegetation closed over their heads, plunging them into a dank cave of near-darkness.

Hereward stepped from the water and rested his back against the cold earth. With relief, the others followed, stamping their frozen feet. 'Night will be here soon,' the Mercian said, 'and this is the best shelter we will find.' He looked around and nodded. 'There is room to light a fire. Its glow will not be seen, and the branches overhead will spread the smoke so that it will be hidden in the dark.'

Acha sank to the ground, burying her head in her arms. Crouching beside her, Kraki slipped a comforting arm round her shoulders. He looked up at Hereward and said, 'I will search for wood.'

'No, you must rest and care for your woman.'

As he watched over Alric, Guthrinc rested a hand on his shoulder. 'You fought well,' the tall man murmured. 'Let no one tell you otherwise. The hopes of the English would have died long ago without your fire.' He gave a reassuring grin. 'Had I been able to see into days yet to come, I would have known you were the right man for this work years ago, when we were lads, and you came to my home and robbed me. And then you came back and robbed me again. And I hung you up in the Barholme oak all night by your feet. And the next night you came back and robbed me again. Nothing stands in the way of your heart's desire.' He glanced down at the faltering rise and fall of Alric's chest and his grin faded. 'Remember that, should times get harder.'

After they had caught their breath, Hereward sent three men out to find kindling, and soon they were all warming their hands around a small fire. While Guthrinc and another man, Ithamar, ventured out with their bows to hunt what game they could find, they took it in turn to keep watch at either end of the cut. Alric lay on his willow bed, unmoving, and the others not on watch huddled in their cloaks near the fire, fitfully dozing. Hereward surveyed them from under heavy lids, worrying what would become of them all. Soon sleep claimed him.

For the first time in days, he saw his father's face, and for the first time ever, it seemed, he thought of Asketil without seeing his mother's body lying before him, her life-blood draining between the boards. Drifting, he wondered if there had ever been a time when he had considered his father with fondness. If there had, he could not recall it. And yet now he felt no threat when he remembered the old man. Nor did he feel that unpleasant churning deep in the pit of his belly where his devil lived. Perhaps it was an omen, he thought, but of what he was not sure.

The scream jerked him from his trance. His men jumped to their feet as one, clutching for their spears and shields. The firelight threw wild shadows up the walls of earth. Acha pressed her hands against her ears as that terrible cry continued without a break, rising and falling, then rising to even greater heights. No one spoke. As Hereward looked around the hunted features he knew everyone there was thinking the same: what agony could draw such a sound out of a man?

Guthrinc had returned. A half-plucked bird hung by its neck from his left hand. But of Ithamar there was no sign. The Mercian's heart fell.

Stalking out of the cut, he cocked his head. The screaming

was not close, but it carried well across the still, night-cloaked forest.

Sighard eased beside him. The snow was still falling, coating his hair and lashes in a white dusting. 'That is Ithamar,' he whispered, his words heavy with dread.

Hereward nodded. 'Harald Redteeth is taunting me.' When he saw the other man furrow his brow, he added, 'The Viking bastard is paying me back for something I did to one of his men nine winters gone.'

'What did you do that could have caused such suffering?' Sighard asked.

Hereward peered out past the ghostly oaks into the deep dark. In his mind's eye, he saw a blade, and a stream of blood, and he remembered the man he used to be before Alric had saved him from his devil. In a voice that seemed to carry no emotion, he replied, 'I skinned his man alive.'

CHAPTER FIFTY-NINE

Branches tore at Kraki's scarred face. His chest burned and his legs felt like lead as he lurched through knee-deep snow. Behind him, his pursuers howled with delight, sensing their prey was about to fall. Ten of them, there were, shaking their axes and swords in anticipation of slaughter.

Skidding down a steep bank, he almost stumbled over a hidden bramble snarled around his ankle. The baying at his back grew louder. He wrenched himself free and clawed his way up the other side of the hollow. As he crested the ridge, he almost stumbled into Guthrinc and Hengist, who were crouching there listening to the wild sounds of the hunt.

'Run,' Kraki bellowed without slowing his step.

He heard the two warriors dash away in opposite directions. Glancing back, he saw that each of his brothers was now chased by four men. But Hengist was wiry and he leapt around the trees like a deer while his pursuers stumbled over hidden hollows. And Guthrinc for all his size was as strong as an ox. The deep snow was as nothing to him.

Grunting with relief, Kraki staggered on through the oaks. He hated fleeing like some frightened rabbit. Would that he could take a stand and test the blade of his axe upon the two bastards still on his tail. But they were silent now, loping like wolves as they ran him to ground. They wanted to trap him, come at him from different sides so he did not have a chance to defend himself.

His breath smoked as he searched the wood ahead. Against the gentle folds of white he glimpsed a thick band of black hawthorn and struggled towards it. Their war-band was scattered across the forest now, torn apart by Redteeth's men. He mouthed a silent prayer to Woden that they all yet lived.

A narrow path weaved through the wall of hawthorn, banks of lethal barbs rising up on either side. Kraki plunged into its midst, pushing his right shoulder forward so he could edge along the track at speed without harm. Even so, he felt the thorns rip through the flesh of his forearm as he brushed past. A trail of blood spattered on the hard-packed snow beneath his feet.

Following the trail of many footprints, he burst from the hawthorn into a bowl-shaped depression. The wall of black thorn continued all around the rim. He was trapped. Sliding into the hollow, he bounded to the other side to make his stand. His feet flew out from under him and he crashed face down in a drift. As he pushed his head up, his beard frosted with flakes, he heard his pursuers yelp and curse as they edged through the hawthorn. He rolled on to his back and fumbled for his axe.

The first man stepped out on to the edge of the hollow. He had eyes like a winter sky framed in the eyelets of his helm. He grinned as he pointed his sword towards the fallen Viking. Behind him, a moan rustled out. For a moment, the warrior paid no attention to the sound, and then, as he realized his companion had not followed him out, he began to turn.

With a hiss like a spitting wildcat, a figure flew from the track through the hawthorn. Cloak flapping behind, it crashed on to the Norman's back, pitching him down into the hollow. He had not even a moment to cry out before his face slammed into the snow. A short-bladed knife rose and fell, rose and fell.

Blood gouted. The stabbing only stopped when the body ceased all movement.

Levering himself up on his elbows, Kraki grinned. 'A well-made plan is a joy to behold.'

Acha looked up with fierce, dark eyes. A line of blood spattered across her pale skin from eye to jaw. The Viking thought that at that moment he would be happy to give his heart to her for ever. 'Two down,' she said. 'The rest . . . ?'

He cocked his head and listened. From across the forest, a peal of cries rolled out from different locations, Norman or English, he could not yet be sure. 'Help me up,' he growled. 'They had the numbers, now let us see if we had the wits.'

CHAPTER SIXTY

The bloody hand stained a crimson circle in the snow. On top of a bank it lay, as if beckoning to the five men who stared at it. After the hunt and the screams, the sounds of men had once again faded from the wildwood. Only the desolate call of the icy wind in the trees, and the creak of branches and the whispers of the stirring holly, remained.

'The *wuduwasa*,' one of the Normans said, crossing himself. He could not tear his eyes from the gory remnant. The two warriors who flanked him looked around with unease, pulling their cloaks tight to them. The snow had started to drift down once more.

'What is the *wuduwasa*?' Deda asked. He crouched so that the hand fell into his line of sight.

'A story as old as time that the English tell themselves around the hearths in midwinter. The wild man of the woods,' Harald Redteeth muttered. The breeze rattled the bird-skulls hanging on the thongs on his hauberk.

''Tis true,' the first Norman muttered. 'In the tavern in Lincylene, a woodworker told how the *wuduwasa* chased him through the woods. It tore his friend limb from limb and gnawed on his bones.'

'"Twas the mead speaking,' the Viking growled. Yet he felt his neck prickle none the less. Beside the fire in the mountains of his home, his father had told him of stranger things.

'The wild men of the woods,' Deda mused. 'That is what the English call Hereward's men. Are they, then, one and the same? Or distant cousins? There is magic in both of them, the English believe.' He smiled, tracing his forefinger in the air. 'A clean cut across the wrist. Unless the *wuduwasa* wields a sword, this is the work of men.'

The knight stood up and looked around. He frowned, puzzled to see that the three Norman warriors were not comforted by his words. 'Men,' he insisted. 'Not stories to frighten children.'

'They are children,' Redteeth snapped. He whirled and shook his axe in the faces of his warriors. 'Do not let the English frighten you. They have torn through us like the wind. Look how many still stand. And all because of our weakness. We were too slow. Too trusting of our own strength. We thought them wounded and broken by defeat, fleeing before our might until we picked them off one by one. We should have known better. They are English. They fight like rats in a corner until their last breath.'

'They outnumber us now,' one of the men ventured. His voice tailed off when he saw the fire in the Viking's eyes.

'We will not be beaten,' Redteeth rumbled. 'I will have Hereward's head.'

Deda strode up the bank. He tapped the severed hand with the tip of his sword and looked out into the white wastes of the forest ahead. It was hard to see more than a spear's throw through the blizzard. 'A trail of blood,' the knight said. 'Would it be wise to follow it?'

'No,' the frightened Norman warrior exclaimed. His two companions nodded and murmured in agreement.

'We move on,' the Northman roared. He stormed up the bank and strode into the teeth of the wind.

Splashes of blood led in a near-straight line, past fingers of yellowing grass waving through the snow, over roots and alongside the rotting hulks of fallen trees.

'Why would the English lure us on?' Deda asked. 'This must be a trap.'

'They try to frighten us,' the Viking replied.

Coming to a halt, the knight looked along the trail. A glistening liver lay on the path. Behind him, one of the men whimpered. 'And it seems they have succeeded,' Deda murmured.

Redteeth swung his leg and kicked the liver deep into the trees. He marched on without another word. A little further on, they stopped in front of a pile of blue-grey entrails, still steaming in the cold.

'No man could have done this,' one of the Norman warriors gasped.

''Tis the *wuduwasa*,' another whispered.

'Stand your ground,' the Viking growled. Even as the words left his lips, he heard the crump of feet racing away through the snow. He whirled to see the three men darting into the haze of white.

Deda rested a calming hand on the Northman's shoulder. 'Even good coin cannot abate a man's fears.'

Snarling, Redteeth whirled and continued along the trail of blood spatters, all caution now thrown to the wind. As he crested another ridge, he found himself peering at a human heart, as big as a man's fist. He snatched it up. It was still warm. With the blood caking his fingers, he threw his arm back and hurled the heart away. 'Come for me now,' he roared into the face of the blizzard. 'Do not hide like whipped dogs. Fight like men.'

Deda caught his arm. 'Do not be hasty. Our position is weak. Let us find shelter, wait until this snow has passed—'

The Viking threw him off. 'I am weary of running and hunting. I would have an end to it. Nine long years I have chased Hereward over hill and bog, across England and Flanders and the whale road. This has become my life now, the two of us caught in a dance that seems to have no end.' He shook his axe as if he would challenge the gale itself. 'Ivar, loyal Ivar, walks the grey path still. Denied the Halls of the Fallen, denied his cups of mead and his handmaidens. Because of Hereward.' His chest heaved. 'Because of my failings. I would have an end to it!'

'Hark,' the knight said, turning his head. He narrowed his eyes, listening.

'I hear nothing.'

Deda held out a hand to silence his friend. In the distance, a lonely cry rolled out, almost lost beneath the moaning of the wind.

Still unsure that he had heard anything, the Viking listened again.

The sound echoed once more, closer this time. A howl.

Redteeth looked down at the blood staining his hands, and the trail of gore reaching out across the forest behind them. The scent of fresh meat hanging in the air: no greater lure to the hungry wolves roaming the wildwood. 'The bastard English,' he cursed under his breath, but a part of him could not help but admire his enemy's wits.

He and Deda spun round as one and raced back through the trees. Behind them, the wolves called to each other, their baying becoming one voice, rushing towards their backs faster than either of them could run.

Redteeth blinked the stinging snow from his eyes. He could hear the pounding of heavy paws close by. Inflamed by the scent of blood, the pack would not relent, he knew. He had seen a man torn to pieces in an instant in the woods near his father's hall.

'There is an oak with branches low enough to climb just ahead,' Deda gasped, 'if only we can reach it.'

The Viking squinted through the blizzard and saw the tree the knight meant, an old man oak, broad and hunched, with strong branches reaching out just above the height of his head. He heaved in a gulp of air to drive him on. The cold burned in his throat.

But then he sensed a blur of movement beside him. He glanced into the burning yellow eyes of a wolf and knew that he would never reach the safety of the tree. Roaring his fury, he whirled his axe and buried it in the creature's head as it leapt for his throat. The impact jolted deep into his shoulder, but the beast's skull split in two and it fell to the ground, dead. He spun round and hacked another one before it could get its fangs upon him. Blood sprayed.

A few paces ahead, Deda turned and drew his sword. The knight could have reached the old oak, but he would not abandon his brother. Redteeth felt warmed by that thought.

Waving their weapons from side to side as the pack circled them, they edged back until they felt the rough wood of another oak at their backs. 'We make our stand here, then,' the Viking growled.

'A good choice,' the knight replied.

Ten grey wolves loped among the trees, waiting for their opening. Their pale eyes reminded Redteeth of Hereward, and that only drove him to greater rage. For long moments the creatures ranged, and then, as if upon a silent signal, they attacked as one, low and fast and powerful. The Viking's vision filled with snapping jaws and fur and gleaming golden eyes. His head rang with their snarling. Fangs sank into his right forearm as he threw it up to guard his face. Ignoring the agony, he hacked with his axe. A spine severed. A head sheared in two. Hot blood gushed down his face and chest. With a roar, he lopped off the head of the beast tearing at his arm. The body fell away, leaving the fangs embedded in his flesh. With a flick of his wrist, the rest flew away into the snow.

More wolves flew at him.

Staggering back, he whirled his blade. Arcs of crimson droplets trailed through the falling snow. Fangs ripped through the flesh of his thigh. From the corner of his eye, he glimpsed Deda beside him, his blade flashing. His face and hands, too, were red.

Blinking away the gore, he realized the snapping jaws were

beginning to thin. Bodies littered the snow around his feet. His agony had started to ebb, his vision closed in. Sounds reached him, dim and distorted. And yet he could hear the whispers of the *alfar* in the branches above as clearly as if they stood beside him. He had been here before. It was the battle-sickness, or Woden's Mercy, numbing him to the pain so he could heal. The flow of blood from his wounds, too, would slow, enough for Deda to bind them.

He hacked another wolf to the ground as it leapt. And then, as if from far, far away, he heard the blare of hunting horns. The surviving beasts paused in their attack and looked around. Their growls died in their throats. Slinking low, they sped away into the swirling snow.

Redteeth leaned against the trunk and caught his breath. His thigh was a ragged mess, and he bled from a score of other wounds. But he had survived. Deda rested a weary hand on his shoulder. The knight's long mail shirt and gauntlets had protected him from the brunt of the savaging. 'Come,' he said, 'we must be away.'

The Viking could not understand the other man's urgency. But then he looked up and saw dark shapes emerging from the blizzard.

Deda sucked in a deep breath of resignation. 'The wild men of the woods,' he said.

The men stepped out of the drifting snow and formed a semicircle around the two blood-soaked warriors. Redteeth looked at the faces. He settled on the one that had haunted his days for so long.

Hereward grinned, his eyes blazing as if a devil looked out of him. 'Now,' he snarled, 'we shall have our reckoning.'

CHAPTER SIXTY-ONE

Harald Redteeth threw back his head and roared his laughter to the heavens. His eyes peered out of a red mask, above a wild red beard. Blood clotted his furs and streamed down his hauberk and his axe into a puddle round his feet. Most of the gore belonged to the dismembered wolves scattered around him, Hereward could see – he had given a good account of himself – but the wounds upon his thigh and his arm were still seeping.

The Northman shook his axe and more crimson droplets spattered across the snow. 'I am ready for you, Mercian,' he said with a mad grin, 'as I have been ready for you these nine long years.'

The wind gusted a sheet of snow between them, and once again Hereward's thoughts flew back across the years to that first encounter. Then he was the one who had been drenched in blood, the one who had no doubt looked mad to all who saw him. His devil had ridden him hard in those days. If Alric finally loosened his feeble grip on this world, would the circle turn once more? Would he become like Harald Redteeth, who had become like him? He felt all the portents fire his deepest fears. He could almost feel the cold breath of death upon his neck. The End of Days was coming, for the world, for England, for him and the Viking and Alric.

'We fight, here, now, and one of us will die,' he called. Drawing his sword, he levelled it at his warriors and swung it in a slow arc. 'Let no man stand in the way of this ending, even if that axe is about to split my skull.' The men muttered with unease at this, but they gave reluctant nods.

'And when I send you to your doom, your men must let me, and Deda, walk free,' the Viking called back, 'and seek no vengeance for your death.'

'Agreed.'

Redteeth rested one foot upon the body of a wolf. 'This battle is a settling of accounts. Your death in payment for my friend Ivar. Only then will he be free to enter the Halls of the Fallen. This was my vow to him.'

'And your death in payment for my friend Vadir, whose head you took in Flanders. A good man, who did not deserve your cruelty.'

'He was a warrior,' the Viking replied with a dismissive shrug. 'These things happen in war.'

'Ready yourself,' Hereward said, gripping Brainbiter with both hands and lifting it.

Redteeth raised one finger to stop him. Without taking his eyes off the Mercian, he dipped one hand into the leather pouch at his hip and drew out a handful of mushrooms. Throwing them into his mouth, he chewed with slow, deliberate movements. When he had swallowed, he grinned and said, 'This is the flesh of Woden. It cures all ills and takes away all pain. On the wings of ravens, I will rise above this battle and then I will smite you down with the fury of the All-Father.'

'Ready yourself,' Hereward repeated.

Still the Viking ignored him. He turned to Deda and said, 'You can drink my piss when we are done, if you like. It will make you fly with the gods.'

The knight bowed. 'My thanks. If the tavern runs out of wine, that will no doubt be my first choice.'

Redteeth stepped over the dead wolves and faced Hereward. As the Mercian neared, he saw the Viking frown and lean in. 'Should the gods have it that this day I journey to the great black sea, never to return,' he whispered so the other men could not hear, 'then take Deda with you. He is a good man, one you could use. And,' he said with a wink, 'the king wishes him dead. He can never again return to William's court. Will you do this thing for me, as we are men of honour and brothers of the axe?'

Hereward was surprised. Never had he seen the Viking show warmth or consideration for any other man. 'Should you die, as you will, I will grant your wish,' he murmured.

The Viking nodded, his fierce face falling for the first time into a pleased smile. He wiped it away in an instant and gave a bloodthirsty grin. Stepping back, he swung his axe high and boomed, 'I wish you a good death, brother.'

'And I you.' Hereward thought of Alric lying a whisper away from his own death, with Acha watching over him. And he thought of the final agonies of Ithamar, who had stood by him since his army had first begun to grow in Ely. He opened himself up to the fury those visions summoned, and he heard the echoing whispers deep inside him. *Come*, he called. *Come. Fill me with your rage.* A devil to fight a devil.

The blizzard whipped around them and the wind howled in their ears so that it seemed they were alone in all the world. Blood showered off Redteeth as he roared and hurled himself forward. He leapt the final step and drove the axe down. Hereward threw himself aside, swinging his sword in an arc. The Viking dropped to his knees as he hit the ground and the blade whisked a finger's width above his head. Rolling aside, Harald hacked for the Mercian's shins. Ready for this strike, Hereward jumped. As the weapon cut through the air beneath his feet, he thrust down, but his opponent was already away and rising to his feet. Snow frosted his beard and his hauberk and furs, but he seemed oblivious of the bitter cold, and of the pain he should surely feel from his weeping wounds. Woden's flesh was working its magic.

Redteeth leaned back and laughed once more. This was a fight to the death, but he was enjoying it as if it were a wrestling bout in the king's feasting hall. Hereward scowled. Death was a serious business.

Growling, he bounded forward. The Northman stood his ground and met him head-on. Sword clashed against axe and sparks flew among the snowflakes. Hereward's head rang with the clang of iron. With their weapons between them, they pressed against each other, Redteeth's face only a hand's width away. Hereward could smell his meaty breath and the sweat rising from beneath his furs. He looked deep into those all-black eyes and for a moment he thought he knew his enemy's deepest secrets. The Viking squirmed under that scrutiny and broke away as if he could not bear to be so exposed.

Locked in each other's gyre, they whirled. Sharp blades nicked flesh, raising mists of blood. But as they danced on and on and no deeper wounds were inflicted, Hereward saw they were too evenly matched. It was as if they knew the innermost workings of each other's mind.

The light grew thin. The cold bit hard. The blizzard enveloped them in a world of white.

Lost to his battle-rage, Hereward had no idea how much time had passed. But then, as he sidestepped an axe strike with ease, he thought it seemed to take all the Viking's strength to draw his weapon back. On the hard-packed snow, he noticed the swirling trail of blood that marked Redteeth's movements in the whirling battle. Line upon line of crimson in a criss-crossing pattern of such complexity that he felt reminded of the illustrated books the monks worked on in the scriptorium.

When he thrust with his sword, Redteeth barely parried the strike, batting his blade away with the axe as if he were swatting a fly. The Northman's step faltered. In those black eyes, Hereward glimpsed a flicker of unease. Harald knew his strength was ebbing. He laughed again, loud and long, but this time it did not ring true. The sound died away and he scowled.

'Fight on,' he bellowed. 'What is wrong with you? Has my

might made you afrit? Have you turned coward in the face of your own death?'

Hereward swung his sword, then caught it at the last. The blade hung in the air for a moment, until he withdrew it and stepped back.

Redteeth shook his axe with fury and tried to bound forward. He staggered and fell to his knees. His face looked the colour of the snow. 'Fight,' he gasped. He tried to shake his axe once more, but it slipped from his fingers. With a juddering sigh, he lowered his chin to his chest. Finally he accepted the truth. He was done.

Hereward sheathed his sword. 'You have not lost,' he said. 'The wolves have ended your days.'

When he looked up, tears glinted in the corner of the Viking's eyes. He reached out a trembling hand to something Hereward could not see. 'Ivar . . .' His voice was barely a rustle. 'I have failed you.' He slumped backwards on to the white ground and stared up at the branches. Flakes settled across his face.

Hereward loomed over him. 'You fought well.'

'This is not an honourable death,' he croaked. 'Not a death in battle. The Halls of the Fallen are denied to me. I will never drink mead with my father again, or my father's father, and laugh, and feast.'

The Mercian winced at the despair he heard in the dying man's voice.

Deda stepped out of the blizzard, his cloak billowing around him. He looked down at the Viking and said in a gentle voice, 'There is still fight left in you, battle-brother.'

Redteeth creased his brow in bafflement. He could barely move, so weak was he from blood-loss, Hereward could see.

The knight glanced at the English warrior for approval and then crouched beside his fallen companion. Grabbing the axe, he pressed it into the Viking's hand and held it there. His feet sliding around on the packed snow, Deda slipped his other hand under Redteeth's armpit and hauled him to his feet.

They stood there, swaying, as if in a ghastly dance of death.

'Fight,' the knight urged.

The Viking licked his dry lips and grinned. 'Come on, you English bastard. Or are you still afrit?'

Hereward drew Brainbiter again. He knew his duty. As he levelled the blade, Deda pressed his friend's hand so the axe tapped against it. In one fluid movement, the Mercian snatched back the sword and thrust it under Redteeth's jaw and into his brain. Blood bubbled out of his mouth, and his eyes glassed over.

As Deda eased the fallen warrior on to the snow, the Viking slid off the blade. Redteeth lay there, staring up, a spark still glimmering within him. How hard he was to kill, Hereward thought. For all the death he dealt, he lived life more fiercely than any other man the Mercian knew.

A smile flickered on his lips. 'Father . . .' he whispered. His breath steamed, once, and then the wind whisked it away. All was still.

And from somewhere overhead came the sound of wings.

CHAPTER SIXTY-TWO

The column of English warriors trudged through the calf-deep snow, heads bowed into the teeth of the gale. Night was falling. Hereward felt more weary than he ever had in the years since he had begun his rebellion against the king.

'You have my thanks for your offer of companionship and shelter,' Deda yelled above the howling wind. He shielded his eyes against the stinging flakes. 'I would not have known where to turn.'

Hereward grunted. 'You will earn your keep.' Glancing at the other man, he added, 'You owe your thanks to that mad Viking. He pleaded for you.'

Remembering the angry vows he had made over Vadir's grave in Flanders, he had expected some joy at Harald Redteeth's death, but there was none, only a curious numbness. The ground had been too hard to bury the warrior, and they would not have been able to light a pyre, so they dragged two fallen trees beside his body and heaped branches over the top in the hope that it would keep the wolves off him.

The knight looked surprised. 'I could not get the measure of him, even to the end.' He hesitated. 'I will not raise my sword against the king. You know that.'

'Even though he wants your life?'

'Even so.'

'Very well. There will be other work for you.' Hereward peered into the storm, searching for landmarks. A part of him did not want to make his way back to the camp beside the stream for fear of what would be waiting for him.

'One other thing,' Deda said. 'I could not in all conscience keep this from you. Your father is dead.' He paused. 'I killed him.'

Hereward jerked round and looked deep into the knight's face. He was not lying. 'Why would you take the life of an old man?'

Deda turned away, choosing his words. 'To save the life of a woman.'

The Mercian looked down, feeling the sting of old memories. 'Then you did well.'

He could feel the knight's puzzled gaze upon him, but he did not meet it, nor would he speak of it again. He was unsure how he felt about Asketil's passing, but he was sure the world was a better place without his father in it.

By the time they reached the camp, he could not feel his face and hands. But once he had stooped under the overhanging branches and reached the safety of the cut, he felt a blast of warmth from the roaring fire. In the glow of the flames, Acha hunched over Alric's frail form. She glanced at him and shook her head. Something in her face seemed to say she did not think it would be long.

Hereward slumped down against the cold wall of earth and sank his head between his knees. He could hear the rhythmic chops of Guthrinc's knife as he butchered the wolf carcass he had carried back across his shoulders. As he drifted into sleep, he thought they sounded like a heartbeat slowly fading into nothing.

Dreams folded around him again, and this time he was holding a babe in his arms, his son, now cared for by the monks at Crowland and whom he had not seen since the day of

Turfrida's burial. He felt at peace, a peace deeper than any he had ever experienced in his life. He blinked, and his eyes blurred with tears, and that, too, was strange.

He jerked awake. Someone was shaking him. His hand leapt to the hilt of his sword and he half lurched to his feet. Fingers dug into his arm. It was Acha. 'No,' she whispered. 'No.' She was smiling.

He looked past her. Lit by the fire's glow, Alric had levered himself up on his elbows and was looking around. 'Food,' he croaked. 'I am hungry.'

CHAPTER SIXTY-THREE

28 March 1072

The king glowered at the three men. 'Ravens, all. You have fed well on the corpse of England. Power, land, gold.' He held out a hand, palm upwards, and slowly curled his fingers into a fist as if he were crushing balls. 'Of all those who have prospered from my victory, you know Hereward the best. You have fought him. And you have been defeated by him. Time and again. I ask you once more: what will stop his rebellion against my rule?'

William de Warenne would not meet the monarch's eyes. He rested his elbows on the table and bowed his head, playing with his cup of wine. Beside him, Ivo the Butcher stared at the boar's head as if it would give him the words he needed. Only Abbot Turold of Burgh returned William the Bastard's gaze, and after a moment's reflection he said, 'He will never stop. It is not in his nature.'

Cloaked in shadows, Redwald peered through the crack in the door at the scene in the feasting hall of the king's new palace in Wincestre. He flinched at the churchman's words. He had seen men killed for less.

When the king plucked the long-bladed knife from the cold pork, Turold all but gasped, the blood draining from his face. He was a big man, broad-shouldered and strong, as much a warrior as a cleric. But the monarch only sawed off a chunk of pork with slow, deliberate strokes, never once taking his gaze from the abbot's flickering eyes.

Taillebois tore off a chunk of bread. 'There is nothing left of the English. They are no threat,' he growled, shrugging. 'Hereward has no more than twenty men left. They flee like startled deer through the forests, hiding among the roots and gnawing on whatever scraps the folk throw them. They are beggars and thieves. But not an army.'

The king stabbed the knife in the meat with such force it rammed into the wood beneath. William de Warenne jerked and spilled his wine. 'There are times when I wonder if any clever men joined me on those ships from Normandy.' He thrust back his bench and wandered round the table. Turold rested his hands beside his cup and stared at them. 'Listen to your own words,' the king continued. 'The folk toss Hereward and his men scraps. Even when they all but starve themselves. Defeat has not diminished him.' Redwald watched him stride behind the three men and stare at the backs of their rigid heads, a flicker of contempt crossing his face. 'The English know he was not defeated by my might. He was betrayed . . . by that cur Morcar who rots in the dark beneath this palace, and by the monks, English monks, who sacrificed their allies to cling on to whatever worldly goods their fingers could grasp. Hereward is my enemy, but he deserved better than the weak bastards who surrounded him.'

William de Warenne moistened his lips and began, 'The English think him—'

'The English think him a hero,' the king roared. Though he had been expecting the outburst, Redwald's heart thundered. He felt fear whenever he was in the monarch's presence, but never had he encountered a man he admired more. William the Bastard bunched his fists as if he were considering hammering them into the base of the noble's skull. He seemed to think better of it, for he unflexed his fingers and walked back round the table. 'They give him scraps now,' he continued, 'and they tell tales of his exploits around the hearths. I know – I have heard those tales. Bear-killer. Giant-killer. A sword filled with God's fire that will take the king's head. My head!' His huge hand swiped a pitcher of wine on to the flagstones. 'And after the scraps, they will ask for his aid against the hated invaders. And they will draw to his standard once again. And the English earls and thegns who have seen their land stolen and given to bastards like you . . .' he yelled the final word, 'will rally to his call. And before I know it, there will be another English army. And another. And another. Until I lie on my deathbed, worn down by constant war and the failings of such dogs as you.'

'We hunt him by the day,' the Butcher muttered, 'and soon we will catch him. And then we will bring his head to you and all will be well.'

'You will never catch him,' William said through gritted teeth. 'Because he has more wits than all of you together. And one thing even greater – the hopes of the English. That will put fire in his heart greater than any lust for gold or land.'

Turold poured himself another cup of wine, his hand shaking so violently that the liquid splashed everywhere, Redwald saw: 'What would you have us do, my lord?'

The king shook his fist. 'We must sever the cord that binds the English folk to Hereward. Never more must they believe they have a champion in their midst.' He looked round the gloomy faces. 'Find me the answer I seek. Or pay the price.'

Redwald stepped away from the door as the monarch began to circle the table once more, like a hungry wolf. He could not afford to be seen. Since the court had returned from Ely he had rarely encountered his master, which troubled him.

He burst out into the cluster of stores and sheds and cook-houses at the rear of the palace. The night was warmer than it had been for weeks. Winter had finally gone, and the spring held hope.

Edoma waited for him beside the slaughterhouse. She had put on her prettiest dress and washed her hair and tied it back with a ribbon. Though she offered him everything he needed, he found that with each passing day she disgusted him a little more. If only he could make her disappear. But he needed her, for a marriage still might earn some favour from the king and bring more attention his way.

'How was it?' she said with a flirtatious smile. She widened her eyes as she looked up at him, hoping it would flatter him. 'Have you learned anything to your benefit?'

'Yes, much,' he replied, putting a hand to his forehead as he thought. 'The king needs my brother dead, but Turold and the others are too slow-witted to give him what he desires.'

'But you are clever,' she said, leaning in close so that her breasts brushed his chest.

He nodded. 'I have failed once to kill Hereward. I cannot do so again. I must find a way to take his life, and then I shall have all the rewards I justly deserve.'

CHAPTER SIXTY-FOUR

10 April 1072

The fat of the newly killed deer sizzled as it dripped into the fire. Sweating, Sighard turned the meat on its oak spit. The smell of the succulent venison drifted across the sun-dappled greenwood, no doubt exciting the appetites of the men hard at work in the makeshift camp. They would eat well this day, and all the better for knowing it was the king's deer, killed on land William the Bastard had stolen and made his own. Hereward looked round at the activity: the cutting of firewood, the whittling and fletching of new arrows, the stripping and curing of the hides. Among his men, there seemed fresh hope now that they had survived the harsh winter months.

For a while every day had seemed to be more running and hiding and sweat and fear as they gave their all to evading the hunting bands that the monarch sent into the Brunneswalde. But as they ventured further into the murky, unforgiving forest, and as the snows came harder, the Norman warriors became fewer and soon days and then weeks would pass without any sign of pursuit.

And when they crept out of the trees into the small

settlements on the fringes, their cloaks smeared with the green of tree and lichen, they had discovered that stories of the wild men of the woods had spread like the fires that had devastated the western fens. The band of men with bow and spear and sword who fought for the downtrodden English against the cruel king, who could sweep out of the greenwood to attack the thieving Normans and disappear without trace only moments later. The warrior who had lost all and still gave more, and his friend the monk. The giant of a man who was as gentle as he was lethal. Heroes all. With the tales had come gratitude, and bread, and ale, and shelter when they needed it. And as the days warmed, and the new buds sprouted, and as Alric regained his strength, Hereward realized he had started to hope too: that the rebellion could begin anew, that a second army could be built and that the English would rise up and heed his call.

On the edge of the campsite, Herrig raised one arm. He had been keeping watch since first light. A moment later, Hereward heard what must have disturbed him: the crack of dry wood. Someone was approaching.

In a flash, the men readied their weapons. Kraki slipped away from Acha and pressed his back against a broad oak, his axe ready. Hengist knelt by another tree, a shaft nocked in his bow.

When a whistle rolled out, they all grinned. Herrig stood up and waved. 'It is only Hunlaf,' he called.

As the men returned to their tasks, Hereward walked from the campsite to where a short man with a wind-chapped face waited. 'Greetings, Hunlaf,' the Mercian called. 'How fares your good wife?' Whenever Hunlaf brought news from the settlements, or gifts of honey cakes or ale or cheese, his cheery mood brightened even the darkest day. Deda had taken to calling him Hunlaf the Drunken in jest, though he was always sober. But as he neared, Hereward took in the man's drooping shoulders and downturned mouth. Beckoning for Alric and Guthrinc to join him, the Mercian said, 'Trouble?'

361

'Aye,' the man replied, 'and worse than I ever feared.' When he looked at the three men, his mouth began to tremble. 'I carry two burdens,' he continued. 'The first – I ask you to follow me so you can see with your own eyes what is to be. And the second – I bring a message from the king himself.'

'William the Bastard has spoken to you?' Hereward said, incredulous.

'Through . . . through his messenger.' Hunlaf sagged, burying his face in his hands. 'They took my wife. They threatened to kill her if I did not come to you.'

The Mercian snatched out his sword and looked around. Guthrinc and Alric too eyed the surrounding trees.

'I did not bring them here,' the visitor insisted. 'I would never betray you.' He held out his hands, pleading. 'You must believe me. The Normans did not care to know where you were camped. They only wished you to know the king's mind.'

'A trap,' Guthrinc said.

Alric nodded. 'They cannot catch us so they would lure us to them.'

'I beg you,' Hunlaf said, his eyes rimming with tears. 'If you do not come with me, they will kill my wife.'

'We will come,' Hereward said, 'but if there is even the smell of a trap, we will be away, and your wife must fend for herself.'

Hunlaf clasped his hands in relief. 'You will see I speak true.'

They fetched Kraki to join them, and set out east through the cool forest. Guthrinc searched among the tangled trees with his clear eyes, but saw nothing. After a while, he put his head back, sniffed the air, and muttered, 'Smoke.'

When they came to the edge of the woods, Hunlaf pointed to where strands of grey twirled up. Charred timbers protruded from the ground in a vast, blackened circle.

'Is that . . . Aseby?' Alric asked.

'The Normans burned it down,' Hunlaf said, his voice cracking.

'What gain is there from such an act?' Hereward asked.

'They were quiet folk in Aseby, and hard-working. No trouble to the Normans.'

'Aye, no trouble,' the other man said. He turned away, unable to look at the remains of the village. 'Good folk, all. That is why they were chosen . . .'

The Mercian grabbed Hunlaf's shoulders and spun him round. 'Chosen? What is this?'

'One village will burn every day, because of you. One village, until there are none left in the east. The king would have you see this so you know he will be true to his word.'

'And once more, what will he gain?' Alric said. 'To make the English blame us for their suffering, to hate us so they will not rise up alongside us?'

'No more villages will be burned if you meet him,' Hunlaf said.

Guthrinc laughed. Kraki snorted dismissively. 'He thinks us mad. We will willingly walk to our deaths? I think not.'

Hereward bowed his head. He had feared this would be the monarch's next step. William the Bastard had never been shy of making innocents suffer to achieve his own ends.

'If you meet him, the king has given his word that you will not be harmed,' Hunlaf said, holding up his hand to silence the ripple of laughter from the other men. 'He has made this vow, before God, in his abbey. And it was witnessed by many, at his request. God will surely strike him dead if he betrays his oath.'

'There is more, yes?' Hereward said.

Hunlaf nodded. 'What you have suffered this winter will be as nothing compared to what is to come. As the villages burn, he will set a price upon your head greater than any man could dream of. Every axe-for-hire in England and beyond, every hungry man, every Dane and Scot and Frank and Norman, will hunt you down. There will be nowhere you can turn.'

After a long moment of silence, Hereward said, 'Did we really think the king would give us all the time we needed to raise another army?'

'After Ely, we thought he would be turning his gaze

elsewhere,' Kraki muttered. 'Filling his coffers, or marking his ledgers. We are a few poor men. No threat to a king.'

'No.' Alric pressed his hands together as though he were praying. 'I see it now. The king is afrit. Not of our numbers, no. But because the tales of you grow in the telling, until now they are bigger than William himself.'

Hereward pressed a silver coin into Hunlaf's palm, to show the Normans if they doubted he had met the English, and then the four made their way back through the forest, saying little.

That night, Hereward called his men to huddle round the fire and discuss what had been said. While the owls shrieked, they argued back and forth, through mouthfuls of venison.

'Why does he want to meet you if it is not to take your head?' Kraki growled, punching one fist into his palm. 'I say again: can he be trusted? Never!'

Hengist stared into the flames, his eyes dull with sanity. 'The king will not let us carry on. Our time is done.'

'Coward,' the Viking roared.

Deda held up his hand to silence them. 'I know William well. He is as slippery as an eel, but he is a God-fearing man. If he has made his vow, he will see it to the end.'

Hereward paced around the circle of men, peering into the dark. 'I will not see any more good English folk suffer on our behalf. Too many in Ely paid the price for our failure. All those long months of want . . . misery . . .' He shook his head. 'We do not have enough men to fight, and may not for long months to come.'

'What are you saying?' Sighard protested. 'That we give up now, after all our struggle?'

The Mercian stepped into the dark beyond the circle of firelight. 'We hear what the king has to say, first. Then we make our choice.'

Guthrinc wiped his greasy hands on his tunic. 'Whichever way we turn, we need to make plans. This peace we have known since the snows melted will soon be long behind us. We must find another stronghold, like Ely. Perhaps . . .' His voice tailed away. No one could find a way to finish his words.

Hereward looked around the faces of his loyal men. They had already given so much, and he knew that if he asked they would follow him to their deaths.

After a while, most of the men drifted away to sleep in their shelters of branch and turf, but Hereward knew he would find no rest that night. As he wandered the camp, turning over his thoughts, he caught sight of Kraki brooding alone beside a great oak. Not long after, he heard the echoes of angry voices. Back at the dying fire, he found the Viking arguing with Acha, Guthrinc, Alric and Deda.

'I will not go,' Acha snapped, her eyes flashing.

Kraki looked up at his leader from under heavy brows. 'Tell her she cannot stay. It is too dangerous.'

Seeing the Mercian's confusion, Acha said, 'He would send me back to my folk because he thinks me some frail flower. As if I have not lived with death ever since I was stolen from the Cymri.'

Hereward was puzzled. As long as he had known her she had wanted nothing more than to return to her home in the west. 'You will meet again—'

'No,' she shouted. 'If I leave here we will never meet again. I am no child. Do not treat me like one. You think you are to die, all of you. And you would see me spared.' Tears brightened her eyes and her face softened. 'I beg you. Do not send me away. If you are to die, I would end my days at your side.'

Hereward looked to Kraki. The Viking's face was like stone, but his eyes were fixed: frightened, the Mercian thought, in a way that he had never seen even in the fiercest battle. He crouched so he could look Acha in the eye, and said as gently as he could, 'I will not let these good men die if it is in my power to prevent it. That is my oath to you here. But if you stay among us, these warriors, your friends, will sacrifice themselves to keep you safe. You know this is true.'

Acha looked away, her eyes glimmering in the firelight.

'If you would aid them, leave here, as Kraki has requested,' he murmured. 'If it is God's will, he will find his way to you again.'

Jumping to her feet, Acha marched away into the dark. She would not let them see her cry.

'I will take her home,' Deda said. 'The road west is hard and fraught with thieves and murderers.'

'Done,' Kraki barked. He softened, adding, 'My thanks.'

Deda bowed.

Beckoning to the Viking, Hereward strode into the shadows beneath the oak. 'You have shown courage this night,' he said quietly, 'though I know it causes you great pain.'

'I did what I must,' Kraki growled.

'Go to her,' Hereward said. 'Make it right with her this night, or as right as can be, so there are no regrets.'

The scarred warrior hesitated for only a moment, and then gave a curt nod and strode after Acha into the dark.

Hereward stirred at first light, stiff from the spring chill. Low voices droned. He crawled out of his shelter to see Deda leading Acha into the trees. By the ashes of the cold fire, Kraki stood like a statue, watching them leave. He did not move, even when his woman glanced back, and held his gaze for a long moment. She forced a smile, her eyes glistening.

And still the Viking stood, watching, even when the forest had swallowed her up.

CHAPTER SIXTY-FIVE

In the last of the fading light, the two beggars trudged through the gates of Wincestre. Their cloaks were stained with mildew and grass from the ditches they had slept in, their shoes and breeches caked in mud. Over their heads, the Master of the Flame chanted his prayer for safe passage to morn as he lit the torches to keep the dark at bay. Soon, the bar would fall and no other visitor would be allowed into the king's town until dawn. The smiths and the woodworkers closed up their workshops. The looms stilled. Bats flitted across the rosy sky. Sleep was not far away.

Amid the rattle of carts and the sweet-sharp stink of horse dung, the beggars wound through the narrow streets towards the king's new palace. At the market cross, the two men paused. Alric raised his head to peer at the tower of the cathedral soaring over the town. He had heard William the Bastard wanted to tear it down and build an even greater monument to God, out of limestone, like the great Norman cathedrals of which Alric had heard so much. How could so cruel a man be so devout, he wondered?

Hereward prowled around the deserted market, deep in thought. Hardly a word had passed his lips on the long journey south from the Brunneswalde. In the camp, the Mercian had fought hard to be allowed to travel alone. For once, Alric would have none of it. He knew his friend's mind better than anyone. Hereward was preparing to do a deal with the king that would sacrifice his own life in exchange for those of his men, Alric was sure of it. Every day on the road he had proclaimed how wrong that course would be, how William the Bastard would surely still come after the remaining English warriors once his greatest enemy's head was on a pole at Wincestre's gates. And still he had little sense of what his friend planned. He eyed the warrior, feeling anxious, but he would pray that he made the right choice.

'You are ready?' the monk said, throwing off his hood.

'Aye.'

'There is still time to turn round.'

'What would we gain?'

'Hmm,' Alric mused. 'Your life?'

Hereward shrugged, as if this was the smallest consideration. 'I will go to the palace. As I near the gates, keep watch for any of the king's men who may be waiting to seize me—'

The monk could take no more. 'Tell me what is on your mind,' he blurted.

Pulling back his own hood, the Mercian raised his face to the cool evening breeze. 'Endings.'

Alric felt his heart sink. He forced a chuckle. 'This is no time for such thoughts. We are on the cusp of new beginnings. The fight goes on.'

'My father is dead,' Hereward said. 'Never did I think I would be free of him. And Redteeth – so long we circled each other with murder in our eyes. Gone, too. Only Redwald remains to drag me back into misery.'

'If your brother knows what is good for him, he will be far from here.'

Hereward shook his head. 'Where power rests, that is where you will find Redwald. Standing in the shadows, plotting. Where is the justice for Turfrida, for you . . .' He held out a hand. 'Your days were almost ended . . . and yet still he rises.'

'We talked of the perils of seeking vengeance . . .'

'I do not want vengeance. Not any more. I have left that behind me.' The Mercian looked round at the monk with clear eyes. 'I only want an end to it. Before we left our camp, I had a dream, of death. My own death. I lay in my grave, looking up at the grey sky.' He glanced around the darkening town. 'All things are coming to an end, monk; that is how it seems to me. If I find Redwald I will kill him—'

'Though it destroy you! You will never escape the guilt of slaying your own brother.'

'Or he will kill me,' Hereward continued as if he had not heard Alric's words. 'This business cannot be done until one of us is gone. And then—'

'And then what?' the monk snapped, his chest heavy with despair.

As the last of the light faded, the Mercian's face fell into shadow. For a long moment, Hereward seemed on the brink of answering. Instead, he only nodded a farewell, and turned and walked away into the night.

CHAPTER SIXTY-SIX

Redwald stood at the entrance to the piss-stinking track beside the tavern, listening to the raucous voices and singing that thrummed through the wattle walls. Apprehensive, he glanced back into the main street leading to Wincestre's palace, a ribbon of silver in the moonlight. All was still. He tried to steady his beating heart, but it throbbed in his head like the hooves of a runaway horse.

When he saw Edoma turn the corner at the far end of the alley and start hurrying towards him, he scrambled quickly along the track and thrust her back into the narrow street with such force that she almost cried out. Grabbing her shoulders, he snapped, 'Why are you late?'

'I was delayed—'

'Never mind.' He looked her up and down. She was wearing a new dress, of finest blue silk, one he had not seen before. Her face had been freshly scrubbed and a new ribbon gleamed in her hair. Pampering herself, when there was so much at stake. He raised his hand to strike her. Edoma recoiled, glaring at him. For that she needed to be punished, but there was no time. 'Let us not fight,' he whispered, feigning a warm smile. 'This night everything will change. I will be raised up to the highest position.'

'You have said those words so many times, I can scarce believe you,' she sighed.

'This time 'tis true,' he said, annoyed by her response. 'And I need your help to make it so.' He peered back down the dark track to the moonlit street beyond. 'I have heard that Hereward has sent word he will meet the king this night. I need you to keep watch by the palace, and when you see him, rush here to tell me so I can make ready.'

'To kill him?'

He nodded. 'The king has taken a vow not to slay my brother. I am not bound by such an oath.'

Edoma frowned. 'This is the wrong course.'

'Who are you to question me?'

'I have thought long and hard about it,' she continued, looking around. 'You are going against the king's wishes—'

'He wants Hereward dead. Of that there can be no doubt.' He formed the words as if he were speaking to a child. 'And if I deliver the head to him, all the better. I will be well rewarded.'

'Can you not see?' she pressed. 'Has your lust for power deluded you? The king does not need your aid to end your brother's days. You clutch at straws because now it is all you have to offer—'

He swiped the back of his hand across her face, harder than he intended. He trembled, stunned that she had dared speak to him that way, and shocked that he could not control his anger. The reason was clear, if he could admit it to himself. He was afraid of losing everything that he had worked so hard for, of once again becoming nothing.

Edoma wiped the back of her hand across her mouth. A bloody smear trailed across her skin. Like a hunted animal, she eyed him.

'No more words from you. You will do as I say,' he snapped. 'You have brought my knife, as I asked?'

She unfurled the fingers of her other hand to reveal the knife with the whalebone handle carved into the shape of an angel, Hereward's knife, which his father had given to him when he was a boy and Redwald had stolen in the days when he had nothing. As he reached out to take it, she folded her fingers around the blade again. 'No,' she said.

'Give it to me.'

'If you bring the king's wrath down upon you with this rash action, I will suffer too. I will not have that.' Her eyes flashed. 'Do you think you are the only one who has struggled and sacrificed to be raised up?'

Redwald smiled, seeing her in a new light. How cunning she had been. She had bent men to her will from the moment she had appeared at Ely's gates, a lost soul whose kin had been killed by Normans, or so she said. First the brothers Madulf and Sighard, and then him. He could not fault her for using the arts God had granted her. He had only done the same. 'We will work well together, you and I,' he said with an approving nod.

Looking back along the dark and lonely track, she sighed and shook her head. 'You are of no use to me now. I have found someone else, a Norman nobleman who will see me well cared for. He wants to make me his wife.'

Redwald recoiled as if she had slapped him. 'I will not allow it,' he blustered. 'Once he has heard the truth about you, he will not sully his hands.'

'As I expected.' She lashed out faster than a striking viper. Only when she stepped back did he realize that his own knife protruded from his stomach. She gasped, her fingers fluttering to her mouth. 'Oh,' she said, flushed, 'I have never killed a man before.' Her eyes gleamed with excitement.

Redwald staggered backwards along the track in shock, clutching at the whalebone handle. He felt numb, even as his blood flowed out to stain his tunic.

As he slumped against the tavern wall, Edoma came to lean over him. 'Die slowly,' she whispered. 'There is gain for me here. I will tell the guards I have slain a traitor to the crown, one who opposed the king's will and threatened my own life too.' She blew him a kiss and then all but skipped along the track into the moonlight.

Pressing his head back against the wall, Redwald closed his eyes – but only for a moment. He felt a seething anger rise inside him. He would not die this way, like a rat on a filthy track. Death had not yet claimed him, and he had survived a worse wound in days gone by. Gritting his teeth, he yanked the knife out. He had his life and he had a blade, and he could still end Hereward's days before the alarm was raised.

CHAPTER SIXTY-SEVEN

The great oak doors loomed up like the gates to hell. On either side, sizzling torches set shadows dancing across the new stone walls of Wincestre's royal palace. Silence hung over the outer hall as Hereward waited. His head was held high, his cold gaze fixed ahead, so that the guard in his hauberk and helm, with his sharp sword in his hand, could see that he was not afraid.

When the doors ground open, William the Bastard's adviser, a thin Englishman in a bright orange tunic, stepped out and bowed. Hereward was pleased that the king had not kept him waiting long. That showed respect.

'King William welcomes you, Hereward of Mercia,' the adviser said with a faint sibilance, 'and grants you fair hearing.' He paused, moistening his lips, his eyes flickering with uncertainty. 'The king believes you to be a man of honour. Is that so?'

'I am.'

The adviser nodded, plucking at his plump lips. 'My lord would see you . . . alone.'

'Without the court? No slithering snakes like you hissing in his ear?'

The adviser pouted indignantly. 'Yes. That is the meaning of alone, is it not?'

Hereward felt puzzled. He had expected at least a degree of humiliation for all the misery he had inflicted upon the Bastard.

'But I would ask you to leave your sword here,' the adviser continued, with an insincere smile.

'In case I am taken by the urge to gut him like a fish?'

The adviser recoiled in horror.

'I am a man of honour. The king has vowed to see no harm comes to me. I have taken an oath not to harm him.' Hesitating, the Mercian weighed the request, then shrugged. 'Very well,' he said, unfastening his sheath and laying it, and Brainbiter, upon the flagstones beside the door. 'See that it is there when I return,' he said, eyeing the guard.

The adviser stepped aside and ushered him into the king's hall, closing the doors behind him. William stood in front of his throne, his hands folded behind his back. For some reason he could not fathom, Hereward had always imagined the monarch with the face of his father, the younger Asketil who had beaten his wife to death with his bare fists. But here was a man, if anything, even more imposing. Broad of chest and as tall as Hereward, with arms that looked as though they could crush a man, he seemed a great oak beside the adviser's sapling. As he sized up his guest, Hereward realized the Bastard, too, must have imagined his own vision of his enemy.

'I expected the Devil,' William said.

'As did I.'

Grinning, the king shrugged. 'Devils are not the leaders of men, but the ones who whisper in their ears, and their faces rarely show their evil.'

'There are some who say the harrowing of the north could only be the work of a devil.'

William's face darkened, but only for a moment. 'Aye, and some say the same of a man who could leave knights' heads on poles outside his father's hall, or set alight the fens themselves.' Lightening, he beckoned. 'Come. Drink.' He walked to the hearth and poured two cups of wine from a pitcher. He handed one to Hereward. 'You have humbled the Butcher, and William de Warenne, and Turold too. My army is feared throughout the world, and yet you held it at bay—'

'And almost brought it to its knees. And I would have, if I had not been betrayed by spineless curs.'

He expected the king to flare in anger, but William only nodded. 'Perhaps. Or perhaps those betrayals were part of the war, weapons used by a clever leader.' He sipped his wine, watching the Mercian over the rim. 'Is it always wise to attack from the front with a spear?'

Hereward sipped his own wine. 'Cunning, then.'

'A king needs to be cunning. Courage is not enough. Strength is not enough.' He swept out an arm. 'Do you think you can hold a country such as England with only axe and spear and sword, and the heart of a lion? Live in Normandy for a while, Mercian, where there is a knife behind every door and poison in every cup . . .' Hereward glanced into his own cup and hesitated. William pushed it back to his lips. '. . . then talk to me about cunning. There, it is about living to see a new dawn. Every day.'

'I see now why you wanted England.' The Mercian grinned.

'And now I have it, for ever more. I am king.'

'You are not my king.'

William the Bastard eyed him for a moment, cold and calculating. Swilling more wine into both cups, he said, again with a calmness that surprised the Mercian, 'No. I will never be your king.' He set the pitcher down and prowled around the hall, staring into the shadows as he chose his words. 'There was a time, not too long ago, when I was ready to offer terms for peace to you and your men. Does that surprise you?'

'Aye, it does. I would have thought a man who could turn the north into a graveyard would never consider finding common ground.'

'The ends matter, Mercian, always. Sometimes a fist, sometimes an open hand, whichever works best.' He walked back to the warmth of the fire. 'Those spineless curs you so despise told me that peace would be seen as a sign of weakness. That the English would think me wounded and rise up. What do you think?'

Hereward peered into his wine for a moment. 'I think they were right.'

'You would not have found common ground?'

'Once, perhaps,' he said, casting his thoughts back to Ely, 'when I feared there would be no England left after our war.'

William smiled and nodded. 'The ends, aye. Leaders always look to the ends.' He waved a dismissive hand. 'I thought my curs were right then. Now, after all I have seen, I am sure. You have found a place in the hearts of the English, Mercian. They speak of you in the west, and the south, aye, and in what is left of the north, did you know that? A king can put a sword through a heart, but he cannot prise out such a thing as that.'

Here was the meat of it, Hereward thought. He rested one foot on the hearth and waited.

'You are more of a problem for me now than ever you were in Ely.' The Bastard studied his face as if he were looking deep inside him. 'If I let you live, the legend will grow, and sooner or later the English will rise up and follow your standard. If I kill you, the legend will grow faster still.' He tapped his right hand upon his breast. 'In the hearts of the English, where I can never reach it. I will never be accepted as king, I know that. You will tower over me in their minds, and grow, and grow. In death, you will unite them as I never could, and then a new Hereward will come along. And another. And another. Each one fired by your memory. And I will spend the rest of my days fighting the same battle, over the same patch of land. That is hell for two devils like us, is it not?'

Hereward nodded. 'Aye, that is a problem, indeed. I cannot live, and I cannot die.'

'Only a clever man could solve it.' The king smiled. 'You *can* live . . . as long as you do not live in the hearts of the English.'

'You said you could not prise me out.'

'I can kill you in another way. The memory of you.' Growing animated, William paced around the circle of light emanating from the fire. 'Would they think you hero if they knew you had taken my gold and fled? Abandoned them to my . . . cruelty?' He fluttered his fingers in the air.

'I would not do such a thing.'

'Not even to save the lives of your men? And the lives of every man and woman in England?' He eyed Hereward askance. His voice hardened as he continued, 'I will not battle for England until my dying day. Nor will I give it up. I would rather see it destroyed. I would do to Wessex, and Mercia . . . everywhere . . . what I did in the north.' He pointed a steady finger. 'The ends, Mercian. The ends. What would you do to prevent such a thing? Or would you rather be the Hereward that was? The one who slaughtered without thought, who would burn the world down rather than admit defeat? Are you that man, Hereward of Mercia, or are you the leader of the English?'

And there it was. The king had him. He turned away, peering deep into the flames.

'Aye,' the king said, his voice softening. 'No man should have to make a choice like that. But we are not any men. We are . . . kings.'

Hereward glanced at him, but William did not meet his eye. 'And if I leave . . .'

'You will take your men with you. I want no trace of you upon this isle. And within a day my messengers will ride out from Wincestre to every corner of this land to slay your legend. You will be as nothing. The English will spit upon your name in the streets. But your men will live. And no villages will be burned, and no men and women will be put to death, and in time the English will grow to love me. You will be forgotten. And I will live on in their hearts for all time.'

Hereward bowed his head. What choice did he have? 'How do I know I can trust you?'

'If a man does not have honour, he has nothing.' The king

glowered into the fire. 'I am not a dog like Harold Godwinson, who promised me this crown, and then took it for his own. You will have my word. Safe passage out of England and into exile. And peace here.'

The logs in the fire sighed. Hereward watched the flames dance, as he had watched the inferno in the fens on the night when he thought he had won. The devil inside him whispered to him to keep fighting. But that devil was shackled now. Alric, his friend, had seen to that, and the monk more than any understood sacrifice. 'Very well,' he murmured. 'For the lives of my men, and for the lives of all the English.'

For a long moment there was silence, and when he glanced up, William the Bastard's hard face had softened. 'You were a good leader, Hereward of Mercia,' the king said in a quiet voice. 'You deserved better than the dogs who ran with you.'

He ushered him to the door and called for his adviser. On the threshold, he turned to Hereward and said, 'Take your sword, and go from here, and make your plans to leave. I will provide a ship for you in the east. Go where you will. But we will not see each other again.' Then he walked away without a backward glance, and the doors slammed shut and Hereward was left once more in the silent hall.

Out in the night, he looked up at the full moon. He felt an odd sense of peace, the like of which he had never experienced before. The fighting was done. His story was over. And now there would be an ending.

Deep in thought, he wandered through the palace gates and on to the road that led past the tavern.

CHAPTER SIXTY-EIGHT

The full moon limned the rooftops of Wincestre. The town was quiet and the air crisp as the monk prowled past dark doorways and shadowed tracks, peering into every one. He felt haunted by a gnawing feeling of dread that something terrible was about to take place.

When discordant voices echoed across the night, he jerked to a halt, listening. A door slammed and the sounds dimmed. He sighed. Only a drunk stumbling out of the tavern. He saw threats everywhere.

Past a pigsty he wandered, the air rumbling with the sound of the beast's snores. As the stink of swill faded behind him, his nostrils wrinkled at another reek, faint but too familiar after the last nine years.

In a shaft of moonlight, a dark puddle gleamed.

His chest tightened. Fearing the worst, he followed a trail of spatters into the track beside the tavern. When he saw a figure hunched against the wattle wall halfway along the path, he almost cried out. Yet as he hurried forward with a thundering heart, he saw that it was not Hereward.

The wounded man turned and looked at him with a face as innocent as a child's. When he smiled, Alric felt his blood run cold.

'Monk,' Redwald croaked, pushing himself up the wall. 'It seems I have had a mishap.' Alric shifted his gaze from the dark patch staining the front of the tunic to the short-bladed knife the other man gripped in his right hand. And then he looked to the far end of the track and the main road to the palace that lay beyond, and he knew all he needed to know.

'Aid me,' Redwald called, reaching out a bloody hand. 'Find me some linen to stem the flow of this blood. I will yet live.' When Alric remained rigid, he added, 'Come – you saved my life once, in Ely.'

'Aye, and damned myself in turn.' His thoughts flew back to that night when Redwald had been wounded in the hut by the walls, when the local men had challenged Hereward's rule. If only he had left Redwald there, to watch his life-blood drain out. But he could not have done so in the eyes of God. Instead he had taken him to the leech, and he had been saved, and Turfrida had died, and misery had been heaped on misery, and all of it because he had been true to God. He closed his eyes and muttered a prayer, shaking as if he were sick.

'Monk,' Redwald called again. 'Aid me, I say. You are a man of God. You cannot turn away from this plea. What if I die?' His face was blank, like a statue, his true emotions unreadable.

'What if you live?' Alric whispered. He knew the answer. He could feel the terrible weight of it crushing him down.

'Then we will praise God. All life is sacred.' He shook his bloody hand once again, beckoning for help.

Alric shuddered; he had no choice. Keeping one eye on the knife, he stepped forward. He eyed the spreading stain, and the wounded man's pallor. He was weak from blood loss. 'You wait here while you slowly die?' the churchman said with an incredulous shake of his head. 'How much do you hate him?'

'Hate?' Redwald replied with what seemed like honesty. 'I do not hate him. He is my brother.' He frowned, realizing he had perhaps given away his intentions.

With a flick of his wrist, the monk slapped the blade from the other man's grip. It bounced along the track and slid into the moonlight at the end. The whalebone angel glowed white. The blade was black.

'No,' Redwald cried. Jerking his head to look at the knife, he reached out towards it in desperation.

Alric lunged. Grasping the man's sodden tunic, he flung him on to the filthy ground and sat astride him.

'Do not do this,' Redwald groaned. 'I am not the man you think.'

Hot tears burned the monk's eyes. He clamped both hands around the other man's neck and squeezed. He felt sickened that a part of him was pleased that he would not have to hear any more lies.

Redwald bucked and clawed at the monk's arms and face. Alric gritted his teeth. His enemy was too weakened now to offer much resistance. He squeezed tighter still, feeling the throat close under his fingers. 'See what you have done to us all,' he sobbed.

Redwald flapped ineffectual hands against the monk's shoulders. He wheezed, his bulging eyes filled with a hellish plea for mercy.

Alric's tears streamed down his cheeks and splashed on the dying man's face. 'I have damned myself this night,' he croaked. 'But I do it willingly, for the sake of my friend.'

Sobs racked him for a moment, and he bowed his head. When he next looked up, he realized Redwald was no longer moving. Still he could not stop choking this man, as if he could squeeze him off the face of the earth and out of the memories of all who had ever encountered him.

Finally, he let go.

Alric looked deep into Redwald's eyes. They looked the same as when he was alive. A stare filled with nothing. A life the same.

The monk clambered to his feet. His chest burned from his sobs. It seemed they would never end, he thought. He wrenched himself away from his terrible crime, but he could not resist one last backward glance. Redwald lay dead, his face still as innocent as a babe's, apple-cheeked, full-lipped.

Broken, the churchman dragged himself out into the street. A figure was wandering down from the palace gates. Alric blinked away his tears and saw that it was Hereward.

The warrior greeted him with a grin. 'All is well, monk,' he called. 'All is well.'

'Aye,' the cleric said, wiping his eyes with the back of his hand. ''Tis.'

As he neared, the Mercian furrowed his brow. 'Monk? Why do you cry?'

'From joy,' Alric replied and realized he meant it, 'for a new day is dawning.'

CHAPTER SIXTY-NINE

The ash trees moaned in the wind. Stark against the vast fenlands sky, they seemed to be calling to the woman who peered to the blue horizon. The sun felt warm upon her face. Spring had returned in force. Bluebells bloomed along the edge of the wood, and for the first time that year the birdsong had been loud enough to wake her. The winter had been raw, with skies like ashes and the snows drifting near to the top of her door. The cold had reached deep into her bones, echoing the frost she had long felt in her heart. But now the world was waking.

After a moment or two, she shrugged and turned away. On the green, where the hens scratched, the boys were fighting with swords, shouting and laughing. The king always died. Hereward always won. She fetched that morning's bread and wrapped it in linen, and took it to blind Rimilda who could no longer cook for herself. For a while, she sat by the hearth, and smiled as she listened to tales of the old woman's husband and his clumsy wooing. Only afterwards did she realize these stories pleased her. She nodded and wondered. Later, she poured a pail of swill into the pig's pen, and cut wood for the fire, and took her bow and hunted for waterfowl but caught none. In the midday sun, she sat on a stool outside her door and sewed a tear in the hem of her best dress. Yet still she could not settle.

Something was coming. Rowena could feel it in her bones.

Looking up, she glimpsed a smudge in the distance on the north road. Her neck prickled. Putting her needle and her dress away, she walked out beyond the village and stood beside the road, watching.

As it neared, the smudge took on shape and became a man upon a horse. She waited.

When the rider passed the milestone, she finally accepted that she had stopped dwelling on days gone by and for the first time since Elwin died had started to think of days yet to come.

A spear's throw away, the man brought his mount to a halt and leaned over the neck and smiled at her. 'I would have my answer,' Deda the knight said.

Rowena smiled back.

CHAPTER SEVENTY

7 May 1072

U nder a silver sky, the crimson-sailed ship strained at its mooring on the swelling tide. Shrieking gulls wheeled across the heavens, and the salty breeze moaned over the throbbing waves. Yet the harbour at Yernemuth was unnaturally still. Sacks of salt, barrels of wine and oil, quernstones, and chests of silk and pottery littered the quayside, unguarded. Baskets of fish from that morning's catch still waited to be delivered to the merchants. Here and there, meals of bread and cheese wrapped in linen lay half eaten. Shipwrights' hammers had been abandoned on the ballast heaps. The world seemed to be holding its breath.

Aboard the ship, the men stood in silence, looking out across Yernemuth's thatched roofs, remembering. They were a rag-tag band, their clothes threadbare and stained with the green and brown of life in the forest, their splintered shields faded and in need of a new lick of paint, their mail shirts rusted and bloodspattered. On their arms and faces, scars mapped lives of struggle.

Not one of them eyed the iron wall of Norman warriors

lining the harbour, keeping the prying eyes of the Yernemuth folk away from what was happening at the waterside. The king's men were dressed for war, in hauberks and helms, their long shields upon their arms, and their hands upon the hilts of their swords or the hafts of their axes. Here was William the Bastard's final show of strength, Hereward thought as he leaned against the mast, a message with clear meaning.

'Where is the monk?' Kraki growled. 'This waiting fills me with fury.'

'Are you so keen to leave our home behind?' Sighard said, sullen eyes lowered. 'You may never see these forests and fields again.'

'Wherever I lay my axe, that is my home,' the Viking snorted. 'You would do well to remember that, you red-headed dog, or you will be whining for the rest of your days.' He eyed the other man askance and softened a little. 'Be sure that wherever we wash up, there will be women with soft skin, and mead and ale and wine. And you will always have good drinking brothers to share them with. What more could you want?'

Sighard sighed, but the Viking's words seemed to have eased his melancholy a little, Hereward noted. That was good. Hard times lay ahead, a battle of a different kind, and they would only find victory shoulder to shoulder. He felt proud of how well his men had taken the news of the king's demands. None of them wanted to leave behind the land they knew, their friends, their kin. But they understood. Once you had taken the life of the spear, the days became ones of hard choices. They could never go back to the fields, or the hearthside, the loom or the smithy. They had given themselves up to death, to blood, to honour, and there was no place for men like that in this new England that William the Bastard was making. Turning, he shielded his eyes from the sun and looked out to sea. If they were to find a place for themselves, it would be out there, beyond the horizon.

Guthrinc loomed over him, sucking on the last shred of meat on a chicken bone. 'Still time to change your mind,' he said. He examined the bone, then tossed it over his shoulder into the waves.

'I have made my choice.'

'It is a brave man who can walk away, knowing that his name will be torn down and pissed upon.' Guthrinc eyed him, trying to hide his concern behind a facade of disinterest. Good Guthrinc, he thought, watching out for him still, as he always had.

'I have been called worse things than coward. If I remember, you called me worse things, back in Barholme when I robbed you.'

The big man laughed silently and clapped a hand on his old friend's shoulder. But then he tapped his nose and pointed towards Kraki standing gloomily by the side, looking towards the west. Hereward nodded. It was not only England they were leaving behind.

'Kraki,' he called. When the Viking came over, scowling, Hereward asked, 'I have a mind not to end our voyage in Flanders. Greater spoils lie out there for men like us. Tell me your thoughts – where should we go?'

The Viking looked taken aback that his opinion had been solicited, but then he grinned. 'About time. I thought you had grown weak since Ely and set your sights low.'

Guthrinc feigned a weary shake of his head. 'I smell misery.'

'Gold, that is what you smell. Riches beyond imagining.' Kraki's eyes gleamed. He leaned in and said in a conspiratorial whisper. 'Constantinople.'

Hereward's eyes narrowed. 'The richest city in the world.'

'Aye,' Guthrinc muttered, 'and the most dangerous. They say every man plots against the other there, and they smile to your face while they slip a knife in your back.'

'Yes!' Kraki said, animated now. He jabbed a finger into the tall man's chest. 'And what it needs is men who know how to wield an axe to cut through all that sly dealing.'

'You think there is a place for us there?' Hereward asked.

'Aye, in the Varangian Guard. The emperor's own army. The best, the fiercest fighting men in all the world. They pay good coin for a strong right arm. And for a man like the great Hereward, whose name crosses the whale road faster than any ocean-stallion, that would be coin whose like we have never seen afore.'

Guthrinc fingered his chin. He eyed Hereward. The Mercian looked back. After a moment, they both smiled. Kraki punched a fist into a palm. 'This is not fleeing, now. This is battle-sport.'

At the prow, Hengist broke away from tormenting Herrig the Rat and gave a shrill whistle. On the quayside, the wall of Normans parted as Alric strode to the water's edge.

'At last,' Kraki growled. 'Now we can be away to better days.'

Hereward eyed the monk. Since they had left Wincestre, he had been worried about his friend. It seemed as if a shadow hung over him, but he would not talk about what ailed him. 'Do not be hard on him,' he whispered to the Viking. 'In heart, he is as much a warrior as any man here.'

Kraki nodded. 'He is a spear-brother. But I can still kick his arse.'

When Alric climbed aboard, Hereward thought he seemed brighter than he had done in days. 'Where have you been?' he asked, suspicious.

'Teaching the children at the church,' the monk replied with a faint smile.

'You and the children,' Kraki snorted. 'What ruin have you set in their minds?'

'Ruin?' This time the monk grinned. 'The ruin of William the Bastard, perhaps.' Wiping his forehead, he flopped down on a bench. The others gathered around him. 'I told the children a tale of the true king, Hereward, who will wait across the waves until the hour of greatest need, when he will sail back and stand by his folk. William may spread his poison through-out the land, but given time it will fade. The children, though, will remember my tale for all time, and it will grow in the telling and spread across all England. Hereward, and all that he fought for, will never be forgotten.'

For a long moment, silence hung over the ship, and then the men cheered as one, and slapped the monk's back. Alric flushed, surprised by the acclamation.

'I told you we needed a man with some wits,' Kraki boomed. 'Now we are well set for the riches that await us. To Constantinople, brothers,' he roared, 'and to glory!'

Soon after, the ship set sail. As it ploughed through the grey waves, Hereward stood astern and watched the land of his youth slip over the horizon. He thought of the suffering, and the deaths, of the victories and the feasts, of Turfrida, and of his son who would grow without a father to ruin his days. And then he turned and looked to the east, and he grinned.

'To Constantinople,' he murmured. 'To glory.'

About the Author

James Wilde is a man of Mercia. Raised in a world of books, he went on to study economic history at university before travelling the world in search of adventure. Unable to forget a childhood encounter – in the pages of a comic – with the great English warrior Hereward, Wilde returned to the haunted fenlands of Eastern England, Hereward's ancestral home, where he became convinced that this near-forgotten hero should be the subject of his first novel. *Hereward* was a best-seller. Wilde indulges his love of history and the high life in the home his family have owned for several generations in the heart of a Mercian forest.